THE QUEST FOR HOME

Book 2 of the Crossroads Trilogy

By Jacqui Murray

When your time comes to die,
be not like those whose hearts
are filled with fear of death…
Sing your death song and die
like a hero going home. —
Tecumseh

OTHER BOOKS BY JACQUI MURRAY

Dawn of Humanity trilogy
Born in a Treacherous Time
Laws of Nature (coming Winter 2021)
In the Shadow of Giants (coming Winter 2022)

Crossroads trilogy
Survival of the Fittest (Book 1)
The Quest for Home (Book 2)
Against All Odds (coming)

Sequel to *Crossroads*
Coming 2023

Cro-Magnon trilogy

Rowe-Delamagente Series
To Hunt a Sub
Twenty-four Days
Book 3 (coming 2026)

Non-fiction
Building a Midshipman: How to Crack the USNA Application

Education
Over 100 non-fiction resources integrating technology into education available from Structured Learning LLC

PRAISE FOR JACQUI MURRAY

For Survival of the Fittest, *Book 1 in the* Crossroads *trilogy*

SURVIVAL OF THE FITTEST is set in times so very ancient that author Jacqui Murray had to delve deeply into past and current research to create the African world in which the book is set. I enjoyed her strong characters, particularly Xhosa, and how they interacted with other humanoid species, some with lesser language skills. Bravo Jacqui! A fine read and meticulous research. —S. Harrison

There are power struggles, deceptions, kindnesses, and wisdom. The world building is a fascinating foray into prehistoric landscapes. Though fiction, Murray deftly brought to life a time we have little record of. Highly recommended. —D. Peach

I'm completely hooked on this moment in history and storyline. I will definitely read the rest of this series and highly recommend it. — Amazon Reader

If you enjoy stories of survival and adventure, this is a must read. I'll be looking forward to Book 2 of this trilogy. —J. Weatherholt

WOW I absolutely loved and enjoyed this book. I found it very hard to put down, held my interest and I can't wait to find the next book in this 3-book series. — Amazon Reader

Through meticulous research, author Jacqui Murray illuminates the gritty details of the lives and world of Homo Erectus as the People trek through Africa and beyond to search for more hospitable surroundings. With wisdom, courage and the ability to learn new ideas, Xhosa is a fierce and memorable character capable of leading the People to their new home. I am eagerly awaiting the second book of this three-book series! — Amazon Reader

I thoroughly enjoyed this well-researched prehistory read. The storyline drew me in and the character development was spot on. The protagonist Xhosa is an amazing leader. No matter the hardships, of which there are many, she always takes care of her people. So grab your coffee or beverage of choice and settle in for an adventure of epic proportions. —S. Cox

Characters are real with emotions that feel accurate. This is fast paced reading that is good to follow. Situations feel real. — Amazon Reader

Really enjoyed this book. Looking forward to reading more books in the series. — Amazon Reader

The story ends with something of a cliff hanger, so I'll have to read the second book in the series to find out if Xhosa manages to befriend some of her enemies or if her band is decimated by them. As with Murray's other books that feature the earliest peoples, I enjoy how her imagination gives us cultural aspects of how our early ancestors may have lived and died. — Amazon Reader

I like this view of how the different species of man might have behaved and interacted. The style and material reminds me of Jean Auel of "Clan of the Cave Bear" fame. The writing tugs me right into the lives of the primitive characters. … Just scan the sample chapters and see for yourself how the stimulating story events will keep you reading until "hand of Sun's travel" occurs many times. — Amazon Reader

Published by Structured Learning LLC
Laguna Hills, Ca 92653

This is a work of fiction. Names, characters, places, and incidents are the product of the author's imagination. Any resemblance to actual persons, living or dead, events, or locales, is entirely coincidental. The publisher does not have any control over and does not assume any responsibility for author or third-party websites or their content.

Printed in the United States of America

ISBN 978-1-942101-42-0

TABLE OF CONTENTS

South shore of the Mediterranean

North Africa, shore of the Mediterranean

Somewhere in modern-day southern France

Close to modern-day Gibraltar

CHARACTERS

Xhosa's People

Ant
Asili
Bone
Danya
Gadi
Ngili
Nightshade
Siri
Snake
Stone
Xhosa

Rainbow's Splinter Group

Bird
Hecate
Kiska
Mbasa
Rainbow
Starlight
Tor

Pan-do's People

El-ga
Lyta
Nak-re
Pan-do
Red-dit
Sa-mo-ke
Wa-co
Spirit
The black wolf

Hawk People (aka, former Hawk People)

Clear River
Dust
Hawk
Honey
Talon
Water Buffalo

Shore Dwellers (originally Raft Builders)
Acto
Qaj
Shaga

Xhosa's Captors
Dreg
Fang
Gak
Ork
Scarred One

Big Heads (Archaic forms of *Homo sapiens*)
Thunder
Wind

The Mountain Dwellers
Dawa
Davos
Deer
Leopard
Viper

Uprights
All Others tribes
Hairy Ones
Lucy

Others
Bako
Ja-card
Koo-rag
Nakhil
Vaya

Big Heads
Hawk's People
Pan-do's People
Rainbow's People
Shore Dwellers
The Mountain Dwellers
Xhosa's People
Xhosa's Captors

The journeys of the five *Crossroads* tribes

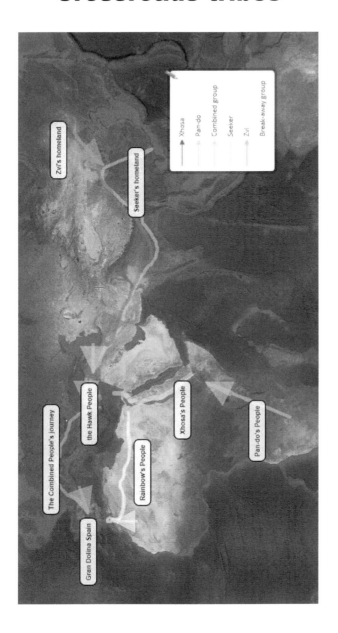

Author's Non-fiction Introduction

Homo erectus, the star of *Crossroads*, is a highly intelligent prehistoric hunter-gatherer who outlasted every other species of man and was the first to spread throughout the Old World of Europe and Asia. He possessed a sophisticated ability to reshape stones into intelligent tools, cross waterways, solve new problems, and make complicated plans. He was smart enough to face-off with dangerous situations and adventurous enough to want to try.

He lived 850,000 years ago.

Why did he thrive? He ate almost any food, made primitive spears to hunt, and used fire (or not, depending upon the expert you talk to—some of mine do because of their cold habitats). His communication was robust and sophisticated though rarely verbal. Instead, he shared ideas, thoughts, directions, and more with a complicated collection of body movements, facial expressions, sounds, and hand gestures. "Body language" today is responsible for about half of communication. In this story, I often refer to it as "motioned" but it's synonymous with the dialog tag, "said".

Homo erectus individuals were more comfortable on two legs than in trees and adept at imagining what they couldn't see. Their vast differences from earlier *Homo* species continues to fascinate paleoanthropologists. For example, their skulls are the thickest of any human species. They left a homeland they dominated and traveled to the far corners of Eurasia. They were a violent people, well-equipped to survive a treacherous world and eager to do so. While the first iteration of man, *Homo habilis* (the star of the trilogy, *Dawn of Humanity*) was timid and shy, you'd never accuse *Homo erectus* of that.

The trilogy *Crossroads* follows five *Homo erectus* tribes who originally lived in the far reaches of Eurasia and come together in the Levant, on the eastern-most shore of the

Mediterranean. Xhosa and her People are from East Africa (the Olduvai Gorge area), Pan-do from South Africa, Hawk from Gesher Benot Ya'aqov in Northern Israel, Seeker from Indonesia, and Zvi from China. They all flee their homelands for various historically accurate reasons, some because man's next iteration, *Homo sapiens*, is determined to eradicate them, others because Nature turned on them. When thrown together by circumstances, they put aside differences, trade knowledge of skills and techniques, and work together to achieve the greater goal of a new home.

Survival of the Fittest is Book 1 in the *Crossroads* trilogy and covers how they come together. This Book—Book 2— follows their journey west and the catastrophes they face as the combined group must flee what they had hoped would be a new home in the Levant. Book 3 shares their new life in an area we now know as Sierra de Atapuerca in central Spain. Life should be perfect after such a long journey but their past comes back to haunt them.

The references to Lucy in Xhosa's dreams are from **Born in a Treacherous Time**, Book 1 of the *Dawn of Humanity* trilogy, where Lucy and her small *Homo habilis* group are forced to leave their home to escape an invading tribe of *Homo erectus*. When an unbeatable enemy threatens Xhosa, Lucy appears to guide her to the future.

Both the *Crossroads* and the *Dawn of Humanity* trilogies explore man's journey from where we started to who we are today. Together, they are part of the *Man vs. Nature* saga which chronicles how the family of man survives from inception to present day. The characters all share the particularly human drive to survive despite extreme adversity, well-equipped predators, and a violent natural environment that routinely asks them to do the impossible.

Questions you might ask

Here are questions I often get from readers about the *Crossroads* trilogy:

What are Uprights and Others?

Uprights *are animals that walk on two legs. It is a general term, like bipedal. That includes these five tribes but also the Hairy Ones* (Homo habilis)*, Big Heads (archaic versions of* Homo sapiens)*, and Giganto (from the extinct species,* Gigantopithecus blacki, *a pre-human apelike creature).*

Others *is a more specific term and refers to only other* Homo erectus *tribes.*

Why are "Uprights" and "Others" capitalized?

Capitalization indicates Xhosa's respect for the individuals or their tribes.

This is also true when animal species are capitalized (like Gazelle or Mammoth). If the characters are referring to a gazelle or mammoth—in general terms—it isn't capitalized.

I don't understand the use of the term "People" (or why it's capitalized)

The label "People" in the Crossroads *trilogy applies to a group organized around a leader—like Xhosa's People and the Hawk People. It identifies the community of shared common experiences, culture, and beliefs. It might be synonymous with the term "Americans" or "French" for people today living in specific geopolitical territories. Since nations didn't exist 850,000 years ago, they are simply the People.*

How do you know these People are as smart as they seem?

Just to be clear, because these predecessors to man lived long before recorded history, scientists have no definitive evidence of their intelligence. We do get hints of its excellence, though, from their toolmaking. The complex thought required to create their stone tools (called Acheulean), the variety of tool types (cutters, choppers, handaxes, cleavers, flakes, scrapers, and more), and their aesthetically pleasing and functional forms make many paleoanthropologists believe Homo erectus *was cerebrally smart. A 2017 study mapped the brains of students as they recreated these same tools and it showed that the work required higher-level motor skills and the ability to "hold in mind" information—much as you do to plan and complete complex tasks (the study compared it to playing Chopin on the piano but I have no idea about that).*

Their speech is too sophisticated.

As a species, Homo erectus *lasted far longer than any other* Homo *species—and there is a reason for that: They were not only highly intelligent for the day but possessed rich communication skills. Their sophisticated tools, especially the symmetry of the hand-axe, suggests to many scientists that they possessed the ability to use language. Since most paleoanthropologists (scientists who study prehistoric man) believe the "speech" part of their brain—the part that allowed them to speak—wasn't evolved enough for verbal words, I present communication often through body language.*

A more convincing argument of why early man didn't want to talk is that voices are noisy and unnatural. That attracts unwanted attention. For these primordial humans, far from the alpha in the food chain, being noticed wasn't good.

Convince me they can communicate as well as it sounds like they do with just gestures, hands, and facial movements.

I get this a lot. Let me give you two examples. First, have you ever been around someone who doesn't speak your language and still, the two of you communicate by pointing, hand gestures, body movements, and facial expressions? Second, think of sign language. Very sophisticated ideas are communicated with just hands and facial expressions. That's how Xhosa and her kind did it.

You used "said"—I thought they didn't speak

In this trilogy, "said" is generic for communicating. It could be verbal but is more likely to be through gestures, body language, or facial expressions. I also often use "motioned" and "gestured" to indicate hand signals that communicate their words.

Could primitive man build rafts as suggested in this story?

Yes, absolutely. They had the brainpower, and the plants and tools required were available at the time but because they were made of wood and vines—-materials that don't preserve over time—no artifacts remain to prove this. Anthropologists speculate this would have been a basic raft made from bamboo and vine. This hypothesis was tested by building rafts using only prehistoric techniques (as Xhosa would have) and then replicating crossings such as the Straits of Gibraltar, through the islands in Indonesia, and even the passage from Indonesia to Australia.

Was there really a giant upright primate like Giganto (Zvi's friend)?

There was! He's called Gigantopithecus blacki. *Extinct now, he was native to southeast Asia, China, and Indonesia where Seeker and Zvi lived originally.*

What does "strong" and "weak" side mean?

Based on artifacts from 850,000 years ago (or longer), paleoscientists speculate that early man had a preference for right-

handedness. That would make their right hand stronger than the left (though they didn't identify "right" and "left" at that time). Because of this, my characters call their right the "strong side" and left the "weak side".

How did early man tell time?

Early man didn't care about hours or minutes. What drove him was how much sunlight remained before he must return to wherever he would be sleeping that night (maybe a cave, a cliff wall, or behind a thistle barrier). As a result, they indicated time in the future by pointing to a place in the sky where the sun would eventually reach. He might say, "Return by this point" to mean, "Return when Sun reaches this point in the sky."

What does a "hand of Sun's travel" mean?

A "hand" quantifies the amount of time it takes Sun to travel the distance of a hand held up to the sky. A finger would be about fifteen minutes and an hour about four fingers, or a hand. This is one of the ways the earliest People measured the passage of time. Test it yourself. Hold a finger up next to the Sun. It will take about fifteen minutes for the Sun to reach the far side of your finger.

What does the term "subadult" mean?

A subadult is a boy or girl older than a child but not an adult. Today, we might call him/her a teenager though without the immature connotations of such an age range. In fact, in Xhosa's world, subadults performed much of what adults did save duties that required scouting, hunting, fighting, or mating.

What is a "homebase"?

This is a permanent location where these people live, what we might consider a neighborhood. It is different than the temporary camps that serve them as they hunt or migrate.

Why are these characters so violent?

The answer to this question is simple: They had to be. If Homo erectus *hadn't been violent 850,000 years ago, he—and we as a species—wouldn't have survived. Man wasn't yet the apex predator. Our skin was too thin, claws too short, and teeth useless for defense. What we did have that those who preyed on us didn't was a thoughtful brain (well, the beginnings of one).*

I am not reading these books in order. Does it matter?

Survival of the Fittest *starts the* Crossroads *trilogy, itself the second trilogy in the* Man vs. Nature *saga. Each trilogy is a stand-alone story; each book in the trilogy fairly standalone in that I include details to catch you up on what occurred in prior books but without most of the drama. They can be read out of order, but you may find the experience enhanced if the three books in each trilogy are read consecutively.*

Foreword

No one told the heroes in *The Quest for Home*—
Xhosa, Pan-do, Nightshade, Wind, Zvi, Seeker, and Spirit—
they represented the leading edge of man's dispersion across
Eurasia. Their willingness to journey into the unknown
marked man's flexibility, adaptability, fungibility, and
wanderlust—hallmarks of an evolutionary fitness that even
back then challenged Nature for control of the world.

As you read the *Crossroads* trilogy, keep in mind these
characters are 850,000 years old. They are pre-everything
civilized. Their rudimentary culture fits broad definitions of
this complicated word because they share behaviors and
interactions, cognitive constructs and understanding, but it
doesn't fit more detailed attributes. Xhosa and those like her
don't wear clothes (though some wear animal skins), don't
marry, and haven't discovered religion, art, or music. They
don't bury their dead—why would they? Other animals don't.
They have no social norms, traditions, societal rules, or
judgmental attitudes toward others. They wear no tattoos,
jewelry, or adornments. They don't count past two. They
prefer descriptions to proper nouns.

Their lives revolve around two simple goals: to survive
and to procreate. To accomplish these, they have become
some of the smartest, cleverest animals in the kingdom. How
else could they endure in a violent world where an angry,
disruptive creature like Nature ruled?

Chapter 1

Northern shore of what we now call the Mediterranean Sea

Pain came first, pulsing through her body like cactus spines. When she moved her head, it exploded. Flat on her back and lying as still as possible, Xhosa blindly clawed for her neck sack with the healing plants. Her shoulder screamed and she froze, gasping.

How can anything hurt that much?

She cracked one eye, slowly. The bright sun filled the sky, almost straight over her head.

And how did I sleep so long?

Fractured memories hit her—the raging storm, death, and helplessness, unconnected pieces that made no sense. Overshadowing it was a visceral sense of tragedy that made her shake so violently she hugged her chest despite the searing pain. After it passed, she pushed up on her arms and shook her head to shed the twigs and grit that clung to her long hair. Fire burned through her shoulders, up her neck and down her arms, but less than before. She ignored it.

A shadow blocked Sun's glare replaced by dark worried eyes that relaxed when hers caught his.

"Nightshade." Relief washed over her and she tried to smile. Somehow, with him here, everything would work out.

Her Lead Warrior leaned forward. Dripping water pooled at her side, smelling of salt, rotten vegetation, mud, and blood.

"You are alright, Leader Xhosa," he motioned, hands erratic. Her People communicated with a rich collection of grunts, sounds, gestures, facial expressions, and arm movements, all augmented with whistles, hoots, howls, and chirps.

"Yes," but her answer came out low and scratchy, the beat inside her chest noisy as it tried to burst through her skin. Tears filled her eyes, not from pain but happiness that Nightshade was here, exactly where she needed him. His face, the one that brought fear to those who might attack the People and devastation to those who did, projected fear.

She cocked her head and motioned, "You?"

Deep bruises marred swaths of Nightshade's handsome physique, as though he had been pummeled by rocks. An angry gash pulsed at the top of his leg. His strong upper arm wept from a fresh wound, its raw redness extending up his stout neck, over his stubbled cheek, and into his thick hair. Cuts and tears shredded his hands.

"I am fine," and he fell silent. Why would he say more? He protected the People. He didn't whine about injuries.

When she fumbled again for her neck sack, he reached in and handed her the plant she needed, a root tipped with white bulbs. She chewed as Nightshade scanned the surroundings, never pausing anywhere long, always coming back to her.

The sun shone brightly in a cloudless sky. Sweltering heat hammered down, sucking up the last of the rain that had collected in puddles on the shore. Xhosa's protective animal skin was torn into shreds but what bothered her was she couldn't remember how she got here.

"Nightshade, what happened?"

Her memories were a blur—terrified screams and flashes of people flying through the air, some drowning, others clinging desperately to bits of wood.

Nightshade motioned, slowly, "The storm—it hit us with a fury, the rain as heavy and fierce as a waterfall."

A memory surfaced. Hawk, the powerful Leader of the Hawk People, one arm clutching someone as the other clawed at the wet sand, dragging himself up the beach.

He was alive!

It was Hawk who offered her People a home when they had none, after more than a Moon of fleeing for their lives through lands so desolate, she didn't know how anyone survived. Finding Hawk and his People, she thought she'd found a new homeland.

Her last hunt with Hawk flashed through her mind—the stone tip they created like the Big Head's weapon, how she had hung by her ankles from a tree trunk to cross a deep ravine. How he grinned when she reached the other side, chest heaving but radiant with satisfaction. He told her many of his warriors shook with fear as they crossed. His pride in her that day glowed like flames at night.

For the first time in her life, she felt Sun's warmth inside of her.

She looked around, saw quiet groups huddled together, males talking and females grooming children. Pan-do bent over a child, whispering something in her ear but no Hawk.

Where is he? But she didn't ask Nightshade. The last time she'd seen the two together, they had fought.

She couldn't imagine a world without Hawk. They had planned to pairmate, combine their groups into one so strong no one could ever again drive her away. She hadn't known there were enemies worse than Big Heads until Hawk told her about the Ice Mountain invaders. They attacked Hawk's People long before Xhosa arrived. Hawk had killed most and chased the rest back to their home, icy white cliffs that extended from Sun's waking place to its sleeping nest, bereft of plants and animals. When he saw where they lived, he understood why they wanted his land.

The children of those dead invaders grew up and wanted revenge.

Someone moaned. She jerked to find who needed help and realized it was her. She hoped Nightshade didn't hear.

He glanced at her and then away. "All the rafts were destroyed."

She shook, trying to dislodge the spider webs in her brain. Hawk's homebase was squashed between a vast stretch of open land and an uncrossable pond. They should have been safe but the Ice Mountain invaders attacked in a massive horde. Her People—and Hawk's—were driven into the water. The rafts became their only escape. Floating on a log platform to the middle of a pond too deep to walk across was something no one had ever done but they must or die. The plan was the rafts would carry the People to safety, away from the Invaders.

That hadn't worked.

"There were too many enemy warriors, Xhosa," and Nightshade opened and closed his hands over and over to show her. "More than I have ever seen in one place."

Images of warclubs slashed through her thoughts, flying spears, the howls of warriors in battle. Many died, beaten until they stopped moving, children dragged screaming from mothers. The giant female—Zvi—sprinting faster than Xhosa thought someone her size could, the children El-ga and Gadi in her arms, a spear bouncing off her back. Her size stunned the enemy, immobilized them for a breath which gave Zvi the time she needed to reach safety.

Almost to himself, Nightshade motioned, "I've never seen him this brave."

Xhosa didn't understand. "Him?" Did he mean Zvi?

"Pan-do. His warriors attacked. They saved us." Nightshade locked onto the figure of Pan-do as he wandered among the bedraggled groups, settling by an elder with a gash across his chest and began to minister to the wound.

"I remember," Xhosa murmured. When the People were trapped between the trees and the water, prey waiting to be picked off, Pan-do's warriors pounced. That gave Xhosa precious time to push the rafts out onto the water. It seemed none of the enemy knew how to swim. Pan-do sliced through the Ice Mountain invaders without fear, never giving ground.

Nightshade motioned, "He isn't the same Leader who arrived at our homebase, desperate for protection, his People defeated."

Xhosa's hands suddenly felt clammy. "Is Lyta alive?"

Since the death of his pairmate, before Xhosa met him, Pan-do's world revolved around his daughter, Lyta. He became Leader of his People to protect her. When he arrived at the People's homebase, Lyta stood out, unusual in an otherwise homogenous group. First, it was her haunting beauty, as though she shone from within, her hair as radiant as Sun. Awe turned to shock when she walked, her gait awkward on malformed feet. She should have been destroyed as a child but Pan-do said he had never considered it. He explained that in Moons of migration, before joining Xhosa's People, Lyta had never slowed them down. He didn't expect that to change if the two groups traveled together.

And then she spoke. Her voice was like bird's song and a gift to People exhausted from the day's work. It cheered up worried adults and put smiles on the faces of children, its melodic beauty convincing them that everything would work out.

It was more than a Moon after his arrival before Pan-do told Xhosa what he valued most about his daughter. Lyta could see truth simply by watching. No one could hide a lie from her, and she never hid it from her father. Pan-do kept it secret because the people it threatened might try to silence her. He only told Xhosa because Lyta had witnessed a conversation about a plan to kill Xhosa.

One of the people Lyta didn't recognize but the other, he was someone Xhosa trusted.

When Nightshade nodded, *Yes, Lyta lives*, Xhosa relaxed but only for a moment.

"Sa-mo-ke?"

Nightshade nodded toward a group of warriors. In the middle, eyes alert and hands energetic, stood Sa-mo-ke.

She sighed with relief. Pan-do's Lead Warrior was also Nightshade's greatest supporter outside of the People. When he first arrived, Sa-mo-ke spent Moons mimicking her Lead Warrior's fighting techniques until his skill became almost as formidable as Nightshade's with one critical difference. While Nightshade liked killing, Sa-mo-ke did so only when necessary.

Nightshade motioned, "Escape came at a tremendous cost, Xhosa. Many died, the rafts were destroyed, and we are now stranded in an unfamiliar land filled with nameless threats."

It doesn't matter, she whispered to herself. *We are good at migrating.*

She jerked her head around, and then motioned, "Where's Spirit?"

The loyal wolf had lived with people his entire life. He proved himself often while hunting, defending his packmates, and being a good friend. An image flitted across her mind, Spirit streaking toward the rafts, thrusting his formidable body like a spear through the shocked hordes. The enemy had never seen an animal treat People as pack. Then, the wolf swimming, paws churning the water into whitecaps, gaze locked onto Seeker. Endless Pond was too deep for him to touch the bottom so his head bobbed up and down, feet paddling like a duck's as he fought to stay above the surface.

Nightshade gestured, "The attackers almost killed Spirit."

She bit her lip, concentrating. "I remember Mammoth's trumpets."

The rare hint of a smile creased his mouth. "Another of Pan-do's tricks. It saved Spirit and probably all of us. He brayed like a herd of Mammoth thundering toward the shoreline. The invaders fled for their lives."

Pan-do is clever.

Nightshade grimaced. "But the storm worsened and the rafts foundered. Many of the People managed to cling to logs long enough to crash onto this shore. Then, they saved others. But many died."

He opened and closed his hands to show how many.

A stillness descended as Nightshade's gaze filled with a raw emotion he never showed. It shook Xhosa. Nothing frightened her Lead Warrior.

She gulped which hurt her insides. Shallow breaths worked better. Rolling to her hands and knees, she stood, making her head swim, and she threw up.

Finally, the dizziness subsided and Xhosa asked, "Hawk?"

Nightshade peered around, hands fidgeting. He examined something on the ground, toed it with his foot. "When the tempest destroyed the rafts, he dragged many to shore, to safety. The last time, he did not return. I tried to find him."

Soundless tears dampened her face. Nightshade touched her but Xhosa focused on a trail of ants and a worm burrowing into the soft earth. Her vision dimmed and she stumbled, fell, and then crawled, happy for the pain that took her mind off Hawk. When she forced herself up, everything blurred but she inhaled, slowly, and again, until she could finally see clearly.

How dare Hawk die! We had plans. Xhosa shoved those thoughts away. Later was soon enough to deal with them.

"His People—do they know?"

Chapter 2

The Hawk People—the former Hawk People, a sprawling proud group of indefatigable warriors, talented hunters, and hard-working females—they would be devastated. Hawk had been Leader most of their lives, protected them from invaders, ensured they always had food, and resolved their squabbles. It was he who found the last homebase with caves for protection and warmth, near water and endless herds, and within a day's journey of the special stones required for tools. It was also he who told the People, when they knew they must leave, to sail the rafts beyond the mountains. There, they would find a good next homebase.

"Yes. The Leads," Lead Warrior, Lead Hunter, and Lead Scout, "are shaken. None has emerged as the new Leader."

That worried Xhosa. Her People were intertwined with Hawk's, pairmated across the groups. Weakness in the Hawk—former Hawk—People would hurt her People. When her father died, both Xhosa and Nightshade stood ready to accept the responsibilities of Leader and engaged in a series of contests that tested their cunning, strength, planning, and battle skills. If Nightshade had won, he would now be Leader, she content to serve as his Lead Warrior.

"The former Hawk People must have a system similar to ours."

In her many discussions with Hawk about melding the two groups, they never discussed his replacement. Why would they? He was young, healthy, and without enemies. Except the Ice Mountain People but he had been sure they were destroyed.

Mentally running through the Leads in Hawk's group, none stood out as capable to replace Hawk.

Nightshade motioned, "No, they don't select a new Leader as we do, with contests to measure the fitness, strength, and ingenuity appropriate to a Leader. Instead, as soon as possible after the death of a Leader, the entire group gathers and a warrior claims leadership. In this case, that means Water Buffalo as he is Hawk's Lead Warrior."

Xhosa's mouth set in a tight line, remembering Hawk's less-than-flattering description of Water Buffalo.

Nightshade added, "If more than one stands to be Leader, the two fight. The winner becomes the new Leader. At any time, he can be challenged by another."

"Hawk never was, not the entire time he led," she motioned and rubbed her eyes. As her father was dying from the injuries inflicted by Big Heads, he made her promise to care for the People, put them ahead of all else. And she would.

"This is none of my business. My attention belongs on the People."

Nightshade hunkered down at Xhosa's side, leg pressed against hers, hands on his thighs.

"It is our business, Leader. The wrong person as Leader will hurt us. But don't worry. I will challenge Water Buffalo."

She perked up. "An outsider can do that?"

"No one will question it if I win. Which I will. Hawk's warriors respect me. More important, they trust me to blend our two Peoples into the group Hawk envisioned, one mighty enough to defeat all challengers be they Ice Mountain invaders, Big Heads, cannibals, or any other."

Her Lead Warrior's muscles tightened and his gaze darkened. Xhosa smelled his greatness, the warrior who intimidated all who dared enter the People's land. The Big

Heads prevailed because of overwhelming numbers, not ferocity or drive.

Nightshade will become Leader of the former Hawk People because he wants not only to dominate but subjugate. He will stop at nothing to Lead them well.

Nightshade read her thoughts. "Or you can challenge, Leader."

She winced as heat shot through her bruised body and pondered what Nightshade suggested. What if Water Buffalo didn't challenge? What if only she and Nightshade stood to lead the former Hawk People? No one ever beat her Lead Warrior one-on-one in a physical fight.

No, if she challenged, she would not only lose but fail in front of the People.

"It must be you, Nightshade."

Her Father in his wisdom wanted a Leader who excelled at not merely the physical but wits, strategy, and perseverance. In the fullness of the challenge, Nightshade's brilliance as a warrior failed to defeat Xhosa's cunning but if strength were the deciding factor, it would be Nightshade.

Xhosa wondered what type of Leader Nightshade would be. Would he try to dominate all groups or treat each as equals?

She nibbled her lip, eyes focused on nothing, turning Nightshade's plan over in her mind. There could be a problem. If Pan-do didn't accept Nightshade as co-leader and left, with him went her most loyal supporters outside of her own People. That would dramatically increase the influence of Nightshade's warriors.

Xhosa motioned to Nightshade, "Have you and Pan-do made amends?"

Nightshade blew out a breath, as close to *No* as he ever got. "He will stay or go, as fits the needs of his People."

Though both were strong Leaders, Pan-do and Nightshade couldn't be more different. Pan-do's brown hair offset his light-colored skin while Nightshade glowed with the dark black of Panther. Pan-do, like Xhosa, towered over Nightshade with the rangy movements of one comfortable with himself. His easy smile told enemies he would destroy them only if they didn't give up. But Nightshade, sinuous muscles as hard as rocks, always looked ready for a fight. The sight of him with his spears and warclub, dark eyes burning with aggression, handfuls of warriors behind him as ferocious as he, made enemies flee. They knew they wouldn't just lose a battle but their lives.

These differences in fighting style had changed their relationship from respectful and equal Co-leaders working toward the same goal to mistrust on Pan-do's side and hatred on Nightshade's.

She mulled over her Lead Warrior's answer. *Maybe if I act as buffer, they can work together until we find a new homebase.*

The two males did share a common belief, that a Leader without fear was feared, but was that enough?

Xhosa dreaded the thought of losing Pan-do. He had stayed with the People despite continual difficulties, maybe because of the unexpected bond that had formed between Xhosa and his motherless daughter. Lyta reminded Xhosa of a female Hairy One named Lucy who appeared often in Xhosa's dreams. Not in appearance—Lucy was short, round, and muscular while Lyta was tall, slender, and slight, and Lucy's movements were graceful where Lyta's were clumsy. No, it was her wisdom, beyond experience, and the way it enabled her to connect signs—clues—until she could identify problems most missed. So, when Lyta warned Xhosa, she took it seriously.

Nightshade, though, saw none of that. He had hated Lyta since the day she refused to mate with him. He treated her as a clumsy awkward cripple who slowed the People. When she promised herself to Seeker with his jumbled words and frenzied movements, Nightshade became openly hostile. It was almost like Nightshade was jealous, which he never was, nor did that emotion have any part in the People's lives. Nightshade knew that.

Xhosa didn't care who mated or pairmated but Seeker and Lyta were both odd and as such seemed a good match.

The People needed babies and Xhosa couldn't imagine anyone else mating with either of them.

What made Seeker especially valuable, and why Xhosa didn't want to lose him, was that he assured her he could find their new homebase. How he would do that had something to do with the movement of the stars. That made no sense to Xhosa but it had guided Seeker, Zvi, and Spirit for more than two handfuls of Moons.

Since Xhosa was entrusted to lead her People and Seeker's plan was the only one she knew of, she needed to understand it.

One cold night, under a dark sky packed with glittering white spots, Xhosa plopped down next to Seeker, in his usual spot beneath the stars, and motioned, "They all look alike, Seeker. How can they guide you?"

"They move, constantly, some more than others. Every night, I sit on the tallest hill I can find and see where they moved and which disappeared—or appeared. Then, I compare it to the prior night. That tells me where we must go to find a homebase."

She stared up into the night sky but saw nothing except bright pulsing lights surrounded by a dark void.

"I don't understand."

He tried again. "Do you see the star there, low to the ground? That's where I'm going. If you are too, we can travel together."

He grinned, bounced once and again, happy that he'd found exactly the right way to explain his method. She hid her continued confusion with a smile which made him clap his hands and then twirl in a tight circle, eyes closed, arms outspread. Xhosa squinted again up into the sparkling sky, still saw nothing and left Seeker to his exultation. She didn't know where to find the People's new home but if Seeker could—and she was as sure as he that he could—she would follow him.

In addition, for such a youngster, he had exceptional instincts. If Xhosa had come across the bumbling, slow-thinking Zvi, wandering by herself, Xhosa would have rejected her as a waste of resources. That would have been a mistake, one that would have meant the death of the handfuls of the People Zvi had saved during the Ice Mountain battle. Seeker had seen her strength, her kindness, and accepted Zvi without expecting her to prove herself in any way. He recognized in her a friend so loyal, she would do anything for him, so devoted, none could sway her commitment to those she called pack.

Seeker told the story of how they met. Zvi had been abandoned by her People at the same time Seeker left his family to follow the stars. When he was seriously injured. Zvi saved his life. Something clicked between them, as though they were two parts of a whole, pups from the same pack, streams feeding into one river. Seeker didn't care that Zvi stuttered and the huge female didn't care that Seeker was curious about... everything... so curious he couldn't walk without stopping to exclaim about a spider's web, a colorful plant, or the brightness of Sun. Together, with the massive blue-eyed wolf, they became pack.

How Zvi found Spirit was a long and complicated story, told and retold often over long nights around a fire. But that Zvi and Seeker earned the loyalty of a wolf was one more reason Xhosa respected both. Spirit had proven more than once that he would give his life for his pack. Without him, Seeker and Zvi probably wouldn't have survived their many Moons of migrating, just the two of them, before they met up with the People. Spirit sniffed out herds well before any hunter and killed prey without spears or throwing stones. Then, he carried as much meat as two full-grown males and was happy to share it with his pack.

Xhosa dragged herself back to the current problems. Though she probably couldn't change Nightshade's mind about Lyta, she could persuade him to tolerate Pan-do if she picked exactly the right words.

She placed an open palm on his arm and met his eyes. "We need Pan-do. His People add size to our group that will prevent attacks."

Nightshade spat on the ground and rubbed the spot with his foot. "He will do what is good for his People, nothing more, nothing less. As will we." But his shoulders drooped. He understood her point.

Sun cast a radiant glow over the shore, its warmth out of sync with her mood or events. From down the shore, a muted howl echoed. Spirit's ears perked and a soft growl rumbled from his chest. Xhosa had one more point to make and then she must leave. Anyone injured would not live much longer.

"When you win the challenge to be Leader of the former Hawk People, you must continue as my Lead Warrior until Snake or Sa-mo-ke can take over."

Darkness shrouded his face, no doubt questioning why she included Pan-do's warrior as a potential Lead. If he couldn't make the connection to appeasing Pan-do, so be it. She didn't have to explain herself and wouldn't.

As the silence between them lengthened, the corner of his eye twitched, followed by his ear, and then an uptick in his lips as he worked through her words and his response.

Finally, he motioned, "As you wish."

There were good reasons Nightshade must remain her Lead Warrior but none more critical than the one he probably thought she didn't know, that he'd once planned to push her from power. She couldn't prove it but believed it. It's what he would do if he sensed weakness. His merciless reputation—at least in part—kept the People safe. She had no desire to change that, just to keep an eye on him.

He stepped close enough she could smell his sweat, the pond plants stuck in his hair, and the sourness telling her he hadn't eaten in a while. She waited, lips thinned, shoulders back, knowing what payment he would require even before he spoke, prepared to accept the price.

"If we pairmate after I defeat Water Buffalo, we join our People with the former Hawk People, exactly as you hoped to do with Hawk. That sends a potent message to all that we are united in our strength."

What she said next could change everything. Her gaze passed over the beleaguered groups of people, trusting she could solve this latest disaster, none more so than Seeker. Oblivious to the broken and dead bodies, shredded logs, tangled vines, and whispering confused groups, he spun in dizzy circles, arms stretched up, body glowing with energy. Watching this odd wild creature, no one would believe he had become integral to the future of her People.

Zvi crouched by Seeker, and with them, Pan-do's young daughter Lyta. Both kept one eye on Seeker and the other on the stomach of a gazelle they were cleaning. To their side lay Spirit, flank pressed against Zvi, head resting between muddy paws. His ears twitched as he looked over the sprawling group that was his pack. He never paused, starting over when he reached the last one. A wet leaf covered the puncture wound in his hind leg caused by an enemy spear. Lyta had bandaged it with honey, moss, and leaves. The sweet syrupy liquid oozed out from holes in the leaves where he had gnawed them.

The wolf sensed Xhosa's attention and fixed his blue eyes on her. His eyebrows bunched in worry but his tail slapped the ground as though to ask how he could help her. She showed her teeth and he settled back to a vigilant rest.

She had planned to pairmate with Hawk as a way to strengthen the People. The same logic should apply when Nightshade led the same group but it felt different. Still, "felt" had no part in her decisions for the People. She flicked the thought away as she would toss aside a weed that couldn't be eaten.

Nightshade shuffled impatiently but she ignored it. This would work best if he had to wait and worry. She rolled around in her mind how to craft a response that he would accept while giving her the time she needed to finish what she must do. Finally, she turned to him, searched his eyes for deceit and saw only hope.

"When you are the former Hawk People Leader, we will find a new home and you and I will pairmate, to celebrate combining our power, to acknowledge the strength of our future."

Nightshade hid his surprise and pleasure with a dip of his head.

She knotted her long hair behind her neck, so unlike the kinky shortness of everyone else's. Sun was high overhead but still climbing. She needed to go or she wouldn't have enough daylight for what she must do.

"We will talk more later," she motioned with a glance and then stared. How had she missed how pale and drawn his face? And fatigue etched lines around his eyes where they hadn't been before?

"Have you slept since we landed, Nightshade?" His teeth ground noisily as he lifted a hand to respond but let it flop to his side. "You're exhausted. Rest. I'll wake you if you're needed."

Her motions were chopped and angry. It did the People no good if he was too tired to think. She doubted he would listen.

After a breath, she added softly, "If you're not going to sleep, decide who will be the People's Second, after you become the former Hawk People's Leader."

This was a critical decision because the Second would become her Lead Warrior when Nightshade transitioned out. Snake had filled the position since Ngili's death because Nightshade said he should. Snake worked the warriors relentlessly, took his responsibilities seriously, and viciously reprimanded those who failed to meet Nightshade's expectations. He was loyal and obedient to his Lead, never questioning, never delaying.

But there was a problem. Since Snake didn't challenge for Second, his leadership didn't come from the loyalty of warriors who had seen him defeat their best. It came from Nightshade. What Snake said was what Nightshade said. Xhosa needed someone capable of making good decisions, creative if needed, in her absence.

The obvious choice to her was Stone. The huge warrior had once challenged Ngili, her father's Lead, now dead. The contest had been who could bring down a water buffalo first. Ngili suggested they work together to separate two animals from a herd and then see who could bring their animal down first. Stone couldn't believe his good fortune. The tricky part, where Ngili excelled, was isolating the animals. After that, physical strength would determine the winner, where Stone had a decided advantage.

It took most of the daylight to trap a pair away from the herd in a dead-end canyon. Ngili and Stone each pointed to the one they would kill and then sprinted forward without another word. Ngili leaped onto the water buffalo's back and stunned it with a blow to the temple and then stabbed a spear through its neck. He planned to hang on until it collapsed which would keep him away from its lethal hooves as it died, but a glance at Stone said waiting wouldn't work.

Stone was in trouble.

Stone's water buffalo had backed the huge warrior up against the canyon wall. One of Stone's spears poked out of the beast's shoulder, the other its side. The animal's hide was so thick with age that the wounds hadn't penetrated enough to do more than anger the beast. Stone's neck sack lay out of reach, his throwing stones scattered. Stone stood fiercely, unwavering, eyes dark and angry, feet spread, gripping his warclub one-handed while the other protected his heavily bruised chest. A deep slash to his upper leg bled freely, probably from water buffalo's horn. He showed no fear, no sign of giving up, and growled at Ngili to stay away. Ngili cocked his head. Stone might win if the spear had punctured a lung but there were no bloody bubbles erupting from the animal's mouth.

Apparently, Stone missed that.

Since Ngili had already won the challenge, he decided the People couldn't risk losing a fighter of Stone's caliber. He tumbled off the dying water buffalo, avoiding its final kick, and sliced open its throat with his cutter. Then, he surprised Stone's animal by grabbing its tail and leaping to its back. It reared and shook but Ngili gripped the long hair on its spine and squirmed up the body. When it turned to bite him, Ngili severed its throat.

From then on, Stone attached himself to his Lead, watching how he made decisions and listening as Ngili explained the strategies behind them. When Ngili was killed by Big Heads, Nightshade made Snake his Second. Stone didn't challenge, telling his pairmate he wanted no part of the crazed anger that often swamped Nightshade.

From that day, when Nightshade made Snake Second over Stone, it was clear Snake would be loyal to Nightshade first, his Leader next. Xhosa needed someone who put her first. If Stone wouldn't challenge, she would ask Sa-mo-ke. He was as good a fighter as Nightshade and as clever as herself.

Chapter 3

In the short time she and Nightshade had been talking, the wind had become blustery. A white cloud now floated from her mouth and nose with every exhale. She shivered and rubbed her arms as another gust off Endless Pond bit through her thin pelt. Even before the raging storm had shredded it, it would have been woefully inadequate for this land's cold. She missed the heat of her homeland, before Hawk. There, her People never needed animal skins.

If Nightshade can locate a herd, they will provide everyone with cold-air pelts.

"Water Buffalo says we are not far from one of the former Hawk People's old camps. We may run into a tribe of Others but it's a small group." He opened and closed both hands to show how few, "We will scout, hunt if we find a herd. Talon and Dust will guide us. Spirit will come, too."

Spirit hunted often with Nightshade. He seemed to respect the male warrior's attitude. The wolf would stay well to the front, return only to alert Nightshade of tribes or herds.

"How many of your warriors lost their spears and warclubs?"

"Almost none. Most tied them to their backs when the tempest hit but many of Hawk's and Pan-do's warriors didn't. They will have to make new ones."

He saw the worry in her hands, on her face. "We will be prepared if needed," and then left to join Sa-mo-ke, Water Buffalo, and a group of males.

Their eyes were red with fatigue, faces gray from exhaustion. All suffered deep gashes and bruises from the battle with the storm but ignored these as they threw out their chests and hardened their faces. Trust in Nightshade, that he would make everything work out, surpassed whatever fear they had for the future and none more so than Sa-mo-ke. Pan-do's Lead Warrior bristled with unbridled power, eager to start, spear in hand and warclub tied to his back. His lips pressed in a tight line, face pale but eyes sharp and bright, he turned—expectantly?—to Nightshade, awaiting direction.

Seeing Nightshade next to Water Buffalo appalled Xhosa. Water Buffalo, Nightshade's equal as Lead Warrior, appeared tense and skittish. The hand gripping his spear shook. The other clenched the warclub too tightly. Nightshade, in contrast, exuded confidence and authority. He sizzled with suppressed energy like an invisible firestorm. He took over the group by doing nothing more than arriving. Conversation stopped and everyone focused on him.

As Nightshade gave directions, Sa-mo-ke edged toward him and away from Water Buffalo, followed within a breath by the rest of his warriors. Surprisingly, so too did several of Water Buffalo's warriors. Nightshade had a fierceness about him, as if the air itself must make way while Water Buffalo looked frightened. When he tried to hide it with anger, it made him appear stubborn. The hunters and warriors— everyone—wanted what had been lost. Nightshade's movements, his attitude, promised to give them that if they followed him.

Feet spread, movements sure, Nightshade directed Water Buffalo, Talon, and other former Hawk warriors to go up the shoreline, Sa-mo-ke with his scouts the other direction while Nightshade, Snake, and Stone led a group inland. No one objected.

What would I do without Nightshade? He was her indomitable force, always had been. With him at her side, threats melted away.

Sa-mo-ke and his group vanished around a bend but Water Buffalo remained, distraught and frazzled, staring after Sa-mo-ke as though unsure where he went and why. His group milled around, baffled, some glancing at Nightshade as though to ask why Water Buffalo wasn't leaving and what Nightshade would do about it. Talon approached Water Buffalo and was angrily waved away.

Maybe the older male resented Nightshade's ability to take charge or maybe it was because Hawk had died. The reason didn't matter. He showed himself as petulant and indecisive at a time his warriors needed courage and confidence, chaotic when events required cohesion.

A moment passed and another until finally, Nightshade strode to the former Hawk People warriors. He motioned something to Talon who answered with a curt nod and headed toward the trees. The rest of the group followed him.

None waited for Water Buffalo's confirmation.

Next, Nightshade led the People's warriors inland, beckoning to Spirit but the wolf stayed with Siri. After a questioning glance, Nightshade left.

Water Buffalo now stood alone. He seemed beaten down by the adverse circumstances with no idea how to rise above. He fumbled for his spear and, with none of his usual swagger, raced after Talon.

Xhosa thought to herself, *Now I understand what Hawk meant.*

Hawk once told her his Lead Warrior was *always loyal but never smart*, and if the day came he could no longer lead, he would pick Nightshade as his successor.

Xhosa shivered as she watched Water Buffalo disappear into the distance. If Nightshade didn't win the challenge, her People must leave.

She glanced up at Sun, now directly overhead.

"I need to go," she mumbled but then heard Spirit whine, loudly, as though to get her attention. She'd never heard the wolf complain before.

Xhosa called, "Siri! What's wrong with Spirit?"

The Primary Female poked at Spirit's muzzle. His tail drooped, legs shook, and he huffed—like he was embarrassed.

Siri motioned, "Spirit has a problem."

Xhosa trotted over, stopped in front of the wolf, and had to bite back a giggle. Porcupine quills covered his face, sticking out of his snout and lips. Even his tongue and inside his mouth had been speared.

Siri motioned, "I once removed these from a child. It must be the same process on a wolf."

Lucy, Zvi, and Xhosa held Spirit in place while Siri pulled the spines out, cautious not to break them off under the skin. The last spine gone, Spirit shook enthusiastically and sprinted toward Endless Pond. He stuck his head into the cool water, raising his muzzle occasionally to breathe while Zvi and Seeker rubbed his back and whispered to him.

Xhosa motioned to Siri, "How are things?"

"I've sent Gadi, El-ga, and other children to collect roots while Wa-co and Clear River pick up the dead fish on the shore. Whoever's done first will get to collect berries."

These treats were rarely found in Hawk's homebase or Xhosa's former home. "The children stuff themselves and then take what they can't eat to share with group members. I let them. They need something happy after what they've been through."

Xhosa smiled. "We have lots of plants, nuts, roots, and other food?"

"Yes, we will eat well."

If the People had a Lead Female, it was Siri. As Primary Female, she organized females and children to scavenge, trained the subadults, and resolved disputes that didn't involve the males. Neither Pan-do nor the former Hawk People had such a female so Siri accepted the responsibility to serve them also. She treated all females with equal respect regardless of their group. When the People managed to blend as one group, much credit would go to Siri.

"I'm glad you recovered, Xhosa. We worried." When Xhosa didn't respond, Siri stepped nearer. "You are better, aren't you?"

In fact, her eyes throbbed as though a cactus spike had been stabbed through them but pain was weakness, to be ignored, not coddled.

She motioned, "I am going down the shoreline to look for survivors. If you hear the hoot of Owl, send help," and she left at a fast trot.

Chapter 4

Yesterday, while she was passed out and then as she recovered, group members straggled into the temporary camp all day, some hobbling by themselves, many supported by others. Xhosa had hoped that by the time daylight ran out, she could account for everyone but there were many she couldn't find. They might be dead but maybe they were simply too injured to reach the camp on their own.

Today, she would find them.

The area where the People now camped sprawled over a wide area, down Endless Pond's coastline and inland until it almost reached the prickly scrub brush and gritty ragged berms that edged the sandy shores. Beyond those were fields overflowing with wildflowers, the reds and blues and yellows choking the crevices between an abundance of rocks and boulders. This continued toward distant mountains whose jagged sides were covered in trees and brush, their tips white as though coated with foam. None spewed black smoke as the Fire Mountains of her homeland did or belched the bubbling red rivers that too often spilled down the flanks and destroyed everything in their path.

Eventually, the People would have to cross these mountains but not until the group was healed and their animal skins replaced.

As Xhosa crossed the camp, Spirit yelped a greeting and then returned to cavorting in the waves along the shore, snapping at white caps while favoring his injured limb. The chill air had heated enough that Xhosa no longer shivered under her tattered animal skin. She greeted those she passed, assuring them the rafts had landed where they needed to be, and promising she had a plan to find a new homebase. Yesterday, most had seemed doubtful but today, well-fed, their Leader healthy, many smiled. They trusted her to fix everything.

Xhosa believed in herself but more than that, she believed in Nightshade. He thrived on chaos, his every movement an intoxicating brew of formidable dominance and indefatigable vigor. Where some wilted under the stress of the storm, the unexpected changes, it energized him.

Just above the skyline, the puffy white clouds darkened. In the distance, the sky rumbled and sent fire to the ground and then pelting rain. It wouldn't be long before it reached the People. Survivors would die if left to the mercy of this storm. Xhosa instinctively reached for her neck sack where she carried everything required for a journey including food, water, throwing stones, and healing plants.

Sacks were usually made from an animal bladder or stomach, this one, Mammoth's. She had cleaned it with sand and then rubbed it with salt to tamp down the odor as well as preserve it. A tendon was woven through small holes punctured at the top so it could be looped over her head. When tendons were unavailable, she used rushes. On her last hunting trip with Hawk, he showed her how to make a neck sack from Mammoth's leg. That was bigger than a bladder or stomach and lasted longer.

Xhosa pushed the memories aside and hurried down the shore, stepping around and over broken branches and dead fish. Tiny shelled creatures darted across her path and buried themselves in the sand just before she could grab them.

She heard a moan and raced forward. It was Cloud, resting awkwardly on her bottom, legs stretched out in front.

"Let me help you."

Though still a subadult, which put her somewhere between a child and an adult, if she had bled, she could mate and that made her valuable to the People. When Rainbow was still part of the People, Cloud had wanted to mate with the charismatic, confident future Leader. He knew it and had invited her to join him when he separated from the People. To his surprise, she refused. She had no family left but Siri and Xhosa had done their best to step in when she needed them. If she left them, she would lose even that. Yes, Rainbow's path appeared much easier than Xhosa's desolate trail edged with bubbling magma pools like those found inside Fire Mountain, but Rainbow had never been a Leader. Why trust him to find a new homebase when she already trusted Xhosa?

Recently, Siri had taken a greater interest in Cloud because as she grew up, she seemed cleverer than most in solving problems, healing wounds, and devising tricks to complete tedious tasks. Cloud had hoped to become the one to help Siri in her varied tasks and even take over for her as Primary Female when needed.

"Can you stand?" Xhosa motioned and got an immediate head shake. "Then stay as still as possible so I can study your injury."

Cloud groaned as Xhosa inspected a deep gash across the bottom of her foot and then a laceration through her calf. Based on her backtrail, the young female had tried to crawl to the camp before she finally quit, too exhausted or in too much pain to continue.

"Why didn't you try to fix these wounds yourself?"

It was a fair question considering Cloud's experience. The injured female panted, tried to answer, face prickled with sweat, and then motioned down her backtrail.

"I … used all … of my supplies … on … Dark."

Xhosa peered down the shore and picked out Dark, or rather his carcass. Green-backed flies burrowed into his skin where they even now deposited eggs that in Dark's case would never hatch. A pack of hyaena had descended on the fresh meat. Some ripped flesh from bones while others guarded the scavenge.

One caught Cloud's blood scent and padded toward her, hackles up, yellow eyes ablaze, fangs gleaming with saliva.

Xhosa locked her eyes on the hyaenas and motioned to Cloud, "We have company."

Hyaena sniffed and seemed to smile, muzzle open, when it realized that one among the prey was gravely injured. He snarled once, again, and then leaped. Instead of backing up, Xhosa dove at the airborne hyaena, wrapped an arm around its neck, squeezed tight while twisting her body against Hyaena's, and they both crashed to the ground. There was an audible crack and the animal went limp beneath her.

Xhosa tossed it aside, growled at the dead animal's pack, and returned to Cloud, not even winded. She scrubbed the female's wounds with moss, filled them with sap, and wrapped them with leaves and tendons. Done, she hooted to call Ant. He would get Cloud to the camp so Xhosa could continue to search for more injured.

By the time Sun reached within two hands of the horizon, Xhosa had treated as many People as fingers on both hands. For some, she filled gruesome wounds with honey, moss, and herbs, and secured them with sinew. Others, she stopped the bleeding with a mulch of roots and stems and covered it in a poultice. If they had no weapons, which made them easy prey, Xhosa stayed with them until help arrived.

Her job completed for the moment, Xhosa climbed to the top of a hill for a better view of the shoreline. The vastness of Endless Pond took her breath away. It stretched interminably forward and back—and across. Its color changed from a dark blue toward the horizon to light blue as it approached the sandy beaches. Waves lapped the shore before receding into white foam.

To her strong side and the direction the People must go, green grass bordered the shoreline, sprinkled with fields of sun-colored flowers and dotted by saplings not tall enough to provide shade. Beyond them were gently rolling hills that abutted rugged spires as tall as the Fire Mountains of her homeland. Rather than tipped with smoke and flames, the peaks glistened white, the flanks an earthy brown and farther down, swathed in green and yellow trees. Xhosa marveled at the nimble animals who sprinted up and down the steep cliffs with abandon. A pair of Eagles, their dark bodies silhouetted against the pale blue of the sky, floated in the valley between two mountains.

Hawk had hoped to pass this mountain range on the rafts. Now, the People must climb over them, including the foreboding white areas. Whatever perils they held, she and her People would face. They must. They had no choice

A voice called, "Xhosa—here!"

She turned toward the sound and saw the youngster El-ga, waving frantically from the side of a huge boulder at the edge of Endless Pond, part in part out of the water. Xhosa remembered the boy. She had saved his life when the People fled the Big Heads.

With a return wave, she raced toward him. "What's wrong?"

"It's my mother," and he pointed to a shivering bundle leaning against the boulder, one leg bent and the other resting in the frigid Pond water. El-ga's mother, Wa-co, shook nonstop, her lips blue and her teeth chattering so loudly, they sounded like one of the tree-eating birds.

Xhosa crouched at her side, unlooping her neck sack from her shoulders.

Wa-co motioned, "I c-can't walk. I t-tried to numb my l-leg in the co-cold water enough for the w-walk to camp but I can't s-stand. El-ga w-won't leave m-me."

Xhosa frowned at the white bone poking through the skin. Wa-co was not going anywhere without help. Xhosa hooted Owl's call, packed the cut with a poultice, and then protected it with moss and spiderwebs. There was nothing she could do for the pain. She'd already used all those plants.

Next, she turned to El-ga. "Are you alright?"

He gulped a yes, too worried to say more.

"If there is a next time, El-ga, go for help."

The youngster's life was as important as the female's. Losing both when one could be saved was wasteful.

Ant panted as he reached them, grinning, slender body damp with sweat. He grabbed Wa-co around the waist and guided her to the temporary camp. El-ga hugged Xhosa and then joined his mother, head hanging, his posture and movements saying how much the future worried him.

Many of today's injuries should have been handled by the victims. Xhosa resolved when the People settled into a new home, all must become more self-reliant.

She sagged behind the boulder where she had found Wa-co. Her temples pounded and the wounds from her own injuries throbbed. She chewed through the last of her head pain leaves, mixing in honey to cut the bitterness, and waited for them to work while listening to the waves lap against Endless Pond's shore. She slit her tired eyes at the sound of paws padding toward her, accompanied by heavy, happy pants.

"Spirit. Why are you here?" Though she guessed it was the Hyaena. Wolves didn't like them.

Or, he might smell his kind.

Spirit sat gingerly on the substantial haunch of his uninjured leg, heaved a sigh, and fixed his blue eyes on her as though to say he knew all about her chronic suffering.

"You must keep my secret, Spirit, even from Zvi and Lyta. No one respects weakness and I can't get rid of this. Now, more than ever, the People need an invincible Leader."

Hidden by the boulder, as she rubbed between Spirit's ears and listened to his contented pants, she grieved for Hawk. Tears rolled down her cheeks and Spirit leaned into her side.

"I miss him, Spirit."

When her People arrived at Hawk's homeland as strangers, he welcomed her. Despite the vast size of her group and the fierceness of her warriors, he never considered them a risk. Over time, he taught her to prepare the pelts everyone now wore and create the fire that protected them at night. Together, they figured out how to make the stone-tipped spears favored by Big Heads. The combined Peoples thrived under their joint guidance.

Xhosa shook her head to clear away the memories and Spirit mimicked her, quivering from muzzle to paws.

"Hawk is gone, Spirit. This," and she flapped a desultory hand behind her, "is where I am now," *an unknown land with undrinkable water and nameless enemies.* "And another storm about to arrive."

A chorus of wolves howled at the redolent aroma of blood. Spirit responded, his voice menacing, as he marked the shoreline with his urine to warn these brothers to leave his territory and his pack alone. The wolves fell silent but Hyaena took up the challenge, angry at the encroachment on their space. High-pitched yelps echoed from the underbrush accompanied by the glitter of yellow.

Spirit leaped toward the noise and snarled, ears pinned back, tail stiff, blue eyes blazing. His substantial feet spread beneath massive muscular shoulders and his bared fangs dripped saliva.

"Spirit!" Pan-do called as his steps thundered toward Xhosa, the night birds whistling in alarm. In the distance, Hyaena chewed noisily on more of the People's carcasses.

Xhosa sprang to her feet and motioned to Pan-do, "Someone may need help," and she flew down the shore, Spirit at her heels, pulling to a stop a spear's throw from a hyaena pack gathered around a bloody carcass. One of the creatures—Spirit's color but smaller, scrawnier, and much less sure of itself— eyed the strangers while chewing into some ribs.

When it was clear nothing but death lay in front of her, Xhosa slid backward. One hyaena padded slowly toward her, blood drooling from wet red teeth, but stopped when Spirit moved in front of Xhosa, growling. In a predator-prey world, Spirit's massive size made him an alpha. Suddenly, easy prey became probable death. The hyaena didn't want live meat at that cost. There were plenty of carcasses.

"Xhosa." Pan-do huffed up to her, his body covered in sweat, still too exhausted from the crash for hard running like this. He pointed toward the dark clouds that filled the sky over the horizon. "We have to go. Siri has a fire going under a ledge."

The wall of clouds had moved much closer than the last time Xhosa looked. They would barely make it to the shelter before the rain fell.

She pointed to wounds on his leg, chest, and shoulder. "Those need to be cleaned, as soon as we reach the camp."

Xhosa didn't look back as they raced away, knowing all she needed to from the sounds of cracking bones, slurping, and territorial snarls. Spirit remained behind, guarding their backtrail.

The last of Sun's rays spilling through the clouds were finally blotted out by the ominous towering blackness. As Xhosa and Pan-do ducked under the ledge, Spirit right behind, the sky barked with anger, threw spears of fire, and dumped its rain. The blazing fire felt good, its warmth and protection welcome. Pan-do followed Xhosa to a corner where she applied a mulch of roots and flowers to his wounds. As she worked, she asked about Lyta.

Pan-do coughed and rubbed his eyes. "I thought I lost her, Xhosa. She dove into the water to rescue Spirit, dragged him to a log. He grasped it with his claws and they paddled toward shore. Zvi hauled them out of the water. That Zvi— she is tougher than any male, even Stone. Many of my People and yours owe their lives to her."

"Does that include you, Pan-do?"

"No. For that, I owe Spirit. What was left of my raft crashed far down the shore. Logs pinned my legs until Spirit found me. He pulled them off one after another and then let me lean on him as I hobbled to the camp. The first thing I did was look for Lyta." He hung his head and scuffed a toe through the sand. "I should have worried about my People but thought only of my daughter."

Xhosa understood, both the emotion and the humiliation. The tears she shed for Hawk, though private, shamed her also.

"Lyta can swim?"

"Spirit taught her."

Xhosa nodded. It had surprised her when the wolf leapt into the water and pawed toward the rafts, and again when he managed to evade all but one of the Ice Mountain spears.

She motioned, "And Seeker?"

Pan-do flashed his teeth. "He must have been a fish once." His smile evaporated. "You know what happened to Hawk?"

"Yes," and said nothing more. The wound was too new to discuss with anyone, even Pan-do.

He continued, "Ant has been worried about you. He doesn't forget your trust in him."

Xhosa welcomed a new topic. "Was he injured?"

"Nothing that bothered him but I think he's oblivious to pain."

While still a subadult, Ant had survived a boil that ate through his calf and had fallen into molten lava that almost burned away the lower part of the same leg. His constant injuries made the male adults consider him nothing but trouble. Even her father wanted to abandon him.

Xhosa motioned, "He deserves my trust, and everyone's. He never complains, always completes his work, rarely questions why, and is well-liked."

Pan-do gestured, "It was he who saved Siri, dragged her from the water. She can't swim." He paused, staring at the People, looking for Siri. "Siri, she has been tireless, assuring everyone that you would awaken with a plan. She reminds me of Ah-ga—"

The name came out a strangled croak. Xhosa suspected the agony of remembering his pairmate's death wasn't worth whatever point he wanted to make.

But he surprised her and after a deep breath, continued. "Ah-ga was my Hawk, Xhosa. I believe I felt her loss as you do Hawk's."

Xhosa grimaced to herself. *Yes, if it felt like slicing your chest open, filling it with honey, and lying on top of an ant hill.*

"Many Moons came and went before I recovered enough to mate."

And then the Ice Mountain enemy killed the female Pan-do chose.

He continued, "But the People grow only through new babies so I must move on. You, too." He placed a light hand on her arm. "Like all wounds, yours will heal."

"Some wounds, like the loss of an arm, never do."

The rain slowed to a heavy mist that tickled her skin, refreshing in its coldness. She turned her back on the fire pit's flames to let her eyes adjust to the darkness. The air flowed over her, wet and swollen, making her breath a cloud that billowed in front of her. She rubbed her arms but couldn't stop shivering, not all due to the cold.

She glanced around. They were alone. Everyone else had moved close to the fire. She might never have as good an opportunity to say what she must.

"Pan-do. Moons ago, you warned me someone plotted against me. I ignored you when I should have listened. I know that now. I want you to know that."

She gulped in a deep, ragged breath and continued, "I need someone who tells me the truth even when I don't want to hear it. There is no one else I trust to do that."

Pan-do fidgeted, uncomfortable with such honesty and he rose to leave.

She lightly gripped his arm. "Here's what I need truth about. I'm not sure what to do about the former Hawk People."

She didn't bother to explain that yes, the next Leader of the former Hawk People was none of her business, that her only concern should be the survival of her People. Because she was pretty sure Pan-do agreed with her that the future of her People—and his—depended on who next led Hawk's group.

When he responded, he skipped all of that as though it had been said and started exactly where her biggest concerns rested. "The warriors respect Nightshade—"

"They respect his power, as do I, but when cannibals threatened us, you're the one who came up with a way to escape without lives lost."

"Shouldn't that always be the goal?"

"The more I'm around you, the more I agree. That's why I ask your advice."

She watched him out of the corner of her eye as he studied something outside of the camp. His dark eyes radiated honesty, caring, and an uncompromising intelligence.

After a breath he answered, hands low and quiet, "Lyta tells me Nightshade wants to lead the former Hawk People. Shouldn't Hawk's Lead Hunter or Warrior do that?"

The former Hawk People combined the job of Lead Scout with Lead Hunter, as Xhosa's People did. After the death of the previous Lead in the tempest, that job fell to young Dust.

Xhosa motioned, "You're thinking of Dust? He didn't even want the job of Lead Hunter. He likes scouting, not ending life. And he doesn't feel competent to make decisions that affect others. When Hawk was Leader, no one expected that of him."

Pan-do grinned. "He is wrong to think himself incapable. Hawk told me a story about Dust's first hunt. They were tracking a herd of Gazelle. The hunters argued that by the time they got there, the animals would be gone but Dust pointed out one who limped, something no one else noticed. Even if the herd moved on, the injured one couldn't follow.

"They set out and as expected, by the time they got to the herd's location, only the injured one remained, nibbling at the grass, holding up her rear leg. The hunters prepared to kill her until Dust stepped in front of their spears.

"See her belly—she carries a fawn!"

"Hunters don't slay pregnant females because they represent future food.

"One hunter argued, *"She limps! Coyote or wolf will bring her down if we don't."*

"But again, Dust noticed what no one else did. He covered his face and arms with the herd's dung to hide his scent and approached Gazelle. Her soft brown eyes latched onto his as though she couldn't look away. She quaked with terror, from her slender legs to the shiver of her ears.

"It's OK, Gazelle. I see the problem."

"He stepped closer, hands out, palms down, as he might show an enemy he meant them no harm. Her huge eyes watched him unblinking, bewildered by the familiar smell of her herd but from an upright animal. He gently lifted her injured leg, turned it hoof up, and saw what he expected.

"A sharp rock was wedged between her claws, so deeply that blood trickled.

"This must hurt, Gazelle. I can help you."

"He pulled his cutter from his neck sack and burrowed the edge into the tender skin, trying to dig the rock out. It didn't budge so he tried from the opposite side. This time, it popped out, leaving behind a smudge of Gazelle's blood and red irritated skin. He placed the injured leg to the ground and backed away.

"She blinked, maybe a *thank you*, cocked her delicate head, and sprinted after her herd, the limp gone.

"If Dust hadn't noticed that slight bump on her stomach, if he hadn't removed the stone from her hoof, she would have died and taken with her the People's future food. He made the right decision. One who is willing to stand up for his beliefs, especially those singly held, can do the job of Leader."

A mournful howl sounded in the night's shadows, answered by Spirit.

Pan-do listened a moment and then continued, "But no. Despite what I've just said, I don't mean Dust."

Xhosa gestured, "The only other option for Leader is Water Buffalo but I have reason to doubt him."

She said enough. If Pan-do had advice he wanted to share, he would.

He pushed to his feet. "Come. Let us show our People the strength of their Leaders."

Chapter 5

The rain drenched the land all night, steady and cold. Two subadults took turns feeding the fire. Xhosa slept at the front of the overhang with the warriors, listening for sounds over the patter of rain, finally falling asleep when she heard nothing.

The silence woke her. The sky had lightened along the distant ridge and Sun's new rays sparkled off the damp leaves and stones. Not a single cloud spoiled the endless sky. Morning was Xhosa's favorite part of the day, a glorious time when the land came to life.

It didn't last long. Siri sent the children to collect palm-sized rocks that would be needed for neck sacks. The excited giggles and the clack-plunk of rocks striking others soon replaced the quiet.

"Greetings, Xhosa." Pan-do found her as she released her water, his voice strong, movements sure despite everything that had happened. With him was Water Buffalo. "Water Buffalo and I ticked off the group members. Each group has lost many—children and females as well as males."

Water Buffalo's insolent scowl said coming here was Pan-do's idea and he wanted no part of working with a female. He turned to leave but Xhosa stopped him.

"How did the scouts do yesterday, Lead Warrior?" Nightshade had told her but she wanted to hear it from the one who wished to be Leader.

"Herds are nearby. Fields of plant food are plentiful. Small groups of Others populate the land but look peaceful."

He wouldn't look her in the eye but his hands moved with none of yesterday's nervousness.

As he turned to leave, she stopped him again. "Water Buffalo. When will the former Hawk People select their new Leader?"

Something flashed across his face but disappeared too quickly for her to decipher.

He motioned, "Soon," and pivoted away before she could ask more, winding his way toward his Second, Talon, and a group of males eager to start the day's tasks. He motioned instructions and Talon trotted off, followed by the group. By snubbing her in front of everyone, Water Buffalo screamed that he didn't need her permission or advice. Xhosa could have forced him to remain but she didn't.

Pan-do stared after him. "He distrusts female Leaders. He will change his mind when he gets to know you."

"It's alright, Pan-do. I am accustomed to gaining respect by proving myself. If he does not come around when he sees the evidence, I will destroy him."

Water Buffalo's report had disappointed her. She wanted to know that all warriors would soon have spears, warclubs, and throwing stones. If he didn't think weapons were her business, he was wrong.

"Pan-do, would you trust Water Buffalo as Leader?"

He grimaced. "To be loyal? Not without being forced."

That was her answer, too, and she turned her attention to matters of her People.

At the side of the camp, Dust was working with Bone and Ant on scouting. They listened to him intently, animated by what he said. When he finished, they swaggered in tight circles, ready to get started.

Pan-do gestured, "Nightshade found prints yesterday. He asked Dust to take Bone and Ant with him and help them learn about scouting. If there's a herd, he'll find it."

"Water Buffalo!" Talon was standing just outside the camp. "Nightshade said there are trees we can use for spears and warclubs," and he gestured to a grove not far down the shore. "We'll go there when we finish hunting."

Making a spear was a lengthy process. The warriors must select a sturdy sapling, shorten it, chop off the branches, and then spend the day scraping and smoothing until it became a serviceable spear. New warclubs took much longer. For these, the warrior must find a hard-wood limb as wide and straight as a leg, trim and smooth it, and then shape the grip to fit his hand. Hawk taught Xhosa how to smooth away the slivers by rubbing it with a grit-covered damp hide from Hare or Antelope. It did a better job than even a carefully applied chopper. Some warriors wrapped plant cordage around the grip while others left the area bare. The best clubs preserved the natural nodes which—if wielded correctly—would puncture an enemy or prey during a fight.

A good warclub required a Moon or more to create. Nightshade had spent most of a rainy season on his new one when the old one cracked. Warriors didn't lose their warclubs.

"No," and Water Buffalo pointed to another grove, farther away and in the opposite direction. "Go there."

Talon looked confused but bobbed his head and sprinted off.

Nightshade smiled and Xhosa understood why. Talon would spend a hand of Sun's journey only to find the trees unsuited for weapons, all because Water Buffalo wouldn't talk to the one who was soon-to-be Leader.

She exhaled. Her Lead Warrior hadn't started the problem but he would finish it. None disrespected him twice.

Whatever happened would. Right now, the People must figure out how to survive long enough to pass beyond the mountains. There, Hawk promised, were abundant herds, bountiful plants, endless groves of trees, and only small tribes of peaceful Others.

Nightshade motioned to Xhosa. "Talon will be back by here and Dust by here," and he pointed to spots in the sky more than two hands farther along on Sun's journey. "If one or both aren't, I will send a party after them."

Nothing about Nightshade said he worried. In fact, when he said, "send a party after them", he really meant "kill anyone who got in their way".

"Xhosa." Siri touched her arm. "I must set a broken bone and I have never done that before."

"Is it Cloud? Did you not help her when Ant brought her to camp last night?"

Siri's brow wrinkled. "No, it's Honey. I didn't see Cloud."

Xhosa had planned to join Pan-do in exploring the area, but now she must find Cloud and then help Honey.

She called to Pan-do, "Go without me. I will catch up or not." She trusted his observations.

"Siri, I'll look for Cloud. She may have been too sick to find you. While I do that, collect clay, big leaves, rushes or bunchgrass, and tree bark. If you can't find bark, two short branches at least as thick as a wrist will do."

Xhosa walked through the group, ticking off on her fingers everyone she saw or smelled and came up with the same list of those present that Water Buffalo and Pan-do did, but no Cloud. Ant said he had placed Cloud outside the overhang because she wanted the rain to wash off the dirt and silt. He knew nothing beyond that. Xhosa checked there and found blood, collected in one spot and then trailing to the edge of camp where it stopped, washed away by the night's rain.

Xhosa sighed. Cloud's injuries would prevent her from migrating for at least a handful of Suns. If they were at the People's homebase, others would help her move about and complete her chores. She would heal and then repay the assistance when someone else was injured. During a migration such as this, a pairmate or family member would carry her on their back. Since she had none, a group member would have to offer. If that didn't happen, and Cloud couldn't keep up with the group, she would crawl away to die alone rather than consume valuable resources and become a burden to the People.

Xhosa would send a scout out later to find the carcass.

She made her way back to Siri and Honey. The young female cowered, her skin prickled with sweat, her mouth tight. A swollen red bump below the knee told Xhosa at least one bone was broken.

At Siri's side hunched Bone, mouth open and eyes so wide white surrounded the color.

Siri motioned, "Bone brought her in as Sun woke."

The young male was a new adult. He'd finished training with a spear just before they fled Hawk's homebase.

Xhosa scowled at him. "Why aren't you hunting as you are trained to do?"

Bone reddened, mumbled something about blood and gore and vomit. Siri motioned him to silence. "I told him to wait. You will want to hear what he found."

Xhosa motioned, "Tell me," hands chopped and brisk.

"When Sun prepared to sleep, I found Honey as I headed for the camp. She-she couldn't walk."

He fidgeted, flicking his gaze from Xhosa to Siri to Honey. "She was alone and wolves were already closing on her. I built a fire to frighten them away. We fell asleep. When we awoke, the fire was out and one wolf was almost on us. I howled like wolf's enemies, tossed Honey onto my back, and fled."

Xhosa dismissed him. "Now go—"

"That's not all, Leader. I found footprints. Of Others. They snuck up on our camp while we slept."

"And left you alive?"

He nodded, head hanging.

They are the ones Hawk warned of, without fear of the night.

Xhosa swallowed the bile burning her throat and waved Bone away. Hopefully, the People's intimidating size, their many spears and warclubs, and the sophistication of their warriors—Nightshade especially—dissuaded attack.

Xhosa put those thoughts aside as she bent over Honey. She was Hawk's favorite until Xhosa arrived. When he stopped mating with her, Honey never said a word. She seemed to understand the importance of the two Leaders pairmating.

"I appreciate your help, Leader Xhosa." Honey's hands showed none of the agony she must feel. A broken limb made even hard warriors howl and hers was inflamed.

Xhosa placed her hands on the swollen bump. "Hold still," and she manipulated the bones.

Honey paled, brows furrowed, but made no sound.

"What I do next will hurt."

Using the healthy bone for reference, Xhosa pulled and twisted the foot until the broken bone ground into place. Honey gasped, stiffened, and fainted. While she was unconscious, Xhosa slathered Honey's lower leg with clay and big leaves, layered one on the other. On top of everything, she molded the bark as tightly as possible around her leg, from knee to ankle, and held it in place with rushes and the tendons Xhosa always carried around her neck.

The skin had split while she worked, allowing blood and pus to drain. Whether that was good or bad, Xhosa wouldn't know until later. Honey's skin would get hot and red or it wouldn't. One would kill her, the other help her recover. Xhosa had no control over either.

Honey awoke as Xhosa finished, her face as white as the foam on Endless Pond.

Xhosa motioned, "It's good you passed out. You missed most of the pain. Now sit while the clay hardens. When it does, you can walk but only with a stick to keep weight off the leg," and Xhosa left.

It was now up to Honey. If she survived, she would someday be an impressive female of the People. Few males stood up to the agony of a broken leg as she had.

Xhosa walked through the People, helping where possible, encouraging where she had nothing else to offer. She stopped by later to see if Honey needed pain plants and found Bone, doing the female's work. Today, that was digging for the tart-tasting bulbs that hid the flavor of meat when it began to green. His body was slick with sweat but he worked quickly, collecting more than a healthy Honey could have.

But he had other duties.

"You aren't with the hunters?"

"They were gone when I left to join them and, well, with Others around…" and his hand motions trailed off.

Bone wasn't a coward so his concern must be he didn't want to leave Honey alone.

Xhosa stooped at his side and motioned, "She is tough. You took care of her. She won't be able to walk for a while. Someone must do her work. Ask others to do this. We need you to hunt."

Bone hugged himself with one arm, rested the other on it and chewed the skin around his thumb, already raw and bloody.

"I'm frightened, Leader Xhosa. We lost everything. Water Buffalo says the tribes here are the most dangerous we've faced, even the Ice Mountain invaders. Will we die?"

Xhosa bit back her fury. What game did the former Hawk People's Lead Warrior play that he would frighten those he was entrusted to protect?

She forced her face to remain impassive. "We confront death every day, Bone, and will do so until it catches us. Every one of your groupmates has lost someone and seen others survive who shouldn't. We cannot live our lives in fear of what may be. We do our best and move on."

When he nodded, she left him to Honey's work and walked among the main group, wanting to see who else had fallen victim to Water Buffalo's dire warnings. Everyone worked diligently, chatting or listening to the melodic beauty of Lyta's bird songs, so Xhosa turned to the task of determining how to get her People out of this place. Zvi's escape plan failed because of the storm, not because of the rafts. Once the People rested, Zvi must collect more logs and create new paddles.

This time, they would leave on a sunny day.

She found the gigantic female talking to Spirit, her chest heaving, hair so wet with sweat she might have been swimming in Endless Pond. She turned toward Xhosa, panting in ragged gasps but grinning as though the day couldn't be better. Xhosa never saw Zvi unhappy.

"Zvi, how long will it take to rebuild the rafts?"

Zvi shook her head and a damp mist flew around her. "Seeker says the trees here are too heavy for rafts. I climbed up the mountains to those forests," and she pointed to a green band on a mountain so far away, even Xhosa's farsight blurred, "but they won't work either."

Xhosa sagged. Spirit padded over and leaned into her leg. A soft whine slipped from his massive mouth.

Zvi motioned, "Don't worry. I haven't given up," and she beamed like a child oblivious to the perils of these unfamiliar shores. Like Seeker, she didn't see problems. She saw adventure.

Xhosa liked this odd, oversized female, as loyal as any of the People.

Talon returned as daylight drained from the sky, head down. The trees where Water Buffalo sent him weren't suited to spears or warclubs. Tomorrow, he would try again, this time following Nightshade's suggestion. When Dust and the scouts returned to camp, they reported small groups of Others around the camp. If they were aware of the People's presence, it didn't show.

The scouts also found Cloud's carcass, torn apart by Hyaena. The scavengers would feast until the People's dead were devoured.

Chapter 6

The People stayed on the shore for a day and another. Food was bountiful giving them time to heal wounds, repair warclubs and spears, and fill neck sacks with throwing stones, choppers, cutters, and travel food. Zvi taught the children how to catch fish trapped in the tidepools created when the waves receded. Seeker showed the subadults—and some females—how to catch the speedy hard-shelled creatures that skittered across the sand, crack them open with a rock, and devour the soft tasty insides. Wa-co hobbled around, supported by El-ga, and Bone nagged Honey about using the walking stick and helped her when Snake didn't have work for him, which was often. Snake didn't like the gentle male. He disliked anyone timid because Nightshade did.

The morning after the second day, Xhosa awoke to the stench of Others not her People. She jerked upright to see a line of warriors inside the trees, a long spear-throw away, elbow-to-elbow, faces gruff. Each carried weapons with more across their backs.

Xhosa sniffed. "There aren't many."

Nightshade nodded, cold gaze fixed on the Others, "This is now our land. They can't stop us."

Xhosa and her Lead Warrior marched toward the intruders, pace long, weapons in hand, while the People's warriors assumed battle positions behind her. When lined up, fully armed, their size was overwhelming, the threat fearsome.

Pan-do joined Xhosa and Nightshade. "They had hoped to frighten us into leaving. Now they see that won't happen. In fact, if they don't back off, they will lose warriors and a battle."

Xhosa motioned, "I will talk to their Leader."

Pan-do stood beside her, feet spread, gaze never leaving the intruders. "We all go. Nightshade will be the warning of what they face in a battle. I will be the alternative. And you, Xhosa—they will know who you are for even here, they have heard of the great female Leader."

This was Pan-do, in command, evaluating the situation, devising a solution. His benign approach and lack of fear would go a long way to convince the Others that the People would avoid fighting if possible but engage if necessary.

A wet nose bumped Xhosa. She kept her eyes forward. "Spirit's presence will show them we are not the normal migrating group."

He nipped at the white cloud that formed with every breath in front of his snout, mystified when it dissolved before he could bite it. He had chewed through the bandage on his wound but he no longer needed it. Though a raw red wound remained, the limp was gone.

The People's Leaders walked forward with slow measured steps. Xhosa picked out the Other Leader and concentrated on him as he studied his opponents. His face went from respect for Nightshade's obvious ruthlessness to disdain for Pan-do's apparent softness, surprise at Xhosa's position of authority, and then fear when the wolf stared at him, fangs exposed. Xhosa kept her face placid, stopping a spear's throw away.

The Other Leader looked first at Nightshade and then Pan-do, not sure who to address. He picked Nightshade.

"Why are you here?"

When Xhosa responded, his mouth dropped open. "Our rafts crashed. We must restock food and weapons in preparation for departure. We have no interest in your land."

Spirit rumbled a low throaty growl. Xhosa smelled his feral scent, the one that warned enemies to back off or suffer the consequences.

She motioned, "Spirit does not like you."

"My warriors will stop him."

"Not before he tears your throat out. Look at him. Do you not see it is you who has his complete attention?"

The Leader visibly shook as he lurched backwards. Apparently, he never planned on being the first to die.

"How many days do you need, intruder?"

Xhosa motioned, "Less than a Moon. More than a Sun. We will not bother you. We want no problems."

To tell him they must replace a Leader and that could delay their departure would show weakness.

After a breath, the Leader motioned, "Go. Soon. We are only so patient."

But Xhosa stood there until the Others drifted back into the tree line. She had no fear of these Others but it would do the People no good to stay here longer than necessary. Water Buffalo seemed to assume he could become Leader without winning a challenge. Xhosa would have to change his mind.

As Sun started its downward journey, she found Dust working alone and asked him why his People hadn't yet selected a Leader.

He fidgeted. "We have never done this. Hawk followed his father as Leader."

"Isn't Water Buffalo an obvious choice?"

"He hasn't announced his intention to lead. We are as bewildered as you."

She stared out at the camp while watching Dust from the corner of her eye. His shoulders slumped, his head bowed, and sweat broke out on his upper lip. Then, he started sighing, heavily, as though he wanted to tell her something but couldn't.

Which told Xhosa what she needed. She clapped him on the back and motioned, "You have been a big help, Dust. Tell your People they must decide by tonight or Nightshade and I will do it for them." She softened her command with a smile and left.

Xhosa cringed thinking of Water Buffalo leading Hawk's mighty People. Her bias—and Hawk's—was always to act. She didn't respect those who let others resolve difficulties.

When day bled into night without word, Xhosa gathered with the rest of the groups around a fire. She and Pan-do squatted side-by-side with Nightshade to Xhosa's side and Sa-mo-ke to Pan-do's, leaving space by Nightshade for Water Buffalo. When Water Buffalo arrived at the fire, Xhosa pointed to the spot saved for him with a dismissive glance. His gaze narrowed to a slit and he refused to sit.

"You are no longer Hawk's pairmate. You won't push my People aside in favor of yours." His hands chopped, shoulders so tense they almost touched his ears.

Inside, Xhosa cheered.

Without looking at him, crunching through a handful of nuts and then a tough root, she gestured one-handed, "You do not act like a Leader, Water Buffalo, so I will not treat you as one."

"And you do not speak for the Hawk People!" he blustered, spraying saliva over the food around him.

After a long pause to finish off a pile of berries, she raised her eyes to his. "Hawk welcomed my People with a hand of friendship. He shared his knowledge as we did ours. When he asked me to pairmate, it was to stand at his side, as Co-leader."

She rose, stepped toward Water Buffalo, and stopped when she was so close the sway of her hair touched his arm. The entire group was so quiet, the chirp of grasshoppers and the hoot of a night bird echoed through the camp.

Xhosa studied Water Buffalo, eyes moving over his face, as a predator did prey.

"Hawk told you to resolve who would lead his warriors, you or Nightshade. You haven't."

Water Buffalo snarled. "You lie—"

"Have you forgotten I was there?"

Spirit growled, hackles up, commanding blue eyes locked on Water Buffalo.

Water Buffalo's gaze flicked to Spirit and then back to Xhosa. "I forget nothing and you are not our Leader."

Some grunted agreement while others maintained their silence, waiting.

"You worry because I am a female. My People will tell you we are as strong now as we were under my father."

Water Buffalo guffawed. "You were driven from your land. You lost half of your People to a rogue warrior. You arrived at our homebase starved and desperate. Why should I follow you?"

He motioned with expansive hands, gaze touching each of his warriors.

"Your Co-leader, Pan-do, takes advice from a subadult female and a crazed boy. Your Lead Warrior infuriates so many, none but his own warriors will ever be loyal to him."

Pan-do interjected, "You are wrong, Water Buffalo, I am proud to align with Nightshade, as is my Lead Warrior Sa-mo-ke. As are many of your warriors."

Water Buffalo sneered. "We will never follow one not of the Hawk People!"

Xhosa expected a reaction from Nightshade but he placed his hands placidly in his lap, eyes hooded, face shuttered. Pan-do too ignored the tirade, whispering to his daughter while smoothing Spirit's hackles.

Her father told her that a bad Leader destroyed good People. Water Buffalo must not be allowed to influence her People.

A deep silence settled when Water Buffalo finished. Xhosa let it bubble, her hands on her knees, fingers relaxed. A tiny crack appeared in Water Buffalo's veneer. He expected his warriors to defend him. Instead, they remained silent.

Time to spring her trap.

"How do you pick a Leader, Water Buffalo?"

"There will be a challenge."

"When?"

Water Buffalo blustered, "It is unnecessary. We all agree who will lead," but none of his warriors would meet his eye.

"I think you're wrong. Let's find out tomorrow."

With that she sat down, dismissing him. The conversation was over. A decision had been made. The group broke into clusters, close enough to the fire for warmth and far enough for privacy.

Pan-do leaned toward her, hands where only Xhosa could see. "You have much respect and support among all groups."

She finished her meal in silence and then retired with her People. The subadults took responsibility for feeding the fire with the twigs and logs that would keep it alive throughout the night.

The next day, subtle changes occurred. The former Hawk People began asking her advice, some questions as simple as whether it was safe to drink from the tidepools and others more involved, like how they would cross mountains that touched the clouds. When she suggested they discuss these with Water Buffalo, they claimed to have tried but he was too busy. Which angered them. They wanted sensible answers to serious questions and the male who wished to lead them couldn't take the time.

To Xhosa, taking time was the Leader's job.

But an elusive subtext wove its way through their faces and gestures that she couldn't quite grasp. When she asked Dust, he explained.

"We respect and like you, Leader Xhosa. We respect Nightshade but don't like him. If either of you challenge and win, the former Hawk People will proudly call you Leader."

As Sun slipped below the horizon, Pan-do appeared at her side. "You will soon become Leader of the combined People."

"You and I, Pan-do, and whoever becomes Leader of the former Hawk People."

His smile died, his face pensive. "Of course, but that is the same."

That puzzled her. Though they never talked about it, she understood why Pan-do didn't want to become the former Hawk People Leader. His focus was on his People—their safety and a new home. She thought he realized that she too had no interest, albeit for different reasons, that Nightshade must challenge Water Buffalo. When Pan-do stood up for Nightshade, she took it to mean that despite their shared reservations, Pan-do accepted Nightshade as the best solution for everyone.

He knew Nightshade wanted the position—Lyta had told him—and he knew Xhosa couldn't defeat him physically. In this challenge, that was the only test that mattered.

She wrapped a tendon around her hair and eased to her knees, eyes gliding over her People—her father's People—picking at the scrub grass growing at her feet, flicking it away one blade at a time. What Pan-do wanted was a shortcut to their goals. All she could offer was a long hard slog. What was the best way to say what he might not like?

She decided on honesty.

"I can't beat Water Buffalo. I would lose not just Leader of the former Hawk People but of my People. He counts on that and I will not let it happen. It must be Nightshade."

When Sun went to sleep, the People gathered, Xhosa and Pan-do side by side, Nightshade to her side and Sa-mo-ke to Pan-do's. Xhosa insisted Siri sit by Nightshade to acknowledge her position as Primary Female. As usual, Seeker and Zvi stayed toward the back. Spirit chose a spot where he could best guard his pack. Tonight, that was next to Nightshade.

The Seconds, the pregnant females, and group members being acknowledged completed the circle. The rest arrayed themselves behind. No one wanted to miss this event.

Water Buffalo sat with his warriors, wrapping himself in their pride and loyalty.

Mounds of meat, plants, berries, and eggs filled the clearing. Someone found a beehive and scraped the honey onto a broad leaf. Group members clustered around the central area, leaving space in the middle for the coming challenge.

When the last group member finished their meal, Nightshade stood. Silence reigned as he began, hands confident, eyes dark pools that bored into one warrior after the next, mouth set, hackles raised.

"I am Lead Warrior of Xhosa's People. I am also Leader of the former Hawk People. I am also Lead Warrior of the former Hawk People. Snake will be my Second. Snake's words are my words."

His voice was low, hands smooth, both so burdened with resolve and strength they vibrated. Impossible to miss was the threat if any disagreed. Snake appeared at Nightshade's side. Talon looked shocked. Water Buffalo sputtered as he stormed to his feet.

Chapter 7

"You cannot do that!"

Water Buffalo stamped his foot like a belligerent child, lips damp with spittle, and strode toward Nightshade. Talon shadowed his Leader, ready to jump in if needed. Two paces from his possible future Leader, Water Buffalo stopped, body hair stiff making him look even bigger than he was. His foul breath washed over Nightshade, accentuated by the stink of a rotten tooth festering in the back of his mouth, darkening his already foul mood.

Nightshade took one pace closer, gaze never leaving Water Buffalo. They now stood a mere hand's distance apart. Water Buffalo dripped sweat though the air was frigid.

Nightshade leered. "Do you challenge Snake to be my Second?"

Snake sauntered forward. "Don't or I will demolish you."

Xhosa hid her smirk. Nightshade had already deftly defined this battle. Mortal danger brought clarity to her Lead Warrior. Physical prowess mattered only to a point. Then, it was about command presence. More talented fighters than Water Buffalo had fought Nightshade. All of them were dead.

Water Buffalo jabbed a finger into Nightshade's chest. It bent at the knuckle. Next, he pushed Nightshade with his palm but he might as well have tried to shove a cliff wall. He settled for spitting a wad of mucous onto Nightshade's lip.

"You are not Lead Warrior. Hawk didn't trust you. My warriors don't either."

Nightshade grabbed Water Buffalo's hand and bent it backwards almost to breaking while using it to wipe the spit from his mouth. When Water Buffalo groaned, Nightshade backfisted him with the same hand, hard. Water Buffalo's head bounced to the side and Nightshade fisted him again on the rebound. The former Lead Warrior's eyes glazed, lids drooped open. After a moment, he shook, trying to clear the wooziness.

The People's Lead Warrior motioned one-handed, "Shall we begin or would you prefer to quit?" When Water Buffalo offered no response, Nightshade motioned, "You are a disgrace to the memory of the great Leader Hawk."

Nightshade loved the physicality of battle, testing his excellence. The bloodthirst that filled his eyes would convince even Cheetah to flee. Xhosa often thought if any could beat Spirit, it would be Nightshade and the wolf knew that. As the People's Lead Warrior, Nightshade had built a reputation for ferocity that persuaded all to avoid him.

Tonight, he had chosen words calculated to goad his opponent into making mistakes, and it worked.

Water Buffalo screamed, "Defend yourself, impostor!" He meant to sound fierce but his words came out slurred and lisping.

Xhosa glanced at the bewildered faces around her and shook her head. Water Buffalo must have forgotten her Lead Warrior's impassioned and deadly defense of the Hawk People against the Ice Mountain invaders. The slew of dead he left in his wake didn't, nor did the many he saved—not just the warriors that fought for Hawk but their pairmates and children. All respected his part in that battle. None would call him an imposter.

Pan-do stood and the buzz of hands and voices fell silent. "Before you begin, understand the rules. "The contenders must stay within the circle. If one steps out, he loses." He gazed from Nightshade to Water Buffalo, making sure they heard him. "Your sole weapon is your body."

He directed the next to Nightshade. "You need not cripple an otherwise valiant fighter who will serve the People well in battle."

Nightshade glowered at Water Buffalo, already woozy, lip split open.

Xhosa motioned, "Water Buffalo, you may challenge another day. It need not be today."

Water Buffalo roared, spitting blood at both Nightshade and Xhosa.

Nightshade showed his teeth. "As you wish."

Sweat poured from Water Buffalo's forehead. He slammed both open hands into the ground. "Prepare to lose, imposter!"

"Begin!" and Pan-do hopped out of the way.

Nightshade squared to his opponent, his arms loose, a smirk on his lips as he smelled the pungent perfume of fear and doubt. His senses sharpened and background noises muted as his body prepared for battle. He listened as the beat inside Water Buffalo sped up and his breathing heightened. His opponent couldn't help but signal to anyone watching what he planned to do and how. There would be no surprises.

The two circled each other, the crowd snorting and howling. Water Buffalo lumbered side to side, preparing his charge, oblivious that he faced the most perilous adversary of his life. Finally, he leaped, arms open, trying to surprise Nightshade with his ferocity and drive him into the crowd. Nightshade nimbly stepped aside and slammed Water Buffalo hard on the temple. Water Buffalo buckled but managed to grab Nightshade. Instead of fighting the hold, Nightshade folded into it and slammed both fists against Water Buffalo's ears. The warrior's eyes popped open and he collapsed.

Drool dribbled from his mouth now. Nightshade stiffened his hand, preparing to slam an open palm against Water Buffalo's forehead, but stopped when his opponent didn't get up. Was he finished? Could it be this easy? Nightshade's instincts screamed at him to finish the warrior off but he pushed them aside, forcing himself to heed Pando's suggestion—that the winner needn't destroy a good fighter.

"Get up or concede, true-imposter. You have lost." He motioned, eyes sharp, hands calm, body poised to continue.

Water Buffalo glared at him, energized by the insult. Blood dripped from many wounds and he seemed unable to hear, but he wouldn't quit. Nightshade respected that. After too long, he finally pushed to his feet and swayed, studying Nightshade, feet shuffling. As though partially blind, he finally punched where his opponent had been, giving Nightshade the opening to kick Water Buffalo's knee. It bent backward and the crowd grimaced. As he fell, Nightshade smashed his nose with a closed fist. There was a crunch and his nose collapsed, but Nightshade hit him over and over until only a soggy bloody mess stretched over his cheeks where a nose should be. When Water Buffalo tried to block one of the punches, Nightshade grabbed the exhausted fighter's hand and snapped his finger like a dry twig.

The scent of blood filled the air. Nightshade breathed it in, leering, invigorated.

"Call me Leader, coward, and I stop!" Nightshade motioned one handed as he pounded Water Buffalo with the other.

Xhosa yelled something that sounded like angry bees. Hands grabbed his arms but he shook them away.

"Call me Leader or die!"

Someone squealed and Nightshade prepared the final punch, to the temple where damage would be permanent and ensure Water Buffalo never again challenged Nightshade's leadership.

Xhosa's voice broke through the red haze. "Do not take his life, Nightshade! He is a valiant warrior. Let him serve you!" She pressed toward the stricken warrior, Nightshade out of reach or she would have grabbed him.

But he paused, glanced sideways at Xhosa, and made a mistake. He relented.

"Quit or die," he whispered into Water Buffalo's ear. "This choice I give you only because the People's Leader asked." No one heard except the former Hawk People's Lead Warrior.

Calling on energy he shouldn't have had, Water Buffalo roared as he grabbed a warclub that had appeared by his hand and swung. Nightshade dove to the side a breath too late and the club thumped against his upper arm. Burning pain stabbed him followed by numbness. Stunned silence filled the room. Water Buffalo cheated. He would be condemned, maybe driven from the People.

Unless he won. Then, no one would question his tactic.

Nightshade stood still, injured arm hanging limply, shoulder swelling even as he stood there.

"You shouldn't have done that." His hands were calm but his eyes smoldered.

And he charged.

Water Buffalo didn't expect that. He swung the club again but Nightshade slid underneath. He bit into the dense muscle of the challenger's stomach and pulled away, tearing out a huge chunk. This he chewed, grinning, and then swallowed. When Water Buffalo threw up, Nightshade kicked him in the groin with all his power. The injured warrior folded, warclub tumbling to the ground. Nightshade slammed his good fist into the side of Water Buffalo's head and kneed him in the mouth. His lip split, teeth clattered to the ground, and Water Buffalo passed out.

Nightshade prepared the kill strike when again, Xhosa's voice broke through.

"No—you won! The former Hawk People are now the Nightshade People. It is over!"

Nightshade stopped just before slamming an elbow into Water Buffalo's already-weakened temple and swerved so the strike crashed into the top of the warrior's head.

Water Buffalo felt nothing. He was unconscious.

Hands flew, retelling the story of how the great Nightshade beat a warrior armed with a warclub. No one could do that, yet he did.

Nightshade rose, eyes on the motionless form in front of him. Fire radiated from his injured arm but his fingers barely tingled. He heard hushed voices, trying to make sense of Water Buffalo's treachery and his own ruthlessness.

When Water Buffalo didn't get up, Snake slapped his Lead Warrior on the back. "Now everyone knows why I will never fight you."

Talon shouldered his way through the group and confronted Nightshade, head thrust forward, fists clenched. "You went too far. He may not recover. We will never call ourselves the Nightshade People!"

Snake crowded into Talon and jabbed a finger into the shorter male's throat. "Water Buffalo disqualified himself when he broke *your* rules. Nightshade overlooked it, treated him with the respect a warrior deserves, and still won. If you dislike winning, get out."

The new Leader of the former Hawk People turned to Talon, sniffing the stench of his fear and snorting his disgust.

"If you want to remain Second, you must beat Snake." Dread flashed across Talon's face, gone as fast as it arrived, but Nightshade saw it. "You don't have the courage, little one. Crawl back to the safety of your other warriors," and he dismissed him with a brush of his hand.

Even after such a ferocious fight, Nightshade's breathing was just above normal. The singular evidence of fatigue was a thin sheen of sweat on his upper lip.

Talon gulped and left.

Nightshade addressed the other warriors, his damaged arm now red and swollen. "Does Talon speak for you? If the defeat of your weak Lead Warrior doesn't make me your Leader, who is a worthy opponent? I will fight him right now!"

No one met his eye though many nodded. Whispers flew around as Nightshade took his seat next to Xhosa. Relief saturated the air, that the merciless Nightshade fought for them.

A hush settled over the group as Xhosa rose, head high and feet spread, hair glistening like a river under Moon's light, glowing like Panther's black pelt in the rain. Pan-do and Sa-mo-ke stood also, matching her stance, joined quickly by Dust and finally Talon. None wasted a glance at the unconscious former Lead Warrior.

Xhosa motioned, "It has been decided. The former Hawk People are now the Nightshade People."

No one said a word, all eyes hooded, hands rigidly at their sides. She could see in their faces they doubted she could fix what had broken this night, but that was because they didn't know her well enough.

"I understand you require more than a simple win to accept a Leader not of your People."

Many nodded, unwilling to relinquish support for the male their dead Leader Hawk designated Lead despite overwhelming evidence he was not up to the job. She paused to catch the eye of every warrior, held it for a moment, and then moved on with a nod. Their expressions showed shock that Water Buffalo lost and fear for a future under her Lead Warrior.

It was time to surprise them and change their minds. "Your new Leader must not just be the victor. He must dominate, control the fight, even conquer his opponent despite deadly odds. That is why I placed that warclub where Water Buffalo could reach it."

Her admission stunned everyone.

She ignored their reaction. "Desperation would drive him to take it but weakness—the nagging doubts he had about himself, and you his warriors—would ensure Nightshade won, even then. Now, you have the Leader you deserve, who believes in you as much as in himself. Can any question Nightshade's right to Lead the Hawk People? Does anyone doubt they are safer with Leader Nightshade than Leader Water Buffalo? He strikes fear in the hearts of any who have seen him in battle. He will do the same for you wherever we settle."

She stepped back, allowing Nightshade to move to the front.

He motioned, "We fight to win, not to honor rules. Anyone who disagrees will not be my warrior."

"I disagree!" Water Buffalo's young pairmate screamed from the back of the group. "You broke a good man! Is this how your People act?"

Xhosa stepped toward the female and glared, disdain thick in her every gesture. "I am surprised Water Buffalo lives. Nightshade rarely shows the mercy he did this evening. No one would have questioned killing a warrior who blindsided an unarmed male with a warclub. Still, when your pairmate recovers, he will be welcomed as a warrior of the Nightshade People. If he doesn't recover, he serves you or us no purpose."

When the female tried to stutter a response, Xhosa stopped her. "You should be bearing children. Why has the great Water Buffalo not put a baby in you, as is his duty? Never mind. The reason is obvious. Tonight, mate with your new Leader. Carry his child. We need new adults who are sturdier than your pairmate."

Xhosa left, Nightshade at her side, trailed by Snake, Dust, and Talon, Water Buffalo's former warriors, and then the People from all the groups. As everyone found their nighttime nests around the camp, Xhosa settled into a boulder bed close to where Water Buffalo lay. She would protect him from predators attracted by the aroma of blood. He had fought hard and with passion. If he recovered, he would serve Nightshade well.

As Xhosa chewed her pain plant, Water Buffalo's pairmate slipped to his side and licked the blood from his face. She would need him once he recovered but tonight, he needed her.

In the night's quiet, Xhosa thought about what had happened. Nightshade now wielded as much control as she and Pan-do. It would either calm him or unleash him. One would allow the People to flourish, the other destroy them.

Which it would be she didn't know, and that worried her.

The Moon had moved far across the night sky by the
time Water Buffalo struggled to sit. His strong arm dangled.
One eye had swollen shut, the other so red, Xhosa doubted
he could see anything. He winced as he took a breath and
then pawed at the ground. He called his pairmate, his voice
garbled and slurred. She limped over from where Nightshade
slept. Xhosa swallowed the bile that rose in her throat. The
female's eye was bruised black, her lip split, and a gash bled
on her cheek.

"Come, I'll help you," and she guided Water Buffalo to
the rest of the warriors.

Nightshade always treated his warriors brutishly, claiming
it made them tough, but in the past, he was kind to his mates,
as were most males. That seemed to have changed. Before
meeting Pan-do, she would have ignored this as none of her
business Now, something deep inside questioned whether her
job as Leader was also to protect those too weak to do so
themselves.

As the two stumbled away, Water Buffalo's pairmate
motioned one-handed, "I mated with Nightshade. He will
give us a strong child."

Water Buffalo made no comment. Once among the safety
of the warriors, he again passed out.

Xhosa was too vitalized to sleep so climbed atop a
boulder with a flat top and lay on her back, entranced by the
twinkling stars. She wished Seeker was here to tell her the
future he saw. To her, the stars all seemed alike.

Not so the Moon. The huge white sphere grew to a full
circle and then shrank to nothing. How or why was a mystery
but the pattern never changed. As a result, Xhosa and her
People used it to keep track of events that took longer than a
day of Sun moving across the sky. For example, a journey to
harvest stones at the quarry might take the full passage of
Moon. Migrating to the dry time homebase took two fingers
of a Moon. When the herds left, they always reappeared

before she ticked off Moon's returns on the thumb, pointer, and middle finger.

No less incredible was its eerie benevolent glow, as though it scrutinized the People and approved.

Zvi plopped at Xhosa's side and shivered. "Seeker says it is cold here because Sun rises from a different location. When we reach the stars' proper positions, it will be warmer."

"Zvi, are you and Seeker doing well?"

"If Water Buffalo had become Leader, we would have left. Water Buffalo does not believe in the stars. But Seeker was sure we would be able to stay."

If Zvi and Seeker left, so too would Lyta and Pan-do. Spirit wouldn't stay without his pack which meant the People would lose a reliable hunting partner, a devoted scout, and a valued guard. More than that, for reasons Xhosa didn't understand, his mere presence made people smile.

Xhosa and Zvi lay side by side in comfortable silence, mesmerized by the brilliant stars, enjoying the cool night. Finally, Zvi started talking.

"Nightshade worries Seeker and me. He enjoys the fight as much—maybe more—than protecting the People."

"That intimidates opponents, Zvi. They think he has no mercy."

"Does he? I don't see it anymore. Well, except tonight when he didn't kill Water Buffalo."

"Battles must resolve not only winners but losers."

"Lyta says Nightshade will challenge you to lead the People."

As though she'd delivered the message that brought her here, Zvi left. What she didn't know, Xhosa kept to herself, that this was the second warning she'd received from one of her trusted few.

Chapter 8

"Snake and Dust are scouting ahead. Sa-mo-ke and Talon are protecting the sides. Stone will watch the backtrail. We are ready to leave."

Xhosa blinked the sleep from her heavy-lidded eyes. Sun glowed dully. "How's Water Buffalo?"

Nightshade gestured one-handed, his injured arm hanging loosely. A deep bruise spread from his shoulder to his chest, "He accepts the challenge as fair. I have assured him he can fight me again when he feels ready." His eyes glittered with pleasure and then he added, "Talon will be the Nightshade People's Lead Warrior. When Water Buffalo recovers, he must challenge for the position."

"How do you feel?"

"I won."

Xhosa had seen Nightshade injured often enough to know he spoke the truth. Only death would stop him.

With her fingers, Xhosa ticked off everyone she could see or smell. Unlike other nights, no one had abandoned the group. Whether they liked Nightshade or despised him, they recognized that his ferocious leadership would keep them safe. Water Buffalo's pairmate wiped herself with moss. Injuries as bad as hers, she might not try again to have Nightshade's child.

Pan-do joined Xhosa and Nightshade at the front of the group and together, they led their People toward Sun's sleeping nest and a new homebase. First, they must cross the mountains. What lay beyond might be where they settle.

Behind, Xhosa heard the murmurs of mothers, the giggled responses of children, and the comfortable patter of the People migrating. Wa-co and Honey walked with El-ga between them. Seeker pranced between Lyta and Zvi, both enraptured by his nonstop stories. Gadi, the orphaned child of Shadow, clung to Siri's hand who moved among the females, assisting where needed. Spirit loped in front of everyone, listening for sounds and scents that would keep his pack safe.

When Pan-do dropped back to be with Lyta and Nightshade to walk with his People, Spirit joined Xhosa. She told him how leading the combined People challenged her and how Zvi and Seeker—and Spirit himself—had also become her People and important to her leadership. As she talked, he wagged his bushy tail as though he understood.

"Something in your eyes, the perk of your ears—you know the right path, don't you?"

At some point during their conversation, Seeker and Zvi had silently joined her. She didn't notice until Spirit looked to them for the answer to Xhosa's question.

Seeker nodded and Zvi shook her head. Spirit huffed.

Zvi explained, "Yes, but his objectives may differ from ours. Ultimately, Spirit must find a mate and raise pups. I don't know if Seeker and I will then be welcome in his pack. So, it is Seeker's decision that matters to me. He never swerves from his goal of finding our new home."

Seeker motioned, "Spirit often sits under the stars with me. We discuss their movement, which spot of light brightened, which is closer or farther from Bright Star or Always There Star, and their positions above the horizon."

Xhosa furrowed her brow. "What is Bright Star and Always There Star?"

Seeker bristled with excitement. His greatest pleasure was sharing knowledge.

"Bright Star hides sometimes but when it appears, it guides me for a handful of days, sometimes a Moon. When it leaves, I look for Always-There. That one is dimmer but has followed me since the day Zvi and I set out from our homeland. It has become a friend."

"Stars have no odors or tastes. How can Spirit use them to find our direction?"

Zvi motioned, "Spirit tests Seeker's path for threats. If Spirit and Seeker both agree, it must be the right choice."

After traveling all day, the People huddled together in a cave, under an overhang, or around a boulder—whatever the scouts found. There, they groomed each other, knapped stones, sharpened spears, shaped handaxes, and finished weapons. When Sun's light faded, they slept, Bone by Honey, Ant by Siri, Nightshade by Xhosa.

Travel began again as soon as Sun brightened the landscape. The mountains loomed far away, their peaks glistening white and the line of trees darkening the slope below, but first, the People must cross the foothills. The best way to do that was to stay along Endless Pond's shoreline.

The trek was never easy. During the day, either the heat of Sun sapped their strength or cold hard rain left them shivering. Sometimes, they found a cave or overhang where they waited until the sky cleared. The land itself varied from wet marshes to rocky hills to damp valleys filled with trees. Often, they had to wade through shallow water to cross from one of what Seeker called an "'island'"—land surrounded by water—to another.

Happily, they ate well. Zvi introduced them to the abundance of food in the tidepools along the shore, from watery seaweed and stranded fish to hard-shelled creatures she called crabs and snails. Besides the water's bounty, the People found small herds and an endless supply of larvae, corms, berries, roots, and many foods no one had ever seen before. The warriors and the scouts explored during the day and protected the camp at night. That no one saw signs of Others didn't matter. The People survived by being prepared.

Talon proved a good Lead Warrior and readily accepted advice. Pan-do's Lead, Sa-mo-ke, taught Talon to move aggressively, think ruthlessly, and win fights in unconventional ways. When Water Buffalo healed enough to challenge for his old position, he chose to remain a warrior under Talon's direction.

One problem that increasingly worried Xhosa was they couldn't find quarries with the special hard stones required for cutters and spear tips. They tried to make what they had last while they searched for other stones that could replace these.

Two and then two more females delivered healthy babies. Water Buffalo's pairmate mated often with Nightshade despite the physical abuse but bled when Moon was full.

Sun was still climbing but would soon start its descent when Xhosa arrived at two trees, both taller than any around, tucked so close to each other their branches tangled. It was here Hawk had told her to turn away from Endless Pond. This she did but Seeker, Zvi, and Spirit didn't, continuing to follow a path that hugged the shoreline. Xhosa chased after Seeker.

"This is where Hawk told us to go inland."

The scrawny, odd boy never slowed as he gestured, "Last night, the stars told me my homebase is ahead, beyond this shore, through a particular pass in the mountains. That's where I must go."

Xhosa's People had stopped, glad for the rest, their heads bobbing between Xhosa and Seeker.

When Nightshade reached her, he motioned, "The scouts say the land found by Hawk is not as good as where Seeker heads but I will go where you wish, Leader."

Xhosa clenched her fists and took a deep breath. "You are Leader of the Nightshade People. What do you think?"

His eyes narrowed as he stared inland. After a moment, his ears tweaked and he licked his lips. "It is too quiet."

She sighed and trudged after Seeker.

Within a handful of days, the colors of the land brightened, the air became damp, and the clouds were more often dark than a wispy white. Water holes spotted the landscape as did inlets from Endless Pond. Finally, their path dipped, often ankle-deep in water and then knee-deep. The People continued, walking on the stones that covered the inlet's bed.

Xhosa woke one morning and motioned the People to rest for the day, take time to repair stone tools, collect travel food, and rebuild their tired bodies. They had reached a flat, dry meadow with caves along the cliff walls and a herd not far in the distance.

"Nightshade. I am out of my pain plant."

While she didn't know the plants in this area, they looked like what she needed.

"I will go with you. Snake and Talon can protect our People."

"We have seen no sign of Others. If I'm not back when Moon has grown this much," and she held her finger and thumb up, close together, "Go. I will catch up."

A sharp wind whipped her pelt against her body as she jogged away from the salted water, tidepools, and marshes. Once she found the plant, Bright Star would guide her back. In a hand of Sun's journey, the sounds of Endless Pond evaporated behind the hills as though never there.

She had only traveled two more fingers of Sun's movement when an out-of-place scrape made the hair on her neck prickle. She maintained her pace, not looking back, but gripped more tightly to her spear. Few would defeat her in a battle. The only way to win would be to surprise her, which wouldn't happen.

Xhosa entered an area of undulating plains, green with bunchgrass and verdant gullies. She skirted it, choosing instead a rock-covered slope that would leave no prints. When hidden from view, she slipped into a narrow crevice between two cliffs. Whoever trailed her would have to pass here and Xhosa could decide then whether he represented a threat.

No one appeared after a finger of Sun's passage so Xhosa assumed her stalker went a different direction and resumed her quest. She rounded a turn and found a field in front of her, bursting with a colorful cacophony of flowers. She grinned.

This is perfect.

The satisfied smile disappeared when dry tinder crunched accompanied by the rancid stench of stale sweat. Blinding pain seared through her head, exploded behind her eyes, and darkness swallowed her.

Chapter 9

Northern Africa, along the Mediterranean Sea

Rainbow wheezed with each labored step. Like every one of his People, exhaustion consumed him. The journey had begun so propitiously when he rejected Xhosa and her leadership, striding confidently—Mbasa called it arrogantly— toward a lush land of green grass, abundant herds, and food aplenty. His steps were buoyant, eyes steadfast, his belief in himself absolute, filling those who followed him with a certainty that they made the right decision in joining him. The landscape at first had been cut with rivers and spotted with lakes, without signs of Others or the vicious Big Heads. Xhosa had been leading the remnants of the People toward a valley filled with bubbling green muck and crumbling dirt, by all appearances, destitute of water, food, and safety.

More of the People than Rainbow expected followed him including most of the pregnant females and their pairmates. Rainbow had hoped Pan-do and his People would come but he stayed with Xhosa when Seeker muttered something about the stars remaining with Xhosa. Though Seeker was worthless, his huge wolf friend—Spirit—would have been invaluable. And Seeker's companion Zvi—she hunted more successfully than a handful of males. Rainbow thought Nightshade would join when he promised to make him

Leader. Of course, Rainbow lied about that but by the time Nightshade realized this, they would be too far away for even the vaunted Nightshade to find Xhosa.

Those first days, leadership intoxicated Rainbow. With Nightshade's reputation for ruthlessness, the native Others stayed away, not knowing Nightshade wasn't with this group. Rainbow led his People—*his* People!—through rolling grassland filled with herds, skirted flat-topped plateaus, and rested by shallow creeks so clear, catching fish required only a grab with the hand or a stab with a spear. Lizards lazily sunned themselves on dusty rocks, easily snatched by subadults for food.

The biggest hazard they faced was snake bites and scorpion stings. Well, Pig gored one hunter. The wound puckered and oozed, eventually rotting the male's leg and killing him because Mbasa didn't know which of the plants in this strange new land would heal it.

Mbasa. What a victory to have her with the Rainbow People. The dark-skinned youthful female had been Nightshade's mate since she bled. Now, she slept by Rainbow. As they progressed, Rainbow insisted everyone call themselves Rainbow's People. Few heeded him until Mbasa suggested it best to leave memories of the Xhosa People behind.

One morning, Others appeared at the edge of the People's camp. Like so often before, Rainbow explained they were passing through, on their way to meet Xhosa and Nightshade, and the Leader allowed them to scavenge and hunt. He assured Rainbow that rich lands lay just beyond the horizon.

Usually, that was true. The glorious wealth of this area never seemed to end. But this time—this time, the Other Leader lied. The farther Rainbow's group trekked, always toward Sun's sleeping nest, the more desiccated the land, and soon nothing more than sagebrush, prickly grass, and the occasional mudhole. There wasn't enough food for the great herds that usually fed the People so the native Others were hungrier and more brutal than those the People had faced earlier in their migration. Their response to Rainbow's greetings became belligerent and hostile despite his assurance that his People only headed for a distant new home. When he mentioned Xhosa and Nightshade, the Others permitted passage but not hunting or foraging. When Rainbow ignored the warning, considering it unenforceable, a mob massacred the best of his warriors. He ordered his new Lead Warrior to train more fighters but the adult, so recently a subadult, didn't know how.

Somehow, all the native tribes soon knew that neither Xhosa nor Nightshade traveled with his group. From then on, Rainbow's People were chased away, often violently. His remaining warriors and hunters were picked off and the pregnant females captured when they couldn't keep up with the fleeing People. No more hunting and scavenging as they traveled. No more frequent rests. They finally reached an expanse of land so dusty and dry, it seemed to have given up on life itself.

No one chased them here because no one lived here.

Rainbow slouched in a sliver of shade, pouting and hungry, scratching at fleas that sucked his precious blood, unable to come up with a plan. Mbasa wanted to change how the People hunted but Rainbow ignored her. Females didn't know how to hunt. Well, Xhosa did but Mbasa wasn't Xhosa.

He closed his eyes, folded his hands in his lap, scratched more fleas, and tried to shut out the world he'd ended up in. There was no meat, no plants to forage, and the children were too hot and tired to play. He panted, mouth open, saliva dripping out of the corners. Sweat soaked his sodden hair so he twisted the strands through his fingers and lapped the tangy liquid off his fingers.

Mbasa nagged constantly about water. Why did she think he knew where to find it when he'd never been here? He always brushed her away, saying he was busy. Once, she told him about an underground pool she and some of the females were digging up. He listened, grunted wisely, and told her to come back if she found water. She hadn't returned.

He popped a pebble into his mouth. Saliva moistened his throat but not for long. He licked his dry tongue over the sweat on his arms even though it made his thirst worse. At least it was damp.

Advice from Nightshade filtered through the murky haze of his thoughts. "Hunger makes males dangerous," another lie from his former Lead Warrior. Thirst made a male desperate long before hunger did.

He rose to his feet and trudged forward, wondering when Mbasa would stop for the night. Sun shone obstinately, stifling and hot. Dust coated his hair, nose, and ears. Unbearable under normal circumstances, here, he must tolerate it. When they had started along this path, he eagerly crested each new berm, excited to discover what lay on the other side. Not anymore. Nothing ever changed. If he weren't so miserable, he'd be bored.

He slapped a flea and popped it in his mouth before it could bite his arm. The salt worried him the most. They ran out of what he took from Xhosa and could find no replacement. Licks had to be here somewhere or where did the animals get salt?

Though he saw no sign of herds.

Really, he blamed Xhosa for his troubles. She made leading the People seem simple—kill the enemy and order people around. He did both with alacrity until it no longer worked. Now, his leadership revolved around one plan: Flee.

"Rainbow. We are being stalked."

He forced his bleary eyes open. Why did Mbasa never tire? "I—the People need to rest."

She huffed. "Then we die."

Again, Rainbow understood the brilliance of Xhosa's father. The territory he had controlled included everything the People required to survive. Never did they need permission to hunt or forage.

"H-how do you know?"

Disgust colored her face. "Their stink."

Rainbow relaxed. "You can't know that," and he shut his eyes, blocking out this treacherous world, enjoying the cool shade cast by her body.

Mbasa looked surprised. "Do you not smell them?"

Rainbow dismissed her with a sweep of his hand. Her steps were strong, her gait a warrior's which was when he noticed the spear across her back.

He called after her, "Give the spear to one of the males."

Without slowing, Mbasa barked, "We have no warriors left."

"It is wasted on you! Don't—"

Before he finished, she pivoted and threw. The spear embedded into the dirt a hand's width from him.

"This is what I do when we stop for the day while you rest. When the time comes we must fight for our lives, I will." Her hands softened. "I may die but not alone."

The next day, Mbasa rousted the People and led them over the flat dry land without a word to Rainbow about the stalker. Knowing about him now, Rainbow couldn't miss the clues—a dust cloud where it shouldn't be, an unusual odor, the occasional Other print, crushed scrub grass, the scurry of scorpions.

Why doesn't he attack? And what would I do if he did?

When they stopped for the day, scouts were posted and Mbasa left the group, spear comfortably in hand. Rainbow quietly trailed after her beyond a small boulder until she reached a field.

"She's going to practice spear-throwing!" He muttered to himself. "I'll offer assistance."

He expected her to struggle with the spear's weight but she effortlessly held it above her shoulder, one-handed, level to the ground, eyes locked on a scrubby bush across the field.

No one can throw that far.

He bit his lip to silence the gasp that threatened to explode when she speared the bush. A handful of throws later, she'd hit the target each time.

"How long have you practiced?"

Rainbow lurched backwards until he had buried himself behind a boulder. He'd been concentrating so hard on Mbasa, he missed Starlight's arrival. The slight female also carried a spear as though she knew what to do with it. He recognized it as that of a now-dead warrior.

"Not long."

"You get better each night, Mbasa. Soon, you will be as good as any male."

"It's easier than Nightshade made it sound. Once you and I can throw well, other females will join us."

As they practiced, they corrected flaws and encouraged each other even when their palms bled and their arms strained to hold the spear upright. Sun went to sleep, Moon arrived, and the females continued. During one of their infrequent breaks, Starlight suggested they quit for the night. Her breath came out in wheezing huffs and sweat glistened off her dark skin.

Mbasa shook her head. "Battles aren't fought when we choose, Starlight. Xhosa said they start when you're tired and get worse when you're injured."

When the stars said night's end approached, they returned to the camp.

As Rainbow lay down, he had to admit, Mbasa was becoming a warrior in more ways than simply her prowess with a weapon. Time and again, she made the difficult decisions for the People about which direction to go, how to avoid local tribes, and where to find water.

He would seek her guidance more often. Then, at least, he could blame her when the plan collapsed.

One day, as the people trudged onward, beaten to lethargy by the heat and monotony, Rainbow realized that Mbasa's stalker had disappeared.

As had Mbasa.

He searched again, as he had a handful of times since the day's trek started, for her long stride or the glisten of her muscular body. When Sun began its long glide to the horizon and still no Mbasa, he wondered if she had been killed. What was he supposed to do? He didn't even know how to find a place to sleep. He squinted into the setting Sun, hoping to find a cave or an overhang. Nothing looked right.

Starlight startled him. "There, Rainbow." Without waiting for his approval, she motioned the group toward it.

When everyone settled for the night and still no Mbasa, Rainbow beckoned Starlight.

"Where is Mbasa?"

Starlight had been docile when she mated with Nightshade, hoping by doing his bidding, he would beat her less and the baby inside of her would live. But when a vicious kick to her stomach caused cramps so violent, she couldn't stand, followed by the gush of chunky brown blood from between her legs, she promised to never again let anyone prey on her.

Though Rainbow was the Leader, Starlight's focus never strayed from the tough root she pounded. "She'll return when she finishes."

"Her work is here, with the People," but Starlight dismissed him without a glance.

When he awoke the next day, Mbasa had everyone ready to leave.

He stomped over. "Where were you? What if I'd risked warriors to find you?"

"We have no warriors."

Rainbow whined, "What if it was I—the Leader—who had to come after you!"

She snorted, eyes flat and hooded. "How, Rainbow? You would track my footprints, the ones I brushed away? Or the scent I hid with mud?"

"Well where did you go?" He recoiled at the pleading tone in his voice.

"The stalker is no longer a worry," and she tossed him a severed finger.

Rainbow's mouth fell open. "By yourself? How—where?"

"Buried where the vultures will not find him." Mbasa leaned over and picked up a well-made spear and warclub. "These are now mine."

Rainbow was stunned into sputtering nothing more than gibberish. Mbasa patted his arm. "I told you when necessary, I would fix it. The time came and I did."

He fought to stifle his anger. And fear. After a few deep breaths, he motioned, "Was he alone?"

Disgust filled her eyes but she answered simply, "He was a scout equipped for battle. I didn't give him the chance to tell me."

"Should we worry his tribe will attack?"

"No, Rainbow. I have a plan."

She motioned to Starlight and the two strode toward Sun's resting place. Every one of Rainbow's People followed.

Rainbow sucked hard on the pebble, thinking hungrily of the burbling river that bordered their homeland. There, he never worried about water. This route should have been cut with streams, not covered in desiccated soil, torturous gravel, and invisible hazards. Something the stalker said right before dying made Mbasa change their direction. Rainbow didn't care, happy Mbasa led. An attack would hit her first.

Suddenly, his nostrils flared and he smelled it—water. He roused himself and trudged as fast as exhaustion allowed toward the aroma. His thirsty People rushed past, one knocking him over, driven by their desperate thirst. He fell trying to climb a ragged dry hill. Mbasa appeared at his side and dragged him to the top.

There, in front of him spread vast fields of green grass, lush plants, and sparkling water. Tears of joy spilled down his cheeks. The entire band rushed downhill and threw themselves into the pond, paying no attention to the other drinkers.

"Drink slowly or you'll get sick."

Those who refused to listen vomited and then drank more water.

"Fill whatever you have for the journey," Mbasa ordered. "Whoever controls the waterhole will drive us away so store as much as possible."

Someone found a gourd to hold water, someone else an animal skull, and another the fresh-enough bladder of a gazelle which they cleaned before filling. The People rested and frolicked in the water for the balance of the day, and then settled in a copse of trees for the night, some in the limbs and others curled against the trunks. All looked safe so Rainbow didn't bother to post a guard.

Mbasa kicked Rainbow awake. He scrambled to his feet, rubbing his eyes, and then gasped. "We're surrounded!"

"I have already talked with them, Rainbow. This is the only water around and they often chase travelers away. There are more of them than us," and she opened and shut her hands more times than Rainbow could keep track of. "We may leave but must do so now."

"There's enough water for them and us!"

"They don't agree."

He glared at the Others and stomped off the same direction his People went every day, toward Sun's sleeping place. Mbasa followed.

She motioned, "They told me we will find water several days away. We are on a corridor that leads from our homeland to an uncrossable pond. It will take this many Moons," and she held up two fingers. "If we survive the tribes in control of each area and stay along Endless Pond's shoreline, we will reach an uninhabited land where we can hunt and forage."

"How did you talk to them?"

"When their scouts arrived at the water hole, I greeted them, spear down but holding my warclub. They confused me with Xhosa. I encouraged that. When they asked me to leave and I agreed, they were friendly."

Dust sifted into Rainbow's nostrils, and the sharp odor of the People's urine made him sneeze. He wilted at the idea of another day filled with heat, dust, and thirst.

"We can go back, Mbasa—

She pivoted and planted her feet in the dirt, muscles taut, spear clenched and ready. "No. Our land no longer belongs to us, Rainbow. We must go forward, no matter how rigorous or deadly, or uncomfortable for you."

Mbasa took his face between her finger and thumb and squeezed. "Xhosa is across Endless Pond. I *will* find a way to reach her."

Rainbow paced aimlessly. "We are too weak. I have made my decision. The next group we encounter, I will offer ourselves as new members, as Pan-do did to Xhosa."

Mbasa scoffed. "Pan-do's People brought strength. Look at us!" She pointed to the bedraggled group that trudged past. "No one will want us."

She fixed Rainbow with her luminous dark eyes. "Here's what we will do."

Rainbow nodded listlessly. What else could he do?

Chapter 10

That night, when the People stopped, Mbasa left the camp with a group of young females. Tired and hungry, beaten down by the muggy hot night, no one paid them any attention. Everyone wanted to rest. This group of females too were tired but more than that, they were curious. Why had Mbasa invited them to join her? The only hint was her cryptic promise that they would save the People.

Mbasa led the group around a cliff wall to a flat patch of ground far enough away that the main group of People wouldn't hear them. Starlight arrived next with more females, most of them panting, many holding their sides.

Mbasa had spent her entire life with warriors, first her father, then mated to Nightshade, and before the groups separated, mimicking everything Xhosa did. Nightshade knew how to fight but Xhosa made sense of it. Mbasa and Starlight had conferred about whether to tell their recruits what most already knew, that Rainbow made good decisions when all went well, abysmal ones when lives were at stake? Or was that too honest?

Mbasa stood silently in front of the group, Starlight beside her. Both waited, heads up, feet spread, until the shuffle of callused feet on dry earth stopped, replaced by a wide-eyed, tense silence. The group sensed they stood on the cusp of a life-changing event.

Mbasa started. "Rainbow agrees we must reunite with Xhosa. That requires two things. First, we must find her. Second, we must survive until then. Finding her requires scouts and survival requires hunters and warriors. Our enemies have slaughtered most of our males who performed those tasks. That makes it our responsibility—you and I." She met the eyes of every female as she talked. "Xhosa showed us that females can do these jobs as well as males and now we must. We have become the final defense against the end of the People.

"Let me be clear: You don't have to stay. No one will think less of you if you leave. If you join us, you commit to protect the People as a scout does, fight for the People as a warrior would, and feed the People using the skills of a hunter. You cannot quit until we find Xhosa or a new home."

Then Mbasa fell silent. No one spoke until finally, one by one, hands rose.

"I came with Rainbow because my pairmate wanted it..."

"I thought this would be easier..."

"I have lost my children and my pairmate. If I can save others, I must ..."

"My pairmate no longer believes in Rainbow's vision..."

"Tell us what to do!"

No one left. The air buzzed with the excitement, expectation, and the enthusiasm that had been lacking for a long time.

Starlight passed out spears scavenged from dead males. When those ran out, the rest got long tree limbs. They would all learn how to shape them into spears.

"The few warclubs we have must go to those who will lead the defense of the People. Who will take that responsibility?"

To Mbasa's surprise, more volunteered than there were clubs.

"You have each been selected because I know you can succeed. Do not doubt that because I don't. I will divide you into hunters, scouts, and warriors based on your abilities."

Mbasa had carefully observed these females since the People lost their last warrior, when the idea came to her that female warriors, hunters, and scouts would solve the problem. She looked for quick reflexes, graceful movements, the ferocity required for battle, the cunning to hide in plain sight, and the ability to sense prey anywhere. The females with those traits stood in front of her, eager to begin.

She and Starlight shuffled them into clusters and Mbasa addressed the first. "You are hunters. You will become expert with spears and throwing stones. Your job is to feed the People."

The females gaped. "But we forage for plants, small rodents, and birds. We don't bring down the herd animals." Most held their spears as they might a digger—hand at the tip rather than the middle. One carried hers wrong end pointed up.

Mbasa brushed the comments away. "You will learn. Who will be the Lead and train the rest?"

Everyone looked around the tired group, each as frightened as the next except one—Hecate. The older female, shoulders back, eyes unblinking, met Mbasa's scrutiny with her own.

"I will. My father taught me. I hunted with Xhosa until she became Leader, then with my pairmate who is now dead."

Mbasa examined her closely. No one except Hecate held a spear ready to throw even though hers was only a tree limb. A memory nibbled.

"You pairmated Ngili who was killed by Big Heads."

Hecate inclined her head and Mbasa gestured, "You are Lead Hunter. That deep fury, the one that burns your stomach and grabs you by the throat, also strengthens you. When I finish, show your hunters how to hold their spears. Help those without real spears to shape their branch into a weapon."

She turned to the second group. "You will be scouts. You will track Others in the same way you find meat. Who will lead?"

One hand rose—Bird, a subadult. Since joining Rainbow's People, her father had been slain and her mother captured. Bird had survived by burying herself in sand, breathing through a stalk of grass until the marauders left. She was so small, Mbasa didn't see her until she climbed on top of the shoulders of another female. The look on Bird's face was brazen and intelligent and not at all frightened.

Those around her giggled. "Bird! You are a subadult." "You are weak, always have been!"

The youngster's face flattened but Mbasa smiled. "You are the one who found the buried eggs? And berries where no one else believed them to be? You will make an excellent Lead Scout. I will show you how and you will teach your group."

Bird stood taller.

Mbasa now turned to the last group, her warrior essence shining brightly. "You are the People's warriors. I will be Lead, Starlight my Second. Our purpose is to deliver death with our spears, destroy the enemy with our warclubs. Nightshade taught me well between beatings."

Mbasa paused to let everyone absorb their new responsibilities. Each scooted closer to those who shared their responsibility.

"Every night, as the others sleep, we practice. That begins now."

Mbasa lined the females up and chopped away their head hair with a sharp cutter. Nothing could hide the breasts but at a distance, they would appear male.

Next, she showed all the groups how to throw spears with enough power to penetrate hide or skin, where to swing a warclub to do the most damage, and how to steal another's meat. When it got too dark to see, they practiced moving by sound and smell.

As the days passed, the females took to walking in their groups and discussing the lessons. At night, Mbasa worked with the Leads and they worked with their groups. The scouts learned to move without leaving any trace. The hunters practiced strategies to drive herds to a slaughter, slip into a pond without causing ripples as Crocodile would, and forage a carcass despite other scavengers. The warriors became proficient at attacks with all weapons—spears, warclubs, and throwing stones—that would end life quickly.

Within a Moon, the females' skills matched or surpassed those of the males. Before another Moon passed, their arms bulged with muscle and they could run at a ground-eating pace without becoming winded.

Rainbow paid no attention to what happened after the People settled for the night. Many left with Mbasa, he assumed for female work and therefore of no interest to him. He did though marvel at Mbasa's growing reputation as a bastion of strength, always ready with suggestions, never too tired to treat wounds, never too hungry to not share her food. At her insistence, every adult carried a spear or a long branch in the manner of a warrior—gripped in the center—whether they knew how to use it or not. To other tribes, the People would appear fierce. No one would recognize the deceit until it was too late.

The critical nature of Mbasa's plan—that the People present themselves as invincible—was tested sooner rather than later. One morning, she awoke to a row of warriors lined along the crest of a hill by the People's nighttime camp. The Others bristled with spears, some with warclubs. If they attacked, many would die, on both sides.

She kicked Rainbow and he scrambled to his feet. He tensed at the sight of well-armed enemy.

His hands shook as he asked, "What will we do?"

But Mbasa ignored him, already sending her warriors to practiced positions and her scouts to determine how many more attackers hid beyond the hill. When the first of the scouts reported back, she beckoned to Rainbow.

"There are too many. We must leave before they realize we are not as strong as they think."

All morning, the people trekked toward Sun's nest with the enemy shadowing their steps. Rainbow walked with

Mbasa, trying to mimic her attitude despite a debilitating worry that the People couldn't withstand even a mild assault.

"How brilliant that you shortened the female's hair." And in the next breath, "Maybe all they want is to prevent us staying here."

Mbasa huffed so he added, "We can explain we are passing through. We seek a way across Endless Pond to be with the rest of our People."

"We—you and I?"

"Well, you're better at it..."

"Lead Warrior!"

Mbasa turned to Bird.

"Good news—there is a way around Endless Pond!"

Lead Warrior? Mbasa? Rainbow grabbed Bird's arm. "Tell me."

She jerked free with a scowl and glanced at Mbasa. A nod and Bird motioned, "Ja-card—one of the Others—told me."

Rainbow couldn't hide his shock. "H-how did you talk to him?"

"I watched him for a long time. He used gestures while joshing with fellow warriors I recognized. He reminded me of Pan-do in some ways. If I could get him alone, I was sure he'd be friendly when I explained we meant his People no harm.

"I got the chance to introduce myself when he relieved himself. He was shocked our People use female scouts. He said they won't destroy us unless we try to remain here or take their food. The land will not support more than their people."

She shuffled, uncomfortable.

Mbasa motioned gently, "What else, Bird?"

"If we give them females, they will provide us food, water, and protection while we pass through their land."

Rainbow bounced. "I'm sure some of our females would like to stay with them."

Mbasa scowled but Bird asked and two agreed.

"These two lost their pairmates and both are pregnant. They prefer to settle with strangers than risk starving."

Mbasa motioned, "Rainbow and I will take them to the Others," but his eyes popped open and he shook so, he dropped his spear. Mbasa sighed. "Better yet, Rainbow, stay with the People in case this is a trap. Hecate and I will go, as will Bird so she can point out Ja-card. Starlight, cover us from the distance of a spear throw."

Starlight nodded, feet spread, piercing eyes locked onto the enemy who stood on the crest of a rise not far from where the People were gathered.

Mbasa started toward them and motioned subtly to Bird and Hecate, "Mimic Xhosa's posture and attitude."

Mbasa paused a spear-throw from the Others, Hecate and Bird at her side. There they stood, shoulder-to-shoulder, heads high, weapons down. Bird looked tiny next to the well-muscled Hecate but no less confident. Behind them, the two females and their children shuffled to a stop, clinging to each other.

Bird stepped in front of Mbasa, her movements graceful, and showed her teeth.

"Ja-card," she motioned to a squat muscular male, hair tightly curled against his skull, skin like the hide of Wild Beast but darker. "Two females with children wish to join you."

Ja-card turned toward an elder, hair white and flowing, a dead carcass draped around his shoulders.

The elder motioned, "Send them forward."

"Stop!" From Mbasa. "I am Mbasa, Leader of this group. How do we ensure you let us cross your territory?"

"Where is Leader Xhosa?"

"We became separated and now travel to her."

The white-haired Leader motioned and several warriors shuffled forward. They carried enough food and water to last the People a handful of days.

"Here is our proof, and my promise."

Mbasa prodded the two females across the divide until the Others swallowed them.

"How do we know you will care well for our group members?"

The Leader chortled. "Females are too valuable to mistreat, Leader-named-Mbasa. See—draw your own conclusion."

As Mbasa watched, the People's females were welcomed, offered sustenance, and surrounded by other females while the males eyed them eagerly.

"They will be honored with their choice of mates."

After a moment more, he motioned, "Ja-card would like the small one you call Bird."

Bird flushed and offered a subtle shake of her head. Ja-card grinned good-naturedly and the Elder grunted. "He understands. Why would one so powerful and valued leave her People?"

When the Other warriors came back from delivering the food to the People's camp, the entire group except two melted away over the hill.

Mbasa motioned to those remaining, "We will be easy to track. We do not try to hide," and trotted back to the People's camp.

Rainbow stood where she left him, eating. Between mouthfuls, he gestured, "How can we trust them?"

Mbasa walked away and motioned one-handed, "I told their Leader that Xhosa led us."

When they passed out of the white-haired Leader's land, the trackers left as promised and Rainbow sent his last hunter, Tor, to find food. Hecate and several females joined him.

Rainbow started to call them back but Mbasa stopped him. "They will help."

"They are females! They can't hunt!"

"And it is unsafe to send Tor alone. Don't worry, Rainbow."

Within a hand of Sun's passage, Tor and the females reappeared and pointed to the ridgeline. There, a warrior stood, spear in hand, warclub tied across his back.

Mbasa gestured, "We must talk to him."

Rainbow's lower lip quivered. "You go, Mbasa. You did well with the last Others. This time, tell them your Leader is Rainbow."

Mbasa pinched her lips between her fingers. "You should come with me," but he slouched and brushed a hand across his thigh—*Do your job.*

Mbasa mumbled to herself, "My fake strength can't be worse than his quaking."

She gave the warclub from the dead warrior to Starlight and hefted Nightshade's old one to her shoulder. It was broader and longer than any other, knobby all over with a smooth grip from constant use. A deep crack would cause it to fail with the first strike but Mbasa figured if she must fight her way back from this meeting, a broken warclub would be the least of her worries.

Mbasa strode toward the warrior, pace measured, spear down. She kept her movements as relaxed as her thoughts were jumbled. The closer she got, the more warriors appeared. Everyone deferred to one, a male young enough that few lines cut his face but experienced enough that wisdom emanated from his deep-set eyes, his peaceful face, and his subdued movements.

His warriors arrayed themselves at his sides, disciplined and prepared. At a signal, they raised their spears, arms cocked. Behind her, the shuffle of ordered steps meant Starlight and her warriors aimed spears at the Other Leader. If his warriors attacked, he would die first.

Mbasa stopped just out of spear range and studied the Leader as he did her. Finally, he stepped forward as his warriors dropped their spears to their sides. Mbasa matched him and heard Starlight respond.

"You are in our land." His hands moved smoothly, using familiar gestures.

"We wish to pass through. Big Heads destroyed our homeland. Many of our people were slaughtered."

"There are no Big Heads here. They are by Sun's awakening place—" He stopped abruptly, gaze beyond the sturdy line of female warriors. "Where is Leader Xhosa and her great warrior Nightshade?"

"There," and Mbasa looked across Endless Pond. "We were separated. We need to get back to them."

He followed her gaze and then turned to where Rainbow stood, bobbing from one foot to the other, hands empty. The Leader's expression soured and he spit as though disgusted by the taste of rotten food.

"The one who quakes and sends a female to do his work, he is the coward you call Rainbow—"

He interrupted himself to spit again. Mbasa gritted her teeth. He'd been watching them.

His eyes blazed. "Everyone smirks as he flees their land. He will get you killed. You and your warriors are brave. Stay with us. One-called-Rainbow—we have no need of him. If he stays, we will kill him."

Mbasa allowed a brief smile to shape her lips. "You may be right, Leader, but Rainbow has few warriors. If I leave, he will have less. Would you do that to your People?"

His gaze narrowed.

She motioned, "You will let us pass?"

He nodded. "You hunt our animals, we destroy you. And, Mbasa, you must lead. I want none to see I permitted a worm such as Rainbow to leave my land unblooded. You, though, any you meet will sense your strength. They will respect you."

Sweat rolled down her arms and dripped from her fingers as she tipped her head in acknowledgement. "You say there are no Big Heads here?"

"They moved to your old land with its rich herds, plants, and water. Nowhere is better. But here," and he waved a hand around his head dismissively, "it worsens the closer you get to Sun's nest."

By the time she returned to her People, shadows were long. Rainbow whined about the arrangement but she reminded him the People lived another day.

Chapter 11

Unknown location north of what is now the Mediterranean Sea

"Get up."

Xhosa's head pounded as though it would split open. When she moved, hot spikes stabbed through her eyes. Her legs felt like tree trunks and her hands didn't even exist. Squinting made her wince but she forced her eyes open.

They were in a cave.

"Wake up." A hand slapped her. She tried to swat it away but her hand wouldn't respond. Dull, empty eyes scrutinized her through dirty tangled hair.

An Other.

The stink of sweat from his body and rotten food in his hair nauseated her. In his hands were her spear and warclub. His hirsute shoulders were broad and muscle-bound, skin as light as hers. His skull was too small and chest too large to be a Big Head.

He might not even be an Other. She saw none of the intelligence that imbued most of her kind. Maybe he was one of the creatures Pan-do described—Hairy Ones.

He motioned, "We waste light."

He bent over, silhouetted against the daylight in the cave's mouth, within biting distance though it didn't seem to worry him, and cut the tendon that bound her feet.

"Don't hope for rescue. Your owner will find it easier to replace you than reclaim you from me."

She sighed with relief. He didn't know her.

"Let me go." Her gestures were those most Others understood, calm though constricted by the tie.

Instead of responding, he dragged her to a stream and shoved her into the frigid water.

"Drink. I won't stop later."

When he yanked her out by the hair, she kicked, hoping to trip him and then choke him with the tendon that tied her wrists. He adroitly avoided the strike and then punched her cruelly. Stars exploded.

"Feisty. Good." He wrenched her head back and studied her smooth hair, long limbs, slender build, and small breasts. "You are scrawny. Your tribe fed you poorly. You will like me better."

He nodded toward her weapons. "Why does a slave have a spear and warclub?" He leered. "Did you slay your owner to escape?"

Xhosa spit at him. He slapped her brutally. Her lip burst and dripped blood. Her cheek burned and her vision swam but she denied him the satisfaction of knowing it hurt.

"What is your call sign?" He motioned.

"Xhosa." Too late to bite back the answer. She didn't ask his because she'd already tagged him—Ugly One.

He did a double take. "A potent name for a slave. I will fatten you so you will serve me well."

She breathed out. He didn't recognize her name. "What is a slave?"

He snorted. "It means you do as I order."

He tethered her with a long vine and then looped a rancid bladder stuffed with meat and plants around her neck. She recoiled at the stench, wondering if it was the food or sack that was spoiled. The answer didn't matter. She'd find out soon enough.

He elbowed her in front. "Move or I will hobble your feet and drag you."

As they walked, Xhosa checked her neck sack. He'd taken not only her throwing stones but her pain plants. That was not good. Her head already throbbed. If she didn't treat it soon, the scorpion inside her head would sting over and over.

Before long, his labored breathing drowned out all sounds. Xhosa could run ceaselessly but pretended she too was exhausted and collapsed under a tree. Its broad leafy limbs shaded her though Xhosa preferred Sun's warmth. He untied her hands so she could eat but secured her feet. Pain ground into her temples, down her cheeks, through her back. It hurt worse than usual. Maybe he hit her too hard.

To distract herself, she asked, "How did you capture me?"

This foul beast moved at the speed of a sick pig and just as noisy, and he made no effort to hide his tracks. How did she miss him?

"I was sleeping. You almost stepped on me when you left the crevice."

Xhosa swallowed, struggling against nausea and the desperate need to lie down. She didn't, refusing to reveal weakness. Instead, she leaned against the trunk and tried to ignore the hot spikes that punctured her eyes and turned the world beneath her closed lids red. She wanted to throw up but forced the bile back.

Finally, she couldn't stand it anymore and motioned, "I need a plant for my pain."

He paused mid-chew. "Describe your pain."

"In my head, grinding into my temples, burning through my eyes. I think you hit me too hard."

"What does the plant look like?"

"It has yellow flowers. The stalk reaches my knees, with hairy leaves. I need the bulb attached to its root..." She peeked at him out of the corner of her eye. "Do you have this?"

He tossed a root bundle to her. Xhosa flipped it over, rolled it between her fingers, tasted it, and then chewed. To her surprise, almost immediately, the pain dulled.

"Where do I find these?"

"We pass a patch before Sun leaves tomorrow."

Tomorrow! "I have to return to my People—"

"Forget them! You are lucky I found you. I treat my slaves well if they behave. The others, when you meet them, they will tell you that." His lip curled into a snarl that revealed yellow broken teeth. "If you try to run, I will cut your feet so you can walk no faster than a shuffle."

"And it will take much longer to reach your camp!" she snapped.

He shrugged. "No, it won't because I will kill you."

His straightforwardness convinced her he meant what he said. He offered no food so she opened the bladder. The food was green with rot and gray with age but she ate it. Her first goal must be to retain her strength so she could flee when the opportunity presented itself. But he must consider her weak and vulnerable. Then, at the right time, she could surprise him.

When he finished eating, he retied her hands, secured her feet, and pushed her along a seldom-used trail. To tell her to turn, he stabbed her shoulder with his spear. After one overly-belligerent jab that drew blood, Xhosa slapped at him, not bothering to hide her anger.

"You leave sign any can find," and with a crunch, she stepped on the leftovers from one of his past meals. "I see your backtrail as does everyone. I'm surprised Others haven't slaughtered you."

He guffawed. "There are no Others here."

They wove through rolling foothills, skirting the base of a range of low mountains, over open valleys with few trees, and in and out of steep canyons that dropped to flowing streams. Her shadow lay to her side, not in front or behind as it did on the People's path. To keep track of her progress, she compared the trail to Sun's movement, identified the position of spider's webs, and memorized the landmarks that would guide her escape.

Because there would be an escape.

"I am thirsty."

The streams had dried up far behind them, replaced by dry cracked ground and rocky cliffs.

"There is no water here."

"You're wrong," and she nodded up to the bluff where profuse green bushes overwhelmed the lip. "It's up there."

He sneered. "How do we reach it?"

Xhosa stored this away. *He can't climb a cliff.* "Let the water come to us. I'll show you."

She found a crack far up the wall no wider than the length of an arm and extended to the top. Below where it disappeared, the rocks glistened.

"We can lick it there," and showed him the shine on the rock face, "or" and moved her finger to the brush along the base of the cliff. "drink from the pool hidden in those plants."

Once she pushed the green fronds aside, a puddle no deeper than a hand appeared, fed by the runoff from some pond or stream at the top of the cliff. They drank what they needed and then continued. The flat barrenness was eventually replaced with trees, swathing their trail in leaves and moss. Birds chattered and brown furry creatures the size of large rats protested the invasion.

"What are those?"

"Squirrels. You have none where you live? They are tasty."

By the time Sun shone directly overhead, the flat plateau gave way again to rocky land with great boulders strewn about as though a giant hand had carelessly tossed them. To one side spread a dry lava bed, to the other, rancid water covered in green slime. Skulls littered the shore.

They didn't stay.

That night, Ugly-One found a cave, so deep the only light that reached their nest in the back came from the glint of his eyes. He trussed her to a rock and left. Rather than eat more rotten food, she caught a rat and snapped its neck. Her stomach satisfied, she slept fitfully. Her toes and fingers numbed in the frigid air.

Pounding rain and the promise of fresh water woke her but her tether didn't allow her to reach the cave's mouth. By morning, the rain had ended so all she could do was lick the damp leaves and slurp water from the small puddles before departing.

The water tasted different—cleaner, lighter even. How could that be? Rain was rain.

The wind blew with such ferocity, she struggled to stand upright as they walked. Any footsteps on their backtrail were erased as though never there. The trees bent to the side, their bare branches whipping in the stormy winds. Every breath stabbed at her throat like shards of rock. Wrapping her hair around herself provided brief warmth until the cold seeped through.

Days passed and then a Moon, each colder than the last. Copses of trees became steep slopes and narrow wooded valleys. They played tricks with the sound or maybe her senses were dulled from the endless migration. At night, he tied her to a trunk or a boulder while he hunted, always returning with meat which they shared.

The creature he called squirrel tasted as good as promised.

Toward the end of another arduous day, the clouds lowered and blackened. Xhosa welcomed rain, desperate to scrub away the bugs that crawled through her hair and made her itch. A flash of lightning broke the sky and then raindrops. She stopped abruptly, not caring he almost tripped over her, and tipped her head back. Ugly One thrust her roughly toward a distant cave. She stumbled, barely avoiding a kick. When he missed her, he lost his balance and fell into a muddy slick. It took the last of her control to hide a giggle.

As the rain became torrents, they tumbled into the cave. He heaved her to the back and tied her feet. She shivered uncontrollably, the cold no less inside than out. Ugly One wore two pelts but never offered one to her.

He must use this cave often because there was a pile of tinder to the side, far enough from the mouth to remain dry.

He gathered pieces and pulled out what must be a fire stone, like Seeker's fire stones.

After many futile attempts, Xhosa hobbled up to the pit on her tied-together feet. "You do it wrong. Give me one of your pelts and I will make fire."

He growled and tried again. "The wood is wet."

She grabbed the stone from his hand, and within a breath, flames leaped.

"The wood is fine. Your skill isn't. Give me a pelt or do this yourself the next time."

He guffawed. "I like your spirit, one-called-Xhosa. You will be worth the trouble," and tossed her an animal skin.

Like the bladder, it stunk. He mustn't have applied salt, nor scraped it well. Xhosa wrinkled her nose and draped it around her neck. The smell wouldn't kill her but the cold might.

With her back turned, he leaped. Her shackles prevented her from defending herself. He muscled her onto her back and forced her arms up. She bit him, slammed her knees into his back and buttocks, and head butted him, all to no avail. Her People mated often but never roughly. This thug didn't care if he hurt her as long as he satisfied himself.

When finished, he left, motioning, "Slaves submit. You'll learn."

Rage churned her stomach. "Your people force females to mate? You are no better than Uprights!"

Ugly One scowled. "You bleed."

She looked down at the blood on her legs. It always started when Moon became a sliver. "I need to clean off, in the rain."

He grabbed her arm and threw her outside, feet trussed. "I am watching."

She breathed deeply to control her rage and collected plants to absorb the flow. Most males avoided females who bled. She hoped Ugly One would.

The rain poured down, hitting her with staggering force and drenching her through the animal skin. A snake crossed her path, eager to escape the frigid air. If it had been one with poison in its mouth, she would fling it at Ugly One and laugh as it bit him. After scrubbing the dirt from her skin with moss and bark, she huddled by the fire. When he tried to push her away, she slapped him viciously.

"I must warm myself."

Her sleep was restless, often broken by a memory of his violence. She shook with fury but if he assaulted her again, the result would be the same. Thankfully, he slumbered without awaking.

They trekked all the next day and the one after. She memorized the landmarks—a lofty waterfall that coated the air with mist, a sunken valley pressed against the base of a mountain, and a far-away ridge. Every night, after they ate, he forced her to mate, oblivious to her bleeding. Every day, her anger intensified and her resolve deepened.

They walked for days through overgrown fields. Birds and squirrels scolded the interlopers with shrill squawks and nonstop chatter. A fat, old skunk waddled across the trail. Ugly One raised his warclub but it lifted its tail and Ugly One fled.

Each day became colder than the previous, numbing her fingers and burning her skin. White clouds from her mouth floated starkly against the blue sky. Nothing stopped her shaking so despite the bile that rose in her throat, at night, she curled next to Ugly One to share his body heat.

After another Moon and as many days as fingers on both hands, traces of Others appeared—footprints, stone shavings, trounced-down grass, and broken twigs at eye level.

"Are these your people?"

He ignored her, forcing her up a steep bluff. Before they crested it, he wrenched her to the ground, scraping her knees over the frozen surface.

"Hide."

Down the slope lay a flat field surrounded by low hills, tall ones in the background, their gleaming white tips edged by dark bands of desolate trees. At their base, tiny figures moved to and from a sinuous stream.

He finally rose and hooted a strange sound. The same call came back and he shunted her forward. She tried to reproduce the noise but couldn't shape her mouth and hold her air sufficiently—which made Ugly One laugh.

"No stranger can pretend to be us. You will learn."

Yes, I will.

As they approached, his people gawked at her straight hair, slender body, and long legs—nothing like these stout light-colored people with fuzzy manes that didn't cover their necks. Xhosa stood a full head above the tallest among them. Ugly One propelled her across the field into a cave and flung her against a back wall where a groupmate tied her feet.

When her eyes adjusted, the cave's size shocked her. The top rose higher than a spear could reach and water dripped from above into vast waterholes. Dark pathways disappeared into deep recesses filled with gray shadows. Gradually, dusty shapes emerged from the dull color of the walls, huddled against each other. These must be the slaves Ugly One referred to.

All smelled alike except one.

She observed cautiously out of the corners of her eyes. Each was bound, all with untreated scrapes, cuts, welts, and bites over their bodies. None seemed familiar.

Eyes shut but mind alert, she listened to Ugly One and his tribe gather to eat and then tell stories like those the People told—the migration of herds, a grove of trees newly bearing fruit, questions about Other hunters who entered their land, and which pregnant slave would soon deliver. If Xhosa closed her eyes, overlooked that her arms and legs were bound, that she was hungry and in pain, she could imagine herself among her own People at the end of a long tiring day.

Someone tossed food at the slaves as her People might toss a piglet to Spirit. The slaves fought over it except for several too weak and Xhosa. Since, her captor left her neck sack, she ate what it held.

Finished with their stories, Ugly One's tribe came up one after another to stare at her, perplexed by her smooth tresses, fawn-colored skin, and over-long arms and legs. Many stroked her with hands that stunk of feces. Finally, she had enough. When the next fetid brute reached a hand toward her hair, she snarled and slapped it away.

"Ha! A feisty one, as you say, Fang!" The brute snagged her arm, thinking to wrench her into submission, but she elbowed him in the temple hard enough to push him off-balance. When she grabbed for his spear, he pushed her off-balance.

The Other males guffawed. "You allow a female to treat you like that?"

The enraged male stood, face rigid, muscles like rocks. He slammed his fist forward and her world dissolved to red and black.

Chapter 12

Somewhere north of what is now called the Mediterranean Sea

"Spirit!" No answer. The wolf always slept with Seeker or Lyta but not last night. This morning, he was nowhere.

"Maybe his kind called him." This from Zvi.

"No. He would tell me."

"Nightshade says we must leave when Moon returns. Xhosa will join us later."

Seeker motioned, sadly. "He's right. It's been a hand of nights since she left. If we stay much longer, we will be discovered."

"And Spirit?"

"He goes where he needs to be. He'll return or not, whichever is best for him."

Zvi sighed. The beginning of the end had arrived.

Chapter 13

Somewhere in what today is Turkey

Xhosa jerked awake with a grimace. Every sound—the buzz of a bee, the pound of rocks against stone, the noisy chatter of voices—made her head throb. When the noises didn't stop, Xhosa squinted. Even that slit of light felt like the stab of a cactus spine. Gray shapes moved, silhouetted by the fire, murky and indistinct.

She sniffed and froze. Whoever belonged to the odor she recognized earlier touched her. A blurry face hovered in the corner of her vision, hair matted and grungy. He dampened a finger with saliva and rubbed it over a bloody gash on Xhosa's cheek, still weeping blood.

"Are you alright, Xhosa?"

She snapped her eyes open and grimaced but warmth filled her body. "Ngili!"

Her father's trusted warrior, the youngest Second ever, Ngili had set the standard for excellence until the day he died at her father's side. No one, not even Nightshade, could beat his skill with spears, warclubs, and throwing stones. His hirsute body kept out all but the most determined biting insects which made him an effective predator. He could lie still in the grass watching an enemy without being bothered by bugs. His crooked nose and wide white scars were all anyone needed to know about his passion for winning and aggressiveness in achieving it. Above all, and what her father valued most, Ngili listened. He adapted as needed during a battle and followed directions without hesitation.

No surprise, he was no longer the sturdy muscular fighter she'd last seen lying motionless on the ground, bleeding from a spear to his chest. Now, Ngili's skin hung on a boney frame, eyes sunken, hair brittle. But the warrior he had been still sparked in his voice and his gestures snapped with delight at seeing her.

He patted his hands on air, palms down. "Shh! No one knows I once fought with the invincible warrior Nightshade and the mighty female Leader Xhosa who saved her people from Big Heads. It wouldn't be good if they find out."

She switched to low hand movements. "How did you survive?"

"The Big Heads healed me to serve as a slave. When they took off after Rainbow, Wind let me go.

"Wind? The one who slaughtered my father?"

"No. His brother Thunder did that. The two are identical in appearance but as different inside as the red-striped snakes. Thunder is Nightshade with an evil streak. Wind is a male version of you."

Xhosa grimaced at the descriptions.

Ngili smiled. "I think you'd like him. Wind was distraught his brother assaulted your father. The People's land provided sufficient food and water for both tribes so why kill your warriors? But Thunder likes killing."

He cast a furtive glance at the captors huddled around the fire but they paid no attention to the slaves.

Ngili motioned, "Does Hecate's new pairmate treat her well?"

Xhosa explained Rainbow's split from the People and how Ngili's pairmate Hecate went with him. Ngili fell silent so Xhosa observed the slaves. A group of subadult females stared at her, eyes frightened but hopeful. One smiled as though to say she trusted Xhosa to fix things. Xhosa responded solemnly with an almost invisible nod.

This youngster had no idea how much would change. Xhosa would die before living as a slave.

Ngili noticed where she was looking and motioned, "They've been expecting you since I shared stories of the mighty female warrior who led my People and would come for me." He grinned at her. The tension in her neck and shoulders melted. She had missed Ngili's positive outlook. "Not because I thought you would but because it kept them from giving up."

"You forgot to say I thought you dead?"

"Well, there is that." He grinned again. "Where would hope come from if not dreams?"

Xhosa motioned, "Ngili. Tell me about these Others."

Ngili motioned, "They are like no tribe I've seen. They control fire and wear the pelts of dead animals. We are their slaves. They ignore us if we do as told, abuse us if we don't. The subadult females," he nodded toward the small group, eyes still fixed on Xhosa, "they were captured together, from one tribe. They will be used for breeding when old enough. The rest, many have been here most of their lives. They don't know where their People are and have no desire to leave."

He leaned back against the wall.

Xhosa motioned, using the People's gestures, "I understand most of their hand signals. They are like a tribe we settled with called the Hawk People, now called the Nightshade People."

Ngili furrowed his brow. Xhosa was about to explain how Nightshade came to lead this tribe when Ngili moved closer to her, turning slightly to place his back to the other slaves.

"That male, over there, he's watching us. Some of the slaves have been here so long, they spy for the Others, all for extra scraps of food or salves for wounds."

To Xhosa's surprise, one of the subadults scooted around to also block the slave's view of Xhosa and Ngili.

Xhosa motioned, "How did you end up with these people, Ngili?"

"When I escaped the Big Heads, I followed your trail from our homebase. I almost caught up when you and the

People took to the water on log platforms to avoid those strange-looking attackers. I followed the shoreline, hoping to catch up when you landed, but the water became too deep to cross. That's where these Others captured me."

Xhosa described the People's time with Hawk, what they learned from him, and how when Hawk died, Nightshade became Leader of the former Hawk People though still acting as her Lead Warrior.

When she finished, she asked, "How do we escape? You must have a plan."

Ngili nodded, face burning with passion, eyes glittering. "It'll be ready soon."

"Will any of the other slaves fight with us?"

Before Ngili could answer, a huge figure bigger than the massive female, Zvi, lumbered over, a club in each hand. He scowled at them, eyes dark, while poking his tongue into the back of his cheek.

"Get up!" he motioned. "Come with me!"

Xhosa and Ngili struggled to rise, stumbling and falling more than once because of the vines binding their feet. As they exited the cave, gusts of frozen wind hit them. For the first time, Xhosa realized she no longer wore her pelt. "My animal skin—it's gone."

Ngili started to say something but Big Male shoved them across the clearing toward a tree. When Xhosa fell, he kicked her until she smacked into the ice-covered bark.

"Try to run, they will kill you," and he pointed toward the Fire Tenders, huddled together, shivering in the frigid air. Xhosa suspected if she ran, they'd let her rather than leave the fire.

She rubbed her hands over her arms as her teeth chattered. "We're too far from the fire," she stuttered, her breath steaming in the icy night.

"You're a slave," and he yanked her hands behind the tree and secured them with a vine. When finished, he leered at her, tongue working the back of his mouth, eyes dark with pain.

She cocked her head. "Your tooth—it makes you miserable. I can help."

He flinched, hand reaching for his cheek but before he could respond, another male called. "Dreg! Get inside—it is cold out here."

Xhosa leaned toward one-called-Dreg. "If I don't help you, one-called-Dreg, the pain will never go away."

For a moment, hope lit his face and then he shut it down. "Don't talk," and left.

Xhosa watched him go, wondering how to use his pain to gain her freedom. Finally, she asked Ngili, "Where is my pelt?"

"When you passed out, the brute you tried to attack kept kicking you. He would have killed you but I convinced the Leader they were stupid to slaughter such a strong slave. He gave your pelt to the brute in exchange for leaving you alone."

Xhosa scooted closer to Ngili, saying nothing but watching everything. A wolf howled. Ngili shivered and Xhosa perked.

Could that be?

"Ngili. What is the plan you have that isn't yet finished?"

He dipped his head and whispered, "When I arrived, I befriended an elder named Dawa. His skin was rough like bark and as wrinkled as one of the great beasts. His hair glowed white with one red streak. He said that was all that reminded him of where he once lived, where most of his tribe had red hair.

"After watching my endless failed attempts, he said he'd better help me escape or I'd get myself killed. I told him death was better than living as a slave.

"We forged a partnership that night, stealing what food and tools we could and hiding them under a tree outside of this camp. Planning our escape was all that kept both of us alive."

Xhosa gestured, "Where is he? He can lead us to his People."

"He's dead."

Xhosa drooped, leaned back against the craggy cave wall, and let Ngili finish his story.

His eyes skittered over the cave, the Others clustered around the fire, and the desperate slaves, before continuing.

"The day before we hoped to execute the plan, the Others found our supplies. They beat Dawa mercilessly and threw him at my feet, saying that would be me if I tried again. Dawa's eyes couldn't focus. He coughed blood as though something inside had broken and his arm hung limply at his side.

"When I left to hunt the next day, he couldn't stand. When I returned that evening, he couldn't move. He told me they had killed him, that I must tell his People he had never forgotten them. He promised they would welcome me.

"As everyone slept, he described in detail the path I must take, words halting and often disrupted by grinding pain. By the time Sun returned, he had died."

A wolf's howl pierced the night, sad and mournful.

Xhosa howled an answer, her voice so realistic, wolves responded from all directions.

"Shut up!" From one of the Fire Tenders.

Xhosa shouted, "I speak wolf. I am warning them away to keep you safe."

The Fire Tender grumbled, undoubtedly believing she lied but hoping she didn't.

Groans and cries from inside the cave overpowered the howls, and then a loud slap, a whimper, and more wheezing pants.

"Do they do this every night?" When Ngili nodded, Xhosa whispered, "We're better off tied to a tree in the cold."

After a moment and a few sidelong glimpses, Ngili motioned, "Have you pairmated with Nightshade yet? I always thought you would."

Xhosa shrugged good-naturedly. "Before becoming a pairmate, I must learn to be a Leader."

One of the Fire Tenders stomped over and fisted Ngili to the side of his head. "Silence!" and then scurried back to the fire, shivering.

Xhosa shut her eyes. Stories the Fire Tenders told each other, trying to stay awake, drifted to her, thinned by the night air like smoke, until she fell asleep.

The welcome warmth of Sun's rays awoke Xhosa. Two warriors dragged a dead female from the cave, one cheek caved in, sightless eyes glazed in death. Many of her fingers and toes were black, her earlobes withered. Chopping food, walking—whatever required hands or feet had become impossible which made her worthless. She was tossed in the ravine used by all to relieve themselves of night water.

Ugly One—Fang—approached Xhosa as he left the waste ditch. "Come," and he wrenched her arm.

Ngili moved to defend her until Xhosa stopped him with a glare that said, "This oaf must consider me weak. Do not change his mind."

She gestured, "I'm hungry, Fang. You promised to feed me."

"You have been traded. You now belong to the Leader. When the hunt ends and we return to our main camp, you will be presented to him. He will enjoy your unusual size and spirit."

Xhosa didn't plan to be here that long but played along. "OK. What will I do today?"

She used the gestures of the Hawk People, just to see his reaction. The Other standing behind Fang howled with pleasure. She met his eye, wondering if he could be an ally. His body was magnificent, all muscle like Nightshade but leaner. His chest was covered in scars as though clawed by Cat and his nose was so small, Xhosa wondered how he breathed.

Instead of Fang's flat dullness, this male's black eyes shone with life. "Fang says your People live in this area but I have never seen them."

"If you let me, I will take you to them."

"Our scouts are excellent and can't find them. It seems they abandoned you."

She kept her expression blank. "Perhaps. I may need a new tribe." She stepped closer. "You have fought many battles, warrior, and won. You must be the Lead."

Since he didn't share his call sign, she mentally tagged him Scarred One.

He pushed Ngili to the group of male slaves who would join the hunters and her to a group of females. She fell to the ground, purposely, on top of plants damp from the night. With her hair shielding her face, she licked as much water as possible before Scarred One kicked her toward a female elder.

"All fear me, as should you. I now own you until we return to the homebase. We can discuss whether you are worthy of my tribe later.

He motioned to the female elder. "Gak will tell you what to do. Don't try to run or you will be hobbled. Like her." He pointed to a captive who walked hunched and slow because her toes had been chopped off.

Elder-named-Gak made room for Xhosa to crouch at her side and then shoved a hide at her.

"Clean it."

Xhosa squeezed in, shivering. "Your call sign is Gak? If I need help?"

Gak snickered. "If you need help cleaning pelts, I will return you to the males."

Xhosa clenched and unclenched her hands. "I can't feel my fingers, Elder. I can work better if I am not freezing."

"Where's your animal skin?"

"Someone took it when I passed out."

Gak grabbed a skin and looped it around Xhosa. Xhosa offered no thanks even as welcome heat seeped into her body, no complaint when its stench filled her nose. She quietly set to her task, using the methods learned from Hawk's females.

After a hand of Sun's journey overhead, Gak slapped Xhosa on the back of her head. "You are too slow. Work faster."

Xhosa glared at her. "You like the reek of rotten carcass? When I remove the decaying meat and clean away the stink, you will like mine better than yours. If you want, I will teach you. If not, leave me alone."

Gak leaned forward, fist raised, but paused to sniff the pelt Xhosa was cleaning. Her eyes burst open and her lips tugged up at the corners.

"Shut up and work!"

Gak returned to her own pelt but watched Xhosa out of the corner of her eye, curious how a stupid slave erased the smell of rot from the pelt.

Xhosa calmly and silently worked. Listening to the chatter around her, she realized this camp served the hunters and was far from the homebase where most of the males, as well as the females and children, lived. Viper, one of the subadults who had watched Xhosa last night, managed to get herself placed next to Xhosa. When Gak was distracted by the other females, Xhosa asked questions and Viper answered. According to her, every morning, someone took the finished pelts to the homebase. He didn't return that day or the next and always looked exhausted.

That meant the main camp was too far away to provide help if it was needed. Xhosa could work with that.

As Sun headed toward its nighttime nest, Xhosa handed the finished pelt to Gak. "This one will last longer and because it doesn't stink, won't attract carrion eaters."

The Elder inhaled, rubbed the inside with her fingers, and tossed it to Scarred One. He snuffled, grunted, and dropped it over his shoulders. "Make another."

Gak motioned, "Tomorrow, show me how you remove the smell."

It took less than a Moon to realize she and Ngili were more skilled as fighters than any here, with the possible exception of Scarred One. The ache to unleash her internal warrior, to fight back against these miserable creatures, to defend herself from each slap or shove or kick became almost unbearable. It took Ngili's constant reminders that their captors must consider them both weak or the plan would fail.

Days passed, Moon grew and disappeared with no change in the routine. Males left early to hunt, returning when they killed enough meat or ran out of daylight. The females spent every day cleaning pelts and preparing food. At night, screams echoed from the cave halted only briefly when one male replaced another. No one forced Xhosa to mate. Apparently, that privilege now belonged to the group's Leader who lived at the main camp.

Xhosa taught Gak to clean the pelts properly and listened to the females chatter about their dull lives. Viper asked every day when they could escape, never expecting she, Deer, and Leopard wouldn't be part of the plan. Xhosa considered their usefulness. They were so devoted to each other that one could be sent on tasks away from the camp without worry she would flee. Because she wouldn't, not without her two friends.

How could Xhosa make that part of the plan?

Each night, the wolves howled, always closer than the night before. When Xhosa answered, they quieted. The Fire Tenders nervously built up the flames. Their furtive glances said though they believed Xhosa could talk to wolves, they didn't know if she warned them away or called them to her.

Everything changed the day Wind walked into the camp.

Ngili lay curled against a tree trunk, eyes closed, claiming to be too weak to hunt. His captors cared nothing if Ngili died. They would just capture another slave. Truth, Ngili got stronger and healthier each day thanks to the bits of meat Xhosa cleaned from the pelts and hid in her skin to share with him.

Xhosa was bent over a hide, fingers busy. She'd heard the strange footsteps long ago and now tracked them as they approached the camp. Her nose twitched at the unusual aroma, part belonging to the wolf Spirit but another part perilous enough to raise the hackles on her neck. The steps belonged to an Upright, a heavy male based on the thump of his feet hitting the ground, but not Nightshade. She wouldn't hear him. Judging by how this Upright slipped through the trees, he was slender.

She heard the bushes part at the edge of the camp. The steps paused and she lifted her head. Nothing prepared her for what she saw.

"Wind," she whispered to herself.

His dark eyes found hers. Pity flashed across his face, immediately replaced by rage. She had never seen him this close but he fit Ngili's description. He was tall as she was, lightly haired over his body, and lean of build but muscular. Power emanated from his every movement. His presence with Spirit's odor shocked Xhosa. Had the Big Head defeated the wolf? She found that impossible to believe but couldn't come up with any other reason.

"There you are!" From Wind. To Xhosa.

Gak jerked upright, hands frozen mid-scrape.

Wind turned soft eyes to the Elder. "You have my slave," and jutted the nob beneath his mouth at Xhosa.

He grinned when Gak looked at him. Had they met before?

"I am here to take her back."

His motions were gentle but firm, as though he expected Gak to return his slave Xhosa now that she knew who owned her. A smile again stretched his lips as though she shouldn't consider this a discussion. More like a friendly order. The strength in his hand gestures made it clear he expected no objection from Gak.

Xhosa's mind spun. Was leaving with Wind safer than staying with these Others? Ngili caught her eye, unable to hide his excitement.

That's right. Wind helped him escape. Ngili trusted the Big Head.

Ngili edged into position to assist Wind. The twinkle in his eyes said he did indeed have a plan though Wind's arrival might not be what he originally intended.

Xhosa motioned, "My new master—the one who enslaves me—is out with the hunters—"

Gak slapped her cruelly. "Shut up!"

Xhosa didn't react, instead, cocked her head at Wind telling him to get started. The tiny upturn of his mouth told her he understood.

"Old master, none here are smart enough to negotiate my release."

This time, when Gak raised her open hand, Xhosa grabbed the wrist and twisted, ignoring the female's squeal.

Wind guffawed, "She is a gutsy one, my slave." After a pause, he motioned, "I need no one's permission to take what I own."

Gak wrenched her wrist free—actually, Xhosa let go— and stood, her full height well below Wind's.

"Leave, stranger. We own her. You are only one male and cannot prevail against all of us," but her voice shook with fear. The other females had stopped their work to stare open-mouthed, eyes bouncing from Gak to Wind. Viper, Deer, and Leopard squirmed bit by bit out of the circle toward Ngili.

Wind stepped forward. The unspoken promise of his skill and the strength of his personality dominated the group.

"I have no wish to hurt you, Elder. Please rethink your decision."

Gak stepped back as though his words pushed her. She searched the surroundings for rescue but found emptiness.

She motioned to Wind, "You are not like us. Who are you?"

As though to answer, the underbrush rustled and Spirit padded to Wind's side, feral gaze on Gak. When she gulped, his hackles rose and tail stiffened. The vibrant blue eyes hardened as a growl rumbled from his throat.

Gak stumbled backward.

Xhosa blinked, unable to hide a smile at the welcome sight of Spirit. He huffed to her, wagged his tail, and then turned back to Gak and growled again, no doubt wanting to reinforce his job as rescuer.

Why does Spirit travel with the Big Head? Time enough later for that answer. Xhosa looped the pelt she'd just finished cleaning around herself, tossed another from Gak's pile to Ngili, and stepped toward Wind.

"Ngili must come also."

With these warriors—Ngili, Wind, Spirit, and herself—the lazy Others would never capture them. Once they were safely away, there would be time to decide whether to stay with the Big Head. As the Elder said, he was but one and Xhosa had never faced a warrior she couldn't beat— except Nightshade.

"Ngili," she motioned, with hand signals of the People. "Spirit is a friend."

Gak stepped back and motioned the rest of the females into the cave. "Use the rocks to defend us!"

Everyone fled except Deer, Leopard, and Viper. "We go with you, Xhosa. We are young but will not hold you up."

"No!" Gak yelled. "You," and pointed to an older female, one of the most brutish with the slaves. "Take them into the cave. They will be dealt with after we recapture this Xhosa. You will rue the day you tried to flee—"

Wind cut her off with a dismissive wave of his hand. "I want my slave. If you wish to get rid of these others, do so now. We must go."

Xhosa understood his hurry. She heard it too—the voices shouting about an intruder in the area, the feet pounding toward the camp. As Xhosa and Wind fled, Ngili and Spirit right behind, the older female grabbed Deer which halted Viper and Leopard. Viper screamed but Xhosa kept going. She would come back for the subadults.

"There—they go there!" Gak yelled and the Other warriors crashed through the underbrush. Spirit fought his way to the front of the small group, nose sniffing out their backtrail. He easily slipped through the bushes, stopping often to encourage his pack with a woof before sprinting onward.

A stone whooshed past Xhosa but another caught Ngili below the ear. His eyes rolled up and when he tried to stay on his feet, he vomited.

"Ngili's hit!" Xhosa grabbed his wrist and dragged him behind her. When he stumbled, she wrapped an arm around his waist and they hobbled onward. "Go, Wind!"

Others flooded from the trees, blocking her way and threatening Wind with their spears.

Scarred One stepped toward her, smirking. "I told you—I own you now!"

Xhosa had no choice but to stop. She pulled herself upright, eyes blazing, feet spread. Before she could snarl a response, a rock crashed into the back of her skull and she plunged into a red fiery darkness.

Chapter 14

An explosion of pain woke Xhosa. She threw up until nothing more came out and then shivered uncontrollably. A thin layer of brittle ice covered her. The cold seeped through her hair and worked its way deep inside. The Others had again tied her arms around the trunk which exposed her body, without the pelt, to the bitter wind.

She wanted to scream but settled for shallow breaths that formed clouds in front of her mouth and nose. Her skin felt as if touched with fire. Beside her, also trussed, were Ngili, Leopard, Viper, and Deer. Though they said nothing, the blue lips and white ears spoke of their extreme cold.

"You're awake." It was Ngili, his voice soft, not loud enough for any to hear except for her. "I worried they hit you too hard. They threw water on you and it froze over your body during the night."

Xhosa wanted the Others to think her unconscious so risked only a quick sideways glance. The side of Ngili's head was bloody and swollen and deep bruises colored his limbs and chest where he'd been struck repeatedly.

She motioned stiffly, "Are you alright?"

He nodded. "It looks worse than it feels. I want them to think I can't walk. They said Wind and Spirit are dead but I haven't seen bodies."

"They aren't." This from Viper. "They complained that the tall stranger and the wolf escaped."

"Were they injured?" Xhosa motioned quietly.

When Viper shook a *No*, Xhosa nodded her thanks. If they killed Spirit, no amount of revenge would suffice.

Viper motioned, leaning past Ngili so Xhosa could see her, "They're going to cut our toes off tomorrow."

Xhosa snorted. "Then we better escape tonight."

Flames flickered in the pit, surrounded by motionless lumps curled in on themselves to conserve heat. The Fire Tenders. They swayed side to side, too chilled and tired to stay awake. The pain from her many injuries ached but she buried it in cold anger as frigid as the air around her. A heavy fog floated above the ground like smoke from a dying blaze. She glanced up once, smiling when the stars winked at her.

Seeker is lying under these same stars, wondering about Spirit. And me.

She tried to think up a plan but the pounding in her head and the nonstop shivering made it impossible. As she fought to control her breathing, she heard a snuffle behind her accompanied by a feral odor. Something cold touched her back followed by a sloppy lick.

"Spirit! I am glad you live."

He huffed and his warm breath on her hands made her sigh with pleasure.

"Loosen these," and jiggled the ties around her wrists where his muzzle must be. How the wolf understood was a mystery but he always did. Maybe because he lived with Zvi and Seeker for most of his life.

The wolf's teeth nibbled at the vines while his damp lips prodded her hands. The Fire Tenders were oblivious, busy melting their hands. As Spirit nipped, Xhosa tugged until the cordage broke and her hands popped loose. The Fire Tenders, slumped forward now, remained unaware of her efforts. Quietly, she untied her feet and Ngili's hands. While he freed his feet, he motioned, "We must take Viper, Deer, and Leopard or they will be killed."

Xhosa blew an irritated breath but loosened Viper's hands, motioning her to do the same for the other two.

While Xhosa worked, Spirit padded to the Fire Tenders and stopped a hand's width away, blowing dank wolf breath over them. When all the captives were ready to leave, Spirit rumbled a growl and the youngest Fire Tender jerked upright. He gasped, then wheezed, but before he could do more, Xhosa raised her hand.

"If you call for help or awaken the other Tenders, you die."

As though to reinforce her words, Spirit snarled, fangs glistening in Moon's light.

One eye on the wolf, the other on Xhosa, the Fire Tender motioned, "I will not stop you, Tall Female! I have been with these Others most of my life and am still treated as a slave. Please, knock me out or they will blame me!"

Ngili motioned, "This is Ork. He tried to help Dawa."

Xhosa stepped forward, took Ork's warclub, and smacked him hard enough to close his eyes but not kill him. That single act awoke the latent power within her. It flowed like water in a flash flood and armed her more than any weapon. She collected the spears of the sleeping Fire Tenders, debated whether to knock them out, and decided against it.

Somewhere, Owl hooted.

Ngili beamed. "Wind's here."

The Big Head appeared and led the group on his backtrail, Xhosa at the rear. The thick fog and dark night would make it difficult to track them.

Deer stepped on a twig. Its snap broke the quiet. Xhosa waved everyone onward. "Spirit and I will handle this!"

Xhosa hoped the Fire Tenders would think sap had exploded in the fire and ignore it but one cracked open bleary eyes.

"Hey," he slurred, hands groggy with sleep. "You're supposed to be tied up."

This male—Young One—was who the older warriors sent to chase porcupines for food. That meant he was often injured and always miserable from the spines. He staggered to his feet while pawing for his spear.

"Is this what you're looking for?" and Xhosa waggled it.

"Give those back!"

Spirit paced forward to within a hand of Young One. Ears flat, tail extended, hackles bristling, he growled.

Young One halted mid-stride, tried to back away, and tripped.

Xhosa towered over him. "Stay there or you will die as he did," turning toward the unconscious Fire Tender. He did indeed look dead.

Spirit placed his paw on Young One's head forcing him to remain flat. A soft snarl rumbled from his muzzle and the hair down his back prickled. Drool dripped from his fangs and fell in gooey strands onto Young One's neck.

Xhosa explained, "He says be quiet or he'll tear your throat out."

Young One shook but agreed. "Why's a wolf here?"

"He's Spirit."

"Spirit?" His voice squeaked and he tried to crawl away but the wolf's curled yellow nails dug holes in his arm.

"He is here for us. Silence, Other, and listen carefully. When you come to, tell your people the Spirit Wolf freed the prisoners. Any who come after us will die," and she bashed Young One in his head. His mouth dropped open soundlessly as he crumpled.

Behind her, a voice hissed, "Go!"

Xhosa jerked. "Wind?"

"Spirit and I will catch up."

When Xhosa touched the Big Head, she felt a tingle. It started with her fingers and didn't stop until it reached her toes. "Alright, but after you convince them to leave us alone, you and I need to talk." And then, "Thank you."

Chapter 15

It wasn't until Sun's morning glow lit the horizon that Spirit rejoined them. Tail wagging, he huffed a greeting and licked Xhosa's hands as though proud of himself for protecting his pack. Next, Wind panted into sight, a spear in hand. Xhosa tensed. What did any of them know about the Big Head? Why would he save Ngili's life, rescue her, and be befriended by Spirit? It didn't make sense.

She watched him from the corner of her eye as she picked burrs from between the wolf's ears. "I am glad you are here, Spirit."

Wind pulled up beside her, breath coming in gasps, eyes bright. "It's a challenge to keep up with Spirit. I've never run with him before!!"

The hair on her neck tingled and instinct told her to flee. Instead, she held her ground, biting back the response that popped into her head.

Of course he runs fast. He's a wolf!

Ridiculous words explained why Big Heads chattered nonstop.

He has earned my patience. Without him, I would still be tied to a tree.

Only in battle had she ever been this close to a Big Head. Spending time with Wind would be a challenge. She eyed him. Despite their desperate circumstances, he radiated confidence, reminiscent of her father. The People's Leader never doubted his decisions or ability to survive, not even the choices that brought his death.

Xhosa wondered if trusting Wind repeated the mistake her father had made.

After a finger of Sun's movement, the trees thinned and they came to a steep slope. At its base ran a burbling stream with a rocky bed.

She motioned, "Let's drink and then stay on the bank where it's not so cold. Viper's pelt is thin."

Ngili nodded and Wind shook his head as he tossed his pelt to Viper. "No. Stay in the shallow water. It will hide our footprints."

Wind made sense. She should have thought of that.

"Ngili. Protect our backtrail—"

Wind raised his hand, palm forward, not even shivering in the cold despite no longer wearing an animal skin "I'll do it while you help him." He pulled several mushrooms from beneath a rotting log and a handful of reeds from the dense thicket along the water. "These will work if you have nothing in your neck sack."

Xhosa had forgotten Ngili's wounds. The warrior never complained nor did his injuries slow him. She closed her eyes, fighting off the head pain. It was worse than usual, probably from the Other's war club slamming into her head.

She smiled her thanks to Wind as he strode back along the traveled trail.

Ngili motioned, "I'm alright, Xhosa—"

She interjected. "We need your fighting skills, Ngili. That means treating your injuries."

The bloody scrape from the Other's rock had already scabbed over. He flinched when she twisted his arm to expose the still-bleeding gash that stretched from elbow to shoulder. His side was a smear of colorful bruises, probably from warclubs and kicks. It must have happened after Xhosa passed out. She chewed the plants Wind had given her until they were soft enough to spread over his wounds.

"Don't move until this dries," and gave him mushrooms for pain before trotting over to Viper, Leopard, and Deer.

When she bent over the subadults, she pursed her lips to keep her anger from exploding. Scabbed cuts, white scars, and bruises—some the purple of fresh contusions and others yellow with age—festooned their bodies. Xhosa could do nothing for the old wounds except make sure the girls were safe. She focused on healing the others.

Viper motioned, "Thank you, Xhosa, for giving us our freedom. I can't tell you sufficiently what that means to us. We will never be recaptured, even if it means death."

Xhosa grunted and then motioned, "I have no time to be gentle, Viper," as she pulled roots and a dried-out orange flower from her neck sack.

When Viper winced, Xhosa slowed her treatment but the subadult motioned, "Just get it done. It won't compare to what we endured as captives."

The more time Xhosa spent with Viper, the more impressive she found the young female. Somehow, adversity and captivity had given her an indomitable core.

As Xhosa worked, Viper asked, "How can Spirit lead when he didn't come with you?"

A tiny smile lifted the corners of Xhosa's mouth. "He doesn't need to know the way. I expect the People stayed along the shoreline but if they didn't, Spirit will find them."

Somewhere ahead, Spirit barked. He wanted them

"We need to hurry."

Viper, Deer, and Leopard didn't have the stamina to keep up so the group paused often to rest. That gave Ngili and Spirit time to check the forward trail and Wind the backtrail.

On one of those breaks, as Xhosa and the subadults nibbled berries and nuts, Xhosa asked, "How did you end up with those Others?"

Viper answered for them, as she usually did. "Our People live where Sun sleeps. Tribes from the Ice Mountains, a frozen land without plants or animals, overran us."

Xhosa motioned, "These same tribes drove my People from our land."

Viper drooped. "We tried to defend ourselves but had only this many people," and she opened and shut her hands. "We had no enemies so few of our males were trained with weapons. The Others massacred our few warriors first, then the males and the children. Females, like Leopard, Deer, and I, they enslaved."

"Should we rescue the rest of the females?"

Viper quivered. "They are all dead. Just Leopard, Deer, and I remain. That is why these Others took you. We can't yet mate though that will change soon. When it does, we would have to stay, for our children. We decided," and she looked from Deer to Leopard and then back to Xhosa, "that we would escape, one way or another, before that day arrived."

Viper's gaze softened. "You should know that I have bled once though I hid the odor with the stink of feces. Since we aren't by any streams, they left me alone until the stench wore off. By the time that happened, my bleeding had ended."

Xhosa smiled at Viper's shrewdness. "Why didn't you leave?"

Viper looked shocked. "I wouldn't go without Deer and Leopard. They wouldn't survive without me."

Xhosa understood that. She wouldn't have left without Ngili.

"Viper, my People migrate toward Sun's sleeping nest. You are welcome to travel with us. Maybe we will find what remains of your People."

"Would we then be your slaves?"

Xhosa shook her head. "My People have no slaves. Everyone works together for the good of the whole. None serves another." Though many females might as well be slaves to their Pairmates. Still, they were free to leave, create a new life with other mates. Viper wasn't.

"How will we know what to do?"

"We have a Primary Female, Siri. She will help you."

Wind appeared, sweaty and agitated, wearing a pelt. "Fang is close. He is furious over losing you. We are easy to follow because we travel the same trail you took to his camp."

Xhosa grinned, knowing Fang couldn't defeat her when she was untrussed and uninjured. "He must be furious that you took his pelt, too. It's one I made and doesn't stink of rot."

"Two broken fingers will slow him down at least. Follow me. Ngili knows an alternate route." and Wind sprinted away.

As Xhosa hurried after him, Viper grabbed her arm. "This Wind. He is different from Others we have seen."

"He saved Ngili's life and Spirit trusts him. The wolf, he has an instinct about who is honest and who evil. That he trusts Wind means a lot. But I promise you, if Wind lies, he won't live to brag about it."

Ngili led them through desolate barren land, up scree slopes with no dry twigs that would announce the group's presence or soft ground that would preserve their prints. Spirit whined once, wanting them back on the scent trail he knew, until he caught Fang's odor. Then, he seemed to understand.

A Moon, maybe more, passed before Xhosa smelled salt. Within a day, she, Wind, and the girls stood on the shore of Endless Pond. She couldn't help but smile. Viper looked out on the water, frowning, shoulders tense, clearly not happy with what she saw.

"There's no sign of them, or anyone."

Xhosa tucked an errant strand of hair behind her ear. "This isn't where we camped when I last saw them but they are here. All we have to do is follow the shoreline."

"Why didn't they wait for you, their Leader?"

Wind gestured, "They are a large group. The local tribes permitted them to stay though not hunt. They had to leave when the People became too hungry."

A twig cracked in the brush. Ngili would never do that. *Someone is tracking us.*

Chapter 16

Xhosa set a ground-eating pace, one hand wrapped around her spear while the other gripped her warclub. Ngili and Spirit covered the back trail while Wind slithered the opposite direction, invisible against the grays and-browns of the landscape.

Xhosa pulled to a stop when the subadults seemed ready to collapse. She sniffed, listened intently, and finally motioned, "We've lost them for the moment. Let's find food and eat quickly before that changes."

She downed a handful of ground birds and several of what Fang called "squirrels" and tossed them into the communal food pile already holding fish Deer and Leopard had caught in a tidepool. They all ate, plenty remaining for Viper and the males.

Ngili and Spirit huffed into camp, each carrying part of a small Gazelle. "We saw no trace of anyone, just Gazelle with a broken leg."

Xhosa motioned, "Eat. We will talk when Wind returns."

Ngili chewed through a leg and finished off the last fish. Viper trotted into the makeshift camp and dropped a ground bird into the pile.

Ngili stuffed a leg and wing, not bothering to remove either feathers or bones, into his mouth, licked the fat from his lips, and motioned to Viper, "Let's work on your spear throwing until the light disappears."

The two moved off to the edge of the camp, using a tree as a target. Xhosa watched as he adjusted Viper's posture and then grip, satisfied that he hadn't forgotten anything during his captivity. Viper listened intently, eager to absorb every word, and practiced relentlessly. Every time Ngili suggested resting, she asked another question. Finally, Xhosa motioned them onward. She couldn't wait any longer for Wind. If he still lived, he would catch up.

The day dragged on as they raced onward. She kept listening for sounds from the backtrail, hoping to hear Wind's return, but nothing. When Sun came within a hand of the horizon, Xhosa started to worry. When Spirit vanished down their backtrail, she quickened the pace. If the wolf and Wind ended up in a fight, she wanted enough distance that she could hide the subadults and then go to their assistance. The subadults started huffing but said nothing. As promised, they wouldn't hold the group up, even if they had to perform the impossible.

By the time the light bled from the sky, every part of Xhosa's body ached. Though there was no sign of Wind or the wolf, they all needed to stop and rest. She, Ngili, and the subadults crawled under a large overhang at the base of a bluff. They ate Gazelle, set up a prickly bush barrier, and Viper, Deer, and Leopard curled together while Ngili faded into the surroundings. Before Sun dipped below the horizon, the girls were snoring.

Xhosa, though, couldn't sleep. Her stomach knotted and her eyes searched every shadow, every dark shape. Down the shore, sky fire sparked, too far away to see the actual streaks rip the sky but bright enough they lit the clouds, usually invisible in the murky night sky.

A storm was coming and Wind, Ngili, and Spirit hadn't returned.

Xhosa chewed a pain plant while climbing a tree tall enough to provide a good view both directions down the shoreline. Usually she could clamber up any tree but now she was so tired, the pain from her last beating still new, it felt like trying to climb a mountain. After settling in the branches, soothed by the lapping waves and the night sounds, she closed her eyes and pretended to be home, before everything fell apart. Before Hawk died.

Sometime later, Spirit woke her, puffing a greeting. Once she caught his eye, he stretched, walked in a circle, and then lay beneath the tree head in his paws. If not for the constant twitch of his nose, she would have thought him asleep.

Then a shadow appeared out of darkness, tall and rangy, moving fluidly toward her, not trying to hide.

"Wind." It must be or Spirit would growl. It was too tall to be Ngili.

Spirit greeted Wind by rolling to his back for a belly rub. Only when the wolf was satisfied did Wind climb into Xhosa's tree nest.

"It's not Fang trailing us. It's Ork, the Fire Tender. He said those chasing us returned to the camp when we climbed the scree slopes, claiming slaves weren't worth the effort. Ork slipped away so he could return to his People. He won't come to our camp because he is embarrassed by how poorly he treated you and Ngili. Ngili and I left him food and a spear, told him to scout our backtrail, let us know if anyone takes up the chase again, until he goes his own way. He didn't understand so Ngili stayed to explain."

Xhosa nodded. Ngili trusted Ork so she did.

Wind ate a dead squirrel while Moon shed its muted light on the vast watery landscape in front of them. When he finished eating, he leaned back and captured her eyes with his.

"Something bothers you." When she looked away, he said, "Ask me anything."

She rubbed the back of her neck, under her hair, wondering where to start. After a breath and another, she motioned, "Why are you here?"

He took her hands and cocked his head, not speaking until she again turned to him. "Xhosa I'll tell you the truth and always will, even if you may not like it." After a deep breath, he continued, "When I let Ngili go, Thunder was furious. He told me to leave or die. I chose the first."

"But your father is Leader?"

Wind's face softened. "He's dead. Thunder and I co-lead much like you and the One-named-Pan-do. I'm like my father—I talk first, attack if that fails. Thunder relies on force."

As does Nightshade, but Xhosa kept that to herself.

"I left my People knowing I would be alone. No tribe would risk Thunder's anger by offering me shelter. I wanted to warn you first and then I'd figure out how to survive. I have no qualms about living or dying alone.

"Ngili told me when I let him go, he was going to find you and warn you about Thunder. I followed his trail just to make sure he succeeded."

Xhosa's knee ached and pain ground into her temples so she ate another pain plant as she motioned, "But you were too late to help him."

Wind barked. "I'll tell you the rest of the story and then you can decide if I'm too late or just in time.

"Ngili's tracks took me through the land of the Leader Koo-rag, across a crocodile-infested river, and to a field where a great battle had been fought. You and your People apparently escaped into Endless Pond."

He glanced at her, a sparkle in his eye. "I'm impressed you could build a raft."

He waited for her to explain but she was too tired to get into Zvi and Seeker and not yet ready to talk to a Big Head about Hawk.

He shrugged and continued. "Ngili arrived after you left. I think he wanted to follow you up the shoreline, figure out where your rafts landed, but was captured by the Others. Their tracks led inland but I stayed along the shore. If Ngili wouldn't be able to warn you, I would. I didn't know how long it would be before Thunder caught up with you so couldn't waste any time. When I'd delivered my message to you, I'd return to help Ngili.

"It took a long time trekking up the coast before I found where your rafts crashed. Your People were still there, trying to decide what to do next. I watched for a long while and never saw you, which is when I figured out your People were not just figuring out where to go next. They were waiting for you.

"One night, hidden in the bushes around your camp, I saw Nightshade arguing with a tall gawky Other about whether they should wait any longer for you. Nightshade insisted they leave, that you would find the People when you returned. The Other wanted to wait longer."

Xhosa motioned, "The Other must be Pan-do. He and Nightshade co-lead, as you and your brother do. I am not surprised Nightshade's decision prevailed."

Wind rubbed his hands down his cheeks and with a tiny smile, motioned, "It was clear, even in that short time watching them, that without you, one-called-Pan-do has the same problem with Nightshade I did with Thunder. There's no compromise from either of them. It's their way or their way."

He picked dirt from the light hair covering his skin and brushed it away. "As I waited for them to leave so I could start tracking you, something strange happened. A boy who flits like a butterfly skipped around One-called-Pan-do, gibbering about someone with the call sign Spirit. He turned to where I hid and stared. At me. Satisfied I'd seen him and understood his message—though I didn't, not then—he spun another time and left. One-called-Pan-do watched him, glanced my way, but said nothing."

Xhosa stifled a laugh. "That's Seeker. And all I can say is, of course he knew you were there."

"When I picked up your trail, a wolf's tracks overlapped your prints. It took many days and a series of strange events before I understood you weren't in trouble, that the wolf also wanted to rescue you."

"How did you befriend Spirit?"

"First, I must deliver the warning." He pivoted her around until she looked into his eyes. "My brother is crazy.

He blames you for deaths you had nothing to do with. He will chase you until he exacts his revenge."

Spittle flew from her mouth as she exploded with fury. "He slaughtered my father and took my land! What more does he want from me?" Rage burned through her, from fingertips to toes, so hot she forgot the ache in her knee and the pounding in her head.

"Thunder cares nothing for your father or the land, Xhosa. He wants *you*! He must *own* you—degrade you, destroy you, and then kill you, all in a misguided effort to get even for the deaths caused by your People so long ago."

Xhosa stilled, stared into the darkness and mulled this over. Except for Wind, every Big Head she'd ever seen considered themselves superior to Others, to animals, to all life around them. They were violent without reason, without respect for life or tribes. Thunder sounded no different except that his vengeance was personal. Her People always pursued actions for the good of the group. Never did they act out of personal animus or she would have revenged her father.

She clenched her fists so hard her arms trembled. "Why?"

Not expecting an answer, she took a deep breath and then another, until the pounding in her chest slowed. Anger did no good.

"Wind. Why do you trust me—and Ngili—if Thunder and your People hate us?"

"I think if I answer your first question, it'll answer your second. There's a story I was told about a time long time ago when your People and mine were not friends but not enemies. Your father was injured—abandoned as dead by his fellow hunters—and brought to one of our camps for care. A female healed him and they ended up having a child together. When your father's tribe came to rescue him, all my People were killed, the female gravely injured. With the last of her energy, she begged your father to raise their child as his own.

A chill passed through Xhosa.

"Because of that senseless attack, Thunder and I grew up hating your People, especially your father and those close to him. Your lands and ours overlapped which meant I saw you often—hunting, traveling, scavenging plants, training your People, and doing whatever you did during the day—and every time, you were calm and reasoned. I never saw you take a life without purpose or lose your temper. That confused me. It didn't match the picture I'd been given all my life about your People, your violent actions, or my brother's vitriolic feelings.

"When Thunder killed your father, he should have felt vindicated but instead, his hate grew. Not wanting it to end, he transferred it to you as though you'd killed our People's tribe and destroyed their homebase. Extinguishing every one of your People and stealing your lands was no longer enough for him. Now, he had to ruin you personally."

Xhosa was appalled by what Wind said. Did that mean this entire vendetta was because of her? She couldn't let Thunder continue to victimize her People. "I will stop him."

"I will help you."

"You should have told me this immediately."

"Would you have believed me?" That she wouldn't make eye contact answered his question. "You needed first to trust me."

She turned away, not wanting him to see the hope in her eyes. "Now tell me how you partnered with Spirit."

At his call sign, the wolf tipped his head up to them, blue eyes shining in Moon's light, and then fell back asleep.

"I had been tracking you for almost a Moon. The trail was easy to follow. Whoever captured you didn't try to hide his path."

Xhosa guffawed. "Fang thought he was alone. He is about the stupidest Other I've ever met—and still, he managed to capture me."

Wind chuckled and then continued, "I could tell I was getting closer. The tracks were fresher, more so each day so I knew I was gaining on you. But I'd lost my spear and hadn't found the right wood to create a new one so I was subsisting on plants and roots. That slowed me because I had to spend too much daylight finding food rather than trailing you.

"One night, I was too hungry to sleep so I lay there against a tree trunk, wondering if I should give up. Of course, that would accomplish nothing because I had nowhere to go. As I rolled that predicament around in my thoughts, a wolf appeared at the edge of my camp. Drool dripped from his fangs and a deep menacing growl rolled from his throat as the hair on my neck spiked. His eyes—whoever heard of a wolf with blue eyes—I've never seen any as ominous.

"I laughed aloud, almost delirious with hunger, and yelled at him that he'd wasted his time hunting me. He wouldn't get enough food from my skin and bones for even a meal. Then, behind me, something squealed and paws scampered away. When I spun around, I saw the backend of a hyaena disappear into the bushes.

"Spirit hadn't been after me. He'd stopped Hyaena from killing me.

"The menace melted from the wolf's body as he padded toward me, dropped a dead rat at my feet, and left. Though covered in wolf saliva and dirt, I devoured it. From then on, he visited often, always with food, once an egg held so gently in his jaws, it didn't even crack.

"Not long after that, I awoke to the feel of hot breath on my face. It stunk of carrion as it wafted across my nose. I reached for my spear—my just-finished new one—but it wasn't where I left it. Later, I figured out that the wolf moved it, knowing I would be frightened when he panted into my mouth. Then, for no reason I understood, he licked me and left. I've seen wolves lick each other but never an Other. It felt good.

"The night I called him friend was unbearably cold— worse than I'd ever experienced. I couldn't find a cave so tucked against a cliff, desperate for anything that would dull the icy wind. My fingers and toes numbed first, and then my nose and ears. The frigid air finally lulled me to sleep and a peaceful warmth settled over me. I dreamt about my father and a time when Thunder and I still smiled at each other.

"I awoke comfortably warm despite the cold. When I opened my eyes, I found the wolf curled against me, snoring.

A story I'd heard long ago floated up in my memory, of a blue-eyed wolf with the call sign Spirit who considered People his pack. When I called him Spirit, he wagged his tail.

"We have journeyed together since. He senses threats I don't know exist and finds food faster than I have ever been able to, though his tastes are not always mine. He's the best partner I've ever had. I know he joined me only to find you but it didn't matter. I have enjoyed our time together. You probably know what a good listener he is. I've told him all about Thunder, my father, and the predicament I have put myself in by helping Ngili and arguing with my crazy brother. I'm sure he understands everything I say."

Xhosa fingered her hair away from her face. Spirit knew he was being talked about and panted his pleasure, muzzle open in a smile.

The days took on a routine. Spirit scouted. Xhosa, Wind, Viper, Deer, and Leopard trailed the People's tracks while Ngili hid their trail. Viper, Deer, and Leopard panted heavily, not used to the fast pace after Moons of inactivity. Every night, after they ate, Ngili worked with Viper—and Leopard and Deer if they chose to join him—on throwing a spear and swinging a warclub. Viper was a natural and quickly became better than most males.

One night, Wind lay on his back next to Xhosa as she watched the stars. "Ork is gone, to his People," and pointed toward a flat dry stretch of land in the far distance. "He invited us to join him, said his People would accept strong warriors such as us."

"You may go, Wind, but I must return to my People."

He nodded. "No, I enjoy traveling with you, Ngili, and Spirit." His brow furrowed and he asked, "If we don't find your People, what will you do?"

"You underestimate Spirit. Seeker, Zvi, and Lyta are his pack, more than I. His job is to find them. If they are dead, this—all of us—will be my new tribe. Maybe we can find Viper's People if any survived the attack, or we can continue to Dawa's People—or the land beyond the mountains that he says would be perfect for us. Spirit is as good a warrior as Nightshade as am I. Viper, Leopard, and Deer—they are committed to survival. They will never quit.

"I have no doubt that whatever happens, we will all be fine."

The silence grew between them. Something about his questions troubled her, as though she didn't hear what he really wanted to know.

And then it clicked. "You are welcome to stay, Wind, whether we find my People or not."

Xhosa wanted to say more but didn't trust herself. She felt drawn to this Big Head but not in the way she had been to Hawk, or Nightshade. He spewed none of the treachery that flamed from his brother or Nightshade. Instead, his voice, his gestures twinkled with curiosity and the same kindness often present in Pan-do. Wind was Nightshade without the fury and as a result, she trusted him more than she ever expected to trust a Big Head.

He fixed her with a luminous smile. "Thank you."

As they traveled, Ngili answered all of Deer, Leopard, and Viper's questions about how to live in a group where they weren't told what to do or beaten when they failed to comply. Ngili explained they must pay attention to what the group needed and then do it, like scavenge plants, chop food, and watch over the children. No one would order them to do anything. The goal was the good of the People. The first proof that they understood this concept happened one night when they collected thorn bushes to protect the group's ground nest without being asked.

Xhosa smiled to herself.

Days later, as Sun prepared to sleep, Xhosa slowed to allow Deer and Leopard to pass and motioned Viper to walk with her.

"Viper, what will you, Leopard, and Deer do once we catch up to my People? Do you want us to help you find yours?"

"Our tribe is dead, Leader Xhosa. We have no one. Ngili said life with your People was fair, even friendly. Siri sounds nice, as does Pan-do. We would like to stay with you." Her hands trembled but her gaze held steady.

Xhosa began her answer before Viper's hands stopped moving. "You are hard workers. You will be welcomed. We have several groups within my People, each with a different Leader. We migrate together for the common goal of safety and to find a new home. You can be part of whichever group you wish."

Normally, the People grew through babies but few of them survived migrations. All the People would welcome hard-working subadults.

Viper motioned, "Our homeland is there, where Sun sleeps. If you go that far, I can help you find your way."

"Whatever you remember will be appreciated. Our group member Seeker has a clear vision of where we're going but he's never been there. He's following stars—I'll let him explain that to you when we find him."

"We are eager to prove ourselves to you, Xhosa. You will not be sorry to accept us."

"You and Deer create fire faster than most. Maybe you'd like to be Fire Tenders."

"I will be a warrior, Leader Xhosa. Like you."

Xhosa and most Others she'd run into could mimic Owl, Wolf, Panther, Mammoth, Cat, and many other animals to warn group members of a threat, food, their return, or something else. She had always believed a natural noise blended into the surroundings but thanks to her captors, she realized that thinking was flawed. A call familiar only to the People would prevent imitators.

She discussed this at the nighttime meal and all agreed. Viper suggested a sound her people used—a cross between

Chimp's call when he located food and a bird's sunrise greeting.

"Teach this call to everyone here. When we catch up with the People, your first job will be to teach it to everyone."

From then on, the small group practiced as they walked. Viper modeled it, showing how to shape their lips and move their tongues, until one after another, all were proficient.

One day, not long after Sun awoke, Spirit's nose twitched. "What is it, Spirit?"

He panted, tail wagging so hard it hit his sides. He raced forward and back, encouraging Xhosa to hurry.

Viper giggled. "What's wrong with Spirit?"

"He found a scent that makes him happy."

Before the day ended, they reached the place where Xhosa left the People to find her pain plant. Spirit inhaled the remnants of the last meal—a buffalo—and the footprints of his pack.

Wind motioned, "At least one of them isn't hiding his— or her—tracks." Footsteps moved through grass rather than along the water where the waves would erase them, and twigs had been broken where every one of the People would have walked around them rather than leave a trail. "In fact, I think someone is leaving us a trail."

Ngili paced in a tight line, nostrils flaring. "Nightshade would never allow this, even for you Xhosa. Unless he's changed. Which I doubt."

Xhosa grinned. "Then we know who it isn't. In fact, we probably know who it is, too."

Chapter 17

Along the Mediterranean, ahead of Xhosa's small group

The rain stopped long enough for Sun's rays to penetrate the dark clouds, a pleasant change from the constant cold. A lone wolf howled his pleasure at a chance to hunt.

The People collected in groups to shape choppers, pound roots, and knap tips for spears while the children played. When their shadows moved, they moved, doing their best to stay in the warm sun as they worked. Nightshade smoothed his war club with fine dirt, the surface damaged when it hit the horn of Buffalo. While he scraped and smoothed, he considered what to do about Xhosa's absence and decided that she shouldn't be replaced. He would continue as acting Leader in her stead but leave her as the official Leader. That would give the People more hope that someday, she might make her way back to them.

To his surprise, Xhosa was well-liked and respected. By being patient, he could transfer the People's loyalty for her to himself. Then, when the People were ready to accept that she would never return, that they required a new Leader, he could simply step into the position without challenges or disruptions.

That night, when the groups gathered to eat—Xhosa's People, Pan-do's, and his—Water Buffalo motioned, "Leader

Xhosa is dead. There is no other reason she would be gone so long," and sat.

Pan-do stood immediately, not waiting for the murmurs to die away. "I am not ready to make that decision. First, I'd like our scouts to do a more thorough search for her, going further inland where she might have been trapped or injured."

Nightshade huffed, not agreeing or disagreeing, simply listening.

As the group broke up, the males to secure the edges of the camp, the subadults to gather protective thistle bushes, and the females to groom the children, Pan-do beckoned Nightshade.

When they were too far into the shadows for anyone to see their conversation, he motioned, "Nightshade, it is time for you to challenge for Leader of the Xhosa People. If you don't, Water Buffalo will. He pretends loyalty to you but behind your back, encourages those who still call the Nightshade People the former Hawk People to work against you. He seethes from his defeat at your hands. I don't think he will ever forgive you for the humiliation you put him through in front of his warriors."

Nightshade picked up a cutter and started to sharpen his spear as Pan-do continued. "Sa-mo-ke says if it comes to a vote, Water Buffalo will back me. You may be the better warrior but—you must admit—I am better liked."

That startled Nightshade. He didn't expect anyone to back a weakling like Pan-do over himself. "You are no match for me or any skilled warrior!"

Pan-do smiled sadly. "You are wrong about that but Water Buffalo agrees with you. He'd prefer to replace Xhosa with someone weak than a warrior he's already lost to. He thinks he could defeat me easily when the time came for that challenge."

Nightshade dropped his spear to the ground and stared into the distance. He hadn't considered that.

Pan-do peered sideways at Nightshade as he smoothed his spear with sand.

Nightshade motioned, "Our difficulties, yours and mine, I have put them behind myself. As you have, I'm sure."

Pan-do waved his hand through the air. "I have no interest in Xhosa's position. I never aspired to leadership and accepted it with my People because no one else would. My group and yours—we are different but I respect you. If you replace Xhosa, I and my People may stay but if Water Buffalo becomes Leader, we won't. Leaving with me will be Zvi, Spirit, and Seeker. Water Buffalo will be Leader of—and you a member of—a much weaker, less threatening group. Considering our goals, I don't think either of us wants that."

Nightshade breathed out, not realizing he had been holding his breath.

Pan-do smiled, eyes widening with surprise. "You are relieved. I should have spoken sooner. I am no threat to you, Nightshade. My People don't forget how you saved many of us from the Big Heads and again from the White Mountain invaders. Sa-mo-ke is a loyal supporter of yours and that means a lot to the rest of my warriors and hunters."

Nightshade tilted his head. "I'm glad we agree. You lead your People and I, everyone else."

"Well, don't disregard the opinions of Seeker, Zvi, and Spirit."

Nightshade motioned, "They will choose what works best for them. Or they will leave."

Pan-do now forgotten, Nightshade joined a group of scouts who were preparing to mark the boundaries of the camp for the evening.

When Pan-do told Seeker and Zvi of his conversation with Nightshade, Seeker giggled and spun. Lyta and Zvi leapt to their feet and twirled in rocking, ungainly circles that carried no less joy than the boy-male's.

When they crumpled into a heap, Seeker motioned, "None of this matters. Spirit found Xhosa and they will be here soon."

The next day, Nightshade ordered everyone onward. No one questioned his authority. Pan-do felt mostly relief that the People had a Leader again.

Nightshade led the combined group well, directing the scouts and hunters, training the subadults in jobs they would perform as adults, and involving Pan-do in decisions. The power of the warriors increased and Nightshade's logic for that was unassailable. In this strange land, risks loomed everywhere. The warriors must always be prepared to protect the People. Everyone adapted without complaint. With each decision, he deepened and broadened his strength in preparation for the position he'd trained for his entire life.

Pan-do, supportive at first, became more suspicious as the days passed. He couldn't shake the feeling that Nightshade liked leading more than he liked being smart. Seeker promised Xhosa was on her way, with Spirit, but Pan-do wondered if it would be too late to wrest control from this increasingly formidable warrior.

Chapter 18

Somewhere along the Mediterranean

Again, Xhosa and her small group spent the night in one of the People's old camps. Spirit had sniffed out where Zvi and Seeker had been lying and, tail wagging—as often happened—found a treat.

Wind motioned, "We're a day or two behind, that's all."

Morning came and they continued, jogging instead of walking, excited that the journey might soon be at an end. Endless Pond remained to one side and wooded hills that sloped to the water on the other, the path they followed the aged-but-worn trail of a large group. Xhosa and her group continued until Sun almost touched the horizon. She was ready to stop when Spirit's tail stiffened. With a bark—part whine, part anticipation, he sprinted away.

"Let's go," and she hurried after the wolf, Wind at her side, followed closely by Viper, Deer, and Leopard. Ngili protected their backtrail even though it was clear any danger lay in front. She wasn't sure what to expect, hoped it was a good surprise, but gripped her spears and was comforted that she had removed her warclub from her back before Spirit took off.

Xhosa pulled up, panting. She would have continued but the area ahead was nothing more than dark shadows and thick brush.

"Let's stay here for the night. It is too dark. Spirit will come back when he realizes we are no longer behind him."

And then familiar voices screeched in surprise. Spirit pounded toward her, howled, and then turned and loped down his backtrail. Xhosa took off, intoxicated by the heady mix of scents she'd missed for too many Moons.

"We found them!" Her voice broke as she yelled.

She plunged into a thicket, not even noticing the jab of spines and thorns, slapping them away on both sides until she tumbled out the opposite side of the patch. She pulled to a stop just in time to prevent herself from stepping on Spirit, started to chastise him for almost tripping her when her eyes focused on what had frozen Spirit in place.

Familiar faces, staring, all looking at her with open mouths. She breathed in their welcome scents as though they were a field of sweet-scented flowers on a breezy day. Tears burned unbidden in her eyes.

"Everyone is here," she mumbled to herself. "Nightshade and Pan-do cared well for the People."

Wind caught up with a huff, slowed, and then stood at her side. She smelled his tension, excitement, but no fear. Her touch to his arm, the set of her face, would tell her People that this Big Head brought them no danger. He had promised her last night that he would accept whatever decisions came from her reunion with the People, even if it meant the end of his time with her and Ngili.

A yip and Xhosa found Spirit, sprinting toward Zvi and Seeker. The two, and Lyta, quickly surrounded him and covered his head, back, and neck with rubbing hands. His tail wagged furiously and his back arched as Zvi scratched from his hackles to his butt.

Xhosa stood tall, arms raised. "I greet my People!"

Her voice formed misty white clouds which then vanished in the chill air. The natural confidence that always filled her gestures and energized her expressions rolled over her People like a wildfire, breathing life into the hopes and dreams of those who depended upon her for their lives, their futures.

"I bring new group members, worthy additions to the People," and she placed an open palm on Wind's chest. "This is Wind of the Big Heads. I couldn't have escaped my captors without his assistance."

He offered those in front of him a smile tinged with cautious curiosity and more excited anticipation than Xhosa expected. Despite the circumstances, he exuded a calm acceptance of what would be.

Then she turned to the other side and motioned, "These are Viper, Leopard, and Deer, also former slaves of those who captured me. They bring a new greeting that will help us identify our group members from all others. Only those in our tribe will know how to make this sound. They will teach you."

Viper stood tall between her two friends, holding their hands, eyeing the group in front of her. Nothing about her communicated fear but Xhosa knew, nothing could be more frightening than what this young adult had already gone through. Other's might see cold suspicion, confrontation in the wide set of her feet, and belligerence in the proud tilt of her head, but Xhosa saw hope for a new beginning, belief in herself, and confidence in her fighting skills. Soon, everyone would, Xhosa had no doubt about that. Deer and Leopard gripped Viper's hands, shaking, their eyes on the ground as Viper dragged them forward.

Xhosa considered standing with Deer and Leopard, in support when the crowd surged, pushing and jostling, and Pan-do burst through. He enveloped her in a tight embrace, something he had never done.

"Lyta told me Spirit found you." Pan-do gulped and then wiped a hand over his cheeks, ignoring Xhosa's surprise. "I am happy you return, Leader. You have been missed," and again gripped her to himself.

"Pan-do, I never worried about the People. If I didn't make it back, you were here. You would take care of them as my father would have."

She placed both hands on his. "It took longer than I expected to free myself. I wouldn't have managed without Spirit and Wind. And Ngili! Imagine my surprise to find him also a captive of the same Others who enslaved me. Now, the People have him back also."

Pan-do looked for Ngili, baffled, started to ask a question but Xhosa laughed. "I'll explain later. Nightshade—he is here?"

Before Pan-do could do more than nod, Nightshade broke through the crowd. His eyes passed over Xhosa, stuttered at Ngili, ignored Viper and her friends, but narrowed to slits when they came to Wind. Muscles bulging, he clenched a spear in one hand, a warclub in the other. Wind's expression never changed but his hackles stiffened. Xhosa picked out the acrid odor of warriors prepared for battle.

As silence overtook the crowd, Wind glanced at Nightshade and then away, as though the Lead Warrior were nothing to him. The expression on Wind's face never changed from the pleasant, inviting gaze that told the People he was happy to be with them. If not Nightshade. Viper edged closer to Wind's side, bristling as she gripped her spear, her work-hardened hands testimony to her ability.

"He does not like us, Wind." Her gestures spoke the language of Big Heads.

Nightshade stopped his forward movement when he was as close to Wind as he could get without touching him, Xhosa smelled the rat he recently ate. Wind turned back to him and offered a brilliant smile as he scrutinized the Lead Warrior. That seemed to anger Nightshade even more.

"Why is he with you?" Nightshade hissed into the silence. His hand motions, stiff with fury, frigid with emotion, addressed Xhosa while staring at Wind.

Xhosa stepped between them. "As I said when I arrived, Lead Warrior, Wind has proven himself a friend."

Wind motioned, hands calm despite Nightshade's contempt, "Of course you are angry, Acting Leader Nightshade—"

"I am Leader of the Nightshade People, the former Hawk-People, one-called-Wind."

Wind nodded congenially. "My mistake," though Xhosa doubted it was. "I believe you confuse me with my brother, Thunder. He has a scar running down his face from an unfortunate encounter with some animal he wanted to kill. I am the reasonable one. It was Thunder who took the life of your Leader and drove you from your homebase. Against my advice."

Shoulders relaxed, feet spread, spear down, he regarded Nightshade with eyes as cold as any warriors who prepared for battle, politely awaiting a response but clearly unworried about what that would be.

Ngili touched Nightshade's arm. That earned him a slap but didn't silence him. "This Big Head—Wind—he saved me, too, when his tribe enslaved me, after the People's warriors abandoned me for dead. Without him, I would be dead. He has earned my respect for his fighting skill and his cleverness."

"Enslaved?" This from Pan-do. "Xhosa also used this term. I'm not familiar with what that means."

Ngili motioned, "One who serves others with no rights of their own. During my time as a slave, I got little food, less sleep, and no privacy. The People are kinder to enemy warriors when we kill them."

Spirit padded up to Wind and licked his hand. Wind responded by scratching under his muzzle long enough to make Spirit sigh.

Zvi motioned, "If Spirit trusts Wind, we all should. I have never seen the wolf wrong."

Seeker spun on the ball of one foot and raised the other to an awkward position waist high. Head back, mouth open, he shouted, "Happy happy!" Zvi and Lyta tried but failed to imitate the intricate balance required to spin, flail, and chatter all at once.

Nightshade mumbled, unconvinced. "Time will tell, Big Head," then, "You are welcome back, Ngili. We have missed your skills."

He dismissed the Big Head with a glare and reached out to Xhosa. "You are welcome here, Leader Xhosa." Spirit nudged Nightshade and the warrior added, "And you, Spirit."

Lined up behind Nightshade, spears down, stood Dust, Snake, Stone, and the rest of the People's warriors, all prepared to do their duty should Big Head warriors storm the People from behind Wind. Water Buffalo and Talon had placed themselves apart from the warriors as did Sa-mo-ke, enabling them a different perspective on an attack should that be needed. Xhosa scratched her arm, confused by the distribution of the warriors. She had expected more of Pan-do's warriors than just his Lead to be the primary defensive group with Nightshade's secondary. After all, Pan-do was Co-leader and should have become the People's Leader in her absence.

But it didn't seem like that happened.

Xhosa motioned, "Did you challenge Pan-do for leadership, Nightshade? Where are his warriors?"

Pan-do stepped forward, hands moving calmly. "We shared responsibilities while awaiting your return, as you and I did before you left. Your People are more comfortable with Nightshade in an authority position than me." After a moment, he gestured, "It has worked well," though his face said otherwise.

Xhosa looked around at her People, happier than she'd been in Moons. She could see in their faces, aside from relief and joy at seeing their Leader that something rested heavily on them and had for a long time. The tension in the arms and chests, the deep lines etched in their faces that only lessened but didn't disappear said although they wouldn't contradict their Leader, something upset them and they weren't sure simply her return would fix it.

She would ask later.

Pan-do motioned, as though seeing her thoughts, "Nightshade and I agreed our Co-leadership would continue only until you returned. I can fill you in on that later."

Nightshade's lips thinned. Xhosa doubted he would accept the changes inherent in her return as amiably as Pan-do.

She motioned, "I have been gone for long. I will rely on both of you until I catch up," and turned away, searching the crowd, finally settling on one face.

"Siri. Will you explain to Viper, Deer, Leopard, and Wind what is expected of them as one of the People."

Xhosa moved through the group, greeting all, applauding those pregnant and those who were new mothers. Everyone showed their joy at having her back but made no effort to explain the tension, as dense as smoke from damp flames, that surrounded everyone.

"Xhosa." Pan-do tapped her arm. "We are ready to eat. The People are eager to hear stories from you and the new group members. I hope it will include a long explanation of this thing you call 'slaves'."

As though she might have forgotten how the nighttime meal worked, Pan-do guided her to the far side of the fire. There the two crouched, Nightshade to her side and Sa-mo-ke to Pan-do's opposite side. Siri steered the newcomers including Wind to positions opposite Xhosa because they would be expected to speak.

Wind started to squat by Deer but Xhosa motioned him to her side, next to Pan-do.

"Come, here, Wind. My People will have many questions for you."

Lyta moved over to make room and Spirit dropped to the ground between the two, his ears perked. Whispers and subtle hand movements from the gathered People approved of Spirit's support of Wind.

As everyone began to eat, Wind motioned, "I have not seen this level of loyalty since my father's death."

She murmured, hands stretched toward the fire, "This— the fire—I have missed how good it feels."

Pan-do looked at her quizzically so she explained, "We couldn't risk one for fear the Others would find us."

The People did well in her absence judging by the robust collection of deer, pig, roots, and berries in the communal food pile. Wind ate silently, observing those around him, nodding occasionally to the scrutiny of one of the warriors, grinning at Viper when she seemed to be scowling too deeply. Xhosa guessed that despite his calmness, he was evaluating her People, trying to decide if they could be his new tribe.

Viper, Deer, and Leopard huddled together, hands on their knees, barely eating until Siri reminded them their next meal wouldn't be until tomorrow, after working a full day. Then, Viper stuffed food into her mouth, Deer and Leopard following her lead until all of them sat back, too full to eat any more.

When all finished, it came time for stories.

Xhosa motioned to Viper. "Please tell the story of how you, Deer, and Leopard ended up in the hands of the ruthless Others."

Viper told of their happy youth in the mountains until the Others arrived. They slaughtered all her tribe's males and children and captured the females. Pan-do quizzed her on the meaning of "slaves" and she struggled to explain it to those who had never even experienced anything called "ownership". Wind jumped into the conversation and explained how his tribe also used forced labor to manage the needs of their large group.

That's how he met Ngili, and why he freed him.

When Viper finished, Wind shared his story of Thunder, a violent crazed brother who considered himself stronger, more deadly, and smarter than anyone else. Death and bloodshed became his tools and cooperation his enemy.

Nightshade smirked. "You no longer have the advantage of the stone-tipped spear. We now know how to make those."

"But we still throw them farther than you."

The Quest for Home

"You're wrong." Nightshade grabbed his spear and beckoned Wind outside. "I'll show you how a real warrior uses a spear."

Xhosa shook her head in confusion. Had Nightshade forgotten the Big Heads who launched spears across the waterhole at her father, farther by far than any of the People had ever seen spears travel?

"Nightshade—"

"It's alright, Xhosa," from Wind as he followed Nightshade. "This has to happen. It will work out as it should."

Seeker followed, bouncing, and repeated Wind's words, "As it should…"

Moon had grown to its full size and bright enough for a challenge. Nightshade handed Wind a spear. Wind balanced it on his hand.

"Which of your warriors created this spear? It is a masterpiece."

Ant tried to hide his pleasure but Wind noticed the satisfied flush and cocked an eyebrow.

"Yours? Excellent job, warrior. The balance point will allow a long throw. Thank you for permitting me to borrow it."

Ant motioned, "I am Ant. I found this spear abandoned after a battle with your kind and repaired it—"

Nightshade bellowed, "Enough! Big Head, I am ready."

Wind inclined his head to Ant as though to say, *We'll talk more later.*

Everyone gathered around the challengers. All expected their Lead Warrior to win and couldn't help but snicker at Wind's calm. Xhosa had seen Wind with spears many times, both training Viper and fighting the enemy. Her warriors, especially Nightshade were in for a surprise.

Nightshade pointed to a spot across the clearing almost lost in the night shadows.

"We will throw this many," and he ticked off each finger on one hand.

He raised the spear and with a stutter-step, threw with the overwhelming force that always impressed opponents.

As it did Wind. "Your throw is excellent, Lead Warrior. Now I understand why you are so confident. I will have to be at my best to beat you." A slight glint sparked in his eye which Xhosa saw but Nightshade missed. She couldn't help but smile. Wind was trifling with Nightshade and her Lead Warrior didn't even know it.

Wind took a deep breath, held it, and threw, barely taking time to balance or aim. It flew as though on wings but to Xhosa's eye, he seemed to be holding back. Why, she didn't know. The darkness made it impossible to determine who won so Wind and Nightshade trotted down the field, joined by Xhosa, Ngili, Ant, and Snake. The first spear was embedded a hand's-width behind the second.

"This is mine," from Ant.

Nightshade won but not by much. The two warriors retrieved their spears and went back to where they started.

When Ngili and Snake measured the second throw, Wind won by a full spear length. Some of Nightshade's cockiness evaporated and he took more time to set up his spear, then flinging it with such power he almost fell forward.

Chapter 19

Wind, as before, picked up his spear, breathed in, and threw, this time winning by two lengths. If Nightshade were Fire Mountain, he would erupt.

As they prepared the final throws, Wind motioned to Nightshade, "May I give you a suggestion?" Nightshade snarled something Wind interpreted as, *Yes, please.* "You replicated our stone-tipped spear expertly. Your problem is the throw. A stone-tipped spear requires a different hold than an all-wood spear. The thumb must extend along the bottom of the shaft like this," and he showed Nightshade his grip compared to what the Lead Warrior used.

"And don't aim. Find your target, point your toe at it, fling, and follow through." Wind demonstrated.

In the back of the crowd, Ant was already practicing Wind's technique.

Contest forgotten, Wind coached Nightshade until the Lead Warrior's distance almost matched Wind's.

As they finished, Nightshade huffing but satisfied, Wind motioned, "You will soon throw farther than I."

Xhosa beckoned, "Let's return to the fire. I believe we'll delay this contest for later."

Everyone returned to the fire, the People chattering about Wind's skill and his willingness to help Nightshade, Ant sidling up to Wind and asking him if his handhold was the right one. This made a perfect opportunity to let the People see why she trusted a Big Head once their enemy.

"Wind, come. Sit with me. Many of my People don't understand why you left your tribe, risked your life to save mine and Ngili's, and why now, you remain with us, ones who have always been your enemy."

He spread his hands, palms up. "The truth, I am not welcome with my tribe, Leader Xhosa. My brother considers me a traitor, to be slain on sight. He has told this to all the other tribes of my kind. Because he carries such power—as you did in your homebase—there is no place anymore that I can call home. If it is among your People, I will count myself lucky. If it isn't, I will move on, happy I could return you to where you belong."

Xhosa gulped. She didn't expect such honesty, had no way to respond to it, so moved on to a different question.

"It seems Thunder has stopped chasing us. At least, we no longer see any signs of Big Heads on our backtrail. Do you know why?"

Wind paused before answering, and then thinned his lips into a tight smile. "He thinks you died when you chose the path through hot boiling muck. He knows it is the most dangerous route you could have chosen and has no food or water. I have seen warriors make it through but my brother had no idea how determined and rigorous you and your People are.

"But, Xhosa, don't mistake his absence for safety. He knows I followed you. When he finds out I lived through it, he will also know you did."

Koorag's warning popped into Xhosa's mind. She tried to tell herself she no longer cared about Rainbow. He'd left the People, took all their salt, and never considered their well-being. But none of that prevented her from asking her next question.

"Did he go after Rainbow?"

"I doubt it. My People know the direness of the route he picked. It might even be worse than yours. Within a handful of days, the herds disappear, water dries up, and anything that could replace meat as food—plants, insects, spiders, even worms—becomes sparse. The Others who live in this area are fiercely protective of their few resources and have no problem killing those who show any interest in taking them. Thunder has seen the strength—and weakness—of Rainbow's group. He has no exceptional warriors, few that are even competent. Those all stayed with you, with Nightshade. Rainbow's hunters are adequate when food is abundant but will fail where they travel now."

Xhosa slumped. This wasn't what she had hoped to hear. "Is there any way Rainbow and his People could survive?"

Wind frowned. "If hunger, thirst, heat, poisonous snakes, and enemies don't kill him, after many Moons, he will reach a channel. There, if he builds a raft, guides it expertly through surging water and crashing waves, he will reach a land of lush grass, abundant herds, and few Others. He should be fine there."

Xhosa scratched her arm and motioned, "Channel?"

"That's a narrow band of water that separates two lands."

Xhosa dipped her head as she chewed her lip, hands running over her arms as though she was cold.

Wind added, "Does he know how to build a raft? As you did?"

Xhosa puckered her forehead, not knowing the answer to that. The People whispered among themselves, quietly. Many had hoped to reunite with Rainbow group members. Now, that probably wouldn't happen.

Finally, Xhosa moistened her lips and asked, "Let's say Rainbow can build a raft and did manage to cross that channel. Would he be where we could find him?"

Nightshade gestured, "Of course not. He went a different direction."

Wind caught Nightshade's eye and gestured, "But don't you think Endless Pond is like any other pond, just larger?"

Nightshade crossed his arms and growled, "What does that mean?"

Wind leaned forward. "According to my tribe's scouts, the path Rainbow chose travels along the opposite side of Endless Pond."

Wind walked toward the shoreline, stopping when he could smell the salt, feel the damp breeze. Then he stared, eyes fixed on the dark line where sky met the water.

"If he lives, he is over there," and he pointed with the bump under his mouth. "He could be over there where we could wave to him if we could see that far. If we both stay along the shore, we will eventually meet where Endless Pond ends."

Xhosa motioned, "What if he doesn't stay along the shore?"

Wind shrugged. "If he takes any other path, he will starve within a Moon. Even Rainbow will figure it out, that he must stay by the water. It was drinkable but did provide a home to lots of animals he can eat."

Xhosa's eyes brightened but when she turned to her People, expecting them to share her excitement, they looked confused, almost angry.

Enough for my first day back!

She stood. Everyone took that as an end to the storytelling, time to sleep. Her head throbbed but she wouldn't eat the pain plant in front of anyone except for Nightshade, maybe Wind. He'd seen her heal the head pains on their journey and never said anything about it.

As she headed toward the sleeping areas, not sure if Nightshade now slept with another female or would be with her, one figure caught her eye.

"Bone!" When he acknowledged his call sign, she asked, "How is your scouting?"

He flushed. "I work with Siri now. I am better at that than scouting."

Xhosa rubbed her eyes. Bone was a natural scout and had loved every part of it—moving like wind over the landscape, eager to see what lay beyond the next hill, quietly observing animals when they thought no one watched. What had changed?

She let him go. That would be something to investigate later. Tonight, she would get the newcomers settled. Siri walked with Viper, Deer, and Leopard. Stone pushed up against Ngili, pointing out where they would patrol this evening.

But she didn't see Wind.

She moved into the shadows at the edge of the group, turned her head, and popped a pain plant into her mouth. While chewing, she raised her arms. "Who will help Wind?"

Pan-do joined her and motioned to the opposite side of the group. "He's with Sa-mo-ke." Xhosa looked where Pan-do pointed to see the two deep in conversation. "I don't think my Lead Warrior will let Wind sleep until he explains how to far-throw a spear. By morning, I expect he'll be expert at it."

Everyone curled behind the thorn bush barrier, the adults quickly snoring and the children falling into a contented slumber. Xhosa struggled to keep her eyes open and gave up. Her last conscious thoughts were that the head pain had left and wondering whether Nightshade would sleep with her.

If he did, Xhosa slept through it, awakening when Sun did, well after many of the People, to the chatter of the children and females for the first time in many Moons.

Nightshade greeted her. "The scouts and warriors left already, Leader. They will tell us if there is trouble though we've had none so far. The rest of the People are on their way."

Leader. How good that sounded.

She and Nightshade worked their way to the front of the group. Siri waved at her as she passed and Spirit panted a greeting, tail wagging with the unbridled elation of being back with his pack. Lyta stopped to lick his muzzle as he did hers. Sa-mo-ke, Wind, and Ngili sprinted into the distance, quickly hidden by a copse of trees.

Xhosa motioned, "It is good to be back, Nightshade. I have missed your competency. Please tell me what has happened in my absence."

He described which of the subadults were preparing to be adults, how many females had their first blood, the impressive changes he'd made for training warriors to fight in an unknown land, and the mysteries revealed every day by the scouts. Talking with Nightshade, strategizing, him knowing what she would say before she formed the thoughts—no one understood her or the People like Nightshade.

They fell into a comfortable silence as had often happened in the past. When they were well-ahead of the group, he glanced at her, then away, and finally motioned, "You must see that Wind is a risk to us."

Just the mention of Wind stirred Xhosa inside. For no reason she understood, the Big Head made her feel as Hawk had, like they could talk, strategize, and build a future for the People.

He continued, "He is here to spy on us, report back to his brother where our new homebase is. Being thrown out of his tribe, befriending Ngili—these are a ruse to gain your trust."

Her face flushed. She kept her eyes forward so he wouldn't see the anger. The silence grew as she carefully constructed her response.

"I would be insulted, Nightshade, that you think I wouldn't see through such obvious subterfuge, but I might feel the same if you showed up after a long absence with a Big Head female. Trust me, that this is the right decision. Wind risked his own life—twice—to save me. There are less dangerous ways to trick me than by tempting death."

Nightshade wasn't convinced. "If his People threw him out, he will want to take over ours. Why else would a Big Head live with Others—"

Xhosa cut him off, trying to hide her irritation. "Ngili trusts him as does Spirit. The wolf hasn't been wrong yet. So far, Wind willingly shows our warriors and hunters his Big Head skills. They all like him but if that changes, we will decide what must be done."

Before Nightshade could respond, Wind caught up with them, spear in hand, filled with a quiet energy. Heat flowed through her body, an unexpected response to the odd-looking male with his long arms, narrow body, stretched out neck, and oversized skull.

"Sa-mo-ke already has the far-throw technique mastered. He and I will work with the rest of Pan-do's warriors on it tonight, after we stop to sleep. Would you like me to include your warriors also, Nightshade?"

"No. They are busy," and Nightshade left without another word.

Nightshade couldn't shake his hatred for the Big Head. Even if he believed Wind condemned his brother's actions, Nightshade's stomach knotted at how he gazed at Xhosa. He didn't care if the two had mated—he expected it on such a long trip. That they hid it infuriated him.

A more important question: Did they *pairmate*? He wouldn't ask. If they did, it would show soon enough as it had with Hawk.

A dark cloud shrouded his thoughts. Her interest in the heathen Hawk had surprised Nightshade and ordained the male's death. If Xhosa continued to mate with the Big Head, he would kill him also.

Or her, if necessary. For the good of the People.

Nightshade had vowed that when Xhosa returned, which he never doubted she would, they must pairmate. She would see his success with the People and the loyalty he enjoyed from all warriors. Even Pan-do deferred to him. There would be no reason to wait.

As they traveled the rest of the day, he had to ignore his warriors' enthusiasm for Wind's new techniques. One after another, they approached him about training with Wind that evening and he told them they had other obligations. He spent the day watching the Big Head, waiting for him to make a mistake, hoping it would happen soon. If it threatened the People, Nightshade could expel him from the group and Xhosa couldn't object.

If Wind made no big mistakes, Nightshade would cause one.

When the group stopped to rest, Wind disappeared. With Spirit. When Nightshade motioned the group onward, he could barely contain his glee that already, he had been proven right. Wind had fled. Spirit was tracking him, maybe to stop whatever his plan was. A hand of Sun's movement later, Wind and Spirit caught up, a bulky pig looped over Wind's shoulders, a fat leg in Spirit's jaws. Hunting a pig this size required a group. How had Wind done it alone?

Ngili raced up. "You found a dead pig? And a fresh one!" His hands were friendly but confused.

Sa-mo-ke joined them. "Did you steal it from another hunting party! Will they try to recover it?"

Nightshade elbowed Sa-mo-ke and Ngili out of the way, steps thudding against the ground in his fury. "You put the People in danger for meat—"

Wind interrupted, grinning, hand raised and palm down, "No, nothing like that, Lead Warrior. Spirit and I wanted to empty our water when he sniffed the pig. It was too easy to pass up."

Nightshade fought against the rage building inside his head. He pressed his palms against his legs as the pounding in his chest sped up. He imagined swinging his warclub at Wind's head, smashing it open as his body folded into a bloody heap.

Anyone was permitted to hunt alone though most considered it risky. In this case, rather than making a deadly mistake, Wind had proven himself a courageous hunter.

"Get moving!" Nightshade shouted. It came out angrier than he intended but he didn't care.

He stomped away, leaving the males to cluster around Wind as they walked, asking how he brought down a giant pig by himself. Wind went into detail, saying he couldn't have done it without Spirit's assistance.

Xhosa listened as Wind patiently explained how he and Spirit stalked the pig, set a trap not unlike what Xhosa did during the Leadership challenge, and then killed their prey. Was it the Big Head way, as it was the People's way, to do what the group needed? If so, they were more alike than she realized. Did her father see that when he convalesced in the Big Head camp? And was that why he didn't attack the Big Heads when he could have?

If so, what she'd always considered a mistake wasn't.

Chapter 20

When Xhosa didn't awake with Sun, as she always did, Nightshade went to check on her. She lay in a curled heap exactly where she'd slept the prior night.

"Leader. It is time to leave."

She struggled to sit, eyes red, face green, chest and neck flushed, and her hair stringy and coated with vomit.

"I am ready," but her hands flapped loosely and she leaned on Nightshade, stumbled, and threw up.

"Did you eat something rotten?" Though everyone ate the same food—the pig Wind had killed—and no one else was sick.

"It's nothing. I'll be fine," but she winced as she stood and had to pause to hold her abdomen, bending over before she could walk.

The entire day, Xhosa struggled, her color changing from green to gray and back. She swallowed the juice from bulbs which Nightshade had seen her give for upset stomachs. It usually helped but seemed to do no good this time. Her face reddened and her stomach bloated as it would if she needed to relieve herself. Siri asked if Xhosa was sick and she mumbled about not sleeping well the prior night and she would feel better once she could lie down. Wind approached but left when she spewed bile over his arm.

When Sun's rays touched the horizon, Nightshade slipped up to her side and motioned toward jagged hills cut by steep valleys. He wasn't sure she was listening but knew if he mentioned stopping for the day, she would figure out how to agree.

"The scouts say these hills in front of us will take a hand of hands to cross. We should stop here for the night, rest, eat, and start again tomorrow when we have sufficient daylight to get through them."

The People sprawled behind a thorn barrier, grooming each other, chattering about how nice it was to stop early for once, but Xhosa slipped away. She found a secluded spot away from the People, somewhat hidden in a copse of trees, and then collapsed without even a cursory check of the surroundings. Nightshade followed—he had to. Her retching drowned out his steps as it would those of a predator who might decide to stalk the sick animal.

His job tonight must be to keep her safe.

While the People rejuvenated from the trek, Xhosa twitched and moaned, never sleeping, hand resting on her stomach. When she stood to relieve herself, her legs shook so, they couldn't hold her and she ended up lying in her own waste. Nightshade decided he had to help. If she breathed in her own vomit, it could kill her. He approached but stayed hidden as long as possible. Just before he had to reveal himself, she staggered to her feet, wheezing, and leaned heavily against a tree as blood gushed from between her legs.

He sniffed and pulled back. It stunk like female blood. But Xhosa always bled when Moon was new—not now—and unlike others, it never made her sick. His eyes snapped open. It smelled like the female blood expunged after mating. This must be from Xhosa's captors.

Or it could be Wind. But if the Big Head forced mating on Xhosa, she would not allow him to join the People.

Unless he didn't force her.

Xhosa crumpled to the ground and crawled to the stream, splashed water over her body, and passed out. Nightshade's eyes narrowed as confusion gave way to something else. When she awoke, he returned to the People.

Thinking about Wind with Xhosa turned what had been simple annoyance into brittle rage. He avoided her when they headed onward that day, snapped at Siri, and swore to himself he would destroy the Big Head. By the time Sun was two hands above the horizon, Nightshade had decided what he must do.

Chapter 21

The day's migration took them through rugged hills and steep valleys and then great open swaths of grassland. These gave way to marshy lowland filled with sinkholes that must be crossed carefully lest the People fall into death sand, be bitten by snakes, or be assaulted by blood-sucking black worms that attached themselves to skin. Those horrid squirmy creatures could only be removed by cutting them away with a chopper.

Xhosa, still weak, mentioned her illness to no one. She'd seen many females expel blood after not bleeding for a Moon or more. It was always worse than usual, as though it had collected inside of them and now, all came out at once.

Siri, though, had other ideas. "Did you not bleed during the last Moon?"

Xhosa shrugged. "I don't remember."

Siri said nothing, as though thinking, and then motioned, "But you mated with your captors." Her hands were low, her face concerned.

"Of course, forcibly." After a pause, she asked, "Are you asking if Wind forced me to mate? No."

"If he did, it explains your sickness." Siri sniffed. "Female blood is on you. Here," and handed over a pungent plant. "Wipe this everywhere it touched. It will clean away the smell and help you feel better."

Xhosa didn't tell Siri how glad it made her the baby was gone. New life was precious to the People but not when they didn't have a home.

Days passed peacefully, pleasantly. If not for Nightshade's uneasy ire, this would be much like a normal migration where the People moved from one area to another, allowing the herds and plants to replenish before moving back. They stayed nowhere so long that they ate all the plants or overhunted the animals.

Many spots they passed seemed perfect for a new homebase—bursting with berry bushes and fruit trees, overrun with tall grass, and empty of Others. Always, Seeker rejected them.

"The stars are not right, Leader Xhosa," he spoke over his shoulder, never slowing.

Pan-do abided by Seeker's choices as did Lyta, Zvi, Spirit, Pan-do's People, and surprisingly, Nightshade. What choice did Xhosa have?

Wind had assigned himself the task of guarding the backtrail. Always with him were Ngili and Viper. Rarely did anyone else join them. While they traveled there, mostly out of sight of the main group of People, Viper picked at Wind to teach them everything he knew about far-throw. Though Wind and Viper clearly cared for each other, Xhosa never saw them mate. At night, Wind slept by himself and Viper with Deer and Leopard.

When he wasn't busy with Viper, Xhosa joined him, asking an endless stream of questions about Big Head defense and offense strategies. She never again wanted to be surprised by a Big Head attack she was unprepared to defend.

As the People walked, they practiced the new greeting. It became Viper's job to decide when a call was good enough. When she wasn't training with Wind, she was teaching them how to reproduce the sound. Lyta got it perfectly quickly but was unable to teach anyone else how to do what she did so effortlessly. Almost a Moon passed before Xhosa heard the first flawless call followed by a whoop of excitement.

Siri motioned, "That was Ant. He now will help Viper help the others."

Moon disappeared and reappeared twice before the perfect land changed. The sweet aroma of flowers gave way to the stale odor of desiccated rotting plants and stifling heat replaced the pleasant cooling breezes that had accompanied the People most days. The ground became too rocky, too hilly, too wet, too salty, or too something else. Wind said his tribe never traveled this close to Sun's nest but Viper must have come through here when captured. When Xhosa asked, she didn't remember. They had been too young.

Xhosa caught up with Pan-do. He slowed enough that Lyta moved forward of him which made her speed up to join Seeker.

"Pan-do. I need advice I think only you can give me."

He flushed but didn't ask why or what. She deserved his silence. She had rejected his guidance in the past when Nightshade had been her most trusted companion, doubting someone as new to the group as Pan-do—and so unfamiliar with their methods—could offer advice to her on how to properly protect her People. Now, in some ways, her Lead Warrior frightened her so she wondered if she could trust him. He had become distant since her illness. He claimed to be scouting at night but instead, stayed with Honey or another female. Why lie? It mattered nothing to her who he spent his nights with.

That niggled at her until finally, she knew what she must do.

She made her first question open, inviting any answer Pan-do chose to give. "How did your People manage in my absence?"

She kept her expression bland, not wanting to influence him, interested in an honest assessment of the People under the co-leadership of Pan-do and Nightshade.

"The People are strong, Xhosa, thanks to you," but his body said he lied.

She mulled over how to force him to be candid and decided on bluntness.

"So, Nightshade was a good Leader. Is he better than me?"

Pan-do, she believed, would tell her the truth even if it hurt. She was afraid of the answer but needed to hear it.

Pan-do said nothing for a long time, choosing instead to watch Lyta and Spirit as they played fetch.

After some time, he gestured with quiet intensity, "Nightshade is a competent warrior who will never lead my People. Should he be in that position in the future, we will move on as I believe Seeker and Zvi will. And Spirit. If Spirit had considered Nightshade the right pack leader, he would not have risked his life to find you. When Spirit disappeared, Seeker assured us he was where he needed to be."

He leaned toward her, the cords on his neck tight. "I've never seen a Leader like you, Xhosa. As long as you guide us, my People will contentedly follow."

Happiness swelled within her for this male who blundered upon her People when she needed him most.

The next day, the land rolled from one valley to another. This forced the People up and down steep rocky hills and around boulders taller than most trees. When Sun reached well overhead, a waterway appeared on their path, too deep to be crossed. They traipsed along its shore a long way before reaching a spit of land that stretched to the opposite shore. Though underwater much of the way, it was shallow enough to cross. The strong current tried to drag them downstream and the slippery rocks that lined the bed made walking tricky but everyone made it.

It became the first of many such waterways—too shallow for lakes, too wide for rivers, and impossible to go around. Always, if they searched far enough, a narrow land bridge showed up connecting them to the other side.

As Sun dipped to sleep, the People found a protected overhang, ate silently without stories, and fell asleep, a few in tree nests, most on the ground. Xhosa beckoned to Pan-do,

Nightshade, Seeker, Wind, and to everyone's surprise, Ngili and headed to a secluded spot away from the sleeping group. Zvi and Spirit trotted after Seeker.

When all were gathered, she turned to Ngili. "Tell them what you told me."

He told of Dawa and how the two had made a pact to escape their captors, how Dawa died before that could happen but not without telling Ngili how to reach his People. He assured Ngili his tribe would welcome the People

"He said his homebase is high in the mountains, surrounded by white peaks that touch the clouds. It abounds in berry bushes, fruit trees, massive herds, endless grass, nuts, and birds. Few live there because to reach it, we must cross frozen mountains, icy valleys, and deep gulleys. He told me how to find it—of the cairns he'd left to mark the path, asking only that I tell his People he never forgot them.

"But he assured me we wouldn't want to live there. It is too cold, too rocky. Only those born to it are happy. What we want is beyond. When we find his People, we must continue going until we pass through the mountains. There, we will find our new homebase."

"I wasn't sure I believed him until now. This land—what we now cross—it matches Dawa's description perfectly."

Seeker gestured, a serene smile on his face, "I've seen it. That is where the stars lead us. We don't want to stop short or go anywhere else."

Pan-do motioned, "How do we get there?"

Ngili pointed forward. "Those mountains match his description of the passage to his homebase. Once we pass through them, we'll find his People."

Seeker broke in, "And beyond that, our new homebase."

Nightshade widened his stance as his nostrils flared. "The hills extend from one side to the other. How can we get around them?"

Ngili smiled. "We don't go around. We go through. Carefully. There is a path and Dawa shared it with me."

No one spoke. Even in the dark, the tall white tips stood out against the dark sky, their rugged slopes intimidating, their crests so high they were lost in the clouds. Xhosa doubted they would look any more welcoming during the day.

Seeker motioned, as though he saw the hopelessness in their faces, "The stars are guiding us. We will be fine."

Xhosa bent her head to the side. "In case it's a cloudy night and we can't see the stars, what instructions did Dawa give you?"

Ngili squatted on his heels. "I memorized them:

> *Find two tall spires separated by a valley. A river runs along the base. Cross it when it is dry, then stay in the foothills until you reach a lowland that wends its way through the mountains. Follow it. Do not climb the mountains! They are too steep and cold for those not born to them. If you find your ears, toes, fingers, nose, lips, and eyeballs freezing, go back. You missed the pass.*
>
> *You will come to a great boulder that blocks your way. Look for my cairns. When you find my People, give them my name. They will welcome you. Tell them you helped me.*"

Seeker leaped to his feet, spun, and then repeated Ngili's words exactly, swaying to his own voice. Without warning, he collapsed in a heap, arms stretched in front, tears rolling down his cheeks.

Zvi, folding her big body next to Seeker's tiny one, ran her fingers through his hair. "He says the stars live in Dawa's homeland but before we reach them, someone will die and someone will betray the People."

Chapter 22

When the shoreline diverted from the mountains, no longer heading toward Sun's nest, Seeker turned inland. First, Zvi, Spirit, Lyta, Pan-do and his People hurried after him, and then, at the back, Nightshade, Water Buffalo, and the former Hawk People-now-the-Nightshade-People. Reluctantly, so too did Xhosa and her People. This path rose steadily toward the white-tipped mountains, leaving Endless Pond far below. No one complained. They were accustomed to difficult migrations. The scouts avoided well-used animal paths because in unknown areas, it was safer to make their own. Nightshade, Xhosa, and Pan-do led, the warriors and scouts arrayed around the group with some hidden, others visible. Ngili, Wind, and Viper secured the backtrail. When it became more treacherous and winding, Stone joined them. That way, they could leave someone at varied points along the trail, make sure no one followed, and then rejoin the group. Always two traveled together with two more left behind.

Hyaena and Wolf howled their dominance in this new area, answered often by unfamiliar calls and sometimes by Spirit. Never did Spirit's kind approach, nor did Hyaena.

And never did they cross paths with Others who might be able to confirm that the People were headed to Dawa's tribe.

They were trekking along a narrow, shallow stream, looking for a spot to stop for the night, when an enormous fur-covered creature trundled out of the trees on the opposite side. His limbs were as big and round as tree trunks, his head larger than a small boulder set atop muscular sloped shoulders. He picked up their scent and rose to his hind legs, standing as tall as a baobab. His sharp claws raked the air and yellow fangs the length of a hand dripped bloody saliva. His roar sent chills through Xhosa.

Zvi stepped toward the monster, mouth open in awe. "She is as big as Giganto."

"She?" *Of course, No penis.* Xhosa pulled Zvi back and motioned one-handed, "Who is Giganto?"

Zvi focused inward, shoulders drooping and eyes distant. Finally, she gestured, "He was my first friend—an Upright, taller than you and as bulky as two of me. He saved my life and died in the fire from the sky. But this can't be Giganto's kind. He eats only bamboo and I see none of that around here."

Xhosa muddled through what kind of plant "bamboo" would be and was about to ask Zvi when Viper strode forward.

She motioned toward the huge animal. "This is Bear. She is at times brown like this one or can be gray or black. She has weak eyesight but can pick up scents farther away than wolf. And despite her bulk, she can run as fast as an angry Panther. If we don't threaten Bear or her cubs," and Viper pointed out smaller versions of the massive mother tumbling through the grass, "she will probably leave us alone."

"Probably?" A squeak from Ant.

"Yes, Ant, though nothing is guaranteed. She could be irritated about something else and take it out on us. Let's hope not. Fighting her, well, spears bounce off her hide and a warclub merely makes her angry."

Xhosa looked around for an alternate path, something amidst the steep canyons and talus covered hills that would be climbable. Even for her who learned to climb from the mountain gazelle, it looked impossible.

"There is no way around," Nightshade motioned. "Any path other than this stream will be too difficult and slow—"

Viper shook her head. "We must avoid the stream, Xhosa. It's where she hunts. If we travel along it, we will make ourselves look like we're a threat. If we pick a path away from the stream, she will lose our scent in the landscape."

Ant moaned.

Nightshade probably resented her intrusion but Viper had been the brunt of his vicious fury so often, it no longer bothered her to contradict him.

"Dust!" Xhosa shouted, not giving Nightshade time to respond.

When her Lead Scout reached her side, she motioned, "Bear is going away from us and we are downwind. Find a path that keeps us far enough from the shore that she can't see us and through plants that will bury our scent."

The group turned away from the water into the heavier timber at the base of the canyons. The scent of wet loam and damp leaves filled Xhosa's nostrils. There were places where the stream had jumped the banks and pooled within stands of trees and around the trunks. Large branches had plummeted to the floor and wedged themselves across the chasm, from one riverbank to the other. The People, led by Dust, picked their way past a waterfall which filled the air with a damp mist and diverted into a forest. The sky darkened as the tree branches closed overhead and blocked out the direct sun.

As the roar of water faded into the background, Asili, an elder, motioned to Xhosa.

"Leader Xhosa. May I walk with you?"

Xhosa beckoned her forward but remained silent as they walked, knowing Asili would speak when she was ready. Xhosa with the spirit of youth and Asili the labored dignity of wisdom, her steps assisted by a stick, traveled beside each other. Their eyes scanned the surroundings, ears perked to every sound, noses twitched to Bear's scent and any other.

Xhosa had seen Asili in Hawk's camp. She did everything the younger females did despite her hunched back, toothless mouth, and red swollen joints. Even at the times when this migration was its most difficult, Asili never complained. Nor did any of the elders. They claimed the more arduous the trek, the more satisfying the new homebase would be.

Never had Asili asked to speak with Xhosa. This would be the first time. Xhosa rarely talked with elders and now asked herself why not. Once they found a new homebase, she would change that.

When Asili finally appeared comfortable, her steps measured, her pace easy, Xhosa motioned, "What can I do for you, Elder?"

A slight smile lifted the corners of Asili's lips. "A day or two at the most, I will be unable to keep up with the migration. Before that, you must hear the story your father told me long ago. At his request, I kept his secret but now, with recent events, you must be told what happened. I think he'd agree that it is time." She paused a moment to breathe deeply and then continued, "You look like her."

That startled Xhosa but she left it alone, assuming Asili would explain what she meant in her own time.

Spirit caught up with the two, sniffed the elder and licked her wrinkled hand with its bent fingers and broken nails. Asili rubbed his muzzle which made Spirit's brows bunch in pleasure. Then, he huffed, whined once, and slipped back to Seeker as though all he'd wanted to do was say hello to an old friend.

She motioned, eyes glancing at Xhosa, "Have you heard of your father and the Big Head female?"

Xhosa nodded. "But not the full story. My father shared little about the time before he led the People."

"When your father was a new hunter, a Wild Beast gored him. His fellow hunters left him for dead but he lived, albeit barely. His moans attracted a small hunting party of peaceful Big Heads who took him back to their camp to be treated even though it appeared he would not survive the injuries. One of the females changed the salves, brought him water, mulched pain plants, and slept at his side to keep him warm. Without her, he would have died."

As Asili talked, Xhosa wanted to ask questions but dared not speak for fear her hands would tremble.

"Your father described the female as tall and lithe with smooth dark hair, like Sun shining off damp rocks. They mated often. When she bore a child, he wanted to stay with her People as her pairmate. It made sense. His differences were accepted by her tribe and his People would not be so tolerant."

As though Asili had come to why she wanted to talk to Xhosa, she placed a gnarled hand on Xhosa's slender arm and turned to face her.

"The female Big Head was killed—how is not important—and your father brought the girl child back with him to his tribe, never explaining her past to anyone. His pairmate raised her as one of the People."

"A female!"

"That was when your father stopped assaulting the surrounding tribes."

Xhosa gulped. "The daughter, she would be my sister."

The Elder's step stuttered but she didn't confirm or deny Xhosa's supposition. Instead, her final comment was less personal but more intimate. "That is all I have to say, except one more thought. For you. Your father believed there are good Big Heads. This Wind and his obvious affection for you, he seems to be one."

She turned to go but stopped. "Leader, be aware, Big Heads are different in more ways than their appearance. The decisions they make are not always for the good of their People. Sometimes, they do things just because it seems to be the right thing to do. Big Heads healed your father and allowed him to stay even though his presence in their camp put them in grave jeopardy."

"Because they considered it right to save a life?"

Asili nodded. "They call what your father and the female shared "love". Your father explained "love" to me as a joyful emotion between individuals that causes one to do the unexpected and the other to do the impossible."

"Like the female saving my father regardless of her safety?"

Asili huffed. "The opposite, as potent as love, they call 'hate'. Your father equated it to how the People rejected Big Heads without reason, what he tried to change, and how this Thunder stalks you regardless of the cost to his People."

Without another word, she shuffled away, back stooped, every step that of one content she'd done what she must with her life.

Asili's story disturbed Xhosa. The People experienced intense emotion—like fear, worry, and anger—but never allowed it to interfere with their actions. If her father knew Big Heads were capable of this thing called "hate", why wouldn't he warn her? And was the child still alive?

Her chest thudded, her head pounding. She chewed and swallowed more of the pain plant, walking slowly, waiting for it to work.

Nightshade approached, unbidden, knowing as usual when she was upset and needed help. "Are you alright? Are you sick again?"

She looked at him, so lost in her thoughts it took a breath to really see him. His eyes were the old Nightshade, the friend she could say anything to, the only one who knew about the stabbing spikes in her head.

"Nightshade." She moved her hands low for privacy. "One of my captors was… different…" she lied. "A slave told me he was the child of a mating between the captors and Big Heads."

His reaction was not what she expected.

"You think Wind mated with Viper? Or Deer or Leopard? Which one, Xhosa? If there is a child, we must kill it and ostracize the female. Was it Deer? He wants her because she is mine!"

This bewildered her. "Why would we kill the child, Nightshade? They did nothing wrong and are like us in many ways."

Nightshade brushed her away. "Which female? You must tell me. We cannot have such an abomination among the

People!" He gripped her arm. First, fear swamped her and then fury. How dare he!

"No! You're wrong—"

"It must be Viper—no, Deer. I will destroy her!"

"No—that's not what I meant!" Xhosa took a deep breath to settle herself. "I will ask Siri," and turned away to hide her shock at Nightshade's reaction. Did it fit what her father called "hate"—to dislike without reason? No wonder her father hid the child's identity. What would Nightshade think if he found out that the trusted, beloved Leader of the People raised what Nightshade called an abomination?

Once Bear ate her fill, she and her cubs loped into the trees on the opposite side of the stream and faded away. The People veered back to the waterway and stayed close all day and most of the next. Soon, Lyta's birdsong accompanied the gurgling splash of water over rocks. Seeker clapped his hands and skipped while Spirit pranced at their side."

Wind motioned, "Her voice—it's beautiful. How does she do that?"

"She mimics the sounds around her or beats out the rhythm with stones or twigs."

Wind laughed.

"We are an unusual group, Wind, unlike any in my father's time."

Now was a good time to ask her unusual question.

"Wind, have you heard of my People wiping out a Big Heads' group?"

To her surprise, he nodded. "We traded females with that tribe. They treated everyone fairly, even Uprights."

Xhosa turned away as though distracted, and asked, "I heard one of my kind mated with one of your kind in that group. I didn't know your people did that. Is it true? Do your People mate with mine?"

He gawked at her, his penis stiffening. That surprised Xhosa and she stepped back. Did he want to mate with her? Some females said it made them tingle; others claimed they slept until finished. Most considered it a duty, necessary to grow the People. When Xhosa mated with Fang and Hawk, one was disgusting, the other a welcome obligation.

She couldn't help but wonder which Wind would be.

"I know it's an awkward question..."

He smiled with a radiance that touched her deep inside. "Yes, it happens. The children are usually like others in the group enough that they don't stand out. Thunder and I are the result of such a mating. None in my tribe considered us different."

Xhosa faced Wind, unable to look away. "How did it happen? The mating?"

"Others forced my mother. She told no one and none suspected." He seemed to want to say more but settled on, "It occurs often."

"Asili, one of the People's elders—"

"Asili is kind, and helpful."

"She tells of a mixed Big Head-Other baby who my father brought back with him. I have no idea if the child survived or who raised it—her. It was female. No one among the People looks different." *Except me.*

Despite herself, her stomach fluttered and her skin tingled. Wind turned away and then back, his gaze a mix of softness and fear.

He motioned, "Such a child would have my general shape, height, hair, with a larger head than Others and a slenderer build. The most prominent difference is what my People call a chin," and he put a finger on the bump under his lips. "Like this," and moved his finger to the bottom of her face. "And this. Anyone with the bump below their mouths must be from a Big Head mating."

She jerked away as though he slapped her. That couldn't be. Her father would have told her! If not he, her mother.

She turned away, eyes burning as she fingered the protrusion beneath her mouth, ignored by everyone among her People.

Wind abruptly stood. "I can't stay," and hurried away, glancing back once but not slowing his pace.

Her mind flooded with unanswered questions about Big Heads, her father's time with them, and the missing child/daughter. Xhosa stilled, seeing nothing, her only movement an occasional thoughtful frown.

When Asili disappeared, no one searched for her. Everyone knew where she was.

As the People walked, they stopped often to fish. At one point, Pan-do was showing Red-dit and Wa-co how to catch the slippery creatures while he juggled an armful and ended up falling into the water.

Xhosa leaped to her feet. "He can't swim! Reach a branch to him!"

El-ga giggled and Lyta motioned, "He swims as well as Spirit now."

And true to her words, Pan-do stroked through the water and plodded his way ashore.

The river narrowed as it climbed the foothills. Smooth rounded stones, some smaller than a man's fist but others the size of a baby hare, soon covered the bed. The adults picked their way along, children on their shoulders, or slogged through the reeds that grew on the water's edge. When the river dried up, the land became a complex combination of hills and depressions. As never before, Xhosa missed the vast openness of her homebase with wide endless plateaus and scattered trees.

The sky, too, tested them, dumping torrents of water that slowed them to a crawl. They often had to shout to be heard above the pounding rain and swirling wind. Then, they sheltered in a cave to await its end. When the last occupants were wolves, Spirit would dance around, chasing his tail, until he picked up a scent. Then, he'd disappear. A day—or days—later, he caught up with the People, tail wagging, exhausted.

Once, what seemed to be an unoccupied den wasn't. The People were just settling to sleep when a twig snapped beyond the mouth of the cave. Spirit's ears tweaked, nose twitched, and he sprinted outside. Xhosa grabbed her spear and chased after him. When she caught up, he stood spread-legged in front of a small black wolf barely to his shoulders. She faced him, tail tucked but standing her ground. Spirit padded forward, whimpering, his head bobbing in rhythm to his pants. She growled, gently, to which Spirit responded with an unusual moan. His long, wet tongue shot out and he licked the air between them. The black wolf offered her rear to Spirit, caught his eye, and scurried off.

He followed.

A day later, he reappeared, the black wolf in tow. He entered the People's cave leaving the female outside, hidden in the underbrush. When they left the next day, she loped along, shadowing them but hidden by the underbrush. Now Spirit traded time between his Other pack and the black wolf.

Chapter 23

Xhosa wrapped her long hair in tendons, hung her pelt on the spear strung over her back, and set out. The sky was clear, Sun hot and bright, and Xhosa already sweating. For days now, they'd been crawling up mountains, slipping down into valleys, searching for Dawa's landmarks or his cairns, keeping Sun's nest always in front of them.

Right now, they were deep in a chasm between two mountains, looking for a path over or through the range. She sighed, wondering if this hot sticky air that clung to her like the stink of carrion was better or worse than the frigid cold of the kidnapper's camp.

As daylight disappeared, the group stopped for the night. Wind approached, his eyes telling Xhosa he had a question. Yesterday's yesterday, they'd seen tracks of Others so Wind and Ngili had been hiding on the backtrail, watching to see if anyone followed. That was difficult in this complicated mosaic of trees, rocks, valleys, and waterways.

She stiffened, prepared for the worst.

He motioned, "Have I annoyed your Lead Warrior?"

OK. Not about Others. Her body relaxed. "No. Why?"

"He takes every opportunity to cause me trouble." His hands were smooth and quiet as he talked. A lone twitch in his eye gave away the stress behind the words.

"Earlier today, when we stopped to rest, he tossed a snake at me. I batted it away but it bit Red-dit's child Nak-re. He screamed, embarrassing himself."

"Why did Nightshade do that?"

Wind turned his attention to the landscape, face impassive. "Its colors were those of a lethal snake. I suppose he hoped I would run in fear, which of course didn't happen. He called it an accident, said he meant to throw it out of the camp."

"So why did Nak-re think it poisonous?"

Wind blew out a frustrated breath and answered with a shrug.

Xhosa offered a grin. "And I thought you two were getting along." When Wind grimaced, she motioned, "Have you interfered with his mating? He thinks he owns the females."

"I've selected a pairmate. At the right time, I will take care of it."

Xhosa's stomach fluttered and she wondered who he'd chosen. Viper? Or Leopard? She mentally shook. It was none of her business.

"He may consider you a threat. Have you mentioned an interest in becoming Lead Warrior?"

Wind's eyes glittered, flat and impenetrable. "He is welcome to that. I spent too much time fighting my brother. He vowed to toughen or kill me and didn't care which. I've had my fill of fighting."

"Does Nightshade know? That you don't want to be Lead Warrior?"

"I have told him."

"Well, everyone I talk to thinks you do."

In fact, it was a favorite topic among the adults when they thought Nightshade wouldn't hear. Wind's quickness, strength, and lack of fear made him the first warrior with a chance to beat the invincible Nightshade. Wind's every movement conveyed physical dominance, surging with potential. He might appear mild but Xhosa knew from experience that he protected what was important.

Xhosa motioned, "Give him time."

"He has had enough but at your request, I will. Not much more, though."

As Wind walked away, Nightshade's dark gaze followed. The Big Head hid his evil intent behind a guileless smile and a weak body. He had explained his few battle scars by saying he always won quickly. His opponent got scars while Wind got only bruises. Nightshade didn't believe him. More likely, he never fought.

Still, a shiver ran down Nightshade's muscular body. Something in the set of Wind's narrow shoulders, the unblemished hairless skin, and his quiet but absolute authority made Nightshade wonder if finally, he had met the warrior with power enough to defeat him. If that was true, so be it. He never ran from a confrontation.

It was time to find out whether Wind or Nightshade was the better fighter.

It happened that night, after eating, when Wind sat quietly, repairing a spear that had broken on the last hunt.

"Wind," Nightshade shouted the Big Head's call sign. "My People reject you as did your own People. I challenge you, coward-named-Wind. If you prevail, you become the People's Lead Warrior. If you lose, I will destroy you."

Wind continued to knap a stone spear tip, didn't even raise his head.

After a long moment of listening to Nightshade's heavy breathing, Wind motioned, "I have no interest in becoming Lead Warrior. You are a good Lead. Your warriors are loyal. Why do you want to change that?"

Nightshade stabbed at Wind with his spear. "You cause problems with my warriors."

Heads turned to see who had difficulties with Wind. In fact, the warrior was generous with his time, showing anyone who asked stronger ways to attach stone tips to spears and more effective hunting techniques. Everyone wanted to learn how to use fire to force herds to the hunters, like how Thunder had forced the People to flee.

When Wind didn't react, Nightshade poked harder, this time drawing blood. The Big Head's lips thinned and the muscles in his jaw tightened but he still did nothing except to ignore the red streak dripping down his chest.

Nightshade leered and spread his feet. "A coward! I knew—"

Wind interrupted, "Walk away, one-who-wishes-to-be-Leader. You want no part of me." His words were low and soft but the warning unmistakable. If Nightshade's fearsome looks had a voice, it would be Wind's.

The Lead Warrior's eyes widened and then narrowed. With a hoot, he yelled, "You are frightened! We reject cowards. There is no place for you among the People. Leave—now, before I force you out!!"

Wind laid the stone tip aside and stood, his venomous attention now locked fully on Nightshade.

"This is your last chance." His gestures were gentle, the only emotion a slight bunching of his arms and chest muscles.

Nightshade growled. "Be ready to lose!"

The People scuttled out of the way.

Xhosa sighed. "Wind, the rules—"

"I am familiar with the rules, Leader Xhosa. No weapons except our bodies. Feel free to hand Nightshade a warclub." He showed no fear, eyes hooded, body steady, cold and confident. "When I win, current-Lead-Warrior Nightshade, will your warriors try to slaughter me?"

A roar sounded behind Nightshade with Snake's voice louder than all. "You insult us! Any who can beat Nightshade will have our respect."

"Do the former Hawk People-still-not-called-the-Nightshade-People agree?" Wind motioned without turning away from his opponent.

"Any can challenge for leadership," from Water Buffalo. "When Nightshade beat me, my warriors gave him their loyalty. The same would apply to you."

A thunderous chorus shouted agreement.

"Current-Lead-Warrior. When I defeat you, I will ask a favor. I want you to agree to it before we engage."

Nightshade guffawed. "It doesn't matter what you ask because you will lose. So, yes, whatever it is you wish, I agree!"

And Nightshade attacked. His lethal fist flew toward Wind but the nimble, leaner warrior ducked, hooked his arm around Nightshade's waist, and dragged him down. Nightshade thudded to the hard pebbled ground and Wind hit him on the forehead with an open hand. When Nightshade stabbed at Wind's throat with the blade of his hand—and missed—Wind pounded him again on the forehead, this time with a closed fist, and the skin split.

Nightshade's eyes glazed over and saliva dribbled from his open mouth.

Wind sprang up and back, freezing in place, eyes locked onto the warrior to see if this was enough to teach him his lesson. The dazed warrior swayed to his feet, shaking his head to clear it. When he found Wind, his eyes flashed.

"You are weak, Big Head. You should have finished me!" and he charged.

Wind deftly dodged the punch and then kicked him in the crotch so hard, his foot buried itself all the way up into Nightshade's stomach. The warrior yelped and folded. As he fell, Wind scooped him up, raised him over his head with unimaginable strength, and hurled him away. Nightshade slammed into the cave wall and slid down into a heap on the floor. Blood sprayed over those around him, covering their faces and hands with a mist of blood. Some even reached Wind. He didn't budge, didn't blink.

When Nightshade stayed down, Wind announced, "He has lost," and settled back onto his haunches to resume his knapping, breathing even, body barely sweating. All of Nightshade's warriors froze in place, stunned. None believed their Lead could lose and wondered what it meant to them.

Except one. When Nightshade didn't move, Water Buffalo, the former Lead Warrior of the former Hawk

People, allowed the slightest uplift of his lips to slip through before immediately hiding it.

Nightshade came to, lying on the cave floor, alone. One eye dripped a foul-smelling mucus, the other throbbed. Purple, green, and yellow painted his skin like wildflowers in raucous bloom. When he touched his lip, it came away dark with blood. A deep gash split his forehead. When he tried to stand, he vomited. He held his head between both hands and squinted as though to keep his skull from exploding.

"You're awake."

Almost alone. "Wind. As soon as I can see, we can finish what we started."

Wind said nothing else, continued whittling the same stone tip he worked on last night, now almost finished. Light spilled into the cave and the outside air smelled clean and fresh.

"Sun shines," Nightshade slurred, his words almost unintelligible.

"I didn't intend to throw you that hard. You were tougher than I expected."

Nightshade pushed to his feet again. His head spun so he balanced against the wall. "Where is everyone?"

"Gone. Pan-do and Xhosa are leading. I told Snake and Talon to take charge of the warriors, Dust the scouts. Water Buffalo—I don't trust him. You and I—we will catch up after we have discussed the repercussions of the challenge."

"The what?"

"You agreed to accept my terms if I won."

Nightshade shook as Spirit might to rid himself of water. He pushed away from the wall, wobbled once and again, and winced.

"You may have Xhosa. I assume that is what you want."

For the first time, anger billowed from Wind. He jabbed a finger at Nightshade and said, "She is not yours to give."

Nightshade yawned. "What then?"

"There are two parts to what you accepted. As the Xhosa People's new Lead Warrior, I appoint you to the position.

Any questions that require the Lead Warrior will go to you. And related decisions."

Nightshade tensed. "You mean like a Second, like Snake?"

"No. Snake is still Second. You are first. I am a member of the group as I have always been. But I will keep an eye on you."

Nightshade fidgeted. "No one will accept that.

"Of course they will. You and I agreed to it before the challenge. Do you remember?"

"What if you disagree with my decisions?"

"Why would I? You are an excellent warrior and an experienced Lead. Nothing I've seen makes me question your ability."

"You defeated me, Big Head. You are not afraid of leading. Why me? Why not Stone as Lead Warrior? Or Snake?"

"You are the most competent. Our goals are the same, Nightshade. Once we stop acting like two scorpions in a hole, we will find clarity and the People will benefit."

Nightshade wiped his hand over his mouth and then rubbed the dried blood down his side.

"What's the next part? You said two."

"We have a truce."

Nightshade agreed with a huff, resigned. "How did you do those moves?"

"I'll teach you. Then you can rechallenge me if you want."

Nightshade walked out of the cave, Wind behind.

It didn't surprise Xhosa that Nightshade swallowed the pain of his injuries. What did surprise her was he continued as Lead Warrior, his warriors' loyalty in him undimmed though their attitude toward Wind changed. Where they once considered him merely a talented spear thrower and hunter, now they sought his agility and competence in hand-to-hand fights as well. And he gained their respect when he didn't push Nightshade—and his fearsome abilities—out.

The challenge emboldened Deer to follow Wind as a female does who wishes to mate. Her breasts were growing which meant bleeding would soon start. She confided to Viper and Leopard her hope that Wind would be her pairmate. Because he kept his selection secret, everyone believed it must be an unbled female.

Deer chose to believe that too.

Days passed, and then Moons. The scouts found the river Dawa referred to. It didn't seem to lead the right direction but Seeker was satisfied.

Periodically, Xhosa found old footprints of Uprights but never Others or Big Heads. She didn't expect problems because the land burst with food, enough for many tribes, everything from sprouts, shoots, beans, and small melons to snails, big ants, and slugs. Digging stones wore out and couldn't be replaced. These hard stones that didn't crack under stress were found near Fire Mountain and its kind. None of those existed in this land nor any the People had passed through so they were forced to use horns or bones instead. Those weren't as sturdy but were plentiful.

The People came across an abundance of strange animals, like those in their homeland but larger or smaller or with thicker or skinnier bodies. They seemed unafraid of the People making them easily hunted.

On one hunt, the males cornered a Pig Beast, larger than any they'd ever seen, sufficient to provide meat for everyone in all groups for a day or longer. The creature roared its fury, pawed at the ground while its milk-filled teats dripped. As the hunters prepared for the kill, Seeker raced up, screeching and flapping his arms.

"Stop! You frighten her!" Seeker placed himself in front of the raised spears, facing the Pig Beast but at a safe distance. "Her piglets will starve if you kill her."

He locked onto Pig's beady eyes and then he slouched, holding out his empty hands.

"Do not worry, Pig. I won't allow them to kill you. I am your friend. One day, when you are old, wolves will drive you into a corner. You will kill many but they will bite your legs, your stomach, and pull you down. You will die but not today, not because of me. First, you must find food, feed your piglets, let them enjoy the land as you have. When your children are grown, maybe then we claim their meat to feed *our* children."

Seeker backed up until he and the hunters disappeared around a bend in the trail.

He motioned, "A small herd of Gazelle grazes beyond that hill. It will fall to Hyaena unless we get there first."

That night, the People ate well. Seeker and Zvi danced in the moonlight and Spirit lay pressed up against the black wolf. When Spirit rose to join his pack, to guard them for the night, the black wolf left. Lyta tried to entice her to stay but she disappeared.

Chapter 24

Moon came and went the tick of two fingers. The scent of Endless Pond had long since melted away, replaced by wet ground, clear water, and the crispness of what Viper called "pine trees". The low hills they traveled in steepened until they became the mountains that once sat on the horizon. The wind blew through the gullies and crevices with such fierceness, it made walking difficult. Still, the People kept going. They must find the two tall spires and the narrow valley Dawa told them would lead to his family and the People's new home, one everyone hoped would be warmer than the mountains.

One morning, Xhosa left their cave to relieve herself. Before she could stop it, both feet shot out from under her. She spun her arms in circles trying to regain her balance but landed with am *oomph* on a cold smooth, almost sticky surface. Siri giggled but not at Xhosa. She was watching the squealing children, led by Ant, as they slid down a hill at the edge of the camp faster than any could walk.

Siri motioned, "The slick clear material you just fell on— it's all over the place! Viper calls it 'ice'."

In fact, the brittle transparent "ice" covered bushes, rocks, puddles, and everything else exposed to the air. Xhosa put a piece into her mouth. It burned for a moment and then turned to water. When she stored a handful in her neck sack, it disappeared, leaving behind a wet stain.

All she could think was, "This is a strange land."

Several days later, the People crouched in a substantial cave, exhausted from another day of trekking up hills and into and out of fissures. Not only was the air freezing but it felt thin. Xhosa had to breathe deeper and more often just to get as much as she usually did.

Which made no sense at all.

Bone found this cave when no one else had been able to. He was turning into one of the People's best scouts. In Xhosa's absence, Nightshade almost expelled him from the People when he found out that Bone threw up at the sight of blood. Siri persuaded the Acting-Leader that she needed help and Bone would be exactly what she needed. Siri had no idea what he could do for her but made sure to keep him busy and out of Nightshade's way. When Xhosa returned, she asked Dust to take Bone as a scout. If Dust was too busy, Spirit could train him. Every day, from then on, Bone mimicked the way the wolf followed scents, listened for sounds, and snuck up on prey. It didn't take long before Bone surpassed all other scouts, even Dust.

Nightshade was alone, feet silent on the wet earth, gaze rolling over his surroundings and then back again. He listened to the quiet of the trees, the whisper of the grass, and tried to find the peace he once relished. He always enjoyed migrations, more so as Lead Warrior. The excitement of exploring unknown lands, of testing his senses against strange surroundings—he relished the challenge. The more difficult the path, the trickier the decisions, the more Nightshade reveled in them. For some, these often ended in disaster but not for Nightshade because he never made wrong choices.

That is, until Wind. Letting him stay was a mistake and a bad one. A Big Head among the People was like rotten meat that must be spit out. He should have forced him to leave. Now, it might be too late. In the short time Wind had been with the People, he'd ingratiated himself into everyone from warriors to females to even the children.

Well, it just meant his departure must be subtle.

Nightshade spread more mud on his face, to tamp down his scent, and bent to finger Gazelle's hoof print. He'd been tracking the animal for most of the day. Its faint but persistent scent tantalized him as it wound over the icy plain, crossed a shallow stream, and climbed the opposite slope into a thicket. When Nightshade exited the trees, he smiled. The animal had disappeared but he'd found where its herd ate. There wasn't enough daylight remaining to track them so he headed back to the People.

When he reached the camp, Sun barely glowed on the horizon.

Snake approached. "Did you find a herd, Lead Warrior?"

Nightshade nodded. "Tomorrow. When daylight returns," and pointed at the sky to describe how far the animals were from the camp.

Snake left to tell the hunters to sharpen spears. Nightshade looked around for Xhosa, to update her on the hunt, but couldn't find her so went to the back of the cave to resupply his neck sack with throwing stones. As he approached the pile collected by the subadults, something shuffled deep in the shadows and he froze. When he peeked, eyes slits, he saw Xhosa standing a hand's width from Wind.

They were talking, hands low and quiet, heads bent together. Nightshade thought about turning away but convinced himself this was an opportunity to see if Xhosa's relationship with Wind was like that with Hawk or something else. Hawk had started as a dalliance, like Nightshade's many mating partners, pursued for the benefit of the People. Hawk's mistake, the one that brought his death, was treating her as more. Xhosa was Nightshade's. He deserved her and would take her by force if necessary.

Was Wind making the same mistake?

He studied the Big Head, snorting again at Wind's insistence Xhosa would decide who she pairmated. The Big Head didn't understand the People.

Xhosa fingered her hair behind an ear and Wind reached to help, hand gentle and tentative. Instead of pulling away as she normally would, a rare smile spread across her face. Anger exploded through Nightshade's body. He and Xhosa—since they were children—were intended to be together. Now, because of the Big Head, the dreams, the promises crumbled.

He would fix this, like any other problem.

From the shadow of a boulder, Pan-do watched Nightshade watch Wind. The Lead Warrior smelled of rage and emotion. Increasingly, his uninhibited anger was central to the group's worst problems. When Pan-do asked Nightshade what he knew about the deep bite marks on Honey's arms and chest, almost through the skin, Nightshade lied. He said he hadn't noticed but he must have. They mated most nights.

Pan-do might have let that go—Honey wasn't complaining—but then Nightshade did what Pan-do couldn't ignore. He started to treat Lyta as a future mate. The act required agreement but Nightshade assumed any female would happily mate with him.

When Pan-do told Xhosa, she glowered. "He knows Lyta wants only Seeker. Have you talked to him?"

Pan-do's brow furrowed and he rocked on his toes. "He will lie. Again. Spirit now stays with Lyta. The only one he growls at is your Lead Warrior."

Xhosa might have thought this just Pan-do protecting his daughter but not after what she experienced the next day. Nightshade, Talon, Ngili, Stone, and Snake returned from hunting, each with a Gazelle looped over their necks. Talon, Ngili, and Snake chattered happily, retelling stories of how they trapped the herd in a ravine and killed them with a shower of spears and stones. Nightshade ignored their good humor, walking a distance to the side, frowning, hands moving as though speaking but the words made no sense. White encircled the deep brown of his eyes and he stared unblinking like a rabid wolf. He jerked toward the sound of El-ga's giggle, spear raised, and then threatened Spirit when the wolf huffed a low growl.

Shadowing the Leader but out of his sight was Stone, a worried frown shrouding what should be bliss over a well-executed hunt. Xhosa wondered if her Lead Warrior, Leader of the former Hawk-People, had already lost control.

Chapter 25

Northern Africa

Mbasa scowled at the flat barren expanse, so hot it should melt her shadow. Her nostrils flared at the aroma of dirt, the stench of tired People, and the tantalizing essence of salt. The slightest breeze, though welcome, sent swarms of dirt into her already-grit-filled eyes and coated her teeth. And there was no food anywhere unless you could break open the spiny fat cactus that adorned the desolate landscape.

The gnawing hunger, the broken earth and its searing heat—no one expected this. Rainbow's plan to save the People now focused on asking anyone they ran into for help. Unfortunately, every group they met in this dry, desolate land wanted to destroy them. Even if they didn't, they were no better off.

Why did anyone stay here?

Mbasa chewed on the remnants of a massive root. By rationing, it had lasted two Suns. The People had found no meat for a long time, over two fingers of a Moon. The last was an emaciated gazelle, too exhausted to outrun the slowest of the hunters. And then, a day later, an old buffalo died before Hecate could even spear it.

Before that, Tor had found a handful of hard-shelled creatures running across the sandy shoreline of Endless

Pond. When cracked open, they revealed soft tasty insides filled with meat and water. There had been enough of the creatures so everyone got one. Tor had never found any more though he kept looking.

And then he bellowed, "Mbasa!"

The People had long ago realized anything requiring a decision went not to Rainbow but Mbasa, and she often leaned on Tor. He had become her rock. He supported her every effort, offered insightful comments about problems, and prepared the warriors as well as could be done with old spears and brittle warclubs. It had been a long time since they came across the sturdy type of trees required for weapons.

"Over here—quickly!"

Tor yelling was unusual. He never made sounds louder than a hiss or a whisper. Nor did any of the People for fear Uprights would hear them.

"What is so exciting that Tor risks discovery?" Mbasa asked herself, partly angry at Tor's recklessness and partly curious.

She wiped sweat from her brow so it wouldn't drip into her eyes. Lately, Tor spent much of the daylight searching for a way across Endless Pond. Was that it? Had he found one?

She struggled to lift her feet out of the loose dirt and gravel, trying to climb the hill that separated her from Tor but too tired to move faster. Behind her, moving even more slowly, came the rest of the tribe.

Behind them dragged Rainbow.

As she crested the hill, she motioned, "Did you find a way across, Tor?"

"I found food—a fish! It washed up on the shore!"

There, part in and part out of the lapping water, loomed a black mound bigger than Mammoth. It didn't move except for a lazy flip of its tail and the lethargic pulse of the fins behind its eye.

Mbasa lurched toward it cautiously. When she toed the behemoth, it quivered. "Why does it rest on our shore?" And then, "It reminds me of Mammoth stuck in quicksand, where it cannot free itself."

Tor motioned, "It lies on its side like Gazelle impaled by a spear. I wonder if something hunted it and injured it so badly, it crawled here to die."

After a breath, watching the fish watch them with a dull unlidded eye, Mbasa motioned, "This will feed us for a Moon if we eat carefully."

Fish were usually shorter and narrower than her arm. This creature stretched as wide as Tor was tall and reached higher than most saplings.

Her breath caught in her throat. "If its herd lives in the Endless Pond, we could eat forever!" And then she slumped. "Except we have no way to hunt it."

The mighty fish lay there, barely moving, defenseless against Tor's pokes, gray-black skin broken here and there by huge fins. Behind the damp eyes flopped rough folds that seemed to move with the air. They fluttered once, again, and then stopped.

Mbasa cocked her head, puzzled. "I don't see any blood. How did it die?"

The glittering eye dulled. Within moments, a fly landed on the murky surface, now blind to the world.

She barked and motioned to the People who struggled toward Endless Pond. "Come—everyone. We eat!"

When they grasped the boundless supply of food that awaited them, they plunged into the shallow water. Mbasa and Tor ate the juicy eyes and the tongue as big as a child. Within a breath, handfuls of cutters slashed open the fish, chopping away its meat and fat, passing it back through the crowd. Despite its huge size and black skin, it tasted like every fish Mbasa had ever eaten.

"Hecate—take the scouts up the hill. I will bring you food."

Hecate left, trailed by a handful of females with warclubs and spears. Mbasa returned her attention to defleshing the massive carcass, filling her arms with food and taking it to Hecate and her hunters. When they had as much as they could eat, Mbasa returned to the giant fish and continued her work of hacking it into pieces. Everyone grinned, eating as they worked, gorging on the fish's mounds of fat. This critical food was in rare supply on the skinny, boney animals that inhabited this land. Without fat, the People became lethargic, dull-witted, and always hungry.

With few bones, the People swiftly cut the carcass into chunks. When all ate their fill, they stowed leftover portions in individual neck sacks for later. If they had salt, it would have been rubbed into the meat to make it last longer. Since they had no other food, preserving the many pieces of the fish didn't matter. They would easily consume all the fish before the green flies and white worms arrived.

Sated, everyone leaned back on their arms or lay prone in the sand, grins spread across their faces for the first time in days. Tor and Mbasa crouched together, staring across the black fish's home.

"I wish it had more blood. To drink."

"At least the fish is moist."

Mbasa searched far out on Endless Pond. "How did it end up here, Tor, when we needed it most? Why give its life for us? It makes no sense."

"It's no different than Gazelle or Mammoth."

Mbasa leaned forward. "Why didn't this massive fish stay out in Endless Pond where it was safe? Why come to our shore?"

"Perhaps it needs to visit land like the hard-shelled creatures but got sick and couldn't return to its water home."

Before Mbasa could respond, a movement distracted her. A graceful broad-winged bird floated in a circle above the water. Its pristine white underbelly made it almost invisible against the clouds until it cawed.

Mbasa pointed. "A bird! We have seen none for a Moon, or more! Where there's a bird, there must be land. They can't live on water!"

Tor's eyes widened in surprise as the bird circled and then banked into a steep, effortless dive, its wings tucked, head now indistinguishable from the plummeting body. It plunged into the water, barely leaving behind a ripple, and emerged moments later with a fish in its beak. It swallowed the writhing creature whole with an audible gulp, dove again, surfacing again with a fish. Instead of swallowing it, the bird flew away.

Tor motioned, "There must be land where sky meets Endless Pond. We just can't see it from here!"

"Boost me up."

Tor placed Mbasa on his shoulders with her feet dangling over his chest. She leaned forward, shaded her eyes against Sun's brightness, and shrieked. "There, a brown-and-green lump—land! This, where we are, must be the crossing!" Mbasa bounced. "It's land, Tor! We will be able to find Xhosa and the rest of our People!"

Water splashed behind them as the People gathered around.

Tor motioned, "Mbasa sees land across Endless Pond. We are near our People! All we need to do is figure out how to cross!"

Rainbow stomped up, hands angry chops as he motioned. "She's said that before and it never is true."

Why such petulance? Rainbow wanted to reunite with Xhosa, too. Rainbow's sullen attitude more than anything drove Tor to join Mbasa's warrior group. He long ago tired of those who believed Others should fear them because they once fought with Nightshade. It worked when they started this migration but now, Others called Rainbow stupid for separating from such powerful Leaders. Tor called him stupid because Rainbow continued to believe something that had been proven false.

Tor had begged Mbasa to take over the leadership. "With you as Leader, we will find Xhosa. Otherwise, we won't. Rainbow has no idea how to search for something, track it, and then bring it to ground."

"No, Tor. These with us, they rejected Xhosa. That's why they joined Rainbow. They won't accept another female Leader."

Mbasa wriggled down from Tor's shoulders and turned to the People. "We must follow the white bird."

Rainbow's face darkened. "How, Mbasa. We have no wings." He jumped to demonstrate and the children giggled.

She hid her anger, knowing it did no good. "Pan-do told me of an Endless Pond at the edge of his homeland. When his People wanted to cross it, they strapped logs together and floated across the Pond. We can do that! If we can get far out on Endless Pond, we can hunt more of this gargantuan fish!"

What Mbasa didn't tell anyone was that Pan-do told none of the rafts were ever seen again. A few reappeared as broken pieces on the shore, the bodies of the rafter-goers crushed beyond recognition or eaten by whatever creatures lived far out on Pan-do's Endless Pond. Finally, none of his People would risk their lives on rafts that either disappeared or killed the raft-goers. When Mbasa asked Pan-do if anyone ever reached the other side, he forced a smile. *I have never talked to anyone who returned.*

Still, in her People's current dire predicament, possible survival must win over starving to death. Shouldn't it?

"We will make Pan-do's rafts. Once launched, the waves can carry us across Endless Pond, to that land I saw."

Rainbow huffed, exasperated. "How is that possible?"

Tor motioned. "Have you not seen logs drift down a river, broken from trees in a rainstorm, Others who fell into the water clinging to them so they didn't drown?"

Hecate shouldered Rainbow aside and asked, "How do we guide these logs that you call a raft?"

Mbasa motioned, "Pan-do told of wood planks called 'paddles'. They were as long as spears but wider and they forced the raft forward by moving the water out of the way."

Mbasa scratched her stomach, searching for the blood-sucking tick that nested in her hair while her mind tried to unravel these things called paddles.

After more discussion and Rainbow's grunting agreement, the People decided to build a raft. There was a grove of trees not far from the shoreline they had sheltered in from the torrid heat. During the day, they laboriously chopped them down with handaxes. At night, before sleeping, they sharpened the dulled tools so they could start again when Sun awoke. Once they felled enough trunks for a raft, they laid them side-to-side and cut the tops and bottoms off to make them the same length. Burly males held them in place while others strapped them together with vines harvested from another grove.

The first raft finished, Hecate and Tor dragged it deep into the water and Mbasa crawled aboard. As the waves pushed her to shore, she shoveled water from front to back with her hands. It did no good and finally, the raft nosed into the sand, grounded.

Mbasa stumbled to her feet. "Now I understand the importance of paddles. Hands can't overpower the waves that drag the rafts back to shore."

It took another day to fashion long spear-length paddles with wide, flat tips. The raft required two because—according to Pan-do—it must be paddled from both sides.

Paddles finished, Mbasa and Tor wanted to test them but Rainbow insisted they send two of the most muscular males.

"Their strength will give them a better chance to battle the water."

The two males launched the raft, paddled, paddled more, crested a wave, and vanished from view.

The People cheered. "We did it!" "Will they come back?" "We will make more so we are ready when they return."

That night, a tempest hit. Thrashing winds tore at the shoreline and blew the trunks away that were to be used for more rafts. Mountainous waves broke over the land and up the shore, beyond the hills that separated the People from Endless Pond. Several children drowned and a few adults were crushed when the high winds slammed uprooted trees against their fragile bodies. The rest fled as far from the Pond as possible.

Mbasa huddled against an old baobab, thinking how lucky those aboard the raft were, safe from the devastating storm.

Chapter 26

The next morning, Sun greeted the land, bright and warm, the sky cloudless and blue as though no storm had ever drenched the land. The People traipsed along the shore, feet sinking into the wet sand, and collected the tree trunks and vines that had blown over the landscape. That took a hand of Sun's travel but they finally finished and were ready to start building the next raft.

"Mbasa! Come!" Hecate motioned from far down the shore, hands erratic and frightened.

When Mbasa reached what looked like a pile of debris, her breath caught in her throat. There, buried in wet plants, vines, and shattered tree trunks was a gray colored hand. Mbasa brushed aside first the detritus and then the flies and crawly creatures.

Tears sprang to her eyes. "It's one of the raft-goers," but she couldn't tell who because predators had eaten away the face. One arm bent at an impossible angle and the trunk was caved in revealing the mushy tissue beneath. "I thought they escaped."

When Rainbow arrived, he paled at the sight of the crushed bodies and then refused to continue the raft-building.

Mbasa stepped in front of him, barely a hand away, and motioned, "We have never seen such violent rain the entire time we have trekked along Endless Pond. There won't be another. We must build the raft or we will die here."

Rainbow pushed her away and stood by the rubble, his neck muscles tight, hair sticking out like a bristled Pig.

"Endless Pond is angry we tried to cross it, like Sabertooth when we place ourselves between her and her cubs." His hands moved with strength and confidence, like the old Rainbow before he gave up, beaten down by events and unsolvable problems. Beneath the outrage, Mbasa sensed his satisfaction in her failure.

No one questioned him. A ragged line of dispirited People trudged forward, their hope shattered that they would ever escape this deadly land and reunite with Xhosa's People.

Except for Mbasa's small group of warriors.

Starlight motioned. "Rainbow's decision will kill us! Fear guides him rather than the good of the People!"

Mbasa raised her hands, palms down. "We must stay with the rest of the People. We are too small a group to survive alone."

Tor motioned, "The People will forget Rainbow's complaints, as they always do. He has too many and never stops from sharing them! Soon, thirst and hunger will again consume everyone and they will expect you to fix it."

Tor walked at her side, arm bumping hers. Sun blazed and their bodies dripped sweat despite a soft breeze. Occasionally, Mbasa mounted his shoulders to scan the distance until the tiny spot of land disappeared. It would have depressed Mbasa but Tor never allowed that to happen. He seemed to have an endless well of optimism.

When she climbed down from his shoulders the last time, head drooping, struggling to come up with any reason to believe her People would survive, Tor motioned, "You will come up with another plan, Mbasa. It's what you do. We all rely on that."

They moved on, he nodding his head in agreement with himself, she searching for a ground shadow that might mark water below the surface. In one hand, she carried a digger, in the other her spear. As always.

The gargantuan fish had been consumed and no other food or water had been found. It took all Mbasa's energy to drag one foot after the other, time and again. Her thoughts became hazier with each new Sun.

"This must be what death feels like," she mumbled to herself.

The noises around her became muted, as though behind a hill or hidden by the buzz of insects, the only loud sounds the voice in her head, telling her this was the end. The rocks under her feet felt like nothing more than sand and a peaceful acceptance that everything would work out replaced the devastating worry that had plagued her for Moons. Death now seemed a delightful alternative to the aching thirst and gnawing hunger. Her brain mused over the different ways she could die, her lips moving as she argued with herself, while her feet slugged forward one step at a time, without guidance or direction.

Someone called her name. She wanted to answer but instead, gave in to an overwhelming desire to let her exhausted legs crumble so she could rest in the soft sand. She was desperate to stop walking, to sleep, but the voice kept screaming, now a shadowy figure in front of her, waving, yelling at her.

Who is that?

Before the question finished forming in her mind, she lost interest. Cramped muscles and bloodied feet made it too miserable to walk

Why am I in this strange place?

Did it matter? Hope had been displaced by the insatiable desire to quit.

That voice again—was it Tor? The memory of Tor brought a smile to her lips.

She didn't recognize anything around her—spotty dry brush, the movement of animals, or the changeless sky.

"Mbasa—open your mouth!"

She wanted to ask the voice why she would do that but truthfully, she didn't have the strength to close it anymore.

Tor bent forward and dribbled water through her parched lips. She gulped, gulped again, and felt energy flow into her arms and legs. She managed to drag herself after Tor—of course, Tor! Her best friend—to a tiny pond. As she relished the wet clean taste of water, he pointed to a twisting crease in the dry, sandy earth. It took a moment to recognize the trail.

"Snake! It's huge!" Her voice lifted at the prospect of meat and blood.

She crawled along the winding path to a boulder bed. There, motionless, lay Snake, coiled deep in a shaded recess, waiting until the blistering heat abated. Mbasa crept forward, spear ready, dazzled by the shine of Snake's scales. The creature latched onto her crouched body and tracked her approach with an unblinking eye.

"I can throw farther than it can strike," *I think*, "so I'll impale it against the rock. If I fail—which I won't—you spear it."

"No, Mbasa. You won't get enough power from that position. I'll distract it. When it comes for me, you spear it!"

Hunger dulled her instincts and drove her to do what reason would have rejected. She raised her spear, prepared to claim her food.

The serpent had other ideas.

It hissed and sprang, coil after coil unleashed from the dark shadows. It flew forward much farther than she expected, never swerving from its focus on Mbasa, and clamped onto her ankle. A vicious bite made her scream as Tor slashed Snake in two with his handaxe. The tail section twitched but the fangs remained embedded in Mbasa's leg.

Pain shot through her in waves, like when she placed a Sun-hot rock on an open wound to stop the bleeding. She shoved the agony aside, knowing she must free her leg before she lost consciousness. With the last of her waning strength, she snapped the jaws open and tossed the head as far away as possible.

That done, she passed out.

"Give me your foot," Tor ordered, words muted as though from far away.

Apparently, she wasn't quite out. She heard the terror in Tor's voice. She gurgled, tried to do as requested but her leg didn't move. Tor didn't wait for her, instead grabbed her leg, sliced the punctures open with his cutter to enlarge them, and then sucked, hoping to pull the bloody venom out before it spread through her body. Then, he pawed through Mbasa's neck sack for snake bite plant, found none, so wrapped the wound in absorbent moss. It would pull the poison out—if it wasn't too dry or too old.

Tor shouted to get the attention of the People. "Mbasa has been bitten by Snake! We must stay until she recovers," and then muttered under his breath, "because she will recover. I will make sure of that!" and moved her to the shade of the same boulder Snake had hidden under.

By the time Sun's light faded from the land, Mbasa knew she was in trouble. Her leg flashed hard and hot from her foot to her hip. Her ankle swelled to the size of her knee and glowed an angry red. She chewed a plant Bird gave her that could help with Snake's bite but it did nothing more than make her stomach heave. Wave after wave of nausea assaulted her and then blissful, welcome darkness.

Mbasa gasped and fire burned her throat. She shook, the slight breeze against the sweat on her face cooling her… No, that was Tor blowing on her… She wanted to thank him but the pain returned, worse than ever. It tore at her leg, radiated up through her body. If she stopped breathing, it would stop hurting, wouldn't it? But Tor wouldn't let her.

He screamed, "You cannot die!" And pounded her chest.

Rainbow tried to continue the migration but Tor wouldn't, nor would Starlight, Bird, and Hecate. Without this influential group, no one else would go so everyone settled by the dry waterhole, sucked on stones, and waited for Mbasa to live or die. Bird and Hecate skinned the massive snake and shared the meat and blood with all. It was thicker than a leg and longer than Mbasa was tall. If she died, her last gift—the snake—saved the lives of her People for at least a handful of Suns.

If they could find water.

Starlight followed a flock of birds to a copse of bedraggled trees. She spent a hand of Sun's travel overhead digging around the trunks, searching for the water that must nourish the roots. The hole became as deep as a child was tall before the soil darkened. She dug faster, pausing only to drink when water dribbled into the bottom. When the puddle grew as deep as her hand, she let the People take turns, sucking up a muddy mouthful, just enough to dampen their mouths and parched throats.

Night came and went and came again. Bird soaked leaves in Endless Pond and spread them across Mbasa's forehead and wounded ankle. Whatever water they persuaded Mbasa to drink, she sweated away, her skin as hot as a stone in the sun. The shallow rise and fall of her chest were the only proof she lived.

Tor slept intermittently, never left her side except to relieve himself, and told everyone who wandered over to ask that she was better than the last time they asked and would soon be recovered enough to walk. He hoped it wasn't a lie.

One morning, as Sun brightened the land and Moon hid, Mbasa's weak voice asked, "Why am I lying in Endless Pond, Tor?"

Tor smoothed her hair. "So you can live," but she had already fallen asleep.

Chapter 27

Rainbow didn't care if Mbasa lived or died as long as it happened soon. All he wanted was to escape this desolate barren patch of land. The only good news was that there were no Others around to kill them or force them away.

When he heard Tor's excited screeches, he silently cheered. Mbasa was awake. The People could move on.

He pushed to his feet and trounced over to Tor. "Let's go."

But Tor motioned back, "No. She can't travel for a day. Or longer. I'll tell you when she's ready."

Rainbow was so angry, he spit, and then wished he hadn't. Water was too scarce to waste. He turned away to release his water. At least then, he'd have something to drink.

In fact, it took two days before Mbasa could walk and that only with the aid of a stick. She refused to use her spear because it must remain sharp to protect the People should the need arise. Instead, Tor found a sturdy limb and covered the top with bark turned inside out to cushion her hand.

As Mbasa walked, Tor at her side, she motioned, "We must practice—"

"Hecate and Starlight have carried on with the training. There wasn't much else to do while you recuperated so they moved from basic skills to strategies. Several more males joined us. Between losing the raft and your serious injury, the People have become more than worried. They're desperate."

"And Rainbow?"

Tor shook his head. "He was a serviceable warrior once and a better hunter. If he practiced with us, it would encourage others to join."

He squeezed his fists and looked away. Mbasa cocked her head, waited for him to speak, and when he didn't, gestured, "What worries you, Tor?"

He motioned low for privacy. "It's not worry. It's excitement, Mbasa. While you were heeling, I spent a lot of time with the group, more than I usually do. I found mistakes."

"Tor, you fought with Nightshade. You know what you're doing. What did you see that we should fix?"

Mbasa welcomed suggestions. Her battle skills were learned from observation where Tor's were hands-on.

"Everyone can hold a spear and warclub well enough to throw it but not with the skill to make them effective. That bleeds the power from the strike. In animals with thick skins, it will bounce off them when it should penetrate. And in hand-to-hand fights, the females are afraid to use the most effective technique, one that will incapacitate male attackers immediately," and he mimed a kick to the groin.

Mbasa swallowed a giggle. "Tonight, you oversee training, Tor. Teach your methods."

When the tired travelers gathered in Sun's fading light, they ate whatever meager food had been found and then most slept while Mbasa's females and a smattering of males practiced. To Tor's surprise, throughout the practice, males dribbled in, some to watch, most to join. None were warriors or hunters but all wanted to learn.

One of the males approached Tor. "I see that you're trying to improve the spear throwing, so it's more effective. I have a trick for warclubs, that will help swing it with more power and accuracy. Let me show you…"

When Tor paused the training for a brief break, Tor asked the male why he had finally joined the new warriors.

"Rainbow promised a new home like our old one with endless herds and fields of grass, bushes filled with berries and fruit, no Big Heads and few enemies. Xhosa made no such assurances, showing us instead a route that led through desolate ground and fire-filled green puddles. I have come to believe what the elders say."

"What is that?"

"They say that under Xhosa's father, the reputation of his warriors for violence—like Nightshade—brought peace with limited bloodshed. Others wouldn't attack because they were pretty sure they would lose."

"Who told you this?"

He thought for a moment. "The Elder, Asili. She stayed with Xhosa though the path was more treacherous because she said Xhosa needed her."

Another listening to the conversation gestured, "Rainbow told me we would find a perfect homebase without working for it. Instead, the journey has been fraught with more risk than I've faced since I was a child, before Xhosa's father took over." He caught Tor's eye and hastened to add, "I'm not angry. I'm smarter. My pairmate carries a baby. I will do what must be done to find our new homebase."

The conversation brought back to Tor the reason Mbasa told him that she left the People. She accepted his vision of a better life, knowing he would fail and she would have to help him. When it became clear that he couldn't lead and someone had to step up, she adopted Xhosa's style. All she had to do was ignore hunger and thirst, evade unknown enemies, battle debilitating insecurity, and turn ordinary males and females into warriors.

One step at a time.

Tor realized he'd clenched his fists and now slowly loosened them. He motioned everyone back to warclub training, watching but his thoughts elsewhere. How would the Rainbow People have survived if not for Mbasa's unexpected strength? Yes, he missed the indomitability of Nightshade, but this—what they had here—felt right.

Listening to the conversation, watching Tor, Mbasa realized how serious these males and females took their preparation and skills. She had complete faith in her Leads— Hecate, Starlight, and Bird—but did everyone? It was time to implement challenges for the Lead positions, make those who held them earn them.

She ran the challenges in front of the People. All warriors, scouts, and hunters—including herself—who wished to be one of the Leads fought for their position. Each day when Sun slept and Moon arrived with its dim light, challenges were held in the temporary camp. Winners battled winners until only one remained. To no one's surprise, Hecate continued as Lead Hunter and Bird Lead Scout. Lead Warrior took longer because so many participated but finally, when Starlight fell to her opponent, only Tor and Mbasa remained. Who won this battle would become Lead Warrior, the loser, Second.

The entire group gathered for the final challenge. Instead, Tor explained why he wouldn't compete.

"Mbasa is an indomitable warrior, wise in the ways of battle with devious strategies that defeat our enemies. If we carried out the challenges Nightshade and Xhosa engaged in, with their test of strength and cunning, Mbasa would win. Every day, she shows it in her actions. I will learn a lot as her Second."

Mbasa became the official Lead Warrior, Tor Second. Starlight became Tor's Second. Every warrior felt pride in being part of this group. The People curled against a cliff, happy with their new strength, dreaming of an easier tomorrow.

Instead, they got trouble.

Chapter 28

Mbasa jerked awake, spitting and sneezing. All around her, the wind howled as it whipped her hair against her face and wrapped its cold arms around her shivering body. Rocky shards stabbed into her skin and stuck to her hair. Scorpions and sand fleas flew past, blown by the whirling storm. The air was so thick with grime, she could see nothing but a brown haze so put her hand over her nose and sniffed deeply, searching for the scents of group members.

The smell of dirt blocked out any scents from the People.

She shouted, "Who is here?" A few close by answered and passed the message along. Finally, grunted call signs accounted for everyone.

Rainbow appeared out of the gloom, one hand on the cliff that shielded their temporary camp. "What should we do, Mbasa?"

A visceral disgust surged but she swallowed it. "We stay here until the storm passes. Tell the People when they relieve themselves, tie one end of a vine around their waist and the other around someone else."

The People huddled together, eyes squeezed shut, hands over mouths and noses to keep the grit out. The arrival of cool air told Mbasa Sun had left and only a lighter shade of black to the landscape announced Moon's arrival. After a fitful sleep, she awoke, confused and uneasy. Blood spotted her cheeks and arms, and her back had been scraped raw rubbing against the sharp rocks of the cliff. A dull brown haze told of Sun's return but the gusts persisted, blowing the dirt and gravel into piles that climbed the cliff wall and forced everyone to dig their way free. With nowhere to move the dirt, they sat on it.

Another miserable night passed before calm returned. The silt they had been forced to eat quickly settled to the ground like a gritty layer of dust. Mbasa breathed deeply without her hand over her mouth for the first time in more than a day and marveled at the crisp purity of clean air. When Sun peered over the horizon, as though it too wondered if the land would greet it, the light and warmth lifted her spirits.

Until she looked around. Mountains of grit, broken tree limbs, and piled up bushes had reshaped the landscape into a barely recognizable world. If not for the Endless Pond to her strong side and the cliff at her back, Mbasa would be lost.

Rainbow scuttled up to her. "Shall we go or will the storm start again?" He jittered from one foot to the other, looking first at her and then into the distance.

She turned away, revolted, that his primary concern wasn't the People. "Is anyone missing?"

A yelp answered her question. Mbasa shook as she stood, trying to shake the grime from her hair and body, and raced toward the sound. A panicked mother pawed through the grunge on the ground. "The vine broke. My child—Kiska— he is lost!"

"Bird!" Mbasa motioned. "Take as many scouts as you need."

Each scout grabbed a spear and raced out. A child was valuable but without tracks and with the boy's unique odor blown away, Mbasa expected little.

Before Sun had traveled a finger across the sky, Bird hooted. The call said her scouts hadn't rescued the boy but did find Others. Mbasa, Starlight, and Tor raced toward the sound, crawled up a hillock, and peeked over. Along its base spread a huge encampment of Other warriors, far more than the People's. Mbasa picked out Kiska in their midst, cheeks wet, a deep blue-purple bruise covering part of his face.

"Tor. Protect me," and she stood to her full height, hands tight around her weapons, and strode down the slope to a position just out of spear range.

Tor squealed his disagreement and then did as asked.

The Others faced Mbasa, neither hostile nor complacent. They seemed curious at this lone female who fearlessly approached a massive collection of well-armed warriors.

Mbasa greeted them as feet shuffled behind her, the People's warriors lining up along the crest of the cliff, spears up, warclubs on shoulders. They would adopt the implacable glare Tor taught them, the one that said they couldn't be defeated because they would never quit.

Without being asked, Tor moved to one side of Mbasa, Starlight to the other. Mbasa sniffed and found Bird and Hecate but not Rainbow.

Good. He would be in the way.

One of the Others—probably the Leader—stepped forward and Mbasa adopted a battle stance, weight over the balls of her feet, prepared to kick, pivot, or run. Her arms were loose and ready, one to swing a club and the other to fling a spear.

She studied the Other who must be the Leader as he studied Tor. This male might once have been a potent force but now appeared to be tired, made desperate by the misery of the land he lived in, his power as thin as the pelt that protected his dangling parts.

As he raised a hand, eyes still on Tor, Mbasa spoke. "I am Mbasa, Lead Warrior of Rainbow's People."

The Leader turned toward her, surprised at her weapons and stance.

He motioned, "Let me talk to your Leader." Mbasa bit back a laugh at what he must consider his intimidating glare.

"He is busy. I have come for our child. He became lost in the storm."

"We found him. Without us, he would not have lived."

Mbasa motioned to Tor in the People's language, "They could have rescued the child."

"Then why not allow him to leave?"

Mbasa gestured to the Other, "He was tethered to his mother. You cut the vine. Return him to us."

Mbasa adjusted her spear as she tightened her grip, sending the message she was ready if they caused trouble. Tor and Starlight did the same and behind, the scuff of feet told her the entire line of warriors mimicked her.

The Other Leader smirked. "We will not release him for free. Do you have food to trade?"

"We are as hungry as you."

He sneered. "Then we will leave, with the child."

Mbasa hardened her face. "Yes, leave, but without our group member." A subtle lift of her hand and Tor raised his spear, as did Starlight.

The Other Leader sneered again. "Your weapons cannot reach us. Why threaten?"

Mbasa kept her eyes forward. "You are mistaken," and Tor's two spears skewered the arms of warriors on either side of the Leader. What she had meant as a bluff became truth. Mbasa covered her surprise, but barely.

Tor gestured broadly to the Leader, arms raised, shouting, "If you attack, we kill your best spear throwers. Yes, some of us will die but most of your warriors will, starting with you, Leader. In the end, we leave with our group member and your People have no one to hunt for them. Do. Not. Challenge us."

"But you are females. You cannot win."

Mbasa offered Tor a dazzling smile and then turned back to the Leader. "Tell that to the warriors our Leader Xhosa fought—oh. You can't. They're all dead."

The Leader stiffened at Xhosa's name. After a breath, and another, he raised a hand and his warriors lowered their spears. A female nudged through the line of males dragging the People's boy forward by his hair. She threw him to the ground and kicked him toward Mbasa. The boy clambered to his feet, eyes red but dry, walking with measured steps toward

Tor as though to tell his captors he was unafraid. As he passed, Tor patted his back and then, with Mbasa and the warriors, backed away until the berm hid them. Bird and a handful of scouts stayed behind while the rest returned to the makeshift camp.

Mbasa eyed Tor with new respect. "You didn't tell me you could far-throw?"

"One of the males who joined while you were sick taught us. He learned it while a captive of Big Heads" After a breath, he added, "These Others, they are trouble."

"And we will be ready."

After hearing what happened, Rainbow motioned, hands defensive, face whiny, "Why imperil us over a child? You are foolish, Mbasa! I am the Leader and I say give them the child. We can make another!"

She wanted to tell him how stupid he sounded but clenched her teeth. She would save that for another time.

Instead, she waved him away dismissively. "This has nothing to do with Kiska."

His face reddened and he took a breath, then another before he could speak. "How many are there?"

Mbasa collected stones by the cliff wall. "This many."

Rainbow blanched, any response he might have wanted to make caught like a stone in his throat. Mbasa took the opportunity leave with Tor to search for a cave. They settled for a cliff, too tall to climb and too wide for a sneak attack. The warriors hid themselves in the surrounding landscape, prepared for the assault all knew would come.

At the meal that night, Tor pulled Mbasa aside. "I need to talk to you."

She followed him to a hidden area away from the group, where no one would hear their conversation. He must have seen the worry on her face.

"Our warriors are well-prepared. This is not about them, Mbasa."

"What then?"

"It's a mindset Nightshade adopted before a battle. He claims it was why he never lost."

"Tell me."

"Don't think you know your enemy."

When he said nothing more, Mbasa cocked her head. "I don't understand."

He looked away, eyes on something in the dark distance, and then returned his gaze to Mbasa's face. "Every fighter judges his opponent. We assume a horde of males with spears and warclubs are accustomed to battle. They assume because we are predominantly females, we can't fight.

"Wrong in both cases. Our warriors are well-prepared and committed to the cause. Our enemy is cocky and has judged us weak. Both are to our advantage. If we remember this, we will win. Like Nightshade did."

Before Moon arrived, the battle began. The Others flooded the encampment, thinking Mbasa wouldn't expect them at night. Their simple plan was to slaughter as many as possible which would force Mbasa and the remnants to flee.

They misjudged her. More importantly, they misjudged the loyalty and passion of her warriors. Had the Others treated this battle as they would one against a feared adversary, the result might have been different. Mbasa's determination to defend the People offset the inadequacy of her warriors. It didn't matter that the only one blooded was Tor. The relentless drills of the Leads—Mbasa, Bird, Hecate, and Starlight—made the fighters stronger than the enemy.

But something else assured victory. If the enemy lost, it was only a battle. If the People lost, it meant the end of everything. No one would let that happen.

Mbasa's warriors, with lethal accuracy, killed one opponent after another. When they exhausted their spears, they used throwing stones and warclubs. The enemy fled when they realized they were losing. The People chased them and massacred every warrior within range. No mercy was shown nor expected.

With Sun shedding only a dim glow over the horizon, the People crested a dry hillock and Tor flung his arm out to the side. Everyone stopped. There below milled the defeated warriors, most bleeding, some from being gouged by spears, others with arms dangling uselessly from savage hits with warclubs. Almost all had deep contused bruises where they had been struck by stone missiles. In front stood the Leader, his mouth hanging open, eyes red from grit, and leaning to the side, his spear now a crutch. When the People's warriors skylined themselves at the top of the cliff, the enemy shuffled into a ragged semblance of order behind the Leader but defeat hung heavy in the air.

They couldn't hide their gaunt hungry bodies, hollow eyes, and skin flaking from lack of water. The Leader approached Mbasa, hand open in peace. She and Tor matched his steps. When they were a spear throw apart, Mbasa raised an arm and her warriors stopped.

The Leader opened his mouth to speak but stopped at a shuffling sound behind him. His warriors moved aside and an elder strode through the crowd, pushed the Leader aside, and stepped to the front. Experience etched deep grooves in his cheeks and forehead. His back was bent and hands crooked from the illness suffered by many elders. Though with few remaining teeth and one eye glazed white, wisdom spilled from the other.

"I am Bako, Leader of the land you wish to cross. You have met my Lead Warrior, injured him it appears. Why are you here?"

Mbasa had no intention of answering questions and asked, "Why did you attack us? We told you we meant no harm. Did you not believe us?"

The Elder huffed. "We have no food. We hoped you did. The smallness of your group with many females—you looked like easy prey." He offered a tiny smile. "The child we captured—we meant to eat him. We are starving and cannot eat our own people."

Mbasa motioned, "We are not staying here. We go to where Sun sleeps, where water stretches along the horizon from one side to the other. That is where the rest of our People are."

The Elder motioned, "We have heard of only one group led by a female."

Tor answered before Mbasa. "You speak of Xhosa. She protects us. We journey to reunite with her. Let us pass or the mighty warrior Xhosa and her Lead Warrior Nightshade will return and take their revenge."

The Elder motioned behind him and all the warriors dropped their spears. "You may pass."

Mbasa held his eyes and frowned. "You have slaughtered some of our People. Their deaths must be avenged."

The Elder bent forward as though he expected this. "We have no food to share but we can provide a guide. You will need one. The land ahead for you is tricky and dangerous. Our enemies are not as reasonable as we."

He motioned and a wiry, scrawny subadult wriggled through the group. His bones pushed against his skin but his eyes sparkled with life and intelligence.

"Vaya lived in the land you wish to reach before he joined us. He can tell you how to get there. When you arrive at what he calls Endless Sea, he must return to us."

Vaya scurried past, grinning, without a backward glance at the Leader, like one who knew he had narrowly escaped a predator.

She motioned to Bako, "What if Vaya wishes to stay with his own tribe when we find them?"

Bako answered without emotion, "He won't. We have his sisters. If he doesn't return, they die," and then motioned his warriors to leave. It didn't take long before they disappeared.

When Mbasa, Tor, her warriors, and Vaya reached the camp, all that remained of the dead was the stink of carrion. Soon, that too would be forgotten.

"Rainbow, we have a guide to help us find where Endless Pond stops. There, we will cross and reunite with the People."

He didn't bother to look at her.

Chapter 29

Somewhere in modern-day Southern France

The journey to the People's new homebase settled into a predictable routine. The local tribes always treated Xhosa and her People well when they realized that this sizable band of weapons-bearing warriors wanted not to take their land but to cross it. In return, Xhosa often allowed small tribes to travel with the People. Though it only slightly increased the People's size, it served the purpose of teaching Xhosa about the areas she and her People would soon be crossing. Most confirmed what she already knew—that the greatest hazard was the land itself, its rugged mountains and frigid deadly terrain.

One such group included a young female named Nakhil. She and her small group—it took less than both hands to tick off all members—were traveling to their alternate homebase where they would live until the primary location's herds and plants replenished. Though she had been blinded by hot lava as a child, Nakhil "saw" as well as anyone by focusing on scents, tastes, touch, and sounds. This intrigued Seeker and he wrapped vines over his eyes to view the world as Nakhil did. With her guidance, he learned to explore even unfamiliar landscape with his senses. He felt the void created in the air by a boulder, smelled the earth disturbed by animal steps, tasted the warning left by Wolf and Panther when they marked their territory, listened to the voices of predators as they echoed off hills and rocks, heard even the slightest rasp of claw on stone, and alerted to the unexpected silence.

When Xhosa asked about it, he explained, "Sight silences what I hear, taste, and feel. It makes me think I know what is out there when I don't. For example, the sight of Wolf only tells me he is there, maybe has seen me. It doesn't tell me if I entered her territory or am close to her pups. Smells and sounds do."

Seeker and Nakhil became inseparable and Xhosa worried Seeker might remain with Nakhil when her group arrived at their new homebase. The bigger question was whether Pan-do would stay, also.

"Pan-do, would you join Seeker if he remained with Nakhil?" She tried to hide how much losing him and his group would weaken the People. He must do what was best, not be influenced by her needs.

"Of course I would, because of Lyta, but that won't happen, Xhosa. Nakhil has a pairmate. She simply repays our favor of allowing her People to travel with us by teaching Seeker her unusual ability. In return, he shares with her his delight for the world."

Xhosa smiled. "No one is more joyful than Seeker."

Pan-do continued, "Seeker wishes to learn what he can from her and then continue his quest for the stars. Wherever her People end up won't be where the stars tell Seeker to settle.

"At least, he doesn't think so."

But Pan-do avoided eye contact as he added, "The stars do change every night, according to Seeker, so I guess we won't really know until the day arrives that she stops migrating."

When Pan-do said nothing more, Xhosa wondered if he silently wanted Seeker to stay with Nakhil rather than follow Xhosa. She had hoped that when Nightshade's attention diverted from Lyta to Honey and Deer, he and Pan-do would regain their amicable if uneasy respect for each other but that hadn't happened. Something about Nightshade worried Pan-do and surprisingly, Spirit also. The wolf no longer hunted with her Lead Warrior and continued to growl at him if he approached Lyta.

Xhosa couldn't deny that during the last Moons, her Lead Warrior had become like a volcano about to erupt and she didn't know how to stop it. Pan-do must feel it too and didn't want his People destroyed when it happened.

To Xhosa's relief, when Nakhil's group reached their homebase, the sightless female and Seeker parted ways without comment. When Xhosa asked, Seeker responded, "I have learned what I needed. The stars move on so I must also."

Xhosa and her People threaded their way among boulders, skirted cliffs too steep to climb, and crossed grass-covered hills broken often by fissures. The one absolute—according to Seeker—was that their shadows must move from behind them to in front, just as Sun moved from its waking to sleeping nest.

The foothills resounded with the bleats and snorts of antelope and pigs falling to the male's spears. The females' stone missiles killed hares, ground birds, snakes, and lizards without the bright colors or pungent odors that meant poison. The children collected berries, tubers, nuts, and seeds, eating them when Viper approved. If she labeled them unfamiliar and Spirit wouldn't eat them, they were tossed. Mushrooms were always suspect and no one ate the orange crunchy roots as fat as a child's arm because some would kill. Xhosa carried a dwindling supply of charred wood for those who ate bad food but it didn't always work. If it failed, they must eat a stinky plant that forced them to vomit.

Graceful floating raptors hunted the plethora of mice who skittered through the brush. Clouds of flying insects made breathing difficult and brittle brown balls the shape of a handaxe littered the ground.

The higher up the hills the group trekked, the colder it got. Xhosa soon shivered despite her pelt and wished it covered her limbs as Spirit's did. Gradually, the air became almost too cold to breathe, burning their throats and insides with each inhale.

When white flakes fell from the sky, Xhosa asked Viper what they were. The young female's mouth softened and tears rolled down her cheeks.

"It is called snow, Leader Xhosa. My People often encountered it at the edge of our homeland. Dawa's People lived in it!" She stuck her tongue out. Flakes landed on it and instantly dissolved. "When it is cold enough to snow, meat lasts longer. The green flies and white worms don't appear as soon."

Soon, snow coated everyone's hair and pelts in white. Around her, as far as Xhosa could see, the land became smooth and white, interspersed with rocks, trees, and the occasional animal tracks. Landmarks Xhosa had picked to guide the back- and forward trail became indistinguishable. Then the wind increased from simply a gentle breeze caressing her skin to the howl of a storm. It whipped lose branches through the air, blowing the snow into piles against cliffs and trunks, forcing the People to plow through drifts that reached their knees and then hips. It became impossible to see and then tiny slivers of rocks filled the air. When those collided with Xhosa's bare skin, they burned like fire. No matter how Xhosa bunched the pelt around herself, or wrapped her arms around her chest, the ice found its way under or through.

"Nightshade." Her hands moved stiffly, her fingertips white with cold. "No one can see in this storm. We need a cave!"

Which was when a mother shrieked, *Danya!*—her child's call sign—and raced into the whiteness.

Xhosa grabbed for her arm and missed. "Stop! Tie a vine around yourself!" But the mother vanished into the swirling snow.

What to do? Was the risk to the People worth saving a mother and child who would most likely soon be dead?

As though Nightshade read her thoughts, he moved his hand waist-high over the ground, palm down. "I won't risk the lives of my scouts looking for a stupid child who should have known better. They can't see what is around them anyway."

Ant motioned, "I will go," but Nightshade dismissed him without a glance.

Xhosa offered a stiff nod of agreement but jerked toward the sound of Wind's voice. He appeared out of the mist, a child over his shoulder, dragging the female through the knee-high snow. He bent into the gale. Snow and ice caked his hair and it hung in frozen clumps but the child and its mother were safe.

She caught up to him. "How did you find them?"

"I followed the mother's prints. She found her child but got turned around when she couldn't see through the snow. Before we could track the prints back, the storm had erased every trace. I listened for the noise of the People, hoping those sounds would lead me here but could hear nothing over the wind's voice. That is, until I heard Spirit bark, over and over. He couldn't find me but knew, somehow, that I would hear him."

At Wind's side was the wolf, panting, mouth open in a grin, ears perked, tail swishing side-to-side through the snow.

The near miss convinced everyone to tie vines to each other. For those who must go beyond the distance of the vine, they built a chain of people. But that wouldn't prevent the People from slowly freezing to death.

Xhosa trotted up to Nightshade. "If we don't find shelter soon, many of the People will die. Have you seen anything?"

As though he heard her, Pan-do shouted, "I found a cave!"

Xhosa's tight shoulders sagged in relief as the People tumbled into the cave, grateful for the quiet reprieve from the wind and the blinding snow. Once her eyes adjusted to the dark, she wandered through, checking for anything unexpected. The hard dirt walls felt damp to the touch. Here and there, roots protruded. Dead leaves and twigs mingled with debris on the floor. To one side, old scratch marks had been etched into the rock, as deep as any Xhosa had ever seen. Doubtless, if the owner of those claws still lived here, Spirit would be growling.

Xhosa nodded to Nightshade. *This looks fine.*

Today, this cave provided sanctuary for the People.

Ant and several other males collected tinder from the corners, swiping away spider's webs so thick and white, none could see through them. As they worked, they crushed a handful of scorpions, chased away a nest of rats, and frightened off a snake sleeping on a ledge.

Ngili lit a fire well back from the mouth. As the wind whistled outside, sneaking through cracks in the cave walls, the People dried their pelts and gathered in small groups while they sharpened cutters and choppers.

But it wasn't enough. The next morning, children's fingertips had turned white from the cold and wet hair had frozen. No one knew how to get warm. Viper who had once lived here said she'd never seen it this cold.

They left the safety and relative warmth of the cave, traveled all day, and found another, no better than the last but a refuge. It was clear that something had to change and it didn't seem to be that the snow and cold would stop.

That evening, as they ate around the fire pit, Xhosa told of her plan. If the People weren't so desperate, they never would have tried it.

"We have fresh skins set aside to be turned into new pelts. We must clean them quickly so everyone can wear two—or more."

She paused as questions about when they would have time filled the air. She didn't answer any of them, motioning to each to be patient.

When the group fell silent, she continued, "We must change our routines. From now on, eat as you walk. When Sun sleeps, we sleep—skipping the group meal like this and the storytelling. When Moon's light arrives, we awaken and clean as many skins as we can before it's time to either sleep again or Sun returns. Even fur from Hare and small ground-dwelling rodents will be scraped and secured around hands and feet with vines.

"We start tonight."

Soon, the new routine became natural. The People rose with Sun, wrapped themselves in pelts, and trudged forward. Breath always a white cloud, ignoring the harsh wind that whipped the bare branches, they tried to rub heat into their arms that weren't covered by pelts, happy they would make more when Sun slept.

The changes slowed the People at first but then not at all. Sooner than Xhosa expected, landmarks once well out of reach moved behind them. The females and children scavenged anything as they walked, the hunters bringing down plenty of meat which was portioned out to all. No one missed the nighttime meal.

Honey sat by Xhosa in a cave, shivering under her pelts but ignoring the cold. She scraped a skin, removing bits of meat and blood, preparing it for salt. Xhosa glanced her way, wondering why she worked so slowly, and gasped. Purple-and-black bruises covered her arms and chest. Ragged cuts, all old, left painful red lines on her legs.

"Honey, where did you get so many injuries?"

She flushed, embarrassed. "I fall often. I am clumsy on hills, Leader Xhosa."

Bone went rigid, his face red with anger, but said nothing. If her injuries came from Nightshade—which Xhosa assumed they did—only Honey could change it. Pain was part of the package if you mated the People's mightiest warrior.

If Honey needed help, she would ask.

Since Nightshade hadn't assigned any duties to Wind, Xhosa invited him to check the cave's recesses with her, to make sure no animals lived or hid there and that none could slip in a rear entrance. She and Wind shuffled through the dirt and dead leaves that layered the passageways, tracked in by earlier inhabitants and wind. They passed many side tunnels, shallow puddles, and what sounded like water deep in one of the crevices, maybe as big as a stream but too far below for them to reach. Moss clung to the damp walls and spongy mushrooms grew in the deep cracks. She collected both, the moss for injuries, the mushrooms for food but she would have to check them in better light.

The whoosh of wings made Xhosa duck. "What bird lives in this darkness?"

"They are called bats—not birds. They are furry rats with wings as sturdy as Mammoth's hide and longer than my forearm, with eyes the size of Gazelle's. They sleep during the day and fly at night so we should be fine.

"Look down," and Wind pointed to soggy white spots glistening around Xhosa's feet. "That's their dung. Now look up."

Covering the cave's roof, what Wind called bats crowded together, wings folded against their bodies as they pressed together.

"Move warily, Xhosa, with no quick actions or sounds. You don't want them to be awakened."

Xhosa did as requested, fearful of how they might react to Upright creatures invading their home while they slept. Truthfully, if the slight breeze she felt on her face and chest didn't guarantee the presence of a rear exit, she would have returned to the front. Instead, they must find it and determine the potential risk for the People.

Avoiding the endless swath of bats overhead slowed the pair's progress as did the darkness in the twisted passages. They often ran into low ceilings and long narrow rocks that grew from the roof or rose from the floor. The roof spires dripped frigid water that collected into ground pools of clean, pure water.

Finally, the whistle of wind and a dim light ahead that grew as they approached told Xhosa they'd found the back opening.

"Good. It's too narrow for anyone to slip through."

Without a wasted breath, they returned to the front and the fire pit. Xhosa walked through the cave, sniffing for group members. The overwhelming odors of refuse, decayed carcasses, and musky fur made it impossible to determine who she found so she simply ticked off each scent on her fingers.

She froze in place, inhaling again, and then mumbled, "Someone is missing," but couldn't tell who until Viper hurried up.

"Xhosa. Deer went to relieve herself and didn't return—"

"But the vine around her waist—"

Viper shook her head. "She promised to stay within view of the cave."

Xhosa bit her lip as Nightshade approached. "Deer is missing, unless you found her in the back passages?"

Xhosa shook her head, pleased he'd noticed Deer's absence so quickly.

He motioned, "We will search for her when the storm ends."

Viper bristled. "She'll freeze!"

"No one should have gone out in these gales alone! If Deer doesn't know any better, Viper should have told her!" and he stalked off, making it clear his scouts wouldn't risk their lives for a female too stupid to take care of herself. Since Viper, Leopard, and Deer belonged to no group, anyone could make decisions for them.

Nightshade surprised Xhosa. Not the decision—that she agreed with—but his reasons. Usually, peril excited him so why not now? If he truly worried about the safety of his scouts, it would be the first time, or was this an opportunity to rid himself of what he now viewed as Deer's unwelcome attention?

"Xhosa." Viper tugged her to a quiet spot in the cave. "Nightshade took Deer outside last night. I snuck after them because I don't trust him. He growled something at her and she shook her head so he shoved her to the ground and left. I helped her up and asked why she put up with him. She said he promised to pairmate.

"I didn't tell her he made the same promise to Honey."

Xhosa sighed, tired of Nightshade and his females and his remorseless violence. She forced herself to respond with, "He wants only to keep the People safe," when what filled her thoughts was that somehow, for some reason, in Nightshade's increasingly twisted world, abusing females had become integral to his leadership.

"Viper, don't worry. Most females are flattered the Lead Warrior selects them for mating, hoping to have his strong baby."

"She is, too, Xhosa. I think she would trust him with her life. Is that what happened, Xhosa? He used her naivete to get rid of her?"

Xhosa motioned, "Of course not," but she wasn't as sure as her gestures indicated.

Viper hurried over to Leopard's side, her friend frozen in place, hands shaking, eyes wide with fear. When Viper wrapped her arms around Leopard, tears rolled down the subadult's cheeks but she made no sound.

Xhosa remained where she stood, now worried as much about Deer's disappearance as her Lead Warrior's strange behavior. Was it her fault Nightshade lost control, because she hadn't yet committed to pairmating? She meant to tell him she changed her mind, ask his patience until they found a new homebase, but it never seemed the right time. Recently, he spent most nights with other females. Why say anything if his interest in her had vanished?

Because hers had.

She mumbled under her breath, "No. I can't pairmate with Wind."

"Why not?"

Xhosa jerked. How long had he been standing there? His scent washed over her like a welcome breeze, his strength mingling with her need. She managed to turn her head away, hoping he wouldn't see the desire that knotted her stomach. In their short time together, Wind more than Hawk or Nightshade completed her. It made her a better Leader and allowed her to serve the People more fully.

"The People won't accept a Big Head as the pairmate of their Leader." She tugged on her hair and motioned one-handed, almost to herself, "What if I anointed Nightshade Leader?"

Wind moved her hand aside and ran her tresses over his palm. It calmed her which didn't make sense.

"Putting him in charge of your People—your father's People—is like allowing Thunder to control mine."

"Yet you did!"

Wind caught her eye. "He may think so but he is wrong."

She looked at him, tried to read his thoughts, but saw only a fixed expression, eyes staring blankly into the distance, dark and foreboding. When he finally faced her again, that was gone.

He motioned, "Your People—they left their homeland to follow you despite treacherous travel, hunger and thirst, and unknown enemies. They stayed when you chose Hawk and fled with you when the Ice Mountain invaders attacked. They trust *you*, not Nightshade. Don't take that lightly. I've rarely seen that in a Leader."

She couldn't deny that something happened in her absence, when Nightshade served as Leader. Relief laced the effusive welcome from her People. Even now, the thrill of a new home that had made every day an adventure prior to her kidnapping seemed to have dimmed. Only one thing she could point to had changed.

Nightshade.

"You're right, Wind. Resigning as Leader is wrong," which made committing to Nightshade the lone option.

Wind studied her for a moment and then gestured, "That–what you are thinking—won't stop the hate and darkness growing in your Lead Warrior. No doubt he once was noble and strong but now, he rots from within."

She huffed. "I must talk to him," and left, finding Nightshade at the front of the cave knapping a spear point. From here, no one came or went without him noticing.

He lifted his head until she could look into his eyes, tired but hopeful. He motioned, "Are you alright?"

His gaze dipped to her neck sack and back, asking silently about her head pain. His tone was the old Nightshade who sensed her moods before she did.

"Nightshade. I have something I must tell you—"

Behind her, Wind slowly exhaled.

Nightshade stood. "I know. We will talk about that soon."

The People awoke to a brutal cold worse than any they'd experienced. A thick layer of snow coated everything and icy flakes swirled through the air. The fire burned in the pit but did little to heat the cave. When Xhosa stepped outside to relieve herself, the wind almost knocked her over. Her water froze as it left her body.

Inside, many of the group suffered frozen ears, fingers, and toes that turned white and lost all sensation. Others shivered nonstop regardless of how tightly they wrapped themselves in pelts or how closely they clustered to the flames. Almost everyone's lips were blue and teeth chattered relentlessly.

Xhosa beckoned Nightshade, Pan-do, Wind, and Ngili toward her. She hadn't spent much time with Ngili since their return. Most of the day, he practiced knapping stone-tipped spears with Sa-mo-ke or hunting techniques with Wind. He gained his weight back and became again one of the best of the People's warriors.

Wind motioned, "Just tell me your decisions, Xhosa. That's all I need," and followed Viper to the murky rear passages of the cave where they would work on stone-throwing in the dark.

Xhosa huffed her displeasure but motioned to the rest, "Dawa warned of the cold if we took the wrong path. Ngili, do you think that's what happened?"

He eased down to his knees and placed his spear to the side within easy reach. "I have no doubt that this is the type of cold he told me I wouldn't be able to tolerate. And he's right."

Xhosa gritted her teeth, unhappy to lose time but eager to escape the bone-chilling cold. "We will backtrack when the sky clears."

All day, Viper and Leopard stayed by the mouth of the cave, searching the landscape for Deer. They were far enough back to be out of the wind but not the cold. Occasionally, Viper strode outside, peered through the storm, and then returned, ice already formed on her eyebrows and hair. She settled next to Leopard only to repeat the same moves later.

The entire group snuggled close to each other, shivering despite the fire, waiting for the storm to end, excited to be leaving this frigid land. Spirit's dense coat warmed Lyta on one side and Seeker on the other. Nightshade slept with Honey and Wind with Xhosa. No one slept alone. Xhosa wondered how Spirit's mate, the black wolf, survived. Spirit should bring her into the cave. Many would welcome her dense fur.

The next day brought more snow and wind. Viper drooped, knowing Deer couldn't survive this chilling cold, but refused to give up. The People remained huddled inside but Spirit left, quickly lost in the opaque whiteness. It didn't take long before Xhosa heard his pants, muzzle shrouded in white clouds, the black wolf at his side. Snow and ice covered both wolves.

Zvi motioned, "Come in, Spirit. Come in, Black Wolf. We will keep each other warm."

Spirit trotted inside and circled through the group. He paused to lick Lyta and Pan-do, huffed to Seeker, and wagged happily at Xhosa and Wind. Only when his pack was secure did he settle beside the black wolf at the mouth of the cave. They curled around each other and Spirit exhaled a gusty, patient sigh. Seeker joined them and cracked away the balls of ice and snow buried deep between the pads of their feet. Then, he rubbed his hands over their eyes and noses, the tips of their ears. Soon, the children and subadults enticed both wolves to join them. When everyone lay down to sleep, the children curled into the wolves' pelts, smiling, warm for the first time in days.

Xhosa murmured to herself, "When Spirit and the black wolf have their pups. Zvi can show how she raised Spirit. It would be good to have more wolves."

Sometime during the night, the snow stopped.

The next day, when Xhosa went to relieve herself, sunlight glistened off the whiteness and dimples spotted the otherwise untouched surface. At the edge of the camp, Spirit licked the black wolf's muzzle and they left together to hunt, paws crunching on the hard snow, her stomach distended.

Nightshade approached her. "The scouts say another storm approaches. We will be caught in the open if we leave now."

The day passed uneventfully and everyone went to sleep early, hopeful that the storm would pass during the night and they could leave tomorrow. Spirit returned with the black wolf, and lay next to Lyta, the black wolf by Seeker. Both curled into tight balls with their bushy tails wrapped over their noses.

Xhosa jolted awake. Outside was still dark. The fire at the front of the cave sputtered, no more than a weak glow as the Fire Tenders dropped twigs and tinder into the pit. A familiar odor drifted by, sweet and rancid like spoiled meat, but she couldn't place it. Spirit's blue eyes jumped between Lyta and Nightshade.

Something was wrong, Xhosa could feel it. She picked her way through the group and was relieved when she could account for everyone. She went outside to release her water, yawning. The storm had ended and Seeker's stars filled the sky. The odd scent was more biting out here, like something that died long ago and now sprouted the white worms.

When Xhosa awoke, the strange odor had faded. Seeker sat at her side in his awkward way of resting on his bottom with his legs crossed in front. The position couldn't be comfortable. A pile of stone shavings lay before him. He'd almost completed the handaxe started last night. His shabby pelt barely hid ribs too narrow for an adult. From him, though, they radiated strength. No one who spent time with Seeker thought him weak. For the first time, Xhosa understood why Pan-do and many of the People trusted this boy-male.

When she pushed herself up, Seeker brightened. "I know where we're going, Leader Xhosa. I will show you," and left. His voice conveyed the pride of a hunter when he finds a herd or a warrior when he repels an enemy.

Outside the cave, the stark shining whiteness of Sun's light bouncing off the icy ground left her half-blind. She closed her eyes to slits and caught up with Seeker.

He continued speaking, his hands eager and filled with energy, "The stars I was looking for showed up last night," and he explained how two—Always There Star and Bright Star—remained constant while the rest revolved through the night sky. Their positions as they moved told him what he needed.

Xhosa scratched under her arm. "I don't understand."

Seeker tried again. "The star-filled sky is to me what your homebase is to you. You recognize everything that lives there, know what grows where, are familiar with all the landmarks that guide you home. Anything out of place, like broken grass or scratched bark, tells you what animals or Uprights have been there.

"The stench from last night—" He caught her eye. "You knew it didn't belong."

Before she could ask if he recognized it, he continued with the original topic. "I have that same familiarity with how the stars spread across the darkness, where each should be, which group grows or shrinks. Those changes tell me where to go."

He grinned as though he'd explained everything perfectly. Xhosa hid her continued confusion.

The People set out, happy the storm had ended. Xhosa and Pan-do led with Seeker a shadow's length behind. Zvi,

Lyta, and Ant came next and then Siri and the rest of the People. Ngili and Wind brought up the rear. No one minded the bitter cold, tempered by the Sun and clear skies, because they were leaving.

Before they'd gone far, a scream shattered the calm. Xhosa rushed toward it and found Viper leaning over something.

"Deer—she's dead," and Viper vomited.

Xhosa edged around the young female and gasped. Deer's caring eyes were glazed and sightless, her skin blue in places, white in others, and her entire frail body rigid with cold. The side of her skull was crushed, the squishy gray matter inside exposed. A leg and arm were missing as though torn away by a predator.

Viper wiped the back of her hand over her mouth and then gently brushed the snow from Deer's face. Tears streamed down her cheeks as she stood. When Nightshade arrived, she shouldered past him, fists clenched, eyes angry slits. Deer had survived the loss of her entire family, the tortures of her captors, and a perilous trek to join a new group with no guarantee of acceptance. She overcame it all by strength of will but couldn't survive what attacked her here, in the frozen mountains.

Xhosa's stomach heaved and she swallowed the bile that threatened to force its way from her mouth. Blood and death didn't bother her—she'd seen as much as any warrior—but something about this scene struck her as wrong. She scanned the body, the surroundings, and sniffed, not knowing what she expected. Did Deer fall so hard, her head exploded when it hit the tree trunk? No, blood didn't speckle the wood, nor was the bark sharp enough to cut skin. Xhosa had seen many skulls cracked in battle. It took immense power to burst one, as Deer's had. No injury Xhosa could think of would do it except for one.

Deer hadn't caused her own death. Someone killed her.

At the edge of the group, Spirit whined. When Xhosa didn't object, he padded forward and smelled the body—not as a predator but as he might to pick up a trail. After a long few breaths, his muzzle rose and pivoted slowly through the open-mouthed group, resting finally on Nightshade. The wolf's hackles stiffened and his fangs glistened beneath curled lips.

The Lead Warrior strode to Deer's body and kicked Spirit aside. "Keep the wolf away," which made no sense. The missing limbs said animals had already fed on her.

Nightshade gestured, "Ngili—you and Bone find her tracks!"

Xhosa doubted any would be found, after the latest snow.

She motioned to him, "This wasn't an accident—"

"A Big Head killed her!" He glared at Wind with such raw savagery, Xhosa cringed.

Wind stepped forward, fists clenched, feral scrutiny on Nightshade. "If my kind was involved, we would have captured her, one-known-as-Lead-Warrior, not killed her. As we did with Ngili. Whoever did this to Deer was so filled with rage, he lost control—"

"He?" Xhosa gestured.

Eyes still on Nightshade, Wind gestured, "Only mating makes a groupmate this angry," and he joined Ngili and Bone to search for a trail.

"Nightshade, Wind didn't do this. In all our time together, he slaughtered only those who captured me and then only because they wanted to kill us. They deserved it."

Pan-do motioned, "Why would anyone execute Deer? Females are valuable not just to us but to all Others. And with her youth, she would have born many babies."

After a pause, he added, "This looks like cannibals."

Xhosa's breath caught in her throat and saw what she had missed earlier. The limbs weren't chewed as a predator would, rather chopped off like those eaten by the cannibals who once captured her and Pan-do. It made her gag.

The smell from last night, like honey poured on a carcass, came back to her with a jolt.

Ngili approached Nightshade. "The snow obliterated the trail. There is nothing to follow."

Xhosa caught Ngili's attention. "Did Dawa mention cannibals?"

Ngili's eyes narrowed. "No."

Lucy appeared in Xhosa's dreams that night, for the first time in a while. The ancient female traveled with her pairmate, two children, and the huge wolf named Ump. The landscape around her was devoid of vegetation, brush, and scrub. The wind whipped the silt as it did the snow in Xhosa's world. Then, without warning, Xhosa was running with Lucy, the rest of her tribe gone. Her breath wheezed, her mouth too dry to spit. As the day's light waned, Lucy flung rocks at a pile of carrion birds. They soared into the air and Lucy sprinted to the carcass, drank the blood while Xhosa slashed away as much meat as the two could carry. A Big Head joined them. When Lucy and Xhosa left, he devoured what remained of the carrion.

He was not Lucy's problem…

The next day, the People put Deer's death behind them. Death was part of life. Everyone had lost family or group members. In Deer's case, most believed a predator killed her—like the giant Bear they'd encountered earlier. That was acceptable because all animals had to eat, as they ate Pig or Gazelle. It also helped that most didn't know her well because she always stayed with Leopard and Viper. She wasn't of the People.

Leopard now shadowed Siri and Viper stayed on the backtrail with Ngili and Wind, armed with her spear, her warclub, and her increasingly angry attitude. At night, when she and Leopard slept beside each other, Viper always had her spear close.

As Sun peaked overhead, the People stumbled out of the frigid mountains into the dry brown foothills. They followed their backtrail far enough to have a good view of the mountain range and where Dawa's passage might be. When they stopped to rest, the children started a riotous game of step-on-the-shadow. Xhosa chewed through most of a soft root and a handful of sweet berries but food did nothing to lessen her unease. It sat like a stone in her stomach.

More like a boulder.

She mentally shook off Deer's death and considered the new problem she faced. Where was the passage?

She approached Seeker. "Dawa must have been confused."

"No, he wasn't. It's right there, Xhosa, where both he and the stars said it would be," and he pointed to a hazy spot nestled between two ridges, almost invisible thanks to a dense layer of saplings.

Tears burned her eyes as she leaped to her feet. "Dawa's gap."

Stride wide, head up, arms swinging, Seeker let out a whoop. Zvi hustled her massive bulk after him while Lyta sang a joyous birdsong. With her walked Pan-do, his group, and Xhosa's People. The former Hawk-People-now-known-as-the-Nightshade-People brought up the rear.

Xhosa couldn't see Viper but knew she was on the backtrail, with Wind and Ngili.

As Sun peaked and began the long trip to its nighttime nest, Xhosa caught up with Pan-do. "How is Lyta?"

"She is fine. Spirit decided to spend part of his time with her and the rest with Leopard but I think he will soon herd Leopard over to Lyta where he can watch both at the same time!"

"Do you think Leopard is in danger?"

Pan-do shrugged. "I don't but Spirit and Lyta must. They can't always explain why but I trust their instincts. And Leopard is frightened she'll be next. Her hands tremble all the time. She won't eat, won't even release her water alone. Spirit senses her need and goes with her any time she must leave the group."

As Dawa's gap grew from blurry mirage to a real destination, the People began to chatter as they had before life-threatening hazards and fatigue became daily companions. Viper and Leopard took over Deer's responsibilities without complaint except for mating with Nightshade. Leopard was too young and Viper too toxic. Nightshade found other options.

When Leopard began to bleed, Viper made it her responsibility to approve mates but none satisfied her. When rejected, no one argued. Her prowess with the spear and her aggressiveness in a confrontation had become legend. Xhosa couldn't help but be proud of this former captive who had been abused and tortured much of her life. Now, Viper had turned herself into a warrior.

What she wanted was to be Lead Warrior.

That wouldn't happen until she challenged Nightshade. Wind, who trusted Nightshade as much as he would a scorpion, counseled patience. The right day would come and Wind would make sure she was ready. Viper reminded him it wasn't death that frightened her. It was not avenging Deer. She and Wind agreed to a compromise. She would challenge Nightshade after avenging Deer.

Both agreed that would likely happen at the same time.

Despite the buoyant spirits of the People and the respect of his warriors, Nightshade grew more irritable each day. Ignoring his truce with Wind, he began poking at the Big Head behind his back. Few warriors agreed with him but wouldn't risk conflict. Xhosa no longer wondered whether the poison in her Lead Warrior would overwhelm the good. She now questioned if she could stop him.

This confrontational and inequitable approach repulsed Xhosa and—she was sure—would have repelled her father. Increasingly, when she needed ideas, she went to Wind. It started when she asked him how to defeat the Big Heads should they again attack. She expected him to push back but instead, he showed her the clever defensive and offensive techniques that had given her enemy the advantage in earlier battles.

Collaboration became respect and then trust. If Xhosa could feel this for one Big Head, maybe she had misjudged them.

One day, as they walked, she motioned, "I thought I hated all Big Heads but maybe I just hate Thunder."

He laughed with a gusto she hadn't expected. "Few of my kind are like Thunder. Many want satisfying lives without blood and battles, like your People."

She motioned, "I still must avenge my father but I think that should be directed at your brother, not your People. Are you alright with that?"

"I will probably join you, Xhosa. Thunder has dramatically changed life for many since my father died and rarely for the better."

When Xhosa caught up to Nightshade and explained her changed thinking, he refused to even listen. That worried Xhosa. It was the first time their differences were irreconcilable and as Leader of the former Hawk-People-now-the-Nightshade-People, his position equaled Xhosa's in both size and power.

He faced her, feet spread, spear in hand. "Rethink this, Xhosa. I don't need to compromise anymore. You do."

Xhosa backed away and snarled, "You do realize your People still call themselves the former Hawk People. Few have forgotten Hawk's respectful, peaceful leadership. You are not either!"

She pivoted and left, not interested in Nightshade's reaction. What she did know was that her focus on Big Heads had clouded her vision. Her biggest enemy was closer to home. She thought back to the whispered conversation long ago where Nightshade made plans with someone to take over the People. Xhosa never knew who that was.

Back then, she had called it impossible. Now, it seemed a matter of time.

Chapter 30

The screech of an owl startled Nightshade as he squatted on his heels in the mouth of the cave. He hadn't been able to sleep. The fire had long since given up the last of its heat but it wasn't the cold that kept him awake. The stars twinkled in the frigid dark. Snow dusted the ground, dotted with prints from Wolf and ground-dwelling birds. Nightshade's breath frosted in a misty cloud in front of him, his body buffeted by a chill breeze. Behind him, the snores of group members drowned out the noise of his movement.

Nightshade burned inside. He never expected Xhosa to turn on him. She had become a prize to Hawk and now, to the Big Head Wind, a way to solidify their control. They were wrong, of course. Nightshade and his warriors—Snake, Stone, Ngili, and the rest—bestowed command. Without them, she had none.

He intended to keep the promise made to Xhosa's father, with or without her help.

"The time has come for us to pairmate. First, I destroy her supporters," he murmured, surprised he'd spoken the words aloud.

Luckily, no one heard, everyone soundly asleep after another arduous climb through the mountains. He would start with the goofy Seeker who followed stars to find their new homebase. Then, it would be the slow-and-dumb Zvi, finishing with the clumsy Lyta. That last would drive away Pan-do without having to battle his warriors. Some of them—like Sa-mo-ke—were talented. With Xhosa's support gone, Nightshade had no doubt the Big Head Wind would flee as he did when his brother confronted him.

Then, Xhosa would come back to him.

His first opportunity to reveal his plan came the next night as the People prepared to share the food collected that day.

Before anyone had begun, Nightshade stood, waited for silence, and motioned, "Any who expect meat must hunt."

Xhosa caught his eye, surprised but didn't interfere. The hunters were Nightshade's job.

Zvi gulped and glanced from Xhosa to Seeker. When neither spoke, Zvi motioned, hands soft, "Which of course doesn't apply to us, Lead Warrior—"

Nightshade interrupted. "This does include you, one-called-Zvi. Things have changed. You must have noticed," he sneered. "Instead of the safety of a homebase, we are traveling unknown territories without dependable herds to feed us."

Zvi's eyes widened and her mouth dropped open. "One-called" was appended to the call sign of strangers.

She sputtered but Nightshade paid no attention. "Why should we feed you if you won't feed yourself? You must agree with the logic."

Seeker spoke, hands calm, "I am not going to argue with you, Nightshade. Zvi, Spirit, and I are able to find our own food—"

"And me," Lyta stood, voice so soft no one would have heard her if they hadn't already been stunned into silence.

Seeker responded benignly. "Of course."

Zvi blew out a slow breath as her shoulders relaxed and her hands unclenched. Seeker always had good solutions to problems.

Nightshade smirked. A crack now split the group, he and his warriors on one side and Xhosa's most ardent supporters on the other.

But he wasn't finished.

"I want to be clear." He let that hang in the already brittle air. Some probably hoped he would offer solace to Seeker and Zvi but those closest to him knew better. Still, none expected his next words.

"You, Seeker and Zvi, are cowards. You refuse to hunt because you are afraid of the herds, frightened of injury. We," and he extended his arms over the entire group, "can no longer support those like you who don't contribute."

Zvi did in fact refuse to join the hunters though the reason had nothing to do with any possible fear she suffered when facing a dangerous animal. Because she didn't. Though an Other, Zvi was raised by Giganto, an enormous Upright with such prodigious strength few could stand against him. Giganto understood Zvi's anxiety over her size—he shared the same worry—so Giganto taught Zvi to view conflicts through the eyes of her attackers and respond with force only when it became the only option.

When Zvi fought, death and injury always followed and she didn't know how to control that outcome.

So, Seeker refused Nightshade's order because Zvi did, even though that decision made both look weak. The People despised weakness as much as cowards. It was culled from the group without mercy. Females wouldn't mate with cowards and none—including mothers—would protect them. In the end, they must change or die.

Now, Seeker and Zvi had been called out.

Most of the People no longer noticed that Zvi was lumbering and clumsy. None had forgotten her impassioned defense of the Hawk People and her tireless rescue of those who would have drowned. Those she saved marveled at her agility and speed and the strength in her tree trunk arms and legs.

But these traits paled in significance to what most had never seen, the quality that made her a greater threat than spears, warclubs, or physical power.

Like her mentor Giganto, when enraged, Zvi fought to win.

The ground vibrated, enough to wake Zvi. Eyes now wide open, senses alert, she felt a dampness in the air that hadn't been there a breath before and then the soft breeze of displaced air. Zvi recognized these as signs that a handful of unskilled warriors were trying to sneak up on herself and Seeker.

They would fail.

She rose silently, making sure not to disturb the nighttime shadows cast by trees, rocks, or bushes, and then roared. The echoing threat in her voice froze her assailants long enough for her to grab two of them by their arms, swing them around, and then release, allowing them to fly wherever they would. They tumbled through the air, once and again, and then slammed into a stand of trees. When they crashed to the earth, they lay there, unmoving. Their eyes didn't even flutter. Two of the other would-be attackers backpedaled at the sight of Zvi's incomparable dominance, appalled that it could have been them lying in a heap at the base of a tree. That gave Zvi the opportunity to sprint forward faster than a creature her size should be able to run and punch her Sabertooth-sized open palms into their chests. She kept her fingers spread to minimize the damage to their bodies. One bounced off a boulder and the other a tree trunk. When they landed, not far from their fellow attackers, they too were silent, bodies still.

Zvi pivoted on the balls of her feet, searching for more attackers, but any others—if there were others—had fled, not wanting any part of this gargantuan female. After a long breath, her arms relaxed and she padded to Seeker's side.

"It ended more quickly than I expected."

Seeker stood, yawning, and pointed to one of the bodies. "His leg shouldn't bend forward at the knee, should it?" Seeker dropped to the ground and mimicked the position of the injured warrior. After a good but failed effort, he rose, shrugged, and turned his attention to the other unconscious figures.

"These two—their chests are too flat—"

"Something snapped when my palm hit them," Zvi mumbled. "I didn't even push him with all my strength, Seeker."

Seeker traced the hollow space under his hand. "Zvi, I don't think they'll bother us anymore this night. We are safe. Thank you for the assist."

With those words, he went back to sleep while Zvi sporadically poked the motionless shapes to see if they lived. They did, though barely.

Zvi hung her head, breathing deep and labored. Spirit plopped down beside her and closed his eyes.

"Was I too rough, Spirit? I couldn't let them hurt Seeker."

The next assault came again at night, as Seeker lay on his back, eyes closed, talking to the stars. He was so wrapped up in the conversation that he missed the out-of-place scent but Spirit didn't. He awoke from a sound sleep curled next to Lyta and Leopard, knowing danger was near. A sniff found only the scents of his extended pack. That confused him. He might have fallen back to sleep but his wolf instinct recognized fear mixed with aggression which usually preceded an attack. And that didn't fit the group members he lived with.

His eyes popped open and he rose, knowing that potent mix of fright and fight always carried with it danger.

Seeker, where he lay, now listening to the stars' instructions for the next day, heard snarls and growls but was too lost in his conversation to do anything. It wasn't until the wet suck of fangs and an anguished cry from a voice he didn't recognize that Seeker forced himself back to the world. Spirit panted up to his side, muzzle spread in a grin, big paw on what was now nothing more than a carcass. Blood dripped from the wolf's fangs and colored the ground below a deep red.

"Spirit! Are you alright?"

The wolf huffed as Seeker checked him for injuries. Finding none, he scratched his fur and rubbed a favorite spot between his ears.

Seeker motioned, "I can see you have it in control, Spirit," and resumed his attentive exploration of the night sky. Spirit stayed with the unconscious and dead attackers until one of Nightshade's warriors arrived to drag him away.

The next night, the attackers avoided Zvi and Seeker, their focus on Spirit. A handful of warriors covered themselves in wolf dung and snuck up on Spirit as he slept with Lyta. They had no problem with the wolf but were told they must kill him. None questioned their Leader.

The plan was to rush the wolf from all sides. A few would be bitten but the wolf would die. Still too far away to attack, a low growl rumbled through the thin night air. It came not from Spirit but across the clearing. The warriors froze as they tried to make sense of how Spirit could be in two places at once. While they ran through the possible answers, rejecting each, Spirit snapped awake. Fangs bared, he snarled and prepared to defend.

"Leave them alone, Spirit. They don't know what they're doing. Maybe I can dissuade them from the mistake they're about to make."

Pan-do materialized behind the warriors. Most he recognized from training sessions not long ago when they were subadults. He placed his hand level above the ground, gaze fixed on Spirit. The wolf huffed as though disappointed.

Pan-do's icy scowl moved on to the disheveled group in front of him. "You're from the former Hawk People. Where are your Leads, Snake and Water Buffalo?"

The warriors shuffled backwards without answering, bodies prickled with sweat despite the cold. One tripped and crawled on his hands and knees, stopping when Pan-do placed a heavy foot on his stomach.

"Did Nightshade tell you killing the wolf served the People?" Pan-do barked a mirthless laugh. "You have much to learn. If you had succeeded, he would have denied any knowledge of your actions. You'd be thrown out of the People to die alone! How stupid are you?"

The warriors jerked as the truth dawned. "We weren't after your daughter, Leader P-Pan-do. Nightshade—he s-said the w-wolf is a th-threat!"

Wind appeared at Pan-do's side, spear in one hand, a rock in the other. Rage seeped from his body like steam from Fire Mountain. The would-be-attackers took one look at him and turned to flee, only to find the black wolf blocking their way, her fangs bared, hackles up. There was no escape for them.

Xhosa strode forward, fists bunched. "What happened?"

Pan-do gestured, "The black wolf saved Spirit, and maybe Lyta."

Spirit skulked to the black wolf's side, ears pinned back, legs bent. He licked her face and nuzzled her neck, all the while whining softly.

Pan-do motioned, "These idiots—Nightshade's warriors—tried to sneak up on Spirit but the black wolf's growl woke Spirit."

The muscles in Xhosa's jaw bunched and she swiped a hand across the group. "Go! I will talk to Nightshade. He will punish you or I will banish you."

They fled like a wildfire in a drought.

Wind shared a glance with Pan-do and then he too left. Lyta fell asleep with Spirit again tucked by her side. Both wolves lay flat on their bellies, heads between their paws, eyes nothing more than slits, and ears perked.

Xhosa and Pan-do slipped out of the camp and climbed a hill with oversight of the area. They hid in a thicket at the crest, ready if Nightshade attacked again. Xhosa saw him sleeping next to Honey, chest rising and falling slowly, hand resting on her hip. Xhosa's head pounded, sharp and heavy, so she chewed the last of the plant from Fang and massaged her temples. Soon, the thudding became a dull ache.

After checking the surroundings and finding no movement, she began to shake. Tears rolled down her cheeks and her lips quivered so violently she bit the lower one until it bled.

"Nightshade has become a stranger to me, Pan-do. He's always been vicious and brutal but in the past, it was only when required. The old Nightshade, the one who sat with me late into the night as we learned from my father, the one who would be my pairmate—he would never hurt his own People."

Pan-do stared into the darkness, waiting until she was silent and then waiting longer.

Finally, he motioned, "I think he's done, Xhosa. He won't risk more failures. The warriors whisper about his blunder— his misjudgment—attacking two as powerful as Spirit and Seeker. They worry Spirit will retaliate, bring not just his mate but a pack of wolves to tear our throats out in our sleep."

He swished his hand through the air, agreeing before she said anything—*That will never happen.*

She motioned, "If he thought he could kill Spirit and Seeker, who's next?"

"I think they're warnings," Pan-do mumbled, as though thinking out loud. "That no one is safe. He does as he pleases—no one controls him."

That sounded right. "He never asked you or me whether we agreed with changing the rules for Seeker and Zvi, just did it, in front of everyone. He knew we'd disagree—"

"As do most of the People. They kept silent because they're accustomed to following what a Leader or Lead says. But the warriors are confused. Zvi saved many in the battle with the Ice Mountain enemy. And Seeker—well, all respect the wolf's power. Now with the black wolf—no, I think Nightshade will wait until we're settled to do anything else."

And then, as though the thought just popped up, he motioned, "But if his plan is to take control, it is working. He earned the loyalty of Hawk's warriors when he fought shoulder-to-shoulder with them against the Ice Mountain invaders. Then he beat Water Buffalo in the challenge and tricked Wind into allowing him to continue as Lead Warrior. Nightshade has proven himself clever and manipulative."

Xhosa gulped in the icy air, reveling in the pain. "Will it take everyone else as long as it took me to see through him?"

"I already do, as do Ngili, Bone, and Ant. Wind has distrusted Nightshade since he arrived. And let's not forget Viper. She still blames him for Deer's death. Her talent with a spear and a throwing stone equal any warrior. You will be glad to have her as an ally should it come to that. The question is, why do we not act against him?"

"Me, I hope he'll change back." Xhosa tapped a hand on her thigh and finally gestured, "How did I let this happen, Pan-do?"

"The simple answer is, our group has grown. It is larger than your father's. The males fight for power and the females squabble over males."

"It's my job to prevent that sort of confusion from devolving to chaos."

He looked at her sharply. "It serves no one to blame yourself. These events were complicated by your long absence, Hawk's death, and admittedly, my mild leadership. I shoulder part of the blame. My approach works with my People but Nightshade uses it against me."

"OK. I'm happy to share blame. The question is what to do." Without giving him a chance to respond, she continued, "You once told me Nightshade was working against me. I didn't listen. I wonder how different things would be if I had. I won't make that mistake again. Tell me what you see."

He shifted slightly, eyes searching the darkness. Xhosa heard the sound too. A shape darker than the night approaching the People's sleeping forms—the black wolf. She carried a dead animal in her jaws. With a huff, she settled into what would be her den this night, where she had a good view of Spirit. A flash of blue eyes said Spirit saw her, too.

Finally, Pan-do gestured, "The People are tired and weary. The length of the migration is one factor but the biggest is your Lead Warrior."

"What do you mean?"

"I think we agree he no longer acts in the best interest of your People. In your absence, he tasted leadership and liked it. When you reclaimed your position, he decided to bide his time as Leader of the former Hawk People.

"And for some reason I can't begin to understand, all of this changed him."

With an effort, Xhosa unclenched her fists and flattened her expression. "I need to replace him as my Lead Warrior. I asked him to consider Sa-mo-ke as his replacement, if that's alright with you. I also suggested Ngili. I need to push him to make that decision."

Pan-do folded his hands in his lap. "Back to your original question, I have an idea that might help with the Seeker-Zvi problem. I think Nightshade insists they become fighters because they will fail—they aren't warriors or hunters—and that will reflect badly on you. You can diffuse this by making Zvi and Seeker Primary Guides, their job to find a path to the new homebase. They can work with you as does Siri. It will give them authority among the People and place them out of Nightshade's reach. He will have to treat them with respect."

Xhosa smiled at Pan-do's cleverness. She should have thought of that.

"I'll announce the change immediately."

Chapter 31

Nightshade crouched in the shadows, the chill wind pelting him with shards of ice, watching as Xhosa elevated Seeker and Zvi to Primary Guides. This must be Pan-do's idea. Xhosa wouldn't think of it on her own.

His anger grew until finally, the seed of an idea sprouted. *Pan-do says he stays because the People's size keeps him safe. What if I change that?*

How easy it had been to kill Deer. When Nightshade told her Viper needed help, Deer hurried out of camp with him immediately, wearing only her thin pelt. She brought no weapons, not even her neck sack, assuming Nightshade would take care of her. She smiled when he took her hand and led her to a secluded area, crumbled when he hit her with his warclub and died when he hit her again.

It pleased him when most of the People blamed a stranger—or Bear. Because she wasn't really part of the People, they quickly forgot about her death even though Nightshade dutifully sent warriors and scouts in a search for the unknown killer. When he found nothing, everyone eagerly moved on, willing to forget the macabre end to the young female's life. Xhosa agreed with him when he said an animal killed Deer. The only one who questioned Nightshade's search was Viper. From that day on, she looked at him as though she knew what he'd done, and because of that, so too did Leopard.

He would take care of both soon.

Nightshade licked his lips and imagined Deer's strangled expression when she realized he meant to kill her, how his penis stiffened when she shrank from him. That he decided her future intoxicated Nightshade.

Something unexpected happened when he sliced the two limbs from Deer. He'd intended to mimic what a predator would do when it tore limbs from a carcass, scavenging the fresh meat, but he lost himself in the pungent aroma of wet tissue still steaming with life from her newly-dead body. He panted as he imagined the hot blood rolling down his throat, could almost taste it on his tongue. Without thinking, he bit into the limb, sucked the fluid out and savored the glorious sweet flavor in his mouth. He'd eaten many kinds of animals but never did they make him feel so filled with life. He remembered his disdain for the cannibals Koo-rag had warned of, that they ate People. Now, he understood.

He expected Deer's flesh to be chewy and stringy, like Gazelle, but the texture was more like Pig, tender like piglets. He guzzled down Deer's leg and then arm, never pausing to wonder who might see him. He didn't care. He'd eat them also. When he finally finished, he cleaned the blood from his face and hands with snow and buried it in drifts away from the ghoulish scene. Then, he snuck back into the temporary camp. He was sure he made no noise but for some reason, Xhosa awoke. Her fist tightened around her spear as she scanned the group, nose twitching. He stiffened when she settled on him and then breathed a sigh when she smiled and moved on, still sniffing, still trying to find the source of the smell that had awakened her.

He looked down at his body, felt around on his pelt. Had he missed a splatter of Deer's blood? That's when he recalled the cannibals and their strange sweet smell, one that leaked from inside of them.

He slept soundly and didn't awaken until daylight broke over the horizon. He rose, stretching, and nonchalantly glanced over at Xhosa. She seemed to have forgotten about whatever had roused her the night before. When Deer was discovered, ravaged and chewed, Xhosa paid him no more attention than anyone else.

Nightshade swallowed the icy air. His plans to take over the People must happen soon. Or he'd need another victim.

Chapter 32

"Spirit agreed to teach me to track prey."

Lyta stood with the wolf, her bright eyes fixed on her father, Spirit panting happily. As Pan-do studied her, Lyta pulled up, wanting to look taller, more capable. When her mother died, Pan-do told her everything would be OK, that he would always keep her safe. She never objected to his guidance until Seeker entered her life. Now, she must prove that when she bled, she could also pairmate.

She motioned, "Spirit has already started."

She knew what her father would say next, that she had work to do. Dawa's path wound through the icy white mountains. If they didn't find a chasm, they must go over. Either way, every animal skin available must be prepared.

"I finished a pelt for myself and one for Spirit, but I need more skins," and then she calmly stroked Spirit's neck and back rather than continue the argument.

Spirit huffed his agreement, brows bunched.

Many breaths passed. She hardened herself, expecting rejection just as her father finally motioned, "Another female disappeared—one of the former Hawk People. Her family thinks she might have tired of migrating, wanted a tribe to settle with, though no one expected her to leave. They fear whoever slaughtered Deer took her."

"Spirit and I will find her tracks, if they are any."

Pan-do knelt in front of the wolf. "I trust you, Spirit. Keep my daughter safe." He pointed to a spot in the sky and glanced over to Lyta. "Return when Sun reaches here," and the pair loped off, never looking back.

The camp was far behind them by the time Spirit found the first prints. Their scent was hidden under mud and dung. Some large animal must have stepped on it after the female left it. Spirit sniffed deeply, padded over to another set, completely unlike the first prints, and sat on his haunches.

"What have you found?" Though based on Spirit's wagging tale, she figured it must be the black wolf.

Then, Spirit's tail stiffened, as did his hackles and his pleased pants turned to growls. From behind a boulder, Nightshade appeared, armed with his spear, warclub, and throwing stones. Lyta didn't need to see his eyes to feel the evil around him. She swallowed her good humor and sidled toward Spirit.

Nightshade motioned, "The scouts report strangers coming this direction. You are too far from the camp. I will show you a shortcut."

His hand motions were benign but his shifting eyes gave away the lie. Lyta sniffed the air for strangers, not expecting any, and found instead the sweet odor that of late wafted from Nightshade, like he rolled in a carcass covered in wildflowers. Spirit did that but she'd never seen the Lead Warrior do it.

She motioned to Spirit in gestures only he would understand, *Not safe. Run,* and then motioned to Nightshade.

"Did Seeker send you, Lead Warrior?"

Nightshade bristled and leaned toward her. "Seeker blathered about an out-of-place star. He makes no sense."

Lyta gasped and then stumbled backward as though pushed. *He might also see strangers. Maybe I'm wrong that Nightshade lies.*

Unless who I must be wary of is Nightshade.

Spirit fixed his malevolent gaze on the Lead Warrior. When Nightshade didn't back away, Spirit growled, canines uncovered, eyes bright.

"Control him or he dies."

Spirit snarled louder, ears flat, and slapped the ground with his paws. Lyta put herself between the two.

"Spirit. Calm," she gestured, palm down and level though not turning from Nightshade. Like Spirit, she didn't trust the male who tasted like evil. Chills sluiced through her body like the fire that shot through the night sky.

Nightshade's lips tugged up but his eyes remained dark and angry. "We will go," and he sped off, crested a bluff, and was gone.

Lyta bit at her lip and motioned, "Something is wrong, Spirit, but I too saw the prints of the black wolf. She could be the one in danger." The wolf shook vigorously, clearly saying they should not go with Nightshade. Lyta nodded. "We will stay alert."

Why Nightshade disliked her so severely, Lyta didn't know. Her father said he once wanted to mate her but calmly moved on to Honey when told she had picked Seeker.

She hobbled after Nightshade, or rather his tracks, in tense silence. Spirit followed but then pulled up, growling, paws spread beneath his powerful shoulders, tail stretched back, hackles raised and stiff. Lyta turned to see where he was looking. An alarming snarl rolled from his muzzle and fangs flashed.

"What—" but that's all Lyta got out before something crashed into her and knocked her down. Hot flames shot through her head and she couldn't move or see. Frantic snarls erupted followed by a *thwack* and a piteous whine. Another violent slam, this to her chest, made her curl inward and everything went dark.

Pan-do paced the edge of camp and squinted the direction Lyta had gone. Sun was well-beyond the point when his daughter should be back. An icy chill shot down his back but he fought to control the terror. Spirit would let nothing happen to her.

Sa-mo-ke padded forward. Together they stood side-by-side until Pan-do could wait no longer.

"Something happened."

"I will go with you." Sa-mo-ke grabbed their spears. Pan-do filled neck sacks with cutters and stones, and both sprinted from the camp.

Not more than a spear-throw away, Spirit appeared on the horizon, hunched to one side, stride graceless. His gaze latched onto Pan-do and he howled, tried to hurry and ended up stumbling, falling, and then forcing himself onward.

"Spirit! What is wrong?"

The wolf limped toward Pan-do, howling with each step, panting harder. Blood glistened on the crown of his head and dripped over his brows, almost blinding him. He whined every time he put weight on his front paw.

"Sa-mo-ke—get help!" Pan-do motioned.

His Lead Warrior raced back to the camp as Pan-do sprinted for Spirit. He got there as the wolf collapsed. His tongue hung out and his tail slapped the ground.

Pan-do knelt over the exhausted wolf, stroking his back and between his ears. "Spirit—where is Lyta!"

He struggled to stand and crumpled. Pan-do had never seen Spirit beaten. Tears came unbidden.

"Pan-do—let me see!",

Xhosa prodded the wolf's leg, rubbed a hand over his great chest, massaging the blood-caked fur, trying to identify the extent of the damage. Pan-do worried Spirit would snap at her but the wolf instead offered a gentle lick as though he understood she meant him no harm.

"Someone beat him with a warclub or a big rock. He trusted this person, enough to allow him—or her—to get close. The pain must have been so extreme that he passed out. The attacker thought him dead which saved Spirit's life."

Xhosa fingered the cut on his head. Even a soft touch made him whimper and lick his lips. "The cut is deep, the blood tacky, not yet congealed. This was recent."

Pan-do motioned, "Can Spirit show us where he was attacked?"

"Let me treat his wounds first."

She dabbed a mulch into Spirit's gashes, sap on top, and then wrapped them in moss and leaves. When Xhosa dug into his cuts, his back leg trembled and his pants came shallow and fast. The pain must be excruciating.

Pan-do stroked the wolf and gestured, "He twitches toward his backtrail. He wants to go after whoever did this." He turned to the wolf. "Soon, Spirit. We will find Lyta and then take our revenge."

Spirit moaned and Xhosa ran her fingers over one of his wounds. Her mouth formed a tight line.

"None of the People—not Nightshade or me—could remain conscious long enough to reach help as Spirit did, not with these injuries."

She mulched roots and let Spirit lap them from her palm. "These are the strongest pain plants I have."

As Xhosa tended to Spirit, Pan-do stared at nothing, fighting his fear.

"She has never been alone. She won't know what to do," and how can she survive one who defeated the invincible wolf?

When Xhosa rolled back on her heels, Spirit wobbled to his feet and winced as he tried to put weight on his leg.

Xhosa tried to push him down. "No, Spirit. You must recover," but he shook her hand off and limped back the direction he had come, tail tucked, one leg raised. When no one joined him, he turned back, barked hoarsely, and hobbled onward, his message clear: *Come or not. I am going.*

"Sa-mo-ke—stay here!" Pan-do motioned to his Lead Warrior. "Until Nightshade returns!" Someone must be there for the People with the Leaders gone.

Pan-do gathered his spear and war club and loped after the wolf, Xhosa at his side.

Spirit stumbled, his steps erratic and unsteady but always headed toward the same spot. Pan-do stayed with the wolf, not moving at the ground-eating pace the wolf usually ran but fast enough. As they sped onward, Pan-do studied the landscape and the deep hidden shadows, searching for those who injured Spirit and probably Lyta.

Sun was well on the way to its nest by the time vultures appeared in the distance, circling over their meal. Spirit's hobble became a fast shamble, punctuated with agonized howls. Pan-do passed him as tears flowed down his cheeks. A wail tumbled from his mouth and he sprinted, Xhosa now with him.

There on the ground, almost hidden by a grove of trees and a low hill, Xhosa saw a body. Pan-do shouted his daughter's call sign but the lump didn't move. Spirit staggered toward it, whining piteously.

"It's Lyta!" Pan-do keened.

She was stuffed into a crevice which protected her somewhat from predators.

Xhosa huffed up to Pan-do's side and motioned, "She's alive or the vultures would be eating."

Pan-do rolled her over and cried out at the slight rise of her chest. Bruises encircled one arm where Spirit dragged her with his teeth to the best safety he could find before going for help. She had curled around herself, one wound crusted with dried blood but other gashes still seeping. This sent the "injured animal" call into the air.

Pan-do folded Lyta into his arms, hugged her to his chest, and sprinted along their backtrail. Spirit sniffed for the black wolf, moaned once, and then hurried after his pack. He wobbled and whimpered often but didn't quit. Nightshade had returned with Snake by the time the group arrived at the camp.

He motioned to Pan-do, "Is she alright? I warned her strangers were close but she wouldn't listen."

Spirit growled a low throaty warning at Nightshade. Xhosa almost did the same. Nightshade's body told a different story than his gestures. Pan-do must have seen it, too. His shoulders bunched up past his neck, his head jutted forward. She had never in all the time she'd known him seen him this angry.

He motioned to Nightshade, "Why didn't you stay with her? Lyta doesn't carry a weapon. She can't even throw a stone with accuracy. She is defenseless without Spirit. Your job is to defend your People!"

He faced Pan-do, feet spread, fists tight. "If someone's at fault, it's the faith you place in that wolf. Why do you trust him to protect Lyta?"

Nightshade forestalled Pan-do's angry response with a dismissive huff. "We waste time. If I go now, I still might catch whoever did this," and he left Sa-mo-ke and a handful of warriors, all fully armed, all committed to finding whoever would attack their People.

Pan-do crouched by Lyta, rigid with anger, cheeks wet, and licked the blood from her hair and skin so it wouldn't attract scavengers. Done, he moved aside, albeit reluctantly, and let Xhosa tend her.

Xhosa motioned, "Your People need you. Spirit will be here," but Pan-do stayed. Sa-mo-ke left to tell Siri what happened. She would tell the groups.

Nightshade didn't return until Sun's last pale fingers of light dissolved. After saying something to his warriors, he joined Xhosa, Seeker, Zvi, and Spirit at Lyta's side.

He scratched his chest, massaged his arm, and then motioned to Xhosa, "We found nothing but will try again tomorrow." He turned toward Lyta. "She is small and vulnerable. Who would hurt her?"

When he reached out to touch her, Spirit snapped at him, almost nipping his hand. The wolf's ears flattened and a vibrating growl rolled up from deep inside. Nightshade jerked back, fury darkening his face but fear making his hand shake.

Seeker fixed Nightshade with a calm, complacent stare. "Stay far away, Lead Warrior of the People. Right or wrong, Spirit blames you. As do I."

Nightshade gestured, "I tried to save her! It's Spirit's fault—he was there to protect her. If he growls at me again, he dies."

Zvi bristled and started to rise but Seeker waved Nightshade away as he might a child. "Stop yelling, one-called-Leader. You are bothering Lyta." His motions, calm but hard, conveyed the unspoken certainty that they both knew why Spirit kept Nightshade from Lyta.

Nightshade stiffened at the insult. Seeker patted Spirit as though the two had an agreement and started to spin.

As Nightshade stomped off, Wind crouched by Xhosa, saying nothing, eyes locked onto Nightshade's back, offering Xhosa his quiet support.

"It's falling apart, Wind. Seeker, one of the kindest most peaceful males I have ever met, just threatened Nightshade. Even Pan-do has reached his limit."

"It's not falling apart, Xhosa. It's coming together."

Lyta awoke to find Spirit tucked against her side, dozing. Her father's face was the first one she saw. Relief spilled from his kind eyes as he smoothed a callused hand over her hair. Tears wet his sun-darkened cheeks.

"What happened, father?"

He told her what he knew and asked what she remembered.

"I remember Nightshade's warning of strangers. He offered to guide Spirit and me to safety, a shortcut he knew about."

"Why didn't he stay, make sure you followed?"

"I had Spirit and the black wolf. What else did I need?" She rubbed a hand through the stiff fur of the wolf, now awake. Just before falling back to sleep, she asked, "Where's the black wolf?"

Pan-do sat at Lyta's side, watching nothing and everything. He took over for Siri and Wa-co who had replaced Viper and Red-dit. Sa-mo-ke wanted to post a warrior but Pan-do told him it wasn't necessary. Sa-mo-ke didn't argue but stayed where he could help if needed. When he couldn't be there, Ant or Stone were but Spirit was the one who wouldn't allow anyone near Lyta other than those Pan-do approved. She was as safe as possible.

Bone and Dust spent much of the time Lyta lay sick in search of the unknown enemy's tracks but the only ones they found were Nightshade, Lyta, Spirit, and another wolf they assumed to be the black wolf. Xhosa gave Lyta and Spirit a day to recover and then another. Though it couldn't be helped, the delay worried her. Dawa had warned Ngili to pass through the mountains before the air became cold and the flowers died. Pan-do said if they had to leave, he would carry Lyta on his back and Zvi would carry Spirit.

One night, as Lyta slept and Pan-do talked with Spirit. everything that had happened since he joined Xhosa snapped into place, like Seeker's stars must when they showed him the right direction. Hawk's death, Nightshade's rise in power, the Lead Warrior's unreasonable demand to mate Lyta—all different events with one goal.

"I know what Nightshade is doing, Spirit."

Spirit yipped, blue eyes fixed on Pan-do, his wounds already on their way to healing. "He wants me to decide staying here is too dangerous for my People so I leave, with my warriors and hunters. Since the remaining warriors and hunters are loyal to him, Xhosa will then be at his mercy."

Spirit's eyebrows bunched. He slapped the ground with his paws and yipped.

"You're right but what can I do?"

A chill ran down his body, thinking how devious Nightshade was. The more he stared at Lyta and listened to Spirit's whimpers, the bigger the lump in his throat and the knot in his stomach, and the more convinced Pan-do became that this enemy must be stopped.

As the group prepared to depart, Sa-mo-ke beckoned Pan-do and the two moved to a secluded area.

Sa-mo-ke motioned, "Another female is missing. That makes Deer and two more from the former Hawk People. All had been mating with Nightshade. The People are worried. I will post extra scouts and warriors but I'm not sure it will help."

"Why not?"

"Because I think Nightshade caused all of this," he signaled quietly, hands well below his waist for privacy. "It would explain why Spirit won't leave Lyta even to search for his mate.

"It's why I will never challenge him, Leader. Nightshade has changed from when we first arrived here. His violence is needless and his temper unpredictable. He frightens me."

Pan-do's jaw tightened. "I will talk to Wind. If we can't prove Nightshade is behind these attacks, maybe the deaths, we can at least be prepared."

Sa-mo-ke motioned, "Ngili agrees, as do Ant and Dust. Water Buffalo also stands with us if necessary."

Chapter 33

Xhosa hated these endless hills that touched the clouds and blocked her sight of anything further than a spear's throw. She couldn't see beyond the next tree or overgrown bush. If anyone stalked the People, she would find out too late.

Viper caught up with her, head bent against the wind. "When Dawa called the trail treacherous, he was too kind."

Xhosa nodded, hugging her arms around her chest. The higher they traveled, the more the wind whipped against their bodies, blowing right through the pelts. Long ago, the cold had exceeded anything she'd experienced.

She motioned to Viper. "Is this where the Others captured you?"

Viper nodded but her confident swagger flagged as though the memories continued to beat her down.

Xhosa gestured, "Shall we send scouts to notify your People of our—your return?"

"My captors said they killed all of them. I have only you, Xhosa."

Xhosa offered a slight smile and they fell into a companionable silence, both probing the trees while sensing for the out of place, spears ready, warclubs slung over their backs, and a supply of throwing stones in the sacks around their necks. Viper had come a long way from the meek creature who fled her captors.

Finally, Viper motioned, "Xhosa. Why does Seeker's path match Dawa's?"

"Seeker says our goals are the same."

"But how? You didn't know Seeker before this migration?"

Xhosa shrugged. "There are many questions I can't answer and that is one." Then, she pointed, "There, a cave. We'll rest for the night."

Pan-do's hands trembled as he jiggled Xhosa awake. "Lyta is sick."

Xhosa shook, clearing the blur of sleep. "Sick? Is anyone else?" She hoped the food hadn't gone bad.

"No. She ate the same as everyone and awoke vomiting."

Xhosa raced to the youngster. She lay unmoving, more like a bedraggled plant than the vibrant energetic subadult Xhosa knew. Spirit huddled at her side, ears flat, tail tucked. Zvi moved out of Xhosa's way and Seeker crouched motionless on the opposite side of Lyta's still form. Her cheeks were flushed and her forehead burned with the heat of a rock too long under Sun's rays. Beside her lay a pile of puke.

Xhosa almost missed the spot of yellow.

"Is this from Lyta—I mean, she didn't vomit on top of a plant?"

Pan-do motioned, "No of course not. I smoothed this area so it would be comfortable for sleeping."

Xhosa breathed in through her nose, searching for a particular odor but smelled only moist earth, the morning-damp grass, and fetid vomit. She dragged her fingers through the thick muck and scrutinized the contents.

Forcing a calm in her voice she didn't feel, Xhosa motioned toward a slender thread from a mushy yellow stem that was mixed in with the vomit. "How did that piece—the yellow plant—get in Lyta's food?"

Pan-do stuttered, unable to make sense of what lay in front of him, "I don't know. It shouldn't be there. Lyta ate with everyone, the same food, but awoke sick. I never left her."

Xhosa wiped the puke from the yellow stem and turned it over once and again, licked it—and then spit fiercely.

"Poison Plant—"

Pan-do gasped. "No, it can't be! Lyta wouldn't eat it."

"It is tasteless and the piece small enough to be missed. If it wasn't on the ground when she threw up, someone put it in her food. That would explain why no one else became sick."

Pan-do stared absently, saying nothing for a long time until finally he motioned, "Whoever did this couldn't have made a worse move. If Lyta dies, they will too." His voice was harder than Xhosa had heard it, his eyes as cold as the ice around her.

She cringed. Pan-do was like a river, curling over the land, sunlight glinting off its rippled surface, a welcome sight because it brought life. But underneath flowed fierce currents. Sharp rocks and treacherous plants filled its depths and it was home to vicious creatures that bit and tore without remorse.

Pan-do, once riled, was no stranger to violence. He used it skillfully when he had no other choice, as a means to the end.

Xhosa motioned, "I need—"

"I am familiar with the plant you need, Xhosa." His hands chopped, brusque and efficient.

"The flowers or bulbs, either will do." She described where to find it—far down the backtrail. Its purposes were few and menace significant so she had skipped it.

"Don't worry, Pan-do. Spirit won't leave Lyta and neither will I."

"I'll go with you." The voice startled her.

"Dust," the former Hawk People's Lead Scout.

He continued, "I know where it is, and I want to help Pan-do. And Lyta."

Xhosa motioned, "I'm sure you have duties."

Pan-do motioned, "I'd appreciate the company," and the two left, Dust trotting in Pan-do's footprints.

Spirit stared until his friend melted into the distance and then dropped his head back between his paws.

Pan-do wouldn't return for a day or more. Xhosa must keep Lyta alive until then.

"Siri!" She called her Primary Female. "I need your help," and explained the problem.

The two of them tried every one of their remedies and a few Viper knew from her tribe. When none worked, they fed Lyta dirt and burned wood, both good at absorbing poison. She didn't improve but also didn't worsen.

Xhosa told everyone they would stay where they were today, maybe longer, and settled to her haunches by the fire knapping a new stone tip for her spear. When the flames dwindled, Xhosa fed it twigs and dried grass. Lyta never awoke, never moved. She could be dead except for the steady rise and fall of her chest.

Stone tools took much time to shape, either from rocks or a handaxe. Every member of the People went through many of these tools chopping plants for food, cutting tough hides, digging in the ground, and other routine tasks. Even the youngest child must know how to sharpen those they had and make new ones.

As Xhosa worked, the youngsters El-ga, Kiska, and Gadi joined her. Each picked up common round stones and mimicked how she held the stone just the right way, the way she struck it, and the exact slat required to chip it correctly. Xhosa knapped first a cutter and then a chopper. When those were done and Lyta still lay peacefully sleeping, she started on a spear tip. That would take most of the night.

The youngsters left at some point while Xhosa worked but Honey and Leopard arrived. The two new adult females crouched across from Xhosa, imitating what she did. It didn't surprise Xhosa that Leopard would be interested in knapping spear tips but Honey—that she hadn't expected. When the two finally left, too tired to concentrate, Xhosa pulled her hammerstone out—a well-used rock the size of her palm—

and chipped flakes from it thin enough to cut through hide. Or in this case, shape her spear.

Moon arrive and everyone slept soundly behind a thorn barrier. Except Xhosa and Spirit. They stayed awake, with Lyta.

Xhosa's head drooped, snapped up when Spirit pawed her and she returned to her work. She had to stay awake until Siri took over, when Sun returned. Her eyes, bleary from fatigue, closed again. A sound dragged her from sleep.

What woke me? Spirit's ears tweaked but without worry.

"It must be the fire."

She shook herself and went back to shaping the stone tip. Again, her lids closed, lulled by her own breathing.

Until a crackle popped her eyes open. She'd spread dry debris so anyone approaching would step in it. Xhosa grabbed her spear as Spirit's tail swished in greeting, the wolf's breath frosting the air under his whiskered snout.

"Xhosa—it's Wind! I'll watch Lyta. You go to sleep."

Xhosa stifled a yawn, too tired to do more than nod.

He settled at her side and heat spread over her. Now, the two alone, this was the time to ask why he sided with her over his brother, but the words wouldn't come.

"Rest. I will wake you if needed." He picked up a caterpillar as long as his forearm, bit off a piece, and chewed while looking for changes in the shadows around them. A comforting darkness engulfed her as he placed a hand on hers.

Unbidden, her worries bubbled out. "Wind. This is my fault, that Lyta is sick. I convinced Pan-do to stay after Deer's death and again after the attack on Lyta. I promised to keep her safe. How did I let this happen?"

"You are not to blame."

"You don't know that."

"Yes, I do. I lived with one of the vilest creatures ever to walk on two legs. That experience taught me how to recognize every trick and then how to defeat them. You are not the evil one here."

"But I have failed to provide safety to my People. That is my job."

Silence filled the space between them until Wind whispered, "I know what you're thinking. If you quit, who takes over as Leader?"

She wandered through that process, mentally and then aloud. "The warriors would engage in challenges, but Nightshade would stand for the position, as he did before. I doubt any would question his right to be Leader. My father trained him and he led the People well when I was a captive."

Saying that put a cramp in her stomach. Was this really what would be best for her People, better than her remaining as Leader?

"Did your People share their experiences in your absence?" Before Xhosa had time to form an answer, he motioned abruptly, "Because when I asked, they described a group as toxic as the one I left."

She leaned into him, her mind churning. When the dull state between sleep and wake took over, the ancient female Lucy appeared, talking to her as though they walked next to each other. Sometimes, Xhosa felt they did.

She motioned, "Xhosa, Nightshade uses Poison Plant to help him sleep."

The next day passed and the one after without Pan-do's return. Seeker assured her Pan-do lived. That was good. Lyta wouldn't survive the loss of her father, despite Seeker and Spirit.

On the morning of the day after the second day after Pan-do's departure, Wind and Spirit stayed with Lyta so Xhosa could wash the stench of sickness from her body. As she rinsed herself in the clear river water, Nightshade arrived to search for knapping stones. They had found none of the quarries where hard rocks lived, the ones needed for durable tools, so river rocks must fill in. She and Nightshade hadn't spoken since Lyta became sick.

Xhosa stiffened as Lucy's warning stabbed her like a spine in her foot, as impossible to ignore.

"Nightshade. We know what made Lyta sick. It was Poison Plant."

He nodded dismissively as though to say he, as Lead Warrior, didn't need this sort of information. The whisper of disquiet that ran through Xhosa increased.

"No one but you use Poison Plant, Nightshade. You use it to help you sleep." Xhosa kept her gestures quiet but firm.

His mouth twitched but he emptied his neck sack on the riverbank. He had cutters, throwing stones, food, healing plants, and no Poison Plant. He dug through the contents, fingers more frantic with each sweep.

"It's missing. I have not needed it as tired as I am—we all are." His gaze held hers, earnest and pleading.

Xhosa touched his hand. "I don't accuse you, Lead Warrior. I know of no reason you would want Lyta sick. My question is who can access your neck sack without your knowledge? That's who wants Lyta dead."

Silently, he left, arms stiff, and made a beeline for the females who were pounding roots for the meal. As though he'd been waiting for Nightshade to leave, Seeker appeared. Without his future pairmate to groom him, his hair bristled with twigs and leaves, matted with dirt and mud. He displayed none of his usual ebullience.

When he said nothing, just stared after Nightshade, Xhosa gestured, "Spirit worries me, Seeker. His tail never wags. He refuses to eat, even Rat—his favorite food. Is he ill also?"

Her energy to handle more problems was exhausted but the question must be asked.

"Poison Plant is not lethal to wolves. Spirit is sick inside, Xhosa. He failed to keep his packmate safe, again. He will not get better if Lyta doesn't. If he dies, Zvi will, too. She survived Giganto's death only because of Spirit."

As Xhosa considered this, Nightshade stomped up. "I found who tried to kill Lyta!"

Stumbling behind him, eyes wild with fear, was Leopard. Xhosa couldn't have been more stunned. Leopard showed nothing but gratitude to the People for taking her in.

"Leopard. Why?"

"I-I-it was an accident. I wanted to help Nightshade, clean his neck sack, and that's when I found the Poison Plant." She jerked, eyes wide with fright, as Nightshade shook her. "I tossed it away, thinking I was helping. It must have blown into Lyta's food."

Nightshade slapped her hard and her lip split. She didn't cry out or staunch the blood flow. In fact, Xhosa saw relief, as though pain salved her guilt.

"Please—I am stupid!"

Viper stomped up and pushed Nightshade away. "Leopard is innocent! You terrorized her and forced the blame on her!"

Xhosa glanced from Leopard to Viper, one abject with fear and the other exploding with fury. Both their pasts were filled with distrust and abuse yet the Leopard Xhosa knew would never hurt a group member. And Viper would never jeopardize her goal of becoming Lead Warrior even for a friend.

Xhosa turned Leopard's face up until her wounded eyes met the Leader's. "It's alright. Tell Pan-do you made a mistake when he returns, as you told me. It is up to him to forgive you. I will tell him I do."

Nightshade threw Leopard to the ground. She fell with a squeal and crawled away until she was far enough and then pushed to her feet and ran to Viper. The two wrapped their arms around each other while Viper glared at Nightshade. The Lead Warrior spat on both.

"If Pan-do isn't back in one more day, he will have to catch up!" With that, he left.

Seeker didn't react, eyes moving from Leopard to Viper to the spot where Nightshade disappeared.

He motioned to Xhosa, "Do you believe Leopard is responsible for the poison?"

"Not for a breath."

Pan-do and Dust dragged into the camp as Sun dipped out of sight. Their breathing was ragged from running, faces grim but satisfied. Both gripped handfuls of the healing plant in their fists. Pan-do collapsed beside Lyta while stuffing leaves into his mouth. He mulched them with water and honey and dribbled the mixture between Lyta's dry, cracked lips. At first, she spit it out but after patient cajoling, she swallowed tiny mouthfuls without throwing up. He did this all night. By morning, her fever broke.

Spirit jerked upright when cold fingers scratched through his fur. He lapped his tongue across Lyta's lips, sniffed her for remnants of sickness, and then snapped up a rat who scurried past, downing it in one swallow before sprinting back to Lyta's side, panting deep contented sighs.

Nightshade told Xhosa it was time to leave but she refused. As did Pan-do.

"Lyta needs one more day to rest. Take the former Hawk People. The rest of us will catch up when she recovers."

Nightshade stomped away and joined a group of scouts just leaving. He didn't include Dust.

The day after the next, Lyta recovered enough to continue and the People left the temporary camp. The canyons became steep and narrow, the walls jagged. The rain made it almost impossible to climb. Mothers strapped their children to their backs with vines, their chubby legs wrapped around the females' waists. Zvi carried almost a handful of youngsters by herself, one on each hip, one in her arm and one on her back. That left an arm and both feet for climbing which for Zvi, was plenty. She deposited her load at the top and descended for more.

Seeker tried to carry Spirit but the wolf, as tall as the slight male and as stocky as Zvi, was too heavy. Wind crouched and touched the wolf's muzzle.

"May I help you, Spirit Wolf?"

Spirit gave a soft huff. Wind layered two pelts over his body to protect it from Spirit's claws and then lifted the full-sized wolf to his back. Front paws drooping over his shoulders, Wind tied the back feet around his waist and completed the long upward climb without a problem.

At one point, the rocks on both sides of a massive waterfall were not only steep but slippery with ice, Xhosa saw no way up or over so searched for a way around. That's when she saw one of Dawa's cairns.

Tears sprang to her eyes. "He places markers where we might give up, as my father did."

Viper looked puzzled so Xhosa explained how her father planned for the day when the People would have to flee by laying out an escape route. The treacherous path often seemed impossible but always, Xhosa found her father's cairns to show them the way.

A whine from the wolf disturbed her thoughts.

Zvi motioned, "I'll find out what bothers him." The two disappeared over the horizon.

Darkness fell before they returned. When Zvi reached Xhosa, sweaty and winded, she motioned, "Dust fills our backtrail. Whoever it is keeps our pace and direction."

"How many?"

"The cloud is huge. More than us by many handfuls."

Chapter 34

Close to modern-day Gibraltar

No matter how much further the Rainbow People traveled along Endless Pond, the earth remained as hard and dry as stone with only a sporadic sprinkling of thirsty trees or shrubs and absolutely no rain. While it was true there were no Big Heads, each new tribe they encountered who called this forsaken land home was more vicious, less trusting, and more intent on exerting their supremacy over the newcomers than the last. No longer did any of them believe Rainbow's lie that his People were part of the group that was led by Xhosa and Nightshade. Rainbow's solution became to flee with the turmoil of a drowned-out anthill.

The occasional scouts Mbasa sent to explore the land that lay to their weak side, inland of Endless Pond, reported nothing but sand. No plants at all and no life of any kind.

Because the Rainbow People were only allowed to cross through the land of the native Others, never to hunt the few herds that roamed the land or forage the occasional fruit and nuts, they were forced to scrounge for scorpions, slugs, termites, snakes, and the big ants and spiders that scuttled across the parched terrain. If not for their guide, Vaya, they would have died.

As bad as it was traveling under the unforgiving sun, nights were worse. The air became frigid and the unremitting wind buried the People in grit.

It didn't surprise Mbasa when Rainbow gave up. He said the group must join the next Others they came across. It mattered little to him that the last one and the one before wanted them as slaves. He said they must beg someone to take them in. She told him that wouldn't happen. She would find an alternative. That suited him well. He was tired of decisions, botched plans, mistakes, and problems without solutions.

Mbasa was tired too but if she gave up, who would lead? Rainbow's People survived because she and her small group of warriors, hunters, and scouts refused to quit.

"Mbasa!" Vaya motioned. "Endless Sea is close!" This was Vaya's call sign for the pond at the end of their journey.

She sniffed. "When will we reach it?"

"Before Moon disappears and reappears."

"Bird! Go with Vaya. I will update Rainbow."

Rainbow shifted foot to foot and brushed Mbasa away, by now a familiar reaction. "This is your job. I must rest."

Moon disappeared as it always did, reappearing a day or two later. As the nights passed, it grew to a round shining orb only to shrink and disappear once again.

In that period when nights were darkest, when Moon didn't appear, moist dirt replaced the desiccated ground and patches of green speckled the landscape until edible plants became the norm, providing food for the People as they migrated during the day. The flat land they had suffered through turned into swelling hills and flowing valleys, many with lines on their steep walls that excited Mbasa. These she had seen often etched into the rock walls of narrow valleys by surging water that filled the valley and drowned everything in its path. Where the People had lived, they were called flash floods and provided a rich source of water where there seemed to be none.

Mbasa would gladly welcome one of those storms now but no matter how hard or long she looked toward the horizon, the sky remained a cloudless blue.

Bird motioned to Mbasa, eyes alight. "We found a cave large enough for all of us and hidden among the cliffs."

As Mbasa considered whether to stay here for the night or continue to Endless Sea, Hecate trotted up, a pig around her sturdy neck and motioned backward to other hunters, each with meaty carcasses hoisted over their shoulders. "Hunting is good here!"

Rainbow strode to her side, his face beaming with the excitement of a journey almost at its end.

He gestured, "Grass grows waist-high here. Your female hunter Hecate has already located herds of Gazelle, Elephant, Mammoth, and Wild Beast. We stay, Mbasa, until we have regained our strength."

Mbasa motioned, "Or until I can find the bridge across Endless Pond. The People might be right over there," and she pointed to the brown mound across the Pond. It had appeared a handful of days ago and now, seemed to get closer with each day.

Rainbow caught her eye, surprised. "We have no need of Xhosa anymore," and he motioned toward the carcasses brought in by the hunters and the dense grass. "This land will make an excellent new homebase."

Mbasa kept her expression flat. "I will scout. You settle the people."

Vaya led the scouting group followed by Mbasa, Starlight, and Tor, each with weapons and throwing stones. Soon, the scent of salt filled the air. As they crested the last of the hills, water stretched from one side of the horizon to the other. Mbasa chopped her hand down swiftly, *Quiet*, and folded into the tall grass.

The shorelines of both Endless Pond and what Vaya called Endless Sea seemed no more than a spear throw apart. The Sea, to her weak side, extended forever with no sign of land, its vastness dappled with scattered white caps and leaping fish. The Sea's shore burst with plants, at times overrun by the hard-shell land-dwelling fish they found along Endless Pond. Caves lined the nearby cliffs. A clear river gushed down the hill, cut through the shore until it dumped its burden of water into Endless Sea.

She gasped. "Look at the opposite side of Endless Pond!"

Even from this distance, Mbasa could pick out the movement of animals through waist-high grass. Birds flew over a carcass and Sun's rays glinted off what must be a waterhole surrounded by a thicket of reeds and cattails.

Tor frowned. "We have reached the end of Endless Pond. But where is the bridge to the other side?"

Mbasa nudged Vaya and motioned, "Vaya. Do you see it?" Did they come this far just to be stopped?

Vaya crawled up the bluff, scanned the horizon, and then motioned, "It is gone."

"Gone? How?"

He scratched his arm. "It should be right there," and pointed toward a narrow straight of white choppy water between Endless Pond and Endless Sea.

Mbasa motioned, "Maybe it's underwater, as parts of Endless Pond are at times. If it's not too deep, we will walk across," though how they could get through the violent cliff-sized waves that crashed through the strait, she had no idea.

Vaya motioned frantically, "We cannot go back. My captors will kill us before they let us stay with them!"

"Vaya. We will never go back."

Before her hands settled back to her sides, a large group of Others emerged from the caves.

Chapter 35

The shore-based tribe, unaware of the People's presence, worked at a frenzied pace. Mbasa looked around but could see no reason why they were afraid. Nor did she see any imminent threat. Some dragged tree trunks from a cave—what Mbasa saw them call "cane"—while others headed toward a pile of woody refuse. They laid the cane logs side by side and wrapped them in vines, much as Mbasa and Tor did when they tried to make a raft. Occasionally, they shook it. If the cane didn't move as one, they added more vines. They repeated this until nothing fell loose.

Mbasa motioned to Tor, "They're making rafts, as we did. I wonder if our rafts failed because we didn't shake them."

The Raft Builders—as Mbasa now called them—then covered the top of the raft with what Mbasa recognized as fibers from grass stalks and some sort of resin. She didn't remember that from Pan-do's description.

Those not building rafts gathered in a separate part of the camp and rubbed sand over what looked like the wide shoulder blades of Mammoth. They'd rub, study the bone, rub a hand over it, and then either continue rubbing or chip an indent into one end. That done, they set it aside and started on the next, not even taking a break.

Mbasa motioned, "I wonder if those are paddles."

Tor gestured, "Maybe they use bone instead of wood."

As they worked, the Raft Builders spoke often to each other, voices mixed with hand motions. Mbasa recognized many of the gestures from Others the People met in their long journey. Sweat dripped from their bodies and no one took breaks to eat or drink.

"They are in a hurry." This from Starlight. "But why?"

No one answered because no one knew.

Often, the Raft Builders looked down the shoreline, faces tense, at something out of Mbasa's sightline, and then worked harder. Mbasa scooted along the edge of the crest until a massive peak came into view. It rose far out on Endless Sea, as wide as it was tall, touching the clouds.

Mbasa motioned to Tor. "It belches smoke and cinder like Fire Mountain does."

When the mountain exploded a fiery red stream of liquid into the air, Mbasa didn't react. She'd seen this many times. Only those at the base of the mountain were in danger. These Raft Builders were far across the water from it.

"I don't understand why they are afraid Fire Mountain's anger will reach them, but I've never before seen Fire Mountain surrounded by water."

Tor didn't respond, eyes tracking the activity on the shore.

The Raft Builders dragged a raft into Endless Pond. When it floated, they cheered and dropped it on the coastline as though stationed for the departure. More cane was hauled from the cave, tied with vines, covered in fiber and beeswax, and then tested in the water. Those that floated were set aside. The others were rebuilt and retested.

Starlight fidgeted. "They want to cross Endless Pond, as we do, but the water is much rougher than we expected. How will they do that without many drowning?"

Mbasa motioned, thoughts churning, trying to understand what was in front of her. "And knowing the treachery, why risk crossing? They are well-fed with good sturdy weapons."

Tor motioned, "If it's one of the Fire Mountains, they should travel up the shore, away from it, or go inland to the caves we found."

Mbasa watched one after another of the Raft Builders glance up the hill where she hid but not at her—farther away. "They act like danger is close. It's not us—they don't even know we're here. It's something else."

Starlight motioned, "The dangerous tribes, we left them far behind—"

Mbasa waved her to silence. "Did we?"

It took most of the day for Mbasa to assemble the clues—the Raft Builders' urgency, their decision to flee, their refusal to move inland—and recognize what was right in front of her. She ground her teeth as reality hit her.

A shiver pulsed through her body despite the heat. "We must go. Now."

Without objection, the group scooted down the hill and sprinted back to the caves. Within sight of the People's camp but well-hidden by tall grass, Mbasa took the measure of her surroundings. Normal insect presence, no unusual sounds or odors, no strange movements—but then why did Rainbow slump outside of the cave without a spear or warclub? She approached silently, rolling from heel to toe, listening for signs of life. He sat so still, he might be dead.

"Rainbow."

He jolted awake, eyes frightened and then angry. Before he could sputter a retort, she explained what they'd seen.

"The Raft Builders are frightened, Rainbow."

He pawed through the dirt, grabbed an earthworm, and then let it wriggle from his fingers. "What does that have to do with us?"

Mbasa clenched her teeth tight enough to hurt and walked away. A visceral dread spread like a sickness through her body.

When Sun awoke, Mbasa had Bird and Hecate stay at the camp while she, Tor, and Starlight returned to Endless Sea.

Again, as the day before, Mbasa, Tor, and Starlight hid in the tall grass at the top of the hill to observe. The Raft Builder males worked the entire day building rafts and paddles while the females stuffed food supplies into neck sacks. She respected these People's strength against horrible options—being burned alive by Fire Mountain, savaged by neighboring tribes, or tumbling across Endless Pond on a raft likely to be destroyed by thrashing waves.

While everyone worked, a boy shambled out of the cave, head hanging, steps unsteady. A female offered him a fresh liver, usually given to those who carried babies. The boy ate a small amount and then curled up in the dirt.

When Mbasa left for her People's cave at the end of the day, he hadn't moved.

After the nighttime meal, Mbasa motioned to Tor. "Tomorrow, I will find out why these Others are leaving."

And help the youngster, if she could.

When Mbasa, Tor, and Starlight arrived the next day, the boy was worse. When he stood, he wobbled. His skin hung loose and he threw up what he ate. Yet, the crusted welts that spotted his limbs made Mbasa happy because they meant she could help.

How do I communicate this?

A plan formed in her thoughts.

Without a word, she walked down the slope to the shore. When Tor grabbed for her, she shook him off.

"Stay here in case I need rescuing."

Tor huffed as Starlight scurried to Mbasa's side and matched her pace. Neither female looked at the other, their full attention fixed on the strangers below. The beat inside Mbasa smacked hard against her chest like a stick banging on a hollow tree trunk. Sweat poured down her back but she kept her gait slow and confident, her spear down, and her warclub loose at her side.

When the Raft Builders noticed her, they first froze as one and then chattered to each other with frantic hands. Someone barked toward those tying the logs together by the shore. One male stopped working and looked at Mbasa and Starlight. He was as stocky as a Wild Beast with bulging muscles, tree-trunk legs, and long thick arms that ended in hands the size of Sabertooth's paws. He grabbed a spear and strode forward.

Mbasa hovered on the brink of panic but controlled it one step, one breath at a time. She greeted Stocky One with a sign of the People. He raised his arms to shoo her away and then slapped his hands palm-down against the ground.

She understood. He meant her no harm.

"I can help him."

She pointed to the sick boy. When Stocky One said nothing, she approached the boy and offered a plant. He refused it, mouth a circle, so she rubbed her stomach with a grimace, ate one of the leaves, waited a moment, and then grinned. The female caring for the child, who must be his mother, blabbered something to Stocky One, pointing from Mbasa to the boy and back. Mbasa didn't understand the sounds but the wide frightened eyes made the mother's message clear.

An Elder strode toward Mbasa, her old spine bent, each step conveying the dignity and fullness of her life. The child's mother ran to the Elder, hands erratic and pleading. Stocky One, still with his spear down, stood quietly, slope-shouldered, breathing harsh and irregular.

The Elder motioned in gestures used by many Others, "If any of us could cure this child, we would. He is Qaj's sole son. Why should we believe you can?"

"Elder, if I do help, he might live. Otherwise, he will soon die." Her hands moved with confidence.

The Elder bobbed her head and Qaj pulled Mbasa closer to the listless boy. Starlight followed, directing a hard glint and a frown at Stocky One, her message clear: *You will be sorry if you try to harm her.* The young female trusted but didn't trust. Those who treated her as a naive subadult lived—or not—to regret it.

The group around the sick boy parted to let Mbasa pass. The boy curled inward but his red watery eyes tracked her. In them, she saw not the youthful delight in life but the dull acceptance that he was dying. Soon. The mother rested a hand on the boy and motioned, "Shaga."

Mbasa placed her palm on her own chest. "Mbasa." She knelt by his side and patted his arm. "I can help you, Shaga."

She took a bite of the plant he had refused, chewed, and swallowed. Then, she handed the rest to the boy.

He scrunched his nose and sneezed. Mbasa tapped her nose. "It smells like decayed carrion and tastes worse but it'll cure the ache in your stomach." She rubbed her stomach and showed her teeth.

Mbasa stayed with Shaga after he ingested the plant. The curing effects took a while to start and she wanted to be there to reassure him and his mother. When he fell asleep, Mbasa used a combination of gestures and mimes to explain to his mother Qaj that Mbasa expected the boy to feel better when he awoke. The tears that tumbled down her cheeks and the hope in her eyes told Mbasa she understood.

Night came and Qaj carried Shaga into the cave motioning Mbasa to join them.

Mbasa caught the attention of the Elder and pointed at the hill. "Our warrior hides in the grass. I will tell him to go."

She motioned to Tor. When he stood, the Raft Builders gasped.

Mbasa motioned, "Go back to the People. We are fine. We will stay with the boy in case he needs more of the plant."

Tor raised a hand, palm forward. "I will wait. If I scream, come help me!" And he melted back into the grass.

Mbasa considered sending Starlight to be with him but decided the danger with the Raft Builders exceeded that from attackers who may not exist. Mbasa and Starlight entered the cave, found Shaga in a separated area toward the back, and squatted by his side. The cave resembled the People's but larger with many pelts for warmth. No one bothered her, grouping together for grooming and sleeping.

Mbasa took the opportunity to memorize the limited range of hand motions and body movements used by these strangers. Soon, she understood most of what they said. When the boy's breathing became soft and level, Mbasa slept.

When Shaga awoke, he jerked upright at the sight of Mbasa, trying to scuttle away from her, but calmed when she greeted him with gestures of his People. His mother offered him water and he drank all of it.

She motioned to Mbasa, "I was awake all night. He never threw up and now, his skin is cool."

Mbasa smiled as broadly as Shaga's mother. The boy scrambled to his feet and ran to join the other children. His gait was steady, steps light. Mbasa motioned Starlight to stay with the boy and she strode toward Stocky One. He was working on a raft but stood to face her when she approached.

"My name is Mbasa. I mean you no harm."

"I am Acto. I am Shaga's father and lead my People. We are Shore Dwellers. Thank you for saving my child."

She allowed a quick smile to raise her lips and motioned, "Why all the rafts?"

He indicated Fire Mountain, the smoke much denser and higher than yesterday. "It will soon explode. We must leave or die. We can't go up or down the shore or inland. The Others will kill us. That leaves only across," and he pointed at Endless Pond. "If our rafts can make it to the other side, we will survive."

That appeared to be more hope than plan. The water, thrown all directions by harsh currents, exploded in frothy whitecaps as though someone churned it with their feet. It was nothing like the calm rivers in Mbasa's homeland.

"Acto, can you even cross this strait?"

He shrugged dismissively, "We must. We won't survive here." He squinted. "You are not those who stalk us, from beyond the caves. They would never offer to heal a child. Why are you here?"

"Malicious tribes drove my People from our homeland. They wanted our land but also our lives. When we fled, we became separated. Our Leader is across Endless Pond." When Acto's face scrunched in confusion, Mbasa explained, "That's what we call the huge waterhole. We trailed it from where it begins, where Sun rises, to here. We need to get to them."

Acto listened to everything before asking a surprising question: "How did you get through the cannibals?"

Chapter 36

Mbasa jerked. "Cannibals? Many tried to destroy us, enslave us, or drive us away. None wanted to eat us."

"Consider yourself lucky to have escaped. Their tribe is massive and growing. I have lived here since a child. Always, we had plenty of food and water. When the Evil Ones—what we call these cannibals—arrived, before we knew they considered us prey, we sent a small group to welcome them. They captured and ate every one of our group. Now they take us one by one. We are peaceful. If we don't leave, they will destroy us."

"Who are they? Where did they come from?" Mbasa had seen none like this group during the People's entire migration.

Acto shrugged.

Mbasa's head buzzed. Her People considered this land without enemies. Those she had left behind at the caves were ill-prepared for the Evil Ones.

Acto studied her for a moment before motioning, "Bring them here. A large group may intimidate Evil Ones. They will not be expecting more than what they have seen so far in our homebase."

Mbasa nodded. "When I return with my People, we will help with the raft building. We have made them—one—in the past."

Acto brightened. "When we realized how evil this enemy was, we collected plenty of logs. Because they have killed many of my group, we now have more than we need."

Mbasa turned without a word, barked to Starlight and Tor, and sprinted toward the caves. Her throat burned, begging her to stop, but her legs screamed to run faster. Starlight and Tor fell behind but Mbasa paid no attention, maintaining her ground-eating pace. At the outskirts of the temporary camp, she hid in the undergrowth where it allowed an unfettered view of the cave. She saw nothing and heard no sounds of the group knapping stones and chopping food, nor any of the children's voices. The only hopeful sign was Hecate and Bird were nowhere. That meant they were either in hiding or dead.

When Starlight and Tor caught up with Mbasa, she motioned at the camp and slithered down the slope like mist through grass, avoiding the loose rocks Hecate had sprinkled as an early warning, eyes scanning for danger.

Footprints of Uprights filled the area in front of the cave. Some of the attackers seemed to search while others explored the surroundings. Mbasa didn't pick up any blood. Nor did she see any sign of a scuffle or that the People fled or were dragged off.

Tor motioned, "The Upright prints leave, go where Sun awakens."

That was good.

Or bad.

Mbasa sounded the call of a ground bird, two times. The quiet changed subtly, as a shadow changes the darkness, and Hecate appeared, Bird just behind, both brown with dust, bodies wary but pleased. Rainbow stumbled out of the cave well behind the females.

Tears sprang to Mbasa's eyes. "Hecate. Bird. You are safe. What happened?"

Hecate motioned, "After you left, I found tunnels deep inside the cave. When the Others came—many of them with spears and warclubs—everyone of us hid. Bird and I and the warriors stayed at the front where the dark made us invisible.

The Uprights who entered were limned against the light and we struck before they could raise their spears."

Mbasa caught her breath, forcing her muscles to relax before responding. No wonder the Shore Dwellers were fleeing to Endless Pond. There was nowhere else to go.

Hecate smiled. "We have time, Mbasa, before they attack. The Others' hand gestures and body motions are like ours. They think we are part of a group called Shore Dwellers."

"We met them. They live on the shore of Endless Pond and warned us these Uprights are violent cannibals."

Hecate thinned her lips. "They planned to assault the Shore Dwellers but when they found us, raced back to their homebase for more warriors. They will return with too many warriors for us to defeat, Mbasa."

Mbasa tightened her fists. "The Shore Dwellers are prepared. I came to get the People. We will go with them."

She spotted Vaya. "Vaya—go back to your People. You have taken us as far as you can. I thank you."

His face whitened and his lips trembled. "I am not going back. Those people—they are horrid. They starve me, abuse me every day. You treat me like your own. No, live or die, I stay with you."

"What about your mother and sisters? The Leader will kill them if you don't return."

He laughed. "He already slaughtered my family. Those he speaks of are his people. They treat me like a slave." He spit in the ground and stomped on the liquid. "That is what I think of them."

Mbasa and her People reached the Shore Dweller's camp while Sun still hung high overhead. Mbasa entered first.

"Shaga—how is he?"

Shaga raced toward her, holding a dead hare by its ears and grinning. "Welcome back, Mbasa!"

She smiled and headed toward Acto. "Not-Leader Acto, my people are there," and pointed to the hill at the edge of the Shore Dweller's camp. "May I invite them down?"

When he showed no objection, she signaled and the People poured over the hill and toward the shore.

Acto stood, slack-jawed, "We do not have room for all of you in our cave—"

Mbasa motioned, "We can sleep outside. We won't be here long. Those you call Evil Ones will be here in less than a handful of days. Can they cross Endless Pond?"

"Only Shore Dwellers know how to create rafts."

A rumble interrupted them, from the Fire Mountain. Smoke billowed from its tip in thick black clouds interlaced with sizzling red streams of fire. It blotted out Sun, covering most of the horizon, and flowed like a river to the shore.

Acto motioned, "That is as big a danger to us, Mbasa. When Fire Mountain finally explodes, it will cover us with lava. It has done this before. Anyone here will die. We must be gone by then. With your help, that will happen."

Once the People knew the routine of cutting the cane, strapping them together, glazing the platform with sap, they worked quickly and efficiently. Working from Sun's first light to its last, one day after another, they finally finished enough rafts to carry the combined group. As the workers prepared to rest, two things happened.

First, Fire Mountain exploded, filling the sky with puffy dark clouds that dumped torrents of sizzling rain onto the People.

Then, the Evil Ones appeared, limned against the crest of the hill. There were hordes of them, so many they stood shoulder to shoulder and still overflowed. All were muscular, naked, and angry. Each carried at least one spear—many with one in each hand—and warclubs strung over their backs. They weren't looking for a peaceful end to the conflict. Their clear goal was to kill every one of the Shore Dwellers, which now included the People.

But Mbasa was prepared. She'd been through this sort of attack once already, with the Big Heads. This time, though, she didn't need to defeat the enemy, just escape them.

Mbasa tried to yell to Tor and Hecate but the Evil Ones were howling so loudly, she could hear nothing over their screeching voices. She finally gave up. Really, anything she would say to her People about fighting and fleeing, they already knew.

With a shake of their spears, the Evil Ones raced toward the shoreline.

"Go—to the rafts! We meet on the opposite side!" Mbasa yelled to anyone who might hear.

Rainbow leaped onto the first raft, knocking one of Acto's People aside. Once the raft filled, the two with paddles propelled it into the violent water with every bit of their combined strength. Gray waves swamped it but everyone managed to stay on board. Those who fell off were retrieved and none of the paddlers quit.

The People were being attacked by the Evil Ones from the shore and Fire Mountain from the Sea. What would destroy them first was a real question.

"Hurry!" Mbasa screamed. The burning rain blistered her skin as she and Tor threw Shaga, his mother, and everyone else aboard rafts. All of them must be launched so they didn't provide the Evil Ones with a way to catch those fleeing.

Finally, Mbasa shouted, "This is the last one, Tor!" She pushed the last handful of People onto the raft and motioned to Tor, "It's time for us to go, now, Tor!"

But before she could reach the raft, one of the Evil Ones grabbed her. When she didn't pull away, he jerked into her. She stepped out of the way and pivoted to face him. He froze, startled a female stood against him. He was young but strong with small black eyes and a nose that hooked to the side. From him drifted a sweet rancid smell like ripe carrion.

Eyes blazing, Mbasa swung her warclub one handed at his head while flinging a throwing stone with the other. Both hit and he crumpled to the ground, unconscious. She jumped onboard the raft and paddled into the channel. Because of the smoke, she lost track of the rest of the rafts but Tor was with her and that would be enough.

The shoulder-bone paddle moved them quickly forward, much faster than the one Mbasa had knapped from a spear. She pulled the vines looped around her neck and tossed them to everyone with instructions to tie one end around their waists and the other to the raft. If they fell off, someone would drag them back aboard.

Just when Mbasa thought it couldn't get worse, a storm rolled in, its dark clouds sending fire down on the land. The air swelled with water, the sky low and gray. Rain swept the land and the air became frigid. She spun back to the shore but the Evil Ones weren't looking at her. Instead, mouths open, they watched helplessly as the tallest wave Mbasa had ever seen bore down on them. Within moments, it exploded on the sand, blew up the hill, and drowned everything in its way.

The cave where the Shore Dwellers had spent most of their lives was now underwater.

Mbasa turned away from the destruction and paddled madly. Harsh salty spray stung her face and hands as waves crashed through the narrow strait and bludgeoned the tiny raft. She wondered for a moment if this type of tempest had destroyed the Rainbow People's raft, launched onto Endless Pond, but the most violent of the waves seemed to be coming from Endless Sea, not the other direction. Hopefully, coating the surface in beeswax and fiber made a difference.

She heard a crack followed by ragged screams but ignored them. Cane logs slammed into her raft but the fragile platform gamely bounced forward from one foamy peak to the next. She paddled furiously, aiming for a brown bump of land she couldn't always see over the immense waves. When it disappeared behind the top of a wave, the paddlers kept the fiery red of Fire Mountain to their weak side. Those who survived must find each other in the new land.

Mbasa paddled onward as did Tor. They balanced themselves on the bucking raft, sometimes standing and other times, on their knees. Within a short time, it felt as familiar as though they had done this often. Her arms burned and muscles cramped but to stop meant death. When one of the People fell overboard, Mbasa glanced long enough to see

Tor still paddling, and then spun back to her task. Horror for those gone would come later. When the gale ripped her paddle away, she used her hands. When a loose log smashed into her arm and cut it from wrist to elbow, she switched places with Tor and paddled with her other arm.

The fragile cane rafts bobbed forward like straw on a tidal wave. Her tired eyes searched one more time and this time, she found it.

"There! That's where we go!"

Shrieks greeted her call. One of the rafts plunged under a monstrous wave and then popped up. Those still on the raft hauled the rest back aboard by their vines.

The first to get across Endless Pond crashed on the rocks. Mbasa couldn't tell if any survived but she adjusted her target, now aiming for what looked to be sand. Mbasa almost cried with happiness when she could finally see the Pond floor but her joy came too soon. The vines that held the cane together exploded. One of the logs slammed into Hecate and she sank into the crashing waves.

Mbasa grabbed her around the chest, swung the limp body over her own back, and sloshed forward. She stumbled under the weight but pushed herself back to her feet, using every bit of her remaining strength to stagger onward and keep Hecate afloat. The harder the struggle, the more committed she became to the truth that she and Hecate would either sink or survive together.

She began to think she wouldn't make it when someone lifted Hecate from her back. She felt her body lift, light, buoyed up by the water, her feet now walking on top of the Pond floor rather than digging into it. She was too tired to turn but her eyes burned with tears of happiness.

Then, Tor's voice, "I've got her," and he hefted Hecate to his shoulder, strode past her and out of the Pond.

Mbasa took her first steps onto the rain-swept shore and stopped. There, in the vast blackness, pelted with burning rain, as her arm throbbed and her legs threatened to collapse from exhaustion, the sizzle of anticipation charged through her.

Or maybe, what she felt was fear.

Chapter 37

Somewhere in what today we call the eastern Pyrenees

Nightshade's warriors spread out while the scouts left to track the invaders. Updates filtered back, none of them good. There were far more of the Others than the People, and all were armed for battle.

"Nightshade, Wind, Pan-do—suggestions?"

"We will surprise them when they get close …"

"Let's listen to what they have to say first…"

"We must burn the grassland once they reach it…"

As they discussed what to do, Leopard and Viper slipped out of camp. Wind noticed but said nothing. In the time he spent with these two, after the rescue and then with the People, he grew to respect their core belief, a need really that they care for their own. In this case, it meant to protect each other from Nightshade.

Viper called him Evil, always said with a snarl. It was a name she never even gave the Others who had captured her after killing everyone important to her. Leopard shook when Nightshade got near to her. He liked her fear and continued to force mating on her. He used to beat her; now he bit her, sometimes taking flesh. Once, Viper pushed Nightshade off Leopard and he threw her across the camp. She almost broke her arm when it slammed into a rock. Without family to stand up for them, she had no protection except Viper.

Wind offered to pairmate Leopard or Viper but both refused. "You have someone else in mind, Wind. Don't worry," Viper gestured. "We have a plan."

Which neither told him.

Siri slipped to Wind's side, arms crossed, but a smile tugged at her lips as she fixed on the same spot he did, the void in the bushes where Viper and Leopard had fled.

Siri motioned, "I wonder if this is their plan." When Wind grunted in surprise, she added, "Yes, I saw them leave, too. They also told me about their plan but not what it was."

"The foul treatment of females must stop, Siri. They are valuable. This is something Xhosa and I agree on and I think you do, too. If I must, I will wrest control of the warriors from Nightshade and persuade Xhosa to change."

Siri barked. "It won't take much persuading."

Xhosa snapped her eyes open, knowing instantly they were under attack. The stench was overwhelming.

Others! Too numerous to tick off on both hands even repeating fingers. She glanced around the camp, not finding Nightshade, Water Buffalo, Sa-mo-ke, or even Snake—none of her Leaders or their Seconds. Her gaze settled on the squirming heap of bodies in the middle of the clearing, so many of the People's warriors and scouts—including Dust and Ant—their feet and hands trussed with vines. But still no Nightshade. Or Water Buffalo.

Or Wind.

Xhosa wobbled to her feet, every muscle weary of the constant fight, the endless trek, and of wondering who to trust. Life had become one confrontation after another, always the choice dire, between death and compromise. It took all her energy to stay strong, to keep her countenance resolute.

Despite the worry, bone-deep fatigue, fury raged. Where was Nightshade? And how did he allow this to happen?

Wind padded to her side. "They could have killed us—you and I, the apparent Leaders—but didn't."

"Do we look frightening? Or clever?"

The two did tower over their opponents but none of them showed any fear. Why would they after defeating Xhosa's best warriors?

Xhosa motioned, "What do they want?"

"Right now, they are waiting."

Wind used Big Head gestures to talk to her, not the People's or Others. He taught her these while they fled her captors, as a way to communicate privately.

"For what? Or who?" But she expected no answer. That would come when the enemy was ready to tell her.

Peace filled her as they waited. Wind at her side brought the confidence she had always felt with her father, the sense that no problem was too great. Nightshade's first solution was always to fight. Today, surrounded and outnumbered, that wouldn't work.

Xhosa assessed who remained among her People. Siri stood with Stone, both as resolute and tireless as ever, a mix of curiosity and boredom painting their faces. Neither seemed to care that behind them were two Other's warriors with spears pointed at their backs. An arm's length away was Ngili, as relaxed as if he were watching a training exercise. Xhosa wondered if that was because he'd been a captive twice. Zvi, Seeker, Lyta, Sa-mo-ke, and Pan-do gathered by him in a clustered group. Seeker was uncharacteristically still, facing the bushes where Leopard and Viper had escaped the day before.

"Wind. Have you seen Nightshade?"

"He and Water Buffalo left to prepare a defense."

"Do you think these Others killed him?"

"If they were dead," Wind motioned, "Their bodies would be with the trussed-up males, where we could see them."

Xhosa motioned, "You're right. Besides, no one can kill Nightshade." She leaned toward Wind and motioned low on her body, "This isn't all of our warriors. I'm sure, right now, Nightshade is mounting an offense."

As though the Others heard her, they flung more trussed bodies into the pile in front of Xhosa—Talon, Bone, a growling Water Buffalo, and a hissing Snake. Xhosa sighed, not bothering to hide her disgust.

Wind huffed. "There goes the surprise offense."

As usual, Wind lightened her mood. "It's time I take charge."

She took one step forward, toward the opponent. Spirit appeared from wherever he'd been hiding and padded to her side, as though he'd been waiting on her. His tail waved, ears erect, and like Seeker, eyes fixed on where Viper and Leopard had been.

At the sight of the wolf, the Others gasped. A few whispered among themselves but none backed away.

"Why isn't Spirit growling?" Xhosa motioned to Wind.

His hands calm, as though he knew something she didn't, he motioned, "We'll have the answer soon."

Xhosa evaluated each invader and settled on a scarred male, face lined with deep crevices, spears in both hands and a warclub across his back, but with kind eyes.

She motioned, "We mean you no harm. We are following the path left by Dawa." Whispers spread through the Others as though they recognized Dawa's name.

Xhosa gestured, "We were prisoners together, captured by a ruthless band of Others." She used the gestures of Others rather than the People's. The male understood.

"I am Lead Warrior of the Mountain Dwellers. We come for justice."

Before Xhosa could wonder what he meant, a hoot rang out. She jerked. That was the People's call. No one else knew it.

She responded in kind and the line of warriors broke open to allow passage for two females, accompanied by a prancing black wolf. It took a moment for Xhosa to recognize them, both in fresh pelts and with a glittery vine— or tendon—around their necks.

"Leopard! Viper!" Leopard's wounds were salved and both seemed well-rested. "And the black wolf!"

Viper and Leopard smiled broadly at Xhosa and motioned to the Lead Warrior, "This is the one who rescued us."

The Lead Warrior motioned, "Leopard and Viper told us we would know you because you would respond to the odd call sign."

Xhosa spread her arms, palms up. "I am pleased they are both happy. We worried about them."

"You might have, Leader Xhosa, but not everyone did."

Xhosa cocked her head, mouth open. "I don't know what you mean."

Viper held a hand up. "These are my People, Xhosa. They are the ones who have been trailing you. They believed you enslaved Leopard and me and were plotting our rescue. When I realized this, Leopard and I left. I had to make them understand that you saved our lives."

Spirit padded up to Viper. She and Leopard held their hands out and he sniffed, licked, and swished his tail before returning to Xhosa, the black wolf at his side.

The massive group of Others again cleared a hole. A muscular male walked through, physique robust but with streaks of red in otherwise gray head hair. Deep scars cut his chest as though clawed by Cat. He stepped lightly, with a happiness Xhosa often saw from victorious warriors. He stopped beside Viper. Pride flowed from his face that belied the angry set to his mouth and the stiffness in his body.

Viper motioned, "This is my father." She overflowed with pride. "The Others lied when they said he was killed. He escaped with many of my People."

Her voice shook and she hung her head but it didn't hide the tear that trailed down her cheek. After a moment, she motioned, "He never stopped looking for me."

If she had been Spirit, she'd wag her tail.

Tears brimmed in the Leader's eyes also which he brushed away. "I am Davos, Leader of the Mountain

Dwellers, brother to Dawa. I am in your debt, Leader Xhosa. You have returned my daughter and Leopard to me. We are a good-sized group but these two are special. Viper will lead if ready when our People are in need."

He handed his spear to his Lead Warrior and stepped forward empty-handed. "You also rescued Deer. Viper tells me she died?"

Xhosa nodded, scanning again for Nightshade, and then frowned. "I am sorry, Leader Davos. My People have crossed many lands, home to handfuls of different tribes. We think one of them took her life."

Leopard started to shake but forced herself to still and then motioned, "That's not what happened, Leader Xhosa."

Xhosa's throat tightened, stunned by Leopard's calm assurance. Many questions came to mind but she settled on, "How can you be so sure?"

"I was there. I know who did this. He is of your People."

Xhosa gasped. "Why didn't you tell me? We do not allow the slaughter of group members. I would banish him—or her!" She allowed anger to soak her words, tinged with distress.

"Would you have believed me?"

"Of course." Her hand motions bellowed and then softened. "You and I spent Moons together, Leopard. Always, you did what you could for me. You have never spoken other than the truth."

Leopard motioned, "What if the killer turned out to be someone close to you?"

Xhosa cringed. She had always feared it was one of the People, worried it was the one she trusted as much as anyone, but hadn't yet been able to admit that to herself.

Now, if Leopard could prove it, Xhosa must not only acknowledge it but administer the punishment.

"No matter who, no matter what position of loyalty, the answer doesn't change, Leopard. Justice must always prevail. If one of the People takes the life of another, such a vile action rots us from within. It destroys not only the wrongdoer but those who keep his—or her—secret. Even if it was me, Nightshade as my Lead Warrior must throw me out."

Her hands wilted. "It must be done, Leopard, no matter how long afterwards it is from the death. Tell me who took Deer's life and I will mete out justice."

Leopard's fury sent a shiver through Xhosa. Clues she ignored—the odd odor, Deer's body, Spirit's reaction—snapped into place with one answer.

One traitor.

Xhosa's vision blurred as heat flared behind her eyes.

Viper mouthed something to Davos, the Leader of the Mountain People. Without turning, he raised his hand and waved his fist forward. The group again parted to make way for a phalanx of warriors, armed for a fight.

Between them, feet dragging across the ground, was Nightshade. He squirmed wildly, muscles bulging with the effort, but failed to break free of his captors, their arms as thick as young trees and as solid.

Xhosa growled, "Release my Lead Warrior!" But her voice conveyed none of its usual strength.

The helplessness of her position gutted her but more than that was the betrayal by someone she spent a lifetime trusting. A dizziness swathed her as though she—and her People— had been mortally wounded.

Wind stepped to her one side and Spirit leaned into her other, providing the support that allowed her to continue.

Leopard scowled. Hate radiated from her like the rattle of a snake. "This is the killer."

A buzz inside Xhosa's head got louder with each breath until it overpowered whatever Nightshade screamed next. Her whole body shook. She squinted, bent over, and then stood, taller than ever.

She breathed in, not wanting any doubt about the weight behind her next words. "Nightshade. Tell me why this isn't true."

Nightshade turned to her, eyes dark and bottomless. Never had she seen him so out of control.

"She lies, Xhosa! Leopard tried to poison Lyta and hates me because I exposed her. You were there when she confessed! Stop her—not me!"

Xhosa willed herself to stay upright as Viper turned her back on Nightshade and stepped toward Xhosa. "He lies. Leopard speaks the truth, Leader Xhosa. I too saw Nightshade. Bloody gobs of tissue dripped from his hair. He cleaned his warclub but forgot the gore splattered on his body from the violent destruction of Deer's body."

Xhosa fought to clear her thoughts, remembering that night, the sweet smell of rotting carrion seeming to come from Nightshade's direction.

Nightshade yelled, "The blood was from Hyaena?"

Viper responded, "Then why try to clean your warclub?"

Wind touched Xhosa's arm. "The cold kept Hyaena inside their dens. The only animal outside was Deer. And her killer."

Nightshade blustered, "I tried to bring the carcass back but wolves stole it. It made me angry!" He wrenched toward Viper and spit out, "You lie because Leopard is your groupmate. We never should have taken you in!"

"I saw it too."

Lyta's voice was scarcely a murmur but Xhosa didn't doubt she too spoke the truth. Not only had Xhosa never seen her lie, she had also never seen her interfere. Any warnings or worries were always communicated through her father.

"Lyta?" From Pan-do. "What are you saying?"

"Spirit and I needed to relieve ourselves and we saw Nightshade with Deer. We hid when he shoved her and bludgeoned her with his warclub. When he cut her arm off and started eating it, we fled."

Xhosa threw up, wiped her mouth, and turned back to her Lead Warrior, Nightshade, the person more like her than any other, the one who would be her pairmate. His lips curved up as though satisfied and his eyes glittered.

She stiffened, the beat inside her chest pounding, sweat dripping from her upper lip. "You did it, didn't you? You tried to kill Lyta—twice."

"No—Xhosa! You have known me my entire life. You know I would never do that!"

Xhosa turned her back to Nightshade and blocked out everything around her other than what had just been said. The silence became so complete that she heard Snake slither through the underbrush and a foot scrape the ground.

Finally, she turned back. "Nightshade, there may be reasons why Leopard and Viper hate you and might lie—though I don't believe they do—but that can't explain Lyta. She cannot hide the truth even to protect herself.

"Worse than that is you lied to me. If you had explained your mistake…" She didn't bother finishing. Nightshade was already interrupting her.

"You should be mine, Xhosa, but you gave yourself to Hawk. I had to stop him—"

It felt like a punch to her stomach. Her throat closed and she struggled to draw a breath. "You told me he drowned!"

"He was trapped under a pile of logs. He pleaded with me to help him. Of course I didn't. I couldn't."

"Nightshade, how—"

"I am a warrior, Xhosa! You never minded in the past when I exterminated your enemy. Hawk was one of the worst. He would have taken over the People, usurped your leadership. I had to correct your bad decisions! You must see that."

Xhosa looked at him as she had so often in the past but this time, all she saw a stranger. "We planned to lead together, bring peace to both groups, ensure safety for all!"

"And we would. I had it all planned! When the Others captured you, I led the People alone, and did it well. I came up with the right choices, made no missteps, agreed to no compromises. We flourished. Pan-do even stopped his petty arguments."

"Because I was leaving, with my People." Pan-do's hands moved with a calmness belied by his words or the circumstances. Only Pan-do, quiet, resilient Pan-do, would face such disastrous events with serenity. "Why argue with you over a future I wouldn't share? But when you returned," Pan-do turned to Xhosa. "Well, I couldn't abandon you to this monster."

Nightshade snorted. "Xhosa was never in danger." He twisted to Xhosa. "Though your return did complicate my plan. I now had to drive away those who supported you. Spirit and Lyta—I never intended they should die. I wanted their injuries to force Pan-do away, for the good of his People. With them gone, my warriors and I would become your sole supporters. You would have become my pairmate, as your father wished!"

Xhosa had heard enough. She caught Pan-do's eye and he nodded. Next, she glanced at Sa-mo-ke and Snake who would be the Lead Warriors. They showed no emotion, eyes fixed on the enemy, not Nightshade.

With that, she focused back on Nightshade, her oldest friend. "You are dead to us, former Lead Warrior of the People, former Leader of the former Hawk-People. You are thrown out of the People. Whatever happens to you is no concern of ours," and she turned away, as did Water Buffalo, Snake, Siri as Primary Female, Wind, and all of the People.

A howl exploded from Nightshade. He fought against his restrainers to no avail as they dragged him away, Xhosa frozen in place until his screams disappeared.

She held her open hands out to Viper and Leopard. "I am sorry. You trusted me to keep you safe. I failed you. I was no better than the Others."

Davos answered for Viper and Leopard. "You are a wise Leader, Xhosa. It takes a strength not often seen to judge those you love. We will leave now. Viper and Leopard will come with us. Nightshade will get the justice his actions earned for him from our People."

The massive group turned and melted into the surroundings.

Xhosa wasted no time to start her People's healing.

"Sa-mo-ke, Snake," and she beckoned them forward. "Untie all of our warriors and scouts. You will share Lead Warrior. Figure out how to make it work."

She didn't ask where their loyalty lay. If not with her, they would be replaced. They grinned and left.

"Pan-do. Why didn't Lyta tell me?"

He shrugged. "She told no one except Spirit."

Lyta tipped her head up and caught her father's eye. "He threatened your life and Spirit's if I told. Spirit guessed it after the-one-who-is-now-nameless attacked him."

Sun crept higher into the sky.

"We must leave."

Epilogue

Every day, the People descended farther down one of the most wretched slopes Xhosa had ever seen. Step after perilous step, Dust and Sa-mo-ke in the lead, chasing the low of Mammoth voices, hoping they traveled a path that would lead to meat. When Sun was no more than a glow on the horizon, the exhausted People rounded another of the endless bends in their winding path and stopped. In the last rays of light, they saw a valley of lush grass and green shrubs. The welcome stench of dung and the sweaty scent of herds perfumed the air. There, already, tiny moving figures—the People's hunters—chased the herd, spears raised.

Xhosa took a deep breath, reveling in the familiar smells, letting them fill her. They were so like home, a great sense of relief flooded her. Beyond stretched a waterhole so vast, she couldn't see the other side. If this verdant land didn't work out, she didn't know what she'd do. No one had the will to continue.

She sat on a hillock, eyes ahead, and listened as everyone plopped to the ground with relieved sighs. Beside her, a ground squirrel sprawled on the rock, no fear that she might view him as food. She looked up at the sky, past Sun, wondering if the stars were pleased.

Seeker bounced up to her, joined soon by a lumbering Zvi and hobbling Lyta. Instead of staring up at the stars, he faced forward, face aglow.

"Do you feel the stars, Xhosa?" But he didn't expect an answer.

At Seeker's side stood Spirit, the black wolf, and Pan-do. Lyta flung her arms around Spirit as he wagged his entire body. Though wolves traveled far in their normal lives, this rocky terrain had shredded their paws. Zvi had covered them with leaves and moss. It frayed and fell away each day, to be replaced each night by their pack.

The wolves, like everyone else, needed to rest. Spirit glanced to the side, as he often did, and caught the eye of the black wolf, stomach hanging, a deep gash almost healed in her side. She was never far from Spirit.

And then Spirit froze. His nose twitched once, again, and he howled.

Preview of *Survival of the Fittest*

Book 1 in the *Crossroads* Trilogy

See where the story started.
Click to Purchase
https://www.amazon.com/gp/product/B07NKM58GB

Chapter One

Her foot throbbed. Blood dripped from a deep gash in her leg. At some point, Xhosa had scraped her palms raw while sliding across gravel but didn't remember when, nor did it matter. Arms pumping, heart thundering, she flew forward. When her breath went from pants to wheezing gasps, she lunged to a stop, hands pressed against her damp legs, waiting for her chest to stop heaving. She should rest but that was nothing but a passing thought, discarded as quickly as it arrived. Her mission was greater than exhaustion or pain or personal comfort.

She started again, sprinting as though chased, aching fingers wrapped around her spear. The bellows of the imaginary enemy—Big Heads this time—filled the air like an acrid stench. She flung her spear over her shoulder, aiming from memory. A *thunk* and it hit the tree, a stand-in for the enemy. With a growl, she pivoted to defend her People.

Which would never happen. Females weren't warriors.

Feet spread, mouth set in a tight line, she launched her last spear, skewering an imaginary assailant, and was off again, feet light, her abundance of ebony hair streaming behind her like smoke. A scorpion crunched beneath her hardened foot. Something moved in the corner of her vision and she hurled a throwing stone, smiling as a hare toppled over. Nightshade called her reactions those of Leopard.

But that didn't matter. Females didn't become hunters either.

With a lurch, she gulped in the parched air. The lush green grass had long since given way to brittle stalks and desiccated scrub. Sun's heat drove everything alive underground, underwater, or over the horizon. The males caught her attention across the field, each with a spear and warclub. Today's hunt would be the last until the rain—and the herds—returned.

"Why haven't they left?"

She kicked a rock and winced as pain shot through her foot. Head down, eyes shut against the memories. Even after all this time, the chilling screams still rang in her ears...

The People's warriors had been away hunting when the assault occurred. Xhosa's mother pushed her young daughter into a reed bed and stormed toward the invaders but too late to save the life of her young son. The killer, an Other, laughed at the enraged female armed only with a cutter. When she sliced his cheek open, the gash so deep his black teeth showed, his laughter became fury. He swung his club with such force her mother crumpled instantly, her head a shattered melon.

From the safety of the pond, Xhosa memorized the killer—nose hooked awkwardly from some earlier injury, eyes dark pools of cruelty. It was then, at least in spirit, she became a warrior. Nothing like this must ever happen again.

When her father, the People's Leader, arrived that night with his warriors, he was greeted by the devastating scene of blood-soaked ground covered by mangled bodies, already chewed by scavengers. A dry-eyed Xhosa told him how marauders had massacred every subadult, female, and child they could find, including her father's pairmate. Xhosa communicated this with the usual grunts, guttural sounds, hand signals, facial expressions, hisses, and chirps. The only vocalizations were call signs to identify the group members.

"If I knew how to fight, Father, Mother would be alive." Her voice held no anger, just determination.

The tribe she described had arrived a Moon ago, drawn by the area's rich fruit trees, large ponds, lush grazing, and bluffs with a view as far as could be traveled in a day. No other area offered such a wealth of resources. The People's scouts had seen these Others but allowed them to forage, not knowing their goal was to destroy the People.

Her father's body raged but his hands, when they moved, were calm. "We will avenge our losses, daughter."

The next morning, Xhosa's father ordered the hunters to stay behind, protect the People. He and the warriors snuck into the enemy camp before Sun awoke and slaughtered the females and children before anyone could launch a defense. The males were pinned to the ground with stakes driven through their thighs and hands. The People cut deep wounds into their bodies and left, the blood scent calling all scavengers.

When Xhosa asked if the one with the slashed cheek had died, her father motioned, "He escaped, alone. He will not survive."

Word spread of the savagery and no one ever again attacked the People, not their camp, their warriors, or their hunters.

While peace prevailed, Xhosa grew into a powerful but odd-looking female. Her hair was too shiny, hips too round, waist too narrow beneath breasts bigger than necessary to feed babies. Her legs were slender rather than sturdy and so long, they made her taller than every male. The fact that she could outrun even the hunters while heaving her spear and hitting whatever she aimed for didn't matter. Females weren't required to run that fast. Nightshade, though, didn't care about any of that. He claimed they would pairmate, as her father wished, when he became the People's Leader.

Until then, all of her time was spent practicing the warrior skills no one would allow her to use.

One day, she confronted her father. "I can wield a warclub one-handed and throw a spear hard enough to kill. If I were male, you would make me a warrior."

He smiled. "You are like a son to me, Daughter. I see your confidence and boldness. If I don't teach you, I fear I will lose you."

He looked away, the smile long gone from his lips. "Either you or Nightshade must lead when I can't."

Under her father's tutelage, she and Nightshade learned the nuances of sparring, battling, chasing, defending, and assaulting with the shared goal that never would the People succumb to an enemy. Every one of Xhosa's spear throws destroyed the one who killed her mother. Every swing of her warclub smashed his head as he had her mother's. Never again would she stand by, impotent, while her world collapsed. She perfected the skills of knapping cutters and sharpening spears, and became expert at finding animal trace in bent twigs, crushed grass, and by listening to their subtle calls. She could walk without leaving tracks and match Nature's sounds well enough to be invisible.

A Moon ago, as Xhosa practiced her scouting, she came upon a lone warrior kneeling by a waterhole. His back was to her, skeletal and gaunt, his warclub chipped, but menace oozed from him like stench from dung. She melted into the redolent sedge grasses, feet sinking into the squishy mud, and observed.

His head hair was sprinkled with gray. A hooked nose canted precariously, poorly healed from a fracas he won but his nose lost. His curled lips revealed cracked and missing teeth. A cut on his upper arm festered with pus and maggots. Fever dimpled his forehead with sweat. He crouched to drink but no amount of water would appease that thirst.

What gave him away was the wide ragged scar left from the slash of her mother's cutter.

Xhosa trembled with rage, fearing he would see the reeds shake, biting her lip until it bled to stop from howling. It hardly seemed fair to slay a dying male but fairness was not part of her plan today.

Only revenge.

A check of her surroundings indicated he traveled alone. Not that it mattered. If she must trade her life for his, so be it.

But she didn't intend to die.

The exhausted warrior splashed muddy water on his grimy head, hands slow, shoulders round with fatigue, oblivious to his impending death. After a quiet breath, she stepped from the sedge, spear in one hand and a large rock in the other. Exposed, arms ready but hanging, she approached. If he turned, he would see her. She tested for dry twigs and brittle grass before committing each foot. It surprised her he ignored the silence of the insects. His wounds must distract him. By the time hair raised on his neck, it was too late. He pivoted as she swung, powered by fury over her mother's death, her father's agony, and her own loss. Her warclub smashed into his temple with a soggy thud. Recognition flared moments before life left.

"You die too quickly!" she screamed and hit him over and over, collapsing his skull and spewing gore over her body. "I wanted you to suffer as I did!"

Her body was numb as she kicked him into the pond, feeling not joy for his death, relief that her mother was avenged, or upset at the execution of an unarmed Other. She cleaned the gore from her warclub and left. No one would know she had been blooded but the truth filled her with power.

She was now a warrior.

When she returned to homebase, Nightshade waited. Something flashed through his eyes as though for the first time, he saw her as a warrior. His chiseled face, outlined by dense blue-black hair, lit up. The corners of his full lips twitched under the broad flat nose. The finger-thick white scar emblazoned against his smooth forehead, a symbol of his courage surviving Sabertooth's claws, pulsed. Female eyes watched him, wishing he would look at them as he did Xhosa but he barely noticed.

The next day, odd Others with long legs, skinny chests, and oversized heads arrived. The People's scouts confronted them but they simply watched the scouts, spears down, and then trotted away, backs to the scouts. That night, for the first time, Xhosa's father taught her and Nightshade the lessons of leading.

"Managing the lives of the People is more than winning battles. You must match individual skills to the People's requirements be it as a warrior, hunter, scout, forager, child minder, Primary Female, or another. All can do all jobs but one best suits each. The Leader must decide," her father motioned.

As they finished, she asked the question she'd been thinking about all night. "Father, where do they come from?"

"They are called Big Heads," which didn't answer Xhosa's question.

Nightshade motioned, "Do they want to trade females? Or children?"

Her father stared into the distance as though lost in some memory. His teeth ground together and his hands shook until he clamped them together.

He finally took a breath and motioned, "No, they don't want mates. They want conflict." He tilted his head forward. "Soon, we will be forced to stop them."

Nightshade clenched his spear and his eyes glittered at the prospect of battle. It had been a long time since the People fought.

But the Big Heads vanished. Many of the People were relieved but Xhosa couldn't shake the feeling that danger lurked only a long spear throw away. She found herself staring at the same spot her father had, thoughts blank, senses burning. At times, there was a movement or the glint of Sun off eyes, but mostly there was only the unnerving feeling of being watched. Each day felt one day closer to when the People's time would end.

"When it does, I will confess to killing the Other. Anyone blooded must be allowed to be a warrior."

She shook her head, dismissing these memories, focusing on her next throw. The spear rose as though lifted by wings, dipped, and then lodged deep in the ground, shaft shivering from the impact.

Her nostrils flared, imagining the tangy scent of fresh blood as she raced down the field to retrieve it, well beyond her previous throw.

"Not even Nightshade throws this far," she muttered to herself, slapping the biting insects that dared light on her work-hardened body and glaring at the males who wandered aimlessly across the field.

"Why haven't they left?"

Another curious glance confirmed that the group looked too small. She inhaled deeply and evaluated the scents.

"Someone is missing."

Why hadn't her father asked her to fill in?

Irritation seared her chest, clouding her thoughts. A vicious yank freed the spear and she took off at a sprint, wind whooshing through her cascade of hair. Without changing her pace, she threw, arm pointing after the spear, eyes seeing only its flight.

Feet pounded toward her. "Xhosa!" Her father's voice. "I've been calling you."

She lifted her head, chest heaving, lost in her hunt.

He motioned, "Come!"

What was he saying? "Come where?"

"Someone is ill."

It all snapped into place. "I'm ready."

She knotted her hair with a tendon and trotted toward Nightshade, newly the People's Lead Warrior. One deep breath and she found the scent of every male who had earned the right to be called hunter except Stone. He must be the one sick.

Nightshade nodded to her, animated as always before a hunt, and motioned. "Stay close to me."

Nightshade's approval meant no one questioned her part—as a female—in this hunt.

A deep breath stifled her grin. "I will not disappoint you, Nightshade."

And she wouldn't. Along with her superior spear skills and unbeatable speed, her eyes possessed a rare feature called farsight. Early in their training, Nightshade had pointed to what he saw as a smudge on the horizon. She not only told him it was a herd of Gazelle but identified one that limped which they then killed. From then on, he taught her hunting strategies while she found the prey.

Xhosa and Nightshade led the hunters for a hand of Sun's travel overhead and then Nightshade motioned the group to wait while he and Xhosa crested a hill. From the top, they could see a brown cloud stretching across the horizon.

Xhosa motioned, "This is a herd but there are no antlers and the animals are too small for Mammoth." A breath later, she added, "It's Hipparion."

Nightshade squinted, shrugged, and set off at a moderate lope. If she was wrong, the hunting party would waste the day but he knew she wasn't wrong. Her father joined him in the lead with Xhosa and the rest of the males following. Nightshade chose an established trail across the grasslands, up sage-covered hillocks, into depressions that would trip those who didn't pay attention, and past trees marked by rutting. At the end of the day, they camped downwind of the fragrant scent of meat and subtle Hipparion voices.

Sun fell asleep. Moon arrived and left, and finally, Sun awoke. Everyone slathered themselves with Hipparion dung and then warily flanked the herd. When they were close, animals on the edge picked up their scent and whinnied in fear, pushing and shoving to the center of the pack, knowing that those on the outside would be the first to die.

Xhosa pointed to the edge of the field but Nightshade had already seen Leopard, lying atop a termite mound, paws dripping over the sides, interested in them only to the extent they meant food. Xhosa imagined the People as Leopard would see them.

"We look benign, Leopard, with our flimsy claws, flat teeth, and thin hide, but we can kill from a distance, work together, and we never give up a chase that can be won. You, Leopard, can only kill when you are close enough to touch your prey—and you tire quickly.

"Who hunts better?"

Leopard answered by closing its eyes, rolling over, and purring.

The battle began and ended quickly, the hunters killing only what they could carry. They sliced the bodies into portable pieces and slept curled around each other in a copse of trees. When Sun awoke, they left for home, shoulders bowed under the meat's weight, leaving the guts for scavengers. Xhosa hefted the carcass of a young Wild Beast to her shoulders. The animal had crossed her path as she chased a Hipparion mare and her colt. One swing of her warclub, the Wild Beast squealed and died. It provided more meat than the colt and would be a welcome addition to the People's food supply.

Sun was almost directly overhead when her father diverted to a waterhole. The weary but happy group dropped the meat and joined a scarred black rhino, a family of mammoth, and a group of pigs to drink. Xhosa untied the sinews that held the Wild Beast to her shoulders and splashed awkwardly through waist-high cattails and dense bunchgrass. Broad-winged white-bellied birds screeched as they swooped in search of food and a cacophony of insects chirruped their displeasure at her intrusion. A stone's throw away, a hippo played, heaving its great bulk out of the water, mouth gaping, snorting and grunting, before sinking beneath the surface. Within moments, the air exploded with engaging dung smells.

Her feet burrowed into the silt as she pulled the tendon from her hair allowing it to tumble down, covering her back, too thick to allow any cooling breeze to penetrate but like Cat's pelt, it kept insects from biting and warmed her in the rainy times.

Nightshade stood close by, legs apart, weight over the balls of his feet. One hand held his spear, the other his warclub. Even relaxing, he scanned the surroundings. When his gaze landed on her, there was hunger in his eyes.

Her breath caught. That was his look for females before mating but never for her. She flushed and splashed water on her head, enjoying the cool bite on her fevered skin, gaze drifting lazily across the pond. Sun warm on her shoulders, breeze soft against her body, scent of the People's meat behind her, the whisper of some animal moving in the cattails—she wanted to burst with the joy of life.

Like that, everything changed.

"Big Heads," she muttered and ticked them off on both hands. "Too many—more than our entire group."

Her father had predicted trouble.

She studied the Big Heads, their swollen top-heavy skulls, squashed faces, brow ridges rounded over beady eyes, knobby growths under small mouths for no purpose she could imagine. Their chests were small, legs long, and bodies lacked the brawn that burst from every one of the People's warriors, and their spears, unlike the People's, were tipped with a rough-hewn stone about the size of a leaf.

She strode to her father, head throbbing, throat rough and dry. He acknowledged her presence by moving a hand below his waist, palm down, fingers splayed, but his gaze remained fixed on the strangers, thoughts unreadable.

After a breath, she motioned, also low to her body, "Why do they constantly grunt, chirp, growl, and yip?" No animal this noisy could survive.

Her father said nothing, calmly facing the strangers he considered enemies, arms stiff, spear down but body alert in a way he hadn't been a moment before. Xhosa wondered if this was what her instincts had been screaming.

Slowly, the Big Heads confronted her father's stalwart figure. One pushed his way through the group, muscles hard, piercing eyes filled with hate. Someone else shouted the call sign Thunder, making the male who must be Thunder snap a call sign—Wind—as though he'd eaten rotten meat.

"Those two must be the leaders," her father motioned. "And brothers."

Both were the same height with thick straight hair that hung past their shoulders. Thunder had a scar that cut his face, making him look resolute and intolerant. For the other, face smooth and young, the word "hopeful" popped into Xhosa's thoughts. Why, Xhosa had no idea, but something told her Hopeful Wind wouldn't win this battle.

As if to prove her right, the Big Heads behind Thunder flexed their arms, waved their spears, and bounced to a rhythmic chant. Someone beckoned Wind but he walked away, head down.

A purr made Xhosa jerk. A hungry Leopard stalked the People's meat. Xhosa started toward it, to protect it, when a scream punctuated the air.

Xhosa snapped toward the sound. One of the People's warriors clawed at a spear lodged in his chest, blood seeping between his fingers.

"They threw that all the way across the pond— Father, how can they do that?" No one was that strong.

"Run!" Her father bellowed.

Over her shoulder, Xhosa heard the pounding of retreating feet but she never considered it, not with the mass of bawling Big Head warriors plunging into the shallow pond, spears thrust forward, rage painting their faces.

"Why do they attack, Father? What did we do?"

He shoved her away. "Go! Get our People to safety! I will slow them!"

"No," she answered softly. "We stay together! *We*, Father. I stand with you!"

His eyes, always soft and welcoming, held hers for a moment as though to object but instead, offered the faintest of smiles and then confronted the onslaught.

Xhosa broadened her stance, picked the closest Big Head, and launched her spear. It flew true with such power it penetrated the male's throat and into the next warrior. Both fell, dead before they hit the water. When a Big Head spear landed at her feet, she seized it, warclub in her other hand, throwing stones in her neck sack.

"I am blooded!" She screamed. "I do not flee in fear!"

Her scalp tingled and her eyesight grew vivid as everything about her grew stronger, harder, and faster. One enemy after another fell to the skill of Xhosa and her father. Her chest swelled with pride. No one could beat them. These creatures would soon withdraw as did all the People's enemies.

She buried a spear in a young warrior's thigh. He screamed, tears streaming down his cheeks.

"You were never stabbed?" With a snort, she yanked the weapon from his leg, eliciting another anguished howl. He was not much older than she. Maybe he too fought his first battle.

She threw the bloody spear at another Big Head who collapsed, blood bubbling from his mouth. Out of spears, she hurled stones from her neck sack, dropping one warrior after another, her barrage so fast no one could duck.

But there were too many. One moment, her father brandished his deadly weapons. The next, the Big Head Thunder appeared, obsidian eyes blazing, white scar pulsing. He caught Xhosa's eye and sneered as if to say, *Watch what I do to your Leader.*

A bellow came from the Big Head Wind, "Thunder! Stop!"

But Thunder jeered. "You are weak, Wind!" And he drove the spear's stone tip into her father's chest, twisting it as he did.

Xhosa's hands flew to her mouth as fury burned through her. Her father, the one who believed in her above all others, pled, *Go.* With the spear thrusting grotesquely from his body, he slammed his warclub into another Big Head who made the mistake of considering her father a walking dead. A loud crack told Xhosa the warrior's chest had caved in. Xhosa started toward him but Nightshade grabbed her.

"You can't help him. We must get the People to safety!"

Body shaking with rage, she shook loose and squared off to Thunder. "I will destroy you! As I did the one who killed my mother!" She gripped her warclub, head high, body blazing with fury, never wavering.

His eyes widened in surprise. He hadn't known.

Her father hurled his last spear and impaled a charging Big Head as another clubbed him. He legs collapsed but he kicked ferociously, tripping one and another before they overwhelmed him, pummeling him with clubs until he no longer moved.

Nightshade forced her away. "We leave our meat. They will let us go," or scavengers would take the food.

To her horror, she chose life over her father and doing so, abandoned her belief in fairness. Her father saw the Big Heads first and let them be. Xhosa would never make that mistake.

Preview of *Born in a Treacherous Time*

Book 1 in the *Dawn of Humanity* Trilogy

If you'd like to learn more about the ancient female, Lucy, who appears in Xhosa's dreams, read her story in the *Dawn of Humanity* Trilogy.
Click to Purchase
https://www.amazon.com/dp/B07CTCR944

Chapter One

The scene replayed in Lucy's mind, an endless loop haunting her days and nights. The clear sun-soaked field, the dying Mammoth, the hunters waiting hungrily for its last breath before scavenging the meat, tendons, internal organs, fat, and anything else consumable—food that would nourish the Group for a long time.

But something went horribly wrong. Krp blamed Lucy and soon, so too did Feq.

Why did Ghael stand up? He had to know it would mean his death.

Lucy wanted to escape, go where no one knew what she'd done, but Feq would starve without her. He didn't know how to hunt, vomited at the sight of blood. For him, she stayed, hunting, scavenging, and outwitting predators, exhausting herself in a hopeless effort to feed the remaining Group members. But one after another, they fell to Snarling-dog, Panther, Long-tooth Cat, Megantereon, and a litany of other predators. When the strangers arrived, Feq let them take her.

By this time, Lucy felt numb, as much from the death of her Group as the loss of Garv. Garv, her forever pairmate, was as much a part of her as the lush forests, Sun's warmth, and Snarling-dog's guidance. Now, with all the other deaths, she could leave his memory behind.

Forests gave way to bushlands. The prickly stalks scratched her skin right through the thick fur that layered her arms and legs. The glare of Sun, stark and white without the jungle to soften it, blinded her. One step forward became another and another, into a timeless void where nothing mattered but the swish of feet, the hot breeze on her face, and her own musty scent.

Neither male—not the one who called himself Raza nor the one called Baad—had spoken to her since leaving. They didn't tell her their destination and she didn't ask, not that she could decipher their intricate hand gestures and odd body movements. She studied them as they talked to each other, slowly piecing together what the twist of a hand and the twitch of a head meant. She would understand it all by the time they reached wherever they headed.

It was clear they expected her to follow. No one traveled this wild land alone. Her reasons for joining them, submissively, had nothing to do with fear. Wherever the strangers took her would be better than where she'd been.

Lucy usually loved running through the mosaic of grass and forest bleeding one into another. Today, instead of joy, she felt worry for her future and relief that her past was past. She effortlessly matched Raza's tread, running in his steps at his pace. Baad did the same but not without a struggle. His sweat, an equal mix of old and stale from the long trip to find her and fresh from trying to keep up, blossomed into a ripe bouquet sending its fragrant scent past her muzzle. She found comfort in knowing this strong, tough male traveled with her.

Vulture cawed overhead, eagerly anticipating a meal. From the size of his flock, the scavenge must be an adult Okapi or Giraffe. Even after the predator who claimed the kill—Lucy guessed it to be Megantereon or Snarling-dog—took what it needed, there would be plenty left. She often hunted with Vulture. It might find carrion first but she drove it away by brandishing a branch and howling. While it circled overhead, awaiting a return to his meal, she grabbed what she wanted and escaped.

Feq must smell the blood but he had never been brave enough to chase Vulture away. He would wait until the raptor finished, as well as Snarling-dog and whoever else showed up at the banquet, and then take what remained which wouldn't be enough to live on.

Sun descended toward the horizon as they entered a dense thicket. They stuck to a narrow lightly-used animal trail bordered by heavy-trunked trees. Cousin Chimp scuffled as he brachiated through the understory, no doubt upset by the intruders. Only once, when a brightly-colored snake slithered across her path, did Lucy hesitate. The vibrant colors always meant deadly venom and she didn't carry the right herbs to counter the poison. Baad grumbled when her thud reverberated out of sync with Raza's, and Cousin Chimp cried a warning.

Finally, they broke free of the shadows and flew through waist-high grass, past trees laden with fruit, and around the termite mound where Cousin Chimp would gorge on white grubs—if Cheetah wasn't sleeping on top of it.

I haven't been back here since that day...

She flicked her eyes to the spot where her life had changed. Everything looked so calm, painted in vibrant colors scented with a heady mix of grass, water, and carrion. A family of Hipparion raised their heads, found no menace, and turned back to their banquet of new buds.

As though nothing happened...

Lucy sprinted. Her vision blurred and her head throbbed as she raced flat out, desperate to outdistance the memories. Her legs churned, arms pumped, and her feet sprang off the hard earth. Each step propelled her farther away. Her breathing heaved in rhythm with her steps. The sack around her neck smacked comfortingly against her body. Her sweat left a potent scent trail any predator could follow but Lucy didn't care.

"Lucy!"

Someone far behind shouted her call sign but she only slowed when the thump in her chest outstripped her ability to breathe. She fell forward, arms outstretched, and gasped the damp air into her tortured lungs. Steps thumped louder, approaching. She kept her eyes closed. A hand yanked her head back, forcing her to look up.

Despite the strangeness of Raza's language, this she did understand: *Never do that again.*

Feq followed until Lucy had reached the edge of her— Feq's—territory. Here, he must let her go. Without Feq, the Group's few children and remaining female would die. She threw a last look at her brother's forlorn face, drawn and tired, shoulders slumped, eyes tight with resolution. Lucy dipped her head and turned from her beleaguered past.

Maybe the language difference made Raza ignore Lucy's every question though she tried an endless variety of vocalizations, gestures, and grunts. Something made him jumpy but Lucy sniffed nothing other than the fragrant scrub, a family of chimps, and the ever-present Fire Mountain. Nor did she see any shift in the distant shadows to signal danger.

Still, his edginess made her anxious.

What is he hiding? Why does he never relax?

She turned toward the horizon hoping whatever connected sky to earth held firm, preventing danger from escaping and finding her. Garv credited Spider's web with this task, said if it could capture Fly, it could connect those forces. Why it didn't always work, Garv couldn't explain. Herds and dust, sometimes fire, leaked through, as did Sun at the end of every day. Lucy tried to reach that place from many different directions only to have it move away faster than she ran.

Another truth Lucy knew: Only in Sun's absence did the clouds crack and send bolts of fire to burn the ground and flash floods to storm through the canyons. Sun's caring presence kept these at bay.

A grunt startled her back to the monotony of the grassland. At the rear of their column, Baad rubbed his wrists, already swollen to the thickness of his arm. When she dropped back to ask if they needed help, his face hardened but not before she saw the anguish in the set of his mouth and the squint of his eyes. The elders of her Group suffered too from gnarled hands. A common root, found everywhere, dulled the ache.

Why bring a male as old and worn as Baad without the root to rid him of pain?

Lucy guessed he had been handsome in his youth with his commanding size, densely-haired body, and brawny chest. Now, the hair hung gray and ragged and a white line as thick as Lucy's finger cut his face from temple to ear. In his eyes smoldered lingering anger, maybe from the shattered tooth peeking through his parted lips.

Was that why he didn't try to rut with her? Or did he consider her pairmated to Raza?

"Baad," she bleated, mimicking the call sign Raza used. "This will help your wrist," and handed him a root bundle from her neck sack. "Crack it open and swallow the juice."

Baad sniffed the bulb, bit it, and slurped up the liquid. His jaw relaxed and the tension drained from his face, completely gone by the time they passed the hillock that had been on the horizon when Lucy first gave him the root.

"How did you know this would work?" Baad motioned as he watched her face.

Why didn't *he* know was a better question. Lucy observed animals as they cared for their injuries. If Gazelle had a scrape on her flank, she bumped against a tree weeping sap so why shouldn't Lucy rub the thick mucus on her own cut to heal it? If swallowing certain leaves rid Cousin Chimp of the white worms, why wouldn't it do the same for Lucy? Over time, she'd collected the roots, blades, stems, bark, flowers, and other plant parts she and her Group came to rely on when sick.

But she didn't know enough of Baad's words to explain this so she shrugged. "I just knew."

Baad remained at her side as though he wanted to talk more.

Lucy took the opportunity. "Baad. Why did you and Raza come for me?"

He made her repeat the question as he watched her hands, body movements, and face, and then answered, "Sahn sent us."

His movement for "sent" looked odd. One finger grazed the side of his palm and pointed toward his body—the backtrail, the opposite direction of the forward trail.

"Sent you?"

"Because of the deaths."

Memories washed across his face like molten lava down the slopes of Fire Mountain. His hand motions shouted a rage she never associated with death. Predators killed to feed their families or protect their territory, as they must. Why did it anger Baad?

"Can you repeat that? The deaths?"

This time, the closest she could interpret was "deaths" without reason' which made no sense. Death was never without reason. Though he must have noticed she didn't understand, he moved on to a portrayal of the world she would soon live within. His location descriptions were clear. In fact, her Group also labeled places by their surroundings and what happened there—stream-where-hunters-drink, mountains-that-burn-at-night, and mound-with-trees. Locations were meaningless without those identifications. Who could find them if not for their surroundings?

His next question surprised her.

"Why did you come?"

Bile welled in Lucy's throat. She must not tell him how she failed everyone in her Group or explain she wanted a better life for the child she carried. Instead, she grunted and pretended she misunderstood.

That night, Lucy slept fitfully, curled under a shallow overhang without the usual protection of a bramble bush barrier or a tree nest. Every time she awoke, Raza and Baad were staring into the dark night, faces tight and anxious, muscles primed.

When Sun reappeared to begin its journey across the sky, the group set out, Lucy again between Raza and Baad. She shadowed the monotonous bounce of Raza's head, comforted by the muted slap of her feet, the thump in her chest, and the stench of her own unwashed body. As they trotted ever onward, she became increasingly nervous. Though everything from the berries to the vegetation, animals, and baobab trees reminded her of home, this territory belonged to another group of Man-who-makes-tools. Before today, she would no sooner enter or cross it as they would hers. But Raza neither slowed nor changed direction so all she could do to respect this land-not-hers was to move through without picking a stalk of grass, eating a single berry, or swallowing any of the many grubs and insects available. Here and there, Lucy caught glimpses of the Group that called this territory theirs as they floated in the periphery of her sight. She smelled their anger and fear, heard them rustling as they watched her pass, reminding her she had no right to be here. Raza and Baad didn't seem to care or notice. Did they not control territories where they lived?

Before she pondered this any further, she snorted in a fragrance that made her gasp and turn. There on the crest of a berm across the savanna, outlined against the blue of the sky, stood a lone figure, hair puffed out by the hot breeze, gaze on her.

"Garv!" Lucy mouthed before she could stop herself. *He's dead. I saw it.*

No arm waved and no voice howled the agony of separation.

"Raza!" Baad jerked his head toward the berm.

"Man-who-preys?" Raza asked with a rigid parallel gesture.

Lucy's throat tightened at the hand movement for *danger*.

"Who is Man-who-preys?" Lucy labored with the call sign. "We don't prey. We are prey." Why did this confuse Raza?

Raza dropped back and motioned, "I refer to the one called Man-who-preys—upright like us but tall and skinny." He described the creature's footprints with the distinctive rounded top connected to the bottom by a narrow bridge. She knew every print of every animal in her homeland. These didn't exist.

"No. I've never seen those prints."

He paused and watched her face. "You're sure Mammoth slaughtered your males? Could it have been this animal?"

"No. I was there. I would have seen this stranger."

Raza dropped back to talk to Baad. She tried to hear their conversation but they must have used hand motions. Who was this Man-who-preys and why did Raza think they caused the death of her Group's males? Worse, if they followed Raza from his homeland, did that bring trouble to Feq?

Lucy easily kept up with Raza, her hand tight around an obsidian scraper as sharp and sturdy as the one the males gripped. Her wrist cords bulged like the roots of an old baobab, familiar with and accustomed to heavy loads and strenuous work. Both males remained edgy and tense, often running beside each other and sharing urgent hand motions. After one such exchange, Raza diverted from the route they had been following since morning to one less trodden. It's what Lucy would do if worried about being tracked by a predator or to avoid a group of Man-who-makes-tools. They maintained a quicker-than-normal pace well past the edge of her world. That suited her fine though she doubted Man-who-preys could be more perilous than what preyed in her mind.

About the Author

Jacqui Murray lives in California with her spouse and the world's greatest dog. She has been writing fiction and nonfiction for 30 years and is an adjunct professor in technology-in-education.

You can find Jacqui Murray on her blog:
https://worddreams.wordpress.com

Twitter:
https://twitter.com/WordDreams

LinkedIn:
https://www.linkedin.com/in/jacquimurray

BIBLIOGRAPHY

Allen, E.A., The Prehistoric World: or, Vanished Races
Central Publishing House 1885

Brown Jr., Tom, Tom Brown's Field Guide: Wilderness
Survival Berkley Books 1983

Caird, Rod Apeman: The Story of Human Evolution
MacMillan 1994

Calvin, William, and Bickerton, Derek Lingua ex Machina:
Reconciling Darwin and Chomsky with the Human
Brain MIT Press, 2000

Carss, Bob The SAS Guide to Tracking Lyons Press Guilford
Conn. 2000

Cavalli-Sforza, Luigi Luca and Cavalli-Sforza, Francesco The
Great Human Diasporas: The

History of Diversity and Evolution Perseus Press 1995
Conant,

Dr. Levi Leonard The Number Concept: Its Origin and
Development Macmillan and Co. Toronto 1931

Diamond, Jared The Third Chimpanzee Harper Perennial
1992

Edey, Maitland Missing Link Time-Life Books 1972

Erickson, Jon Glacial Geology: How Ice Shapes the Land
Facts on File Inc. 1996

Fleagle, John Primate Adaptation and Evolution Academic
Press 1988

Fossey, Dian Gorillas in the Mist Houghton Mifflin 1984

Galdikas, Birute Reflections of Eden: My Years with the
Orangutans of Borneo Little Brown and Co. 1995

Goodall, Jane In the Shadow of Man Houghton Mifflin
1971

Goodall, Jane The Jane Goodall Institute 2005
http://www.janFriendshipegoodall.com/chimp_central/
chimpanzees/behavior/communication.asp

Goodall, Jane Through a Window Houghton Mifflin 1990

Grimaldi, David, and Engel, Michael Evolution of the Insects
Cambridge University Press 2005

Human Dawn: Timeframe Time-Life Books 1990

Johanson, Donald and Simon, Blake Edgar From Lucy to Language Simon and Schuster 1996

Johanson, Donald and O'Farell, Kevin Journey from the Dawn: Life with the World's First Family Villard Books 1990

Johanson, Donald and Edey, Maitland Lucy: The Beginnings of Humankind Simon and Schuster 1981

Johanson, Donald and Shreve, James Lucy's Child: The Discovery of a Human Ancestor Avon 1989

Jones, Steve, Martin, Robert, and Pilbeam, David The Cambridge Encyclopedia of Human Evolution Cambridge University Press 1992

Leakey, Richard and Lewin, Roger Origins E.P. Dutton 1977

Leakey, Richard The Origin of Humankind Basic Books 1994

Leakey, Louis Stone Age Africa, Negro Universities Press 1936

Lewin, Roger In the Age of Mankind Smithsonian Books 1988

McDougall, J.D. A Short History of the Planet Earth John Wiley and Sons 1996

Morris, Desmond Naked Ape Dell Publishing 1999

Morris, Desmond The Human Zoo Kodansha International 1969

Rezendes, Paul Tracking and the Art of Seeing: How to Read Animal Tracks and Sign Quill: A Harper Resource Book 1999

Savage-Rumbaugh, Susan, et al Kanzi: The Ape at the Brink of the Human Mind John Wiley and Sons 1996

Spencer Larson, Clark et al Human Origins: The Fossil Record Waveland Press 1998

Stringer, Chris, and McSahn, Robin African Exodus: The Origins of Modern Humanity Henry Holt and Co. NY 1996

Strum, Shirley C. Almost Human: A Journey into the World of Baboons Random House 1987

Tattersall, Ian Becoming Human: Evolution and Human Uniqueness Harvest Books 1999

Tattersall, Ian et al Encyclopedia of Human Evolution and Prehistory, Chicago: St James Press 1988

Tattersall, Ian Fossil Trail: How We Know What We Think We Know About Human Evolution Oxford University Press 1997

Tattersall, Ian The Human Odyssey: Four Million Years of Human Evolution Prentice Hall 1993

Thomas, Elizabeth Marshall, The Old Way: A Story of the First People Sarah Crichton Books 2008

Tudge Colin Time Before History Touchstone Books 1996

Turner, Alan, and Anton, Mauricio The Big Cats and Their Fossil Relatives: An Illustrated Guide to Their Evolution and Natural History Columbia University Press NY 1997

Vogel, Shawna Naked Earth: The New Geophysics Dutton 1995

Vygotsky, Lev The Connection Between Thought and the Development of Language in Primitive Society 1930

Walker, Alan and Shipman, Pat Wisdom of the Bones: In Search of Human Origins Vintage Books 1996

Waters, JD Helpless as a Baby http://www.jdwaters.net/HAAB%20Acro/contents.pdf 2001

Wills, Christopher Runaway Brain: The Evolution of Human Uniqueness Basic Books 1993

READER'S WORKSHOP QUESTIONS

Setting

- What part did Nature and the land play in Xhosa's ability to survive and thrive?
- How does the setting figure as a character in the story?

Themes

- Discuss Xhosa's respect for all animals. Why do you think she felt this way?
- Why did Xhosa and her kind survive Nature's challenges?
- We know *Homo erectus* died out, replaced by the more-advanced human, Archaic *Homo sapiens*. What characteristics and traits in this story help to explain why?

Character Realism

- What traits made Xhosa a survivor?
- Do you relate to Xhosa's predicaments? To what extent does it remind you of yourself or a woman you know struggling to attain respect, fit into a 'man's' world, or survive a toxic environment?

Character Choices

- What moral/ethical choices did the characters in this book make? Discuss why the animals are referred to as "who" rather than "'that" and why often they are addressed by proper nouns rather than simple nouns.
- Discuss the dynamics between Xhosa, Nightshade, Hawk, and Pan-do. How did the People raise children? Do other primitive tribes handle families in this way?
- What events triggered Xhosa's evolution from passive to warrior?

Construction

- Discuss how Xhosa communicated—with body language, gestures, facial expressions, and the rare vocalization. How effective do you think it was? How is it relevant today? What present-day animals communicate with methods other than words?
- Discuss why Xhosa's People didn't use proper nouns to describe places.
- Discuss Xhosa's lack of a number system and how she described quantities (such as "Sun traveled a hand" or "ticked them off on her fingers"). Discuss the limited number systems used by some primitive tribes even today.
- How did early man make sense of the moon disappearing and reappearing over and over?

Reactions to the Book

- Did the book lead to a new understanding or awareness of how man evolved to be who we are today? Did it help you understand something in your life that didn't make sense before?
- Did the book fulfill your expectations? Were you satisfied with the ending?

Other Questions

- What do you think will happen to the characters in Book 3?
- Discuss books you've read with a similar theme or set in the same time period.

Printed in Great Britain
by Amazon

55448419R00210